REPUBLIC UNDER SIEGE

Threat from Within

By Michael J. Brooks

Wars of the New Humanity

Book Two

About this Book

Content Warning

Republic Under Siege: Threat from Within is an action-filled science fiction book that contains violence, strong language, and detailed scenes of lovers making love.

Content Meter

Medium

Low   **High**

2025 Edition

You are reading the 2025 edition of *Republic Under Siege: Threat from Within*.

Copyright © 2022 by Michael J. Brooks

Edited by Xyana and Leilani Dewindt
Illustrations by Ann (anygoart on Instagram)
Original cover design by Ida Jansson: http://www.amygdaladesign.net/
Cover update by Mahi: https://www.fiverr.com/mahii_creations

This book is a work of fiction. All names, characters, events, and places are the result of the author's imagination or are used fictitiously. Any resemblance to actual persons (living or deceased), events, locales, organizations, etcetera, is purely coincidental.

Paperback ISBN: 9781737929345
Ebook ISBN: 9781737929352

Library of Congress Control Number: 2022918518

Printed in the United States of America

Michael J. Brooks
Mount Rainier, Maryland 20712
www.authormbrooks.com

2025 edition

Praise for
Republic Under Siege:
Threat from Within

"The second book in the sci-fi series Wars of the New Humanity combines elements of thriller, social inspection, and sci-fi to produce a riveting, refreshingly original story . . . packed with moment-by-moment reactions to pain, surprising twists and turns, and journeys towards healing and revised destinies. Libraries seeking solid sci-fi replete with social and psychological inspections that move from the aftermath of world-changing war into the motives and experiences of young people who would forge new lives and worlds will find the social inspections in *Republic Under Siege: Threat from Within* compelling. It will attract a wide age range, from young adult to adult readers. Ideally, book clubs will also consider *Republic Under Siege: Threat from Within* for its many enlightening moments about the kernels of social change as individuals experience healing, transformation, loss, and novel opportunities."
—**D. Donovan, Senior Reviewer,** *Midwest Book Review*

"Memorable characters, passionate prose, riveting action, graphic combat scenes, and steamy romance make this technothriller a standout read for new adult audiences. Brooks deftly explores social justice themes related to misogyny, racism, classism, and the balance between revolutionary ideals and maintaining functioning governmental systems while keeping his audience thoroughly entertained with the characters' intertwined conflicts, romantic liaisons, and destinies."
—**Kate Robinson,** *The US Review of Books*

Glossary
(nonalphabetic order)

Earth Era: the era of humanity before intergalactic migration from Earth

Commonwealth: humanity's star nation consisting of four planets —Eden and satellites One, Two, and Three

Eden: humanity's utopian motherworld inhabited by three-fifths of the human population

Satellite One: humanity's dystopian secondary world inhabited by two-fifths of the human population

Advanced Exascale Global Information-collection System (AEGIS): the AI computer system created during Earth Era to divide humanity between Eden and Satellite One

Satellites Two and Three: vacant worlds belonging to the Commonwealth, used for military training exercises and mineral excavation

Edenite/Eden citizen (synonymous terms)**:** human beings living on Eden, whether born on the planet or during Earth Era

Highborn: a moniker referring specifically to human beings born on Eden

Colonist/colony citizen (synonymous terms): human beings living in the colonies of Satellite One, whether born on the planet or during Earth Era

Commonwealth Defense Force (CDF)/Defense Force (synonymous terms): the Commonwealth's military force

Guardian: a soldier in the Commonwealth Defense Force

Cadet: a Guardian in training

Shell: a mechanized, armored combat suit used by Guardians

Commonwealth Government/central government (synonymous terms): the governing body of the entire Commonwealth, which includes the Parliament and Chief Executive's Office

Republic of Unified Colonies (RUC): the republic formed by colonies One, Four, and Six after they declared sovereignty from the Commonwealth

The Three-Week War: the war initiated and won by the Commonwealth Government to reclaim colonies One, Four, and Six after they declared sovereignty from the Commonwealth

The Coalition of Rebel Factions/the Coalition (synonymous terms): a coalition of rebel factions formed by the remnant fighters of the RUC to continue combating the Commonwealth Government

The Quad: the Chief Executive's Manor, Parliament Building, Supreme Judiciary, and Defense Force Academy, on Eden, which are situated in a Quadrangle in the middle of Eden's capital, Cornerstone City

Operation Hammer Fall: the Coalition's operation to invade the Quad, commandeer the Parliament Building and use its broadcast center to cast files exposing government corruption across the net

The Battle of the Quad: the historic battle between the Coalition rebels and CDF Guardians during Operation Hammer Fall

The Interplanetary Union: the intergalactic alliance consisting of the Commonwealth and planets Ghanrax, Dhalgratt, Varsh'Ru, Zirkran, Rumanoah, and Taramassia

****The [   ] symbol represents translation from a character's native language****

Author's Note

In *Republic Falling: Advent of a New Dawn* (Wars of the New Humanity, book 1), humanity is divided between two worlds. The first is Eden, a utopian paradise and the motherworld of the New Humanity's intergalactic republic, the Commonwealth. The second is Satellite One, a dystopian world that serves as the Commonwealth's resource hub. The colonists of Satellite One exist primarily as resource harvesters, essentially government laborers. They live in colonies with subpar conditions and are denied the technological luxuries available to Eden's citizens. By design, they occupy the bottom rung of the Commonwealth's socioeconomic hierarchy.

However, the Commonwealth's immigration lottery system offers colonists a chance to escape their circumstances and live on Eden. Those selected become "immigrants"—ironically labeled, considering they are already citizens of the Commonwealth.

For *Republic Under Siege: Threat from Within* (Wars of the New Humanity, book 2), I asked myself, What happens when someone is transplanted on Eden with hopes and dreams, only to face continued marginalization under a class system? That question gave rise to the character of Akane Sugimori, a nineteen-year-old immigrant introduced in the book's prologue.

To tell Akane's compelling backstory while advancing the present-day adventure, which picks up where book one left off, I structured the narrative with chapter interludes. These interludes transport readers back to Akane's immigration journey, chronicling how she arrived at where she is presently. The story follows a rhythm of present-day chapter, then interlude, and so on.

While Akane is essential to the plot, I was careful to ensure she didn't overshadow our main hero, Randal Scott. At the same time, I continued to advance the arc of Stacie Spencer, who is now Randy's ex.

In the previous book, Randy left the Commonwealth Defense Force (CDF) to side with the colonies' Coalition of Rebel Factions, an alliance he initially saw as nothing more than treasonous insurrectionists. After the Coalition executed their trump card, Operation Hammer Fall, they succeeded in opening the door for colony and immigrant equality.

Now, with no Coalition fighters being prosecuted for war crimes, Randy returns to the CDF branded a pariah, and it seems Akane is one of the few Guardians he can trust. Or can she be trusted?

Akane tries to recruit Randy, one of the colonies' liberators, into what appears to be a social-activist organization fighting for immigrant equality. Thanks to the chapter interludes, readers get to witness how Akane herself was recruited, as she leads Randy through a parallel experience. But there may be far more to this organization than meets the eye.

In many ways, Akane became the linchpin holding the story together, and I hope readers will enjoy following her journey as much as I enjoyed writing it.

Republic Under Siege delivers the same thrilling gunfights and mechsuit battles featured in *Republic Falling*, though the setting has shifted. The last book unfolded during a brutal war; this one takes place in the war's aftermath. It's more of a techno-thriller than a war story, but it continues to explore the themes of rebellion, classism, discrimination, and more. Enjoy!

Intro

"I've been marginalized by an oppressive government system, by a system designed to keep people like me down. But I decided to fight back. You may not approve of my methods, but I really don't give a damn."
—*Akane Sugimori*

PROLOGUE

BEFORE THE THREE-WEEK WAR

Planet: Satellite One
Colony Three
Immigrant Departure Station
(Receiving Area)

Lucky, *damn* lucky. That's what eighteen-year-old Akane Sugimori was. There were colonists who'd kill to be in her shoes. She'd scored the opportunity to untether her future from a destiny of grueling labor—an opportunity to rise beyond a dour life of second-class citizenship. To no longer be lumped with the "lesser" of humanity was a privilege, one that was nearly unattainable.

Eden, the utopia of humanity's intergalactic republic, the Commonwealth, awaited her. So why the fuck was she down in the dumps? This was a dream coveted by nearly every denizen of Colony Three.

Clad in denim shorts, fashionably ripped fishnet stockings, and a black crop top, she sat Eden-bound on the frontmost bench in the receiving area of Colony Three's immigrant departure station, mood somber.

Arms clenched around herself, she tapped the heel of her sneaker boot against the floor in a nervous staccato. She loathed every second that ticked by, waiting for her citizen registration number (CRN) to be announced over the intercom. Soon, her undesired voyage to Eden would begin.

She dreaded being torn away from friends and family. Who would she laugh, dine, and share the pain and pleasures of life with? As inferior to the motherworld as it was, Satellite One would *always* be home in her heart.

To her left, Dad. To her right, Mom. Benjiro and Akari Sugimori were loving parents who'd made substantial sacrifices for her well-being. She wouldn't *dare* ask more of them. They had worked tooth and nail to give her the best upbringing possible. Toiling in the caverns and agricultural fields of Colony Three as government-employed resource harvesters—or, to some, government serfs—was no easy job.

Akane had caused her parents' blood pressure to skyrocket more than once, secretly working the black-market commerce system at age sixteen to ease their burdens. Peddling hard-to-get luxuries to residents of Sector 07 had come with serious risk.

Migrants from former Japan populated the sector, earning it the name NeoJapan. They had preserved their language, culture, art, and history in the era of the New Humanity, during a time when colony selectees had banded together for survival and community, resulting in the emergence of assimilated cultures.

Due to her devil-may-care attitude, Akane had to admit she deserved the scoldings she got from her parents. But, especially now that she'd graduated into adulthood, the obstinate youth refused to let anyone, even Mom and Dad, police her individuality.

Her attitude, mouth, and parent-disapproved fashion choice, right down to the pierced navel, were staying put.

As Akari and Benjiro each anchored an arm around her to console her, she couldn't help but wonder: Was she swapping one hell for another? She knew how to survive in this hell. The new one? Not so much.

She'd heard stories of colony immigrants, lottery beneficiaries like herself, having their once-bright dreams crushed by the harsh realities of life on Eden. The Commonwealth Government had proclaimed the planet a haven of peace, comfort, and prosperity, but Eden's high society, it seemed, wasn't receptive to certain groups of people. Immigrants were issued ten thousand living credits and expected to survive with minimal support or transitional assistance. Even so, for many colonists, Eden citizenship was the prize of a lifetime.

Two staff members walked by. One had blue hair, and the other had brown.

The blue-haired one said, "I betcha some colonies are gonna declare independence soon."

"And ignite a war with the Commonwealth Government? Doubt it. That'd be a stupid move."

After overhearing the two men, Akane glanced at each of her parents. "[Do you guys believe the rumors? Do you think some colonies might actually declare independence and form their own republic? If a civil war starts, you could be at risk. What if—?]"

Benjiro said, "[Don't worry about us or what's happening in the colonies. Your future is on Eden.]"

"[And what if I end up like so many others?]"

"[You won't,]" Benjiro replied confidently. He had faith in his daughter.

As the two staff members headed for the exit, the brown-haired one said, "Can't wait to get back to Eden. I'm tired of this shithole colony already."

The blue-haired one replied, "The immigration lottery's only once a year. Someone's gotta do these temp assignments."

"Yeah, hopefully it's not us next year."

"Registrant C-Nine-Eight-Eight-Seven, proceed to Decon to prep for boarding," a young woman said over the intercom. "I repeat, proceed to Decon."

Scrolling across the wall's massive info display: C-9887 REPORT TO DECON.

Akane ran a fidgeting hand through her short, unruly black hair. *That's me.* Depressed about separating from her parents, she was on the verge of tears.

Two men in their early twenties and a woman Akane's age sat four benches behind the Sugimori family. They were dreamers, anticipating a wondrous life on Eden.

The young man with short auburn hair wore a sleeveless white hoodie and blue jeans. The other had neck-length jet-black hair and was dressed in a T-shirt and cargo pants. As a devoted Mercedes Gardner fan, the woman wore the pop star's T-shirt paired with magenta palazzo pants. She had even styled her platinum-blond hair in pigtails, just like Mercedes often did.

Waiting to be called to Decon, the trio regaled each other with friendly banter and stories of their childhood. The woman was the bubbly one—always smiling, animated gesticulations, laughing often, voice bursting with optimism.

The Sugimoris stood. Akane's chin tilted downward, and her shoulders sagged. She was *so* not feeling this moment.

Akari tenderly framed her daughter's melancholy face with small hands calloused from intensive labor. "[We'll miss you, Akane. But this is your day, a special day. Be joyful.]"

Be joyful? Inside, Akane was crumbling to pieces. *Easy for her to say.*

Benjiro placed a soft, comforting hand on Akane's shoulder. Like her mother, he'd often worried about where and with whom Akane spent her spare time. Much of it had been consumed by socializing with youth outside NeoJapan. She'd adopted non-native behaviors and a non-native patois from her social excursions.

Rebellious since childhood, she only grew more defiant of all authority—parental or otherwise—over time. Tell her not to do something and she'd do the opposite. But because of her rebellious nature, she had become a strong, resilient young lady.

Benjiro was beyond happy for her, and it showed in his wide-set eyes. "[We are proud of you, Akane,]" he said. "[A new life awaits you on Eden, a *better* life. There will be hardships to overcome, of course, but you will persevere.]" Street-smart, resourceful, and armed with exceptional survival skills, Akane knew how to weather tough times, how to roll with life's punches. "[As soon as we're permitted travel passes, we'll come see you.]"

Memories of parental love and affection bum-rushed Akane. "[Thanks, I love you guys.]" She sniffled and bit her lower lip. "[And thanks for putting up with all my harebrained mischief.]"

Peeved, the woman on the intercom repeated herself. "Registrant C-Nine-Eight-Eight-Seven, report to Decon *at once.* What the hell are you doing?"

Akari kissed her daughter's tear-slick cheek. "[We love you too. Now off you go.]"

Akane wiped her glassy eyes with the back of her hand. She snatched her hot-pink backpack from the floor, the cartoony skull on the back fading with age, and slung it over her shoulders. Her main luggage had already been loaded onto the shuttle.

She took off running toward the lone terminal before the

intercom lady could get even more livid. Looking back, she caught one last glimpse of her parents. Who knew when she'd see them again? She waved a tearful see-you-later.

Vision poor from laboring in health-hazardous subterranean caverns, Akari watched her baby girl fade into a blur. A lump of sadness swelled in her throat. *May good fortune smile upon you wherever you go, my daughter.*

The next traveler was summoned over the intercom. "Registrant C-Six-Five-Five-One, report to Decon. I repeat, report to Decon."

"That's me!" the woman with pigtails exclaimed. Überexcited, she bolted from the bench.

Midway down the terminal, Akane encountered a towering, bulbous woman clad in an all-white uniform.

The woman's pudgy, pockmarked face twisted into a scowl of pure detest.

I guess she would be the boarding proctor, Akane thought. *Why the hell couldn't her lazy keister come escort us?*

The proctor wasn't going to fetch the beneficiaries from the receiving area herself. No way. She was an Edenite, on duty; "nadir" had to come to her.

"Call me Ella," the huge woman said in an inhospitable tone. She glowered at the petite eighteen-year-old in front of her. "I'll be your boarding proctor, *pissant*. Do everything I say, and keep your *stinking* mouth shut unless spoken to." Her thick lips expanded into a wry grin. "And don't do anything that might *tick* me off, unless you'd like your Eden citizenship registration revoked. Which, honestly, would make my day."

Geesh, what bug crawled up this fucking asshole's pants? Akane's brows drew together. She subdued the impulse to cuss out Ella.

Ella's forehead creased. Her demeanor radiated the irrepressible enmity harbored in her soul. She despised that yet another "nadir" had been granted access to the upper echelon of the New Humanity. In her eyes, "nadir" belonged here on Satellite One, the New Humanity's resource hub, as nothing more than resource harvesters.

In a belittling timbre, Ella said, "Please acknowledge understanding, registrant C-Nine-Eight-Eight-Seven." She didn't even deign to use Akane's actual name. To her, Akane was nothing more than a CRN.

"Yeah, I gotcha." Akane stayed cool, even though she wanted to go the fuck off. "You won't get *annnyyyy* trouble from me." She was eager to get away from this doofus and get the joyride to Eden underway.

The bubbly blond woman moseyed up, her stride carefree.

Ella's saggy features twitched, and her lips pursed. "Hey, Ms. *Lah-di-dah*, quit dragging your feet!" Startled, the woman tensed up and froze. "Move! Put some pep in your step!"

A flutter of nervousness eclipsed the woman's sunny disposition. "Uh . . . coming right away, ma'am!" She kicked her pace up to a jog and brought herself to a halt in front of Ella.

Ella studied the info displayed on her tablet. Then she swung her hard gaze back up at the blond. "Registrant C-Six-Five-Five-One, Skylar Grace. Correct?"

The woman nodded quickly. "Yes, ma'am," she replied, her usual pep gone. She was more reserved in the proctor's menacing presence.

The two young men who had sat with Skylar in the receiving area rushed up.

Ella checked her tablet again. "Registrant C-One-Seven-Nine-Two, Jacobi Johnston."

"Here," the auburn-haired man replied.

Next, Ella read, "Registrant C-Zero-Eight-Nine-One,

Desmond Castillo."

"That's me," the black-haired dusky-skinned man said, loud and proud.

Ella clipped the tablet to her oversized belt. "Alright, follow me," she ordered. "I'm taking you to Decon so you can disinfect. Don't want you nadir contaminating the motherworld."

Jacobi frowned at the slur. *Nadir? Butt-ugly snob.*

The proctor and her group of beneficiaries veered left into another corridor. Like this entire government facility, it was flawless, squeaky-clean, and sterile, unlike the outdated, lackluster structures common on Satellite One.

Jacobi wandered closer to Akane, encroaching on her personal space. "*Psst*, hey, what's your name?"

His proximity made Akane cringe. "Why?" she replied flippantly. Coping with the pain of leaving behind her friends, family, and everything familiar, she wasn't in the mood for conversation.

Jacobi offered a polite shrug. "We might as well get acquainted. We're all on the same journey, right?"

"All mouths are to remain closed, Mr. Johnston," Ella snapped, shepherding the group forward with a slow, lumbering gait. That was Jacobi's warning shot. Next time, she might not be so merciful.

Jacobi went silent. *What a bitch.*

One-third of the way down the corridor, there was a set of doors to the left and another set to the right.

Ella barked instruction. "Gents, that way." She pointed left. "Ladies, that way." She pointed right. "Once inside, you'll receive further guidance. *Make sure you follow it to a tee.*"

Why do we have to get "decontaminated" like we're infectious, diseased rodents or something? Akane wondered. Well, she had no choice but to comply.

Akane and Skylar stepped into the ladies' Decon. Twelve compact examination pods, connected to a series of pipes, were built into the spheroid wall of the white nondescript space.

The doors whooshed shut behind them, and a disembodied artificial voice said, "Welcome to Decon. Extract all apparel and place it in deposit bins for sterilization." Two rectangular bins ejected from wall lockers. "After discarding apparel, proceed to the sterilization pod of your choosing."

Akane dropped her backpack on the bench in front of the bins, and she and Skylar began unlacing their footwear.

After tugging off her high-tops, Skylar turned to her new traveling companion, sporting a sweet smile. Time to bond. "So, what's your name?"

"Akane." The drab way she answered sent a clear message: She wasn't happy and didn't give a crap about schmoozing right now.

Skylar jerked her shirt overhead and dumped it into deposit bin zero-one, uncovering a silky pink bra.

Squeamish about undressing in front of strangers, Akane blushed and shyly eased her shirt up over her head.

"Why so glum?" Skylar inquired. "We're headed to Eden. We're headed to *paradise*." She spread her arms wide on "paradise." "I hear it's a lot like Earth." Born after Earth Era in Colony Five, she'd never laid eyes on humanity's lost homeworld. She had only seen imagery of its former glory, from a time before Armageddon devastated its environment.

Akane discarded her shirt in deposit bin zero-two, along with her backpack. "I'm just . . . not sure how things are gonna shake out. I mean, what are the odds of us immigrants actually . . . you know, prospering on Eden?"

Skylar threw a monkey wrench in Akane's skepticism, spieling some truth. "Oviereya Amaechi became a Chairwoman of the

Parliament and Chancellor of the Supreme Judiciary. Arson Scott became one of the Commonwealth's most revered war heroes. He earned the pinnacle of military commendations. Arson and Oviereya were able to adapt to Eden culture, overcome hurdles, and shatter barriers.

"Anything's possible, Akane." With bravado, Skylar pumped her fist. "*Motherfucking* anything." She flicked a hand dismissively, as if fanning away the doubt percolating in Akane's mind. "Come on, girlfriend!"

Akane had a tendency to expect the worst. It was her way of shielding herself from disappointment. But that reminder, the reminder that colonists such as herself had risen to prominence in the Commonwealth, elicited a small hopeful smile from her. Albeit small, it was still a smile—a sign she wasn't all doom and gloom.

"I guess there is hope for us, huh?" Akane said thoughtfully.

Skylar punched a fist upward. "Yep!" she chirped. Her animated body language practically screamed "now that's the spirit!"

While the two finished undressing, they shot the breeze, and Akane gradually loosened up. Fully unclothed, they approached the pods, bare feet quietly slapping the spotless floor.

Akane, following closely behind Skylar, cast a quick glance down at her own slender frame, then up at Skylar. Her cheeks burned with envy and admiration as she noted how Skylar's hips jutted out from her narrow waist.

Akane thought Skylar looked like a supermodel. Her fine bone structure, cute heart-shaped bottom, and ample breasts made her a jaw-dropper. And all of it was one hundred percent natural. No black-market body mods.

Self-conscious about her own straight-figured frame, Akane couldn't help but compare. *Why is her bod so fucking perfect?*

Everything about Skylar's body made Akane retreat inward, from the radiance of her skin to the subtle bounce of her curves, both front and back. Not to mention those magnificent legs, which seemed to go on forever. She was a work of art come to life.

The two entered neighboring decontamination pods, ending Akane's bout with her insecurities.

"Initiating sterilization sequence," the automated guide notified them.

A cylindrical vat in the room gurgled to life, releasing a cool chemical mist into the pods through the spinning applicator mounted to their ceiling.

Skylar pivoted toward Akane's pod, pressing her hands against the glass. She was so excited about going to Eden that her sapphire eyes gleamed. "So, whaddya think having our brains modded with a cerebral implant is gonna be like?" She raised her peppy voice over the loud hissing mist gusting against her skin.

Akane pursed her lips, eager to get out of this glass chamber thing and not in the mood for "shower talk" with a hyperactive woman who couldn't stop running her mouth for one second. Not how she thought preboarding would go. Life was so unpredictable.

She replied, "You're able to . . . do some mental Bluetooth thing. Link, that's what they call it, right? Sync your mind with someone else's. Hear their thoughts. See their memories. Experience their emotions. Become one with someone and all that jazz." Her muscles coiled as she imagined Linking minds with someone. "*Souunnnddds* kinda fucking creepy, if you ask me."

"*Nuh-uh*," Skylar said. "Linking is supposed to be a gateway to deepening relationships. It's a way to bond, to form closer ties and expand your cognitive awareness of another person's innermost feelings." In a sultry "Oh, I can't wait!" kind of tone, she added, "A way to manifest an extraordinary sex life too."

Akane's shoulders gave Skylar a "meh."

Skylar sighed. They were talking about one of humanity's greatest technological breakthroughs, and all Akane could offer was a lukewarm reaction?

The unending mist continued to swirl around them, cleansing away foreign bacteria, microbes, and parasites.

Skylar kept the conversation going. "So, what's your goal in life, Akane?"

Akane blinked slowly, as if she were confused. "Huh?"

"You know, the thing that motivates you. That gives you a sense of purpose. That gives you the will to wake up and deal with the muck of life day after day. The thing *you* feel is your reason for breathing."

My ikigai? Akane thought, then replied, "Right now I'm just focused on keeping my head above water and steering clear of trouble on my soon-to-be new homeworld."

"You've gotta aim high, Akane. If you don't know your purpose yet, find it. Me? I'm destined for *stardom*. I'm gonna be a famous singer, like Mercedes Gardner!"

Mercedes was famous alright. The entrancing sound of the pop star's vocals had captivated audiences across Eden and Satellite One. She had also performed on Mission Worlds to boost the morale of Guardians deployed on planetary-impact missions. And her vids usually racked up millions of views.

Akane lifted her eyebrows mockingly, finding it hard to believe that Edenites would embrace an immigrant superstar. *Yeah, right.*

Skylar's expression hardened. She was sick of Akane's pessimism.

Her tone shifted to something not so friendly, a departure from her usual bubbly self. "I know what you're thinking. You're thinking that's a lofty goal for an immigrant, right?" The rising aggression in her voice warned Akane that her bleak outlook had struck a nerve. "You think I should take a step back and conform to reality, isn't that right?"

Akane kept her mouth closed, listening quietly. She didn't want to further piss off her traveling companion.

Skylar's face tightened more. "Friends have told me the same stupid thing. They think I'm some zany airhead, a fucking birdbrain, or ditsy. But it's the conformists who stay content being doormats for the Commonwealth Government. Prosperity seekers like *yours truly* become trailblazers."

Akane heard her mother's words of encouragement echo in her mind: *"Remember, Akane, even the most herculean feats can be conquered."* Her parents had raised her to never cast a shadow on anyone's dreams.

"You're right. I'm sorry," Akane said.

Skylar's features instantly unkinked, softening. "No prob, girlfriend. We're good."

The mist finally stopped. Next, a gelatinous decon chemical lathered them from head to toe. Thirty seconds later, a shower of water rinsed it away. Then the drying cycle activated. After that, the pods' three metal rings spun, emitting purple X-ray beams. A chirp from the medical sensors declared them healthy for travel.

Decon completed, Akane and Skylar retrieved their clothes from the deposit bins and dressed.

Exiting the doors, they saw Ella, Jacobi, and Desmond waiting for them. Ella proceeded to lead the group to the ship hangar, where a single passenger carrier was docked.

The beneficiaries hurried up the boarding ramp, relieved to at last part from their crude, mean-spirited chaperon.

A bulkhead separated the cockpit from the passenger compartment, giving the group privacy. There was seating for up to twenty-five people, so the cabin felt spacious for just four.

The pilot, a woman wearing the standard orange jumpsuit, wrapped up her launch checks and spoke over the intercom, sounding cheerful. "Alright, ladies and gents, this is Deloris, your pilot speaking. We are a go. Sit back and enjoy the ride."

The roll-up hangar door reeled open, and the shuttle rolled out onto the tarmac. Its propulsion system powered up. Engine cycling from a low purr to a high-pitched whine, the shuttle climbed into the sky, giving the group a sweeping overhead view of the colony.

Jacobi stared through a porthole, an aggrieved look in his eyes. A hodgepodge of stacked tenements, small living pods, dilapidated MHUs, and rusting girders of long-unfinished structures—promised to be completed years ago—shrank into specks as the surface grew distant.

A montage of childhood memories flooded his mind. He remembered his parents talking about sitting in auditoriums of resettlement centers as children, government hubs designed to assimilate colonists into the New Humanity's socioeconomic framework, a framework crafted by the Advanced Exascale Global Information-collection System—AEGIS.

The centers' "indoctrination" programs prepared colonists for their roles in society. They were told being resource harvesters was an honor and that the New Humanity rested on their shoulders. The programs conditioned their minds to accept second-class citizenship, an attempt at social engineering. Megascreens displayed images of the lush metropolises to come; Satellite One was supposed to replicate Eden eventually. The Commonwealth Government filled colonists' minds with hope.

After the Phazharian and Bhalkran wars, the Commonwealth Government led the colonists to believe the financial toll from those wars was why the vision promised hadn't come to fruition yet. It was the reason they had to tolerate years of insalubrious living conditions. In actuality, colonists were victims of systemic degradation.

Jacobi turned red just thinking about the squalor of impoverished zones in his sector, colonists' cries for equality discredited by the government and the media. The government seemed to always control the narrative.

The colony labor force was keeping the Commonwealth afloat. They harvested invaluable resources that ensured humanity's star nation remained a thriving republic. *We're the lifeblood of the New Humanity,* Jacobi thought. *But we're treated like spokes on a wheel. We're told our purpose is to be manual laborers for the government and megacorporations.* This was his chance to stick it to the system designed to keep colonists at the bottom of the socioeconomic ladder. This was his opportunity to be the maker of his own fate and honor his mother.

The fatal infection his mother had contracted from the toxins in the mines she had worked in doomed her to a premature death. He watched his emaciated, bedridden mother wilt away, intubated to a shabby life-support system in an underfunded intensive care ward. Mrs. Johnston had wanted her only child to live a life of abundance. Obtaining Eden citizenship was Jacobi's chance to make that life a reality.

As the shuttle emerged into space, its hull juddered.

Skylar sat by a window, stargazing in amazement. *Holy fuck, outer space!*

Akane lounged back in her recliner, her hands resting behind her head. She pondered what trials awaited her on Eden. Knowing a lot of suck was in store for everyone aboard, she'd suggested that

Skylar temper her excitement, but nothing seemed to dampen the jolly optimist's enthusiasm.

Jacobi walked over to Akane's seat, hands tucked into his hoodie's pockets. "Hey, Akane, what's the first thing you're gonna do when we get to Eden?" He was obviously trying to lure her into a social chat.

"Dunno," Akane replied in a barely audible, flat tone.

As someone who'd envied lottery beneficiaries, Jacobi was angered by Akane's apparent lack of appreciation for this golden opportunity. She should've forfeited her lottery win and let a more grateful entrant take her spot, he thought. Scads of admittance factors, some as minuscule as physical and mental disabilities, disqualified colony selectees from Eden citizenship. Some selectees simply didn't meet the IQ requirements. To maximize the human race's survival probability, only the best of it was meant to inhabit Eden. Yet Akane, one of the privileged few who had secured Eden citizenship, was acting all petulant.

"Well, you don't seem all that thankful for this fortunate position we've lucked into," Jacobi said. "This is our chance to no longer be pigeonholed to a lifetime of marginalization. What gives?"

Akane sat upright and went on the defensive, facial expression intense. "Listen, pal, my parents prayed for me to win Eden citizenship, and I intend to honor them. But I'm a realist. That's all. I'd rather serve myself a dose of reality now than psych myself up for major disappointment.

"So, yeah, just because I'm not jumping through the roof right now doesn't mean I don't value this opportunity. I'm just a down-to-earth type of girl. Now stick a fork in it. Beat it."

"I see." Jacobi backed off and took a seat beside Desmond across the aisle.

"So what's up with her?" Desmond aimed a thumb in Akane's direction. "Why is she such a grinch?"

"Hey, I heard that, you jerk!" Akane shouted.

"Sorry!" Desmond bellowed. He then lowered his voice to a whisper. "Why is she so moody?" he asked Jacobi.

Jacobi dropped his volume to "covert level" as well. "She's just trying to stay level-headed. And I get it. Things will probably get worse for us before they get better."

"Hey, you guys talkin' about me?" Akane yelled over at them, suspicious.

"Uh, no, not at all," Jacobi replied. *Geesh.*

Desmond shifted the conversation. "So, what's your dream, man?"

"Knowledge excites me. I want to enroll in one of the universities. I want to study abroad on other planets and commingle with different races, then take that knowledge and do some good." Wanderlust and enthusiasm held Jacobi in their thrall.

"You're the scholarly type, huh?"

Jacobi shrugged. "I guess so. What's your dream?"

"I'm gonna join the Commonwealth Defense Force, enlist in the Land Combatant Corps."

"A friend of mine, a lottery beneficiary, told me the physical challenges at BCT are supertough, as one can expect. But then immigrants like us have to deal with bigoted drill sergeants on top of that. You ready?"

Desmond's overconfident smirk suggested he was beyond ready. "All fine by me, brother. I live for a good physical challenge. It gets me thrilled. And I play all sorts of contact sports in my sector. A buncha prick drill sergeants aren't gonna intimidate me." Desmond liked to get rowdy, roughhouse, and loved weapons. Knowing their son well, his mother and father supported his decision to join the CDF. They thought it was a good career choice for him. "Yup, the military's where I belong, bud."

"Well, you've certainly got the drive. I'll say that much. I'm sure you'll do well."

"Thanks." Desmond's eyes glanced to where Skylar was sitting, behind Akane. Usually extroverted and energetic, she'd finally run out of juice and was now sound asleep. And Desmond found the sight of a peacefully sleeping Skylar adorable. "Hey, just so you know, I got dibs on Skylar."

Jacobi laughed. "You can have at her all you want. I'm not auditioning for 'boyfriend' for either of those two."

"Is that why you keep prowling around that Oriental chick?"

A flush crept into Jacobi's complexion. "It's not what you think. My interest is *strictly* platonic."

Desmond's internal lie detector went off. "Yeah, right, sure it is," he said archly. "Tell me you're not jockeying to get into her underpants."

Jacobi tried to hide the fact that Akane's presence quickened his pulse and set butterflies loose in his stomach. "I'm not in pursuit of anything beyond cordial relations, my friend."

"Uh-huh. Liar."

Her body overtaken by lassitude, Akane closed her heavy eyelids. Thoughts of her parents and the looming possibility of civil war swirled in her mind. Then sleep finally claimed her.

The hull vibrated, and shifting patterns of multicolored light gleamed outside the windows as the shuttle transitioned into Hyperspace Leap.

"Akane, wake up! Wake up, Akane!" Skylar hollered.
Akane groaned tiredly as a pair of hands rocked her from her

slumber. She awoke to the sight of Skylar leaning over her.

Akane's mouth turned downward, and her features pinched at Skylar's annoyingly chipper smile. She was on the brink of shoving Skylar to the floor. "What is it, damn it?" She sounded pouty.

Exuberantly, Skylar replied, "We're close now! It's almost time!"

Akane rubbed the grogginess from her eyes. "Really!" Her heartbeat raced.

Skylar retook her seat, her whole body on edge. This was it, the day she'd been waiting for. At last, she was going to see Eden.

"Eden inbound," the pilot reported over the intercom. The planet's single green-and-brown continental landmass grew closer on her viewport screens. A countdown blinked on the console. "Atmospheric entry in three . . . two . . . one."

Piercing Eden's atmosphere, the shuttle rattled and began its descent. It soared above sublime towering feats of architecture, while surfing the turbulence stirred by headwinds.

Conical, pyramidal, and domed edifices with shining windows blurred past, along with other structures alien to a colonist.

Akane leaned into the starboard window, plastering her palms against the glass.

She watched colorful flyers dart over the solar-paneled roadways, amid masterworks of engineering constructed of glass, metal, and phyocrete. "*Holllyyyy* fucking shit!"

The clean-swept surface below teemed with activity. Tiny figures of pedestrians strolled across or rode slideways. They entered and exited a mélange of shops and restaurants.

In awe, Akane trembled. *This is incredible!*

Exclamations broke out from the group. Fingers pointed at this and that.

The shuttle streaked past golden spires spearing the sky. After five more minutes of flight, it decelerated, banked downward, and leveled off smoothly. Its undercarriage repulsors fired as it began a steady vertical descent, touching down on the outdoor landing deck of the immigrant reception station just outside Myrtle City.

The engines gave a final gasp before falling silent. Cooling metal creaked in the hush that followed.

The pilot pressed the intercom button. "Ladies and gents, your trip has come to an end." A panel of blinking instruments dimmed, and the viewport screens showing the outside went dark. "You may now disembark."

The fuselage's door unsealed, and the boarding ramp extended onto the airstrip to let everyone off the shuttle.

The beneficiaries walked down the ramp into the brilliance of a cloudless sky and vivid sun.

A burly, fully bearded porter was unloading their luggage bags from the storage hold—four duffle bags that could be worn on the back or carried using their straps. "Hurry up. Come get your stuff so we can get moving," he barked.

The beneficiaries collected their luggage and followed the porter to a white commuter van.

"My name's Finnegan, by the way," he said as he climbed into the driver's seat. "I'll be dropping you off at Central Square. You can find lodging there and just about anything else you need."

Skylar slid into a window seat. Akane claimed the spot beside her. Across from them, Jacobi and Desmond settled into the same row.

Finnegan input the destination into the van's onboard navigation system, letting autodrive take the wheel.

As the autonomous van made its way to Central Square, throngs of men and women bustled through the city. There were no dirt roads, compact row homes, living pods, and stacked tenements here. The contrast between Satellite One and Eden was stark, like night and day, heaven and hell. On Satellite One, there were no aerial vehicles, and colonists didn't have any of the technological boons that Edenites took for granted.

The van purred to a stop at a red light in the entertainment district. Skylar's starstruck eyes stared at the giant hologram of Mercedes Gardner projecting from a skyscraper's roof. The superstar's ginger hair cascaded past her hips.

That's gonna be me. I know it! Skylar thought.

Skylar pictured scores of fans screaming her name as the concert's MC introduced her: *"Without further ado, the one you've all been waiting for, Skylarrrr Graaccceeee!"*

The van jerked into motion, giving the beneficiaries a rolling view of a strip mall.

High-end storefronts of haute couture infected Skylar with the shopping bug. One sign said OUT-OF-THIS-WORLD GLAM CENTRAL. Another said SO-FINE GALAXY APPAREL. The stores' window displays exhibited extraterrestrial fashion.

Skylar's intrigued eyes twinkled. "Tomorrow, you and I *have* to come back here, Akane."

"*Uh*, shouldn't we be preserving our *credits*?" Akane's brow furrowed.

"Aw, come on, don't be a spoilsport. We've got like four to six months' worth of living credits. And this isn't some backwater world. This is Eden! It won't take us long to get on our feet, not in the land of milk and honey. Live a little, Akane."

"Well—" Akane was close to caving.

Skylar playfully nudged Akane's shoulder with her knuckles. "Oh, don't be a party pooper!"

Akane finally relented to peer pressure. "Okay, fine, but let's not go overboard tomorrow."

"Cool! A girls' day out tomorrow! Yaasss!"

Akane shook her head derisively.

It took only seconds for Skylar to dive back into conversation. "So, have you given it more thought: your purpose, your life mission?"

"My people often refer to it as ikigai. And no, I haven't. I'm focused on staying off the street and making sure I don't go hungry. I'll worry about my *purpose* later."

Skylar offered some unwanted encouragement, ignoring Akane's nonverbal cues, which clearly expressed her irritation with the subject—the facial tics, mashing of her lips together, and grinding of her teeth. "Don't worry, you'll find it," Skylar said.

Akane grunted. She wasn't concerned about finding "it" right now.

The van hissed to a halt at the beneficiaries' destination, Central Square. "This is the drop-off point. Good luck to ya," Finnegan said.

The van's doors unlocked and slid apart to release the beneficiaries into the hustle and bustle. Once everyone had gathered their luggage and exited, the van hummed away.

The city's pristine condition amazed the beneficiaries.

Myrtle City, like other metropolises on Eden, boasted high air quality, spotless streets, and first-rate housing. Not even one building was run-down. The city provided idyllic living.

Skylar watched sanitation golems sweep, scrub, and sterilize streets, slideways, and building windows. "Cool, robots!"

She darted toward a storefront display, drawn in by the flashy apparel. Her foot stepped onto a sensor panel beneath the window, and a colorful cyclone of eye-catching pop-up holos burst to life around her—a swirling three-dimensional showcase of skirts, pants, blouses, and lingerie.

Her eyes glittered with fascination as they flitted left and right. *Superfucking cool.* She tapped the advertisement graphic in one of the floating frames. Instantly, the dress in the advertisement shot out and wrapped itself over her body in a projection of light. She was wearing the hologram over her clothes. "Holy shit."

The holowords BUY NOW circled her head.

Jacobi stared, stunned. It was unlike anything he'd ever seen.

Skylar stepped off the sensor panel, and the entire holographic brochure dissolved, along with the outfit she'd been "wearing."

Desmond canted his head skyward. Above the eateries, boutiques, and corner stores were glass-walled balconies of ultramodern living complexes, and there were tiers of open-air walkways connecting towering retail centers.

Citizens were in high spirits. They seemed carefree, laid-back, and easygoing, unencumbered by the hardships colonists faced. And suicides caused by depression were virtually nonexistent.

Akane had never been gullible enough to view Eden through rose-colored glasses, and now the city's glitz and glamour were wearing thin. The honeymoon was over. Reality had reared its ugly head—exposure therapy. She and her new friends had been transplanted into a world of technology and culture they knew nothing about. They had to fend for themselves and claw their way up the broken rungs of the ladder of immigrant success.

Young Highborn fashionistas, clad in garish smartwear, strutted past Akane. They spoke in unfamiliar jargon while operating wristcoms, playing sim games on gamecom pads, and using other gizmos Akane couldn't even name.

A suffocating feeling welled up in her chest. She felt like an Earth Era relic, light-years behind the curve on mankind's technological evolution, and she felt so uncultured.

Anxiety tightened her muscles, and the pit of her gut churned.

Her fear response was to flee back to Colony Three to cower inside its refuge. But the daughter of Benjiro and Akari Sugimori was no wimp. She steeled her composure and drowned out the voice of weakness in her head.

Eden was her home now, and she'd confront her discomfort and fears head-on. She was going to honor her hardworking parents, who wanted nothing more than to see her flourish on the New Humanity's motherworld.

Curious eyes scrutinized the beneficiaries. Some people stared with repulsion.

Though the beneficiaries were part of the Union's human community too, they were foreigners on this world, and they stood out like a sore thumb—the way they moved and dressed was telling.

Two women walked past Akane, hand in hand. They wore matching attire: light-up miniskirts, short tops that exposed their flat midriffs, and ankle boots. Floating helper golems followed the couple, lugging their overstuffed handbags.

To Akane, this world felt surreal, like a dream.

Questions arose in the back of her mind. What would she and her new friends do for employment? How long would their credit vouchers last before they hit rock bottom? How could they connect with other lottery beneficiaries?

Blithely unconcerned about the severity of their situation, Jacobi, Skylar, and Desmond stood amid a tide of humanity, frissons of excitement prickling their flesh. They saw intergalactic tourists and day-trippers, wearing language translators around their necks, commingling with humans. While the sight was commonplace for Edenites, it was alien to colonists.

People chatted beneath pedestrian shelters, waiting for air-cabs. Teenagers riding hover scooters laughed. Land vehicles honked. Flyers roared overhead. Roads and air lanes buzzed with moving traffic. So many sounds. So much activity.

As her friends soaked in the city's energetic atmosphere, Akane thought, *This is where life kicks you in the ass and gives you a major wake-up call.*

CHAPTER ONE

PRESENT DAY

Star Palace (space station)
Specialist Randal Scott's Cabin

The warm, soothing mix of pristine water and chemical relaxant sluiced from the shower jets, soaking Randy's golden-brown hair and cascading down his well-built frame. He exhaled, relief washing over him as his melancholic mood began to subside. Pressing his palms against the sleek tiled wall, he leaned into the spray, letting it pound his shoulders and back.

He expected to get chewed out by his task force leader, Lieutenant Breckenridge, for the physical altercation he'd started with his teammate last night. To Randy, the mouthy dumb prick deserved a beating.

Randy had returned to the CDF after a three-month hiatus, granted by the few top-ranking allies who still supported him.

Most had turned their backs on him after his "treason." But he had no regrets about switching sides and fighting for the colonies. The civil war's aftermath brought the imprisonment of corrupt government officials, the rise of an interim Chief Executive with morals, and promises of colony reform.

Upon returning to the CDF after his short vacation, he had two career trajectories to choose from: join one of the ongoing planetary-impact missions or be assigned to the CDF's Expedition Task Forces (ETF).

The ETF appeared to be the best choice. Gallivanting across the universe to dispatch human and intergalactic bandits, marauders, traffickers, and ruiners of lives sounded like a good change-up from being stationed dirtside in a combat zone. Been there, done that. But whichever path he chose, one thing was certain: He'd need to get reacclimated to the CDF—a post-civil-war CDF—and get reacclimated to being "Randal Scott."

Before Operation Hammer Fall, he was the young Guardian full of piss and vinegar hellbent on restoring honor to his family's revered name by killing the man who'd tainted it, his father, Arson Scott.

Back then, many lower and upper-ranking Guardians sympathized with Randy and respected him. His sphere of supporters had included brass in the CDF and law enforcement. Favors he requested got approved without hesitation. Now—post-war, post "treason"—the privileges, respect, and reverence attached to his family name were gone. Not that he gave a damn, though; he was still the same man, with or without such prerogatives.

Fellow Guardians now kept their distance. When near, they gave him the silent treatment and condescending side-glances, like he was some contagious vermin, not their brother-in-arms. To them, he was just a traitor, a bastard who'd forsaken the Oath and sided with insurrectionists that brought their campaign of terror to Eden soil.

Now he and other defectors who'd rejoined the CDF were getting the same disrespectful outsider treatment that immigrant Guardians had been enduring for years. These immigrants hadn't committed treason to warrant such treatment; it was because AEGIS had deemed them unfit for Eden citizenship. They were "nadir" meant to be resource harvesters only and were "contaminating" the prestige of the Defense Force.

The disrespect hit a new low when civil war erupted between the Commonwealth Government and seceding colonies, a war that finally ended, after months, with the Battle of the Quad.

Since the war's conclusion, with no Coalition fighters being tried for war crimes, there'd been an upsurge in the mistreatment of immigrants within the CDF: mysterious hangings, rank delays, bullying, harassment. Rigged investigations were doing little to apprehend the culprits. They were protected by a culture of immunity.

Mistreatment of immigrant Guardians and citizens had reached unprecedented levels. Anger was being taken out on Eden's immigrant population because it was their people, those living on Satellite One, who had ignited the New Humanity's first civil war.

The war's end seemed to bring out the worst in the worst of human beings. And in truth, it felt like a civil war was still being waged, a discreet, weaponless one—a war of ideologies and beliefs being fought in the political arena, between compatriots, and among Guardians.

This was supposed to be peacetime, but Randy knew that peace was fragile—brittle. It'd only take a spark to set the Commonwealth ablaze.

He'd hate to be the Chief right now. On one side of the dilemma, immigrant activists were demanding a crackdown on hate crimes. On the other, disgruntled and bereaved nonimmigrants—the majority of Eden's population—were rioting for retribution over the service members killed by the Coalition. Mysterious fringe groups had even posted names and faces of former Coalition fighters on the net, spurring lone wolves to travel to Satellite One and go on a witch hunt.

Times were tumultuous. Chief Executive wasn't a job Randy would ever want. All things considered, Oviereya was holding the Commonwealth together quite well.

Still thinking about the mistreatment of immigrant Guardians, he found the division within the CDF insane, and it was only growing worse. Guardians were supposed to be brothers and sisters. Now, more than ever, that ideal felt like a lie.

Upon his voice command, the shower disengaged and the drying cycle activated, blower vents whistling. Once dry, Randy stepped up to the mirror and wiped away the condensation obscuring his reflection. He examined the shiner around his left eye, a receipt from the brawl he'd started.

Emotions compounded. "Damn it!" he blurted.

He'd just given his task force commander, Captain Valentina Narvaez, a reason to write up a negative counseling statement in his service sketch. And now higher-ups had even more ammunition to screw with his rank promotion, one he was sure was already being blocked by some big-shot officer way above his pay grade. No doubt because he was a "treasonist."

Like all Coalition fighters, including CDF defectors, Randy had been absolved of war crimes by Chief Executive Amaechi. So in a perfect world, his comrades and society wouldn't shun him. The Union leaders themselves had declared the Coalition's rebellion justified. But this wasn't a perfect world, was it? The exoneration of Coalition fighters had only poured fuel on the fire, stoking the anger of many Guardians and Eden citizens.

Passing his fingers over the bruised flesh encircling his eye, Randy cursed the asshole who'd pushed his emotional triggers to the brink of violence, Paul Shaffer.

Randy had thick skin. He knew how to stay cool and ignore petty bullshit. But Paul's cryptic verbal jabs and vexatious teasing had gotten on his last nerve. Enough was enough. He'd tried to deck the prick but missed. That sparked the brawl. Paul took his shot and nailed Randy in the eye. Luckily, Captain Narvaez had stumbled onto the scene and broken up the fight, because Randy was sure he would've kicked Paul's ass into next week.

Paul was definitely someone he'd have to be on his p's and q's around. Not only did the irritant hate so-called traitors, he hated that immigrants were allowed to enlist in the CDF.

Randy stared into the mirror for a long time, the wheels in his head turning. He mulled over who he could actually trust on the nine-man task force he'd been assigned to, Vanguard Alpha.

Lieutenant Carl Breckenridge, the team's field-combat leader, seemed trustworthy. Randy was still feeling him out, but Carl didn't seem to subscribe to the same invidious behavior that Paul did, at least not while in uniform. Maybe he was just putting professionalism before personal bias. Sergeant Jenny Pines seemed cool so far too.

Of the remaining six teammates, Paul and his two buddies, Sergeant Mark MaCallum and Corporal Dan Maddox, were the ones who'd earned permanent spots on Randy's watch list. He'd have to be a fool to trust any of them. Hell, he didn't even want to count on them in a firefight. And that was a crying shame.

Still getting to know the other three—Sergeant Sam Guthrie,

Specialist Jamie (Jay) Lister, and Private Akane Sugimori—Randy felt confident only about Akane. After all, she was an immigrant, from Colony Three *(which had the highest population of Asiatic migrants)*. She understood what it was like being hated.

Akane had welcomed him with generosity from day one of this new mission assignment. And even though she wasn't his usual type—white, blond, athletic build with decent curves—he had to admit that the tomboy wasn't hard on the eyes. She was cute. And reading between the lines, she was a little smitten with him. Infatuated, even. Understandably so. They'd developed good chemistry and vibed naturally. They forced nothing. Their interactions flowed organically.

Given the emotional strain he was under from being ostracized, Akane's presence was a relief. He was fond of her and gravitated toward her upbeat, chill demeanor. Her lively energy was a breath of fresh air. But he had to be careful. At just nineteen, she was young and impressionable. The last thing he wanted was to mislead her into thinking their friendly dynamic was a prelude to romance.

Nope, no romance was brewing. Not now, not ever. It didn't matter how cute he found Akane to be. Getting emotionally entangled with another woman wasn't in the cards. His relationship with Stacie Spencer, virtually the woman of his dreams, had gone up in flames because of him. He'd made the mistake of his life, a mistake he owned.

Because he'd been Linked with Stacie, getting over her wasn't easy. Shared memories, emotions, and sensations from their time together remained ingrained in his cerebral implant. Just thinking about her now, he could practically feel her all over him—her touch, her lips, the soft, creamy press of her naked body as they cuddled. The phantom sensations were so palpable that his spine tingled.

Strengthening intimacy through Linking was always an intrinsic risk. If a long-term relationship crashed and burned, romantic partners could experience a short-term case of relationship withdrawal referred to as Cerebral-attachment Syndrome, a constant recycling of feelings, emotions, memories, and sensations. Even recurring dreams of their ex-lover occurred. Thanks to the mnemonic power of a cerebral implant, Cerebral-attachment Syndrome could last from weeks to months.

Trying to move forward with his life, and get past the syndrome, he had tested the waters with Kesley Whittaker. The sex was off the chain, but fantastic sex wasn't enough to sustain a long-term intimate relationship. She just wasn't the woman he wanted to cocreate a lifelong partnership with, so their fling fizzled out. But they remained on good terms. They'd be friends for life, after everything they'd survived together.

Randy shoved thoughts of Stacie out of his head, left the bathroom, and headed for his closet. His cabin wasn't anything to write home about: a fold-out wall bed, an armoire, and a table. Still, it was roomier than the cabins aboard Vanguard Alpha's ship, the *Nightingale*.

From the wardrobe of CDF uniforms and civvies inside the closet, he took out a sleeve and stepped into it. Pulling the thin flex material over the defined muscles of his body, he slid his stout arms into the armholes. Then he yanked up the zipper, drawing the single-piece suit snug over his chest.

Movement for today's op was slated for zero-eight-hundred hours. That gave him a little over an hour until showtime. It was a direct-action mission. Vanguard Alpha had been tasked with raiding the compound of a human-trafficking racket that had abducted several of the Commonwealth's women, along with women from planets outside the Union, adding to an emerging intergalactic diaspora of rescued victims.

The traffickers were also dealing guns, mechsuits, weaponized vehicles, and anything else that would fetch a profit on the black markets of the universe. Human criminals had been lining their pockets off the burgeoning intergalactic trafficking industry since Earth Era and showed no signs of slowing down.

First order of the morning for Randy was chow, as usual.

The two halves of the motion-activated door split as he approached, and he exited his quarters. Crossing the corridor, he ran into Mark MaCallum and Dan Maddox, Paul Shaffer's cohort. The two were having an animated discussion, peppered with profanity.

Mark gestured wildly as he spoke to Dan. "Can you believe this soft-ass Chief? Ethics investigations into CDF culture? Suspending planetary-impact missions *she's* not cool with? This is her idea of . . . reformation." He scoffed.

"Yeah," Dan replied, "she should focus on solving the Commonwealth's debt crisis and leave the CDF out of her reformist warpath."

They heard the sound of boots coming in their direction.

Mark caught Randy in the corner of his eye. He twisted around, a sneering smile playing on his lips. "Well, well, if it isn't Randal Scott—Warrior Extraordinaire, son of the infamous war hero Arson Scott, and most of all, a *traitor*."

"Excuse me," Randy said casually. He made a detour around them.

Dan chuckled. "How's that black eye?" he asked, taking a dig at Randy to waylay him. "Maybe next time, learn how to throw a punch"—he mimicked how to throw a "correct" punch—"before taking a cheap shot at Shaffer."

Jaw clenched, eyes forward, Randy distanced himself from the troublemakers.

"What's wrong? Not in a talkative mood?" Dan said. Randy surged ahead with a relaxed stride, disregarding them, acting unbothered. "Look at you, pretending to be all calm and collected, but deep down, you're just a testy little punk kid, aren't you? Not to mention, you're also a *murderer*." Dan was doing his best to bait Randy into a fight. He was itching to beat down the ex-Coalition fighter, the "traitor."

Randy paused. Miffed, he curled his hands into fists.

Pushing the boundaries of Randy's self-restraint, Dan said, "If you don't like what I'm saying, do something about it. Your move, or are you just a pushover?"

Randy kept his emotions in check. He unclenched his fists and moved on, resisting the urge to kick off another fistfight. No need to give Lieutenant Breckenridge another reason to bust his chops. "I don't have time for your childish antics."

"All bark and no bite," Mark said. He and Dan went back to chatting.

Randy rode an elevator pod down to the mezzanine ring of the Star Palace, the CDF's way station in the X-Quadrant. It consisted of three annular tiers, each lined with wraparound windows.

The mezzanine's concourse was alive with restaurants, entertainment venues, rec areas, and commercial vendors. Many nonhuman merchants had set up shop at the Star Palace, with permission from the Commonwealth Government.

The mezzanine ring functioned like a microcity. The lower ring housed the shipyard. Quarters and a few lounges occupied the upper ring.

These space stations served as rest stops for some task forces and as one-to-three-month lodging for those carrying out multiple missions within their assigned quadrant. Vanguard Alpha had been at the Star Palace three days now, prepping for their op. It would be a short stay. After they rescued the abductees, they would set course back to Eden.

Randy strolled through the busy concourse.

The aroma of exotic cuisines pervaded the air. Guardians ate and bantered with noisy exuberance.

Randy's ears caught snippets of underhanded barbs from Guardians who recognized him as they walked past, some in casual wear, others suited up in sleeves. "There's the traitor . . . Rebel scum . . . Murderer . . . Coalition filth . . . He should be in the grave, not those Guardians . . ."

Randy's watchful eyes scanned his surroundings. He was half-expecting someone to stab him in the back at any moment. Paranoia had him walking on pins and needles. *Is this what it's boiled down to?* he asked himself. *Sizing up my fellow Guardians like they're rabid dogs just waiting to tear into me?*

With the majority of the CDF made up of nonimmigrant Edenites who opposed the colonies' rebellion, Randy felt like a pariah among what was supposed to be his military family.

Up ahead, he spotted Akane sitting with Jay and Sam. The three were feasting on bowls of something flavorful.

They were suited up in their sleeves for the mission. Sam, always upholding an Earth Era soldier's clean-cut image, was freshly shaven and had his hairline high and tight as usual. Randy could tell they were a close-knit trio, bonded by battle.

"Hey, Randy, over here!" Akane called out, voice bright and lively, eyes of adoration glued to him. She jumped from her chair, a mop of straggly bangs tumbling over her forehead. Waving her hand, she flagged him down. "Come join us!"

Randy couldn't help but smile at his admirer's warm invitation. After considering her offer to sit and break bread, he joined his teammates at the dining table. He settled into a chair—Jay to his left, Akane in front of him, and Sam to his right.

From the neighboring tables came laughter, casual chatter, and the clattering of trays and utensils.

Within seconds, a server golem on four wheels rolled up to Randy to take his order. The bot had a cube-like body and a domed head.

Randy chose whatever everyone else at the table was having, and the golem buzzed away.

"Randal Scott, the man who helped liberate the colonies from oppression!" Jay said in a jovial tone.

Randy looked toward the young swarthy man with long dreadlocks. Funny how things turned out, he thought; he was a hero to some Guardians, albeit a few, and apparently a bastard to others. And not being a spotlighter, the "hero" stuff meant nothing to him. He didn't think of himself as some war legend or crave any tribute.

In truth, the Battle of the Quad wasn't a simple tale of "good guys" versus "bad guys." Certainly, there were scumbags in the CDF—a lot of scumbags—but not every Guardian was one.

To Randy, the real villains were the corrupt politicians and the avaricious Eight Elite. The Coalition fighters and Guardians who fought the Battle of the Quad were just soldiers following orders on that abominable day. There were heroes on both sides. In his eyes, the Battle of the Quad had simply been one big, unavoidable catastrophe.

"How was it? What was it like fighting in the Battle of the Quad?" Jay asked. He lounged back in his chair, laced his fingers behind his head, and crossed his ankles.

Flashbacks of Guardians going down pulled Randy's mind back to the horror of the battle. He'd done his best to preserve life but hadn't been able to avoid killing some Guardians. It was war, after all. Composing himself, he replied pointedly, "Hellish." That was the best word for it. "Definitely not table talk for me, know what I mean?" No sense in being retraumatized.

Jay uncrossed his ankles and sat upright. "Gotcha," he said, his levity gone. "I know how damaging combat can be to the psyche. Believe me, I've seen a lot of gruesome violence in the hell zones I've been deployed to." His own mind hadn't come out unscathed; planetary-impact missions were rarely pleasant. "Sorry," he added, apologizing for not being more mindful.

"It's okay."

The server golem returned to the table, carrying Randy's entree and a tumbler of fizzing blueberry peppermint chiller on a tray. After setting the tray on the table, it left to take more orders.

"So, where are you and Sam from, colony or Eden?" Randy asked Jay, making casual conversation—and gathering info to assess who he could trust. Sure, Akane trusted Sam and Jay, and he trusted Akane, but he made his own calls. For now, he'd stay guarded.

"I'm from Colony Six. So is Sam," Jay replied.

Knowing they were colony immigrants put Randy at ease. All immigrants respected the Coalition rebels, which meant Jay's admiration was genuine, not pretend or just an icebreaker.

On a screen in the concourse, an anchorman in his late fifties—with silver hair and a dimpled chin—said, "All votes have been counted. Ron Burchardt, a pro-reform dark horse, has defeated the anti-reform candidate Todd Sieger."

This was the third of several special elections being held to choose successors for the Parliament members jailed after the Coalition exposed their corruption. "Pro-reform" had become the media term for candidates committed to accelerating colony development and addressing the surge in immigrant mistreatment. "Anti-reform" referred to those who favored the current gradualist approach to improving colony life and were reluctant to address the challenges immigrants continued to face.

Boos reigned throughout the concourse, most Guardians there being anti-reform. The applause for Ron Burchardt was tepid at best.

The anchorman said, "It seems like a completely illogical victory, based on pre-election polls. Sieger has demanded a recount, and authorities say they'll be investigating suspected voter fraud."

Guardians angry at the election results grumbled.

The anchorman continued. "Now here is our interview with Damien Sykes, who announced his candidacy for Chief Executive three days ago. If elected, he would become the second youngest Chief in history, at thirty-two."

A handsome golden-tan man with slicked-back dark blond hair appeared onscreen. The Sykes family was one of the Seven Elite, formerly Eight, until Stacie Spencer withdrew from the conglomerate. Like the children of the other slain family heads, Damien had inherited the reins of his parents' criminal empire.

The Seven's bylaws forbade family heads from holding political office, as doing so would undermine the conglomerate's balance of power. But Damien was the odd man out. Now in control of his parents' enterprise, he intended to do whatever he damn well pleased.

Randy and his comrades watched the screen. The interview drew the attention of other Guardians as well.

Damien was regarded as a major front-runner for the Chief Executive seat in next year's election. He was gaining traction, and as a staunch proponent of the current socioeconomic status quo, he had become the poster boy for Eden's anti-reform base. Election analysts predicted he would overtake Oviereya and any other candidates who jumped into the race.

The interviewer, a brunette woman in a pantsuit, asked, "What is your message to the people of the Commonwealth, Mr. Sykes?"

Damien, with a snicker and a sly grin, radiated villainous energy. "Simple. We need justice. A bunch of colony insurrectionists started a civil war and invaded our soil, killing Guardians. Not since the Bhalkran War has there been an attack on Eden. Families are grieving. They deserve to see their loved ones' murderers incarcerated, or better yet, executed.

"A lot of people say the Coalition coming to Eden and removing corrupt politicians was a *good* thing. Okay, hear me out. If I went above the law and killed some psychopathic wife beater, would people be pissed off about it? Of course not. But does that mean I just get to walk away scot-free? No, it doesn't.

"So if someone who goes all vigilante is subject to the consequences of the law, then how the hell do a bunch of treasonists get to skate free?" His bronze eyes glared into the camera. "Tell us that, Amaechi. *Huh?* Tell the emotionally devastated widows and parentless children why their loved ones' killers are loose. It makes no fucking sense.

"Eden's people deserve better. And I understand their anguish; my parents, far from perfect, were murdered by the Coalition. Let's face it, these treasonists could've employed other strategies for accomplishing their colony-equality objective. Instead, they ignited a civil war and invaded humanity's motherworld."

"Well, in the Chief Executive's defense, the Union declared the colony rebellion justified, and she has the authority to exonerate anyone she chooses, just like any other Chief," the interviewer said, unknowingly about to set off a tirade.

Damien's brows quirked. The controversial public figure went off. "Exonerate? No, this is different! So don't give me that nonsense! As for the Union playing Big Brother, to hell with their . . . so-called ruling. We need to unseat Amaechi. She's a peace-loving Coalition panderer who needs to be kicked outta office!"

Memories of the Battle of the Quad, refusing to lie dormant, besieged Randy's mind with vivid flashes of combat casualties. His features pinched. Guilt and remorse, for the few lives he'd taken, etched themselves into his face. Then his chin touched his chest.

Jay's green-dyed eyes flicked over at him. "You letting that slimeball get in your head?"

"I'm fine," Randy said flatly, playing down the pain. He sipped his drink, his guilty expression remaining unchanged.

Again, images of the Battle of the Quad slipped into his mind, but he fought them away.

Damien's aggressive tongue continued putting Oviereya on blast. "She's even been promoting the idea of giving the colonies unfettered access to trading partners. You know why that's a dumb idea? Easy, it means Eden would be competing for resources with its own colonies. *Duh.*

"There's a reason things are the way they are. There's a reason we didn't—and shouldn't—deviate from the blueprint AEGIS fashioned for the New Humanity. The system's creators—Doctors Cyrus Kline, Jagr Vlcek, and Atticus Hancroft—knew what they were doing. Oviereya is dismantling our society in a very, very bad way."

After finishing her pink bubbling beverage, Akane slammed her cup on the table and expelled a sigh of disgust. "Damien Sykes, just another fucking Gould."

"Worse," Sam opined. "Gould was well-spoken. He was a

skillful politician. And he was low-key compared to this loudmouth. Sykes is more flamboyant—more of a hothead, more outspoken. He's a demagogue who doesn't give a shit about censoring himself to appeal to the less-extreme or just to save face. Gould articulated himself with finesse. This guy? Not so much. Sykes doesn't play it safe at all, and unfortunately, people are flocking to him."

The thought of Damien becoming Chief put a foul taste in Akane's mouth. "You don't think he'd actually win the election, do you? He's the son of one of the Eight, and the Coalition exposed the family heads for what they were when they published those files on the net. They proved the Eight were just a buncha crime moguls."

Sam said, "Yeah, but Damien's been proven guilty of *nothing*. He's playing dumb, and he's promised to disband all criminal activity. An obvious lie, but in this new era of colonist hate, he's the savior a lot of Edenites are clamoring for. They're energized by this loose cannon, so they overlook what's staring them right in the damn face: the possibility that he's no different from his parents.

"The crazy thing is that I think he has a real shot at unseating the incumbent Chief next year, according to polls.

"Oviereya is soft. This guy's a bloodthirsty, rampaging bull; she's a dove." He sipped his drink. "Oviereya needs to go on the offensive, not just play defense. You try to be passive in a fistfight, your face eventually gets mauled. You've gotta get aggressive in politics, *really* aggressive. Maybe that's not her style, but like on the battlefield, if you don't adapt to your enemy's offense, you're dead."

Listening to Sam, Randy got the impression that he was not only the oldest of everyone at the table but the most insightful and combat-seasoned.

Jay contributed to the convo, saying, "Yeah, but I just can't see some Purist sicko like Sykes becoming the Commonwealth's head honcho." A reproving scowl flickered across Sam's face when Jay said the word "Purist," as if it were forbidden. "We know he's one of 'em," Jay continued, having not noticed Sam's fleeting expression. "He's gotta be. There're even rumors floating around about it now."

Randy raised a brow. "Excuse me, a what?"

"You don't know?" Jay seemed surprised.

"Is there a reason I should?" Randy retorted.

"I guess not. People who *do* hear about Purists usually think they're just fiction, some conspiracy theory cooked up by groupies on the net. Since you were a Coalition rebel, I figured maybe you'd heard about them and that—"

"Sorry, I've never heard of these . . . Purists."

Akane chimed in. "Yeah, understandable. Almost no one knows about them."

"So who are they?"

Akane replied, "They're followers of an extremist movement dedicated to colonist and immigrant oppression. Like Jay said, most people who hear about them think they're just made up. But that's exactly what they want."

Randy listened intently to Akane.

She rested her forearms on the table. "Purists stay incognito. They don't give away who they are. You're not gonna see membership ads on the net or recruitment posters posted around town.

"These people are rotten to the core, the worst of discriminators. Gould was a fucking saint compared to them. These hive-minded, cult-like idealists are *die-hard* believers in AEGIS's social stratification of humanity, like the damn thing was God. They think Eden selectees were 'the ordained' or something.

"Their mission is to preserve the status quo and keep colonists and immigrants down. They've got their slimy tentacles in politics, the government, and even the CDF."

Randy took in everything Akane was saying, but the idea of a clandestine brotherhood of extremists infiltrating all of society's institutions was a lot to accept. Sure, he knew there were extremists out there, but on this scale? He wanted to call bullshit. Maybe Sam, Jay, and Akane thought this . . . hate group was way bigger than it actually was.

Akane said, "All they wanna do is acquire power and gin up fear." Anger flashed in her eyes. "We think Purists within the CDF are behind most of the rank delays, hangings, and harassment of immigrant Guardians. Their keep-the-hate-alive movement is catching fire, attracting followers."

The edge in her voice sharpened. "*Purists* are the ones who used the net to broadcast the identities of Coalition fighters to the public, calling for wackos to hunt them down. Our hunch is that even Sergeant Shaffer's one of—"

Sam craned his head toward Akane, brows knitted. She fell silent, cutting herself off.

Randy, observant and incisive, tried to decipher the enigmatic message on Sam's face. He wasn't quite sure what it meant. It came off as a reprimand, a signal to shut up, as if Akane might be disclosing too much.

"Akane, I think Randy's heard enough," Sam said in a reproachful tone. "Some of this may be a lot to digest. We don't want him thinking we're nuts or something, now do we?"

Everyone became quiet.

Randy's eyes swept over the frozen faces at the table. Not one mouth moved. To diffuse the awkward atmosphere, which was dragging on, he said, "The meal was delicious." He got up. "I'm going to head to the *Nightingale*. I'll see you guys there." He walked away.

Slapping her hands down on the table, Akane pushed herself up from her chair. "Let me talk to him. He might even be able to convince Arson Scott himself to lend us a hand." To emphasize such significance, she added, "War hero. Coalition icon. Reza's *top* commander. *Hell-oh*."

"You think we can trust him fully?" Jay asked, turning his head from Sam to Akane with a skeptical look. "He killed Reza, after all. The Purists had Gould to believe in, we had Reza. And he and his dad took Reza from us."

Sam twined his fingers. He spoke thoughtfully, relaying his opinion. "Jay, Reza was my hero too. And I think he had the right idea, eliminating the Eight family heads and the corrupt officials. Some call it murder; I call it justice. But the fact of the matter is that Reza's change in course was going to end in defeat.

"Him doing a one-eighty and crowning himself sovereign ruler of the Commonwealth would've caused the Coalition's assault force to implode, those for the change and those opposed to it fighting each other. Then the CDF would've taken advantage of the infighting and crushed the assault force entirely. Even if the rebels had stayed united, there was *absolutely* no way they could've overpowered the CDF.

"Hammer Fall was supposed to be a quick op: take over the Quad, release the corruption files to the public, and call for peace. With Reza's new plan, the Coalition would've eventually lost the Battle of the Quad, unless he had some secret ace up his sleeve.

"And don't think Guardians or Eden citizens were going to praise Reza as a savior just because he exposed government corruption and the mistreatment of colonists. Bullshit."

Jay shifted uncomfortably, absorbing Sam's words.

Sam said, "Yeah, it's a tough fucking pill to swallow, but the Scotts made the right call, killing Reza and paving the way for Amaechi to become Chief Executive.

"Don't get the wrong idea, though. I listen to Reza's orations nearly every day. I teach my kids about him, so they'll know the revolutionary he was, not the tyrant most of Eden portrays him to be. But Reza let power poison his head. You take over things internally, not always by force. You infiltrate sectors of the government and military. You game the system. You mete out justice not by public executions but in the most discreet way possible—a way that doesn't draw attention to yourself, a way that leaves no footprints. Plausible deniability. Reza's downfall was himself, Jay."

Jay leaned into the backrest of his chair and took a moment of silence, coming to terms with the truth. "But do you think Randal Scott would cede to our ideals, our way of doing things?"

A driven woman, Akane remained persistent. "Just let me talk to him. I can persuade him to join us." She fixed her eyes on Sam, seeking approval. "Yea or nay, Guthrie?" Her irritation rose as she alternated her thumb between thumbs-up and thumbs-down. "C'mon."

Sam's pale-blue eyes stared at Akane. He could see she was passionate about enlisting Randy's help for their mission. "Alright, he's your assigned prospect now. Feed him info in small doses. No need to overdo it. Use sound judgment."

Akane nodded in understanding and raced off after Randy, a smile tugging on the corners of her mouth.

Jay said to Sam, "Akane's drooling over Randal Scott a little too much. She's getting way too attached. I respect the guy for airdropping onto the Quad and risking life and limb to emancipate the colonies from systematic oppression, but he's not part of our trusted circle yet. It's too early for Akane to be getting *that* cozy."

"Honestly, Jaime, I don't care who Akane gushes over. As long as she's deadass sure where Scott's mindset is at before letting him through our door, she can get starry-eyed over him all she wants."

While navigating the jam-packed concourse of D-Block to catch up to Randy, Akane hollered, "Hey, Randy, wait up!" She jostled shoulder after shoulder. "Excuse me . . . Sorry . . . Pardon me . . . Comin' through."

"Hey, watch where you're goin'," a man snapped as Akane shoved past him.

"Randy!" Akane called out.

Randy paused and wheeled around. "Akane, what's up?"

Akane caught her breath. "We still got some time before the strategy brief. Stroll with me, 'kay?"

I wonder what her aim is. Curious where the conversation might lead, Randy accepted her offer. "Sure, okay. Why not? Like you said, we've got some time, and I'd like to get better acquainted with my teammates."

"Awesome." Eardrums pestered by raucous idle chatter, Akane scanned for a quieter venue. Taking notice of the environmental recreation-domes, she said, "How about a park sim?"

"Yeah, that'll work."

They approached one of the silver dome-shaped constructs. The doors chirped and hissed open. Inside was a hydroponic biosphere simulating a park, complete with fancy white benches, misting fountains, and walk bridges arched over artificial ponds.

The sky was a hyperrealistic holo, bright and blue with puffy white clouds. Piped-in sound effects mimicked birdsong. The plant life, like the colorful flower beds, was organic, grown synthetically.

Good replica, Randy thought as he and Akane began their nature walk. The simulation definitely felt real.

His cerebral implant pinged. Akane had forwarded a Link request. "Yeah, right." He rejected it, shutting down her hopes for a deeper connection—one of the most intimate connections of all.

Akane hadn't expected him to accept a Link request this early in their budding relationship, but it was worth a try. "C'mon, I want you to trust me, Randy. We're already friends, right? So what's the big deal?"

Whoever said we were friends? "Let's cross one bridge at a time. Besides, why the heck would you want to be inside my head?"

Akane gaped. "You're fucking kidding me, right? You participated in one of the greatest acts of heroism in Commonwealth history! The liberators who airdropped onto the Quad that day are rock stars to immigrants like me, especially you and your dad!"

Randy furrowed his brow. Was that why she wanted to Link? To get closer to a so-called "colony hero"? To learn from him? To get an orgasmic thrill from being psychically connected to someone she had a major crush on? The last thing he needed right now was a one-girl fan club.

As they sauntered under a trellis threaded with green vines, Akane said, "Thanks to you and your dad, the ceasefire happened. It's because of you two that Amaechi became Chief and started the Colony Restoration Initiative." While they strolled, holos of Earth Era animals materialized: rabbits, tortoises, squirrels, and others. "Who the fuck *wouldn't* wanna Link with you, man?"

This kid's head was in the clouds, Randy thought, and it was time to bring her back down to reality. He paused their walk right at the trellis' exit and censured her. "Believe me, there's a lot up here"—he pointed to his temple—"that you *don't* want to see. That you don't want to experience. You can't comprehend the chronic trauma the Battle of the Quad cursed me with, faceless dead forever memorialized in my mind.

"You haven't encountered true pain, Akane, *my* pain—the pain of killing fellow Guardians, combined with the pain of killing Coalition fighters I believed were the enemy before I joined them. The mental anguish never fully goes away. You can't outfight it. Its echo always returns to torment me. The strife I live with, Akane . . . you don't want to know.

"And sure, I could've refused to participate in Hammer Fall. I could've just gone back to Eden and sat on the sidelines, joined neither the CDF nor the Coalition, to protect my conscience." He sighed. "But I don't regret participating in Hammer Fall. I can't pull a time machine out of my ass and rewrite history, anyway.

"But because of that battle—because of the sacrifice I made—I can't even live out my own fucking military career in peace. I'm always having to keep my head on a swivel, fearing a Guardian will knife me in the back for revenge. Best you protect the sanctity of your mind from any spillage of my unpleasant misfortune."

In an offended tone, Akane struck back. "Hey, *wiseass*, save the roasting for some newbie fresh out of Basic. I already know something about living with pain." The headstones of Skylar Grace and Desmond Castillo flashed in her mind, along with the headstone of a woman dear to her. Akane Sugimori wasn't a newcomer to pain and suffering.

"Do you?" Randy questioned her.

"Yeah, and I know what it's like to live with paranoia too. I'm an immigrant, a target for Purists inside and outside the CDF. And you're a target as well, because they hate every rebel who fought for Satellite One, us immigrants' homeworld."

Randy rolled his eyes. "Here we go with this 'Purist' psychobabble again."

An outrush of emotion burst from Akane's mouth. "They're a real threat, *goddammit*, to people like *you* and *me*!"

She grabbed Randy's sleeve at the chest, twisting the fabric in her fist. "Those lowlifes took someone special from me, so don't ever *fucking* lecture me about pain." The acrimony in her voice, the fire in her eyes—Randy had never seen her in such an incensed state. "I don't wanna see you, one of our heroes, found hacked into a million pieces by these shitbags. You get me, Randy?"

Though he wished she'd drop the "hero" stuff, her passionate outburst firmed Randy's features. He now regarded the youngster more seriously.

Akane said, "Purist groups all across Eden are plotting to dominate central and region state government, law enforcement, and the CDF. Cliques of these people exist in all our institutions, but you wouldn't recognize them, not blatantly. Remember, these people aren't just stuck-up Eden citizens with a high-and-mighty attitude. These people are *dangerous*."

"So, these Purists are like a . . . shadow society or something, operating under everyone's noses."

Akane uncurled her fist, letting go of Randy's sleeve. "Bingo. A lot of Purist groups are independent, but they're all acting in solidarity toward a common goal: to keep Eden free of immigrant integration, continue exploiting colonists as servile resource harvesters, and ensure the current immigrant population remains at the bottom of society.

"They inspire leaderless resistance, lone actors committing acts of violence in the name of their warped manifesto. Our republic is under siege by Purist groups. But they've got opposition, people working to counter them."

So, some sort of shadow warfare's going on? Randy thought.

"The opposition espouses Reza's ideals but rebukes his late methods of executing those ideals," Akane said. This talk of warring sides gave Randy déjà vu. "It's a game of chess, an arcane war between two diametrical mentalities that—"

Okay, enough with the crumbs. It's time for real answers, Randy thought, fed up with Akane's cryptic behavior. "Just how do you know all this, Akane, *huh?*" he pressed, interrupting her.

Akane's wristcom chirped. "Aw, man! It's almost showtime. I can get into the nitty-gritty later. Right now, we gotta haul ass if we don't wanna be late for the mission brief. And trust me, we don't wanna piss off Breckenridge." She jetted out of the dome, ending the conversation on a cliffhanger.

"To be continued, then," Randy muttered to himself. *Who are you, Private Sugimori?*

Akane wasn't a quick study. There seemed to be a lot more to her than met the eye.

INTERLUDE ONE

FIVE DAYS INTO THE THREE-WEEK WAR
Planet Eden

Akane strolled through an empty construction zone, dressed in embellished jeans and a black T-shirt. Around her were substructures, half-finished buildings, and idle construction equipment.

Rejected again! she thought. *I can't even land a fucking assembly-line gig at some golem factory. Because my citizen registration number flags me as an immigrant. Because AEGIS decided I should be just a lowly resource harvester chucking dirt somewhere. It's clear the corporate execs who control the private sector here don't want an immigrant like me "stinking up their joint."*

I'm sick of this asinine bullshit. I thought coming here was supposed to turn my life around, Mom and Dad. I thought coming here was supposed to be my big break.

Homesick, she longed for Sector 07, NeoJapan: grimy alleyways, ramshackle living units stacked one atop the other, no modern tech, none of Eden's scenic beauty. A colonist might think she had a few screws loose for wanting to return to that place.

The lottery's just a sham. Caught in a fever of anger, she kicked over a trash receptacle. "I fucking knew it!" Her ears might as well be steaming.

The receptacle tumbled across the phyocrete, flinging litter.

A roving police golem on three wheels sped toward her. Its antenna bulb, round eyes, and rectangular voice slot flashed as it admonished her. "Warning, warning!" it said, waving its tubular arms. "There is a one hundred credit fine for vandalizing public—"

"Shut up!" Akane kicked the four-foot blocky robot onto its side and let out an exasperated huff.

A policeman had witnessed the misdemeanor while sitting nearby in his interceptor, a black-and-white hover vehicle. He pressed the accelerator and glided over to Akane, parking beside her. His coarse, throaty voice tore through the air. "Hey, you! Stupid girl!"

Akane recoiled, panic taking hold of her. She knew she was in deep trouble.

The policeman climbed out. His thin lips, set beneath a dark mustache, compressed into a grim line. "It's illegal to vandalize public property and assault a policing golem." Behind dark shades, his eyes radiated antipathy for miscreants.

Perspiration slickened Akane's brow. "Yeah . . . I, uh—" Head bowed, she hooked both thumbs between her belt and pants. Like a child who'd just been scolded by an adult, she toed the dusty ground.

"You want to go to jail?" The policeman thrust a finger at her. "What the heck's wrong with you, kid?"

Akane raised her head, gathered her courage, and spoke her mind. "It's just that lottery beneficiaries like me have it tough. We're given a measly ten thousand credits to make ends meet and told, 'Go make a life for yourself. Shoot for the stars.'

"This planet's supposed to be the Zion of humanity. But immigrants like me are treated as if we're inferior to everyone else. Why do people wanna make us feel like we don't belong?"

The policeman's eyebrows came together, his features contorting.

What are you frowning about, dickwad? Akane thought.

"So, you're one of them, one of those ungrateful immigrant degenerates," the policeman said. "Just a wannabe Highborn from some ghetto, cesspool colony who's got a chip on their shoulder. Even if you were handed the world, you'd still find something to bitch about. 'I don't get this. I don't get that. I don't get what the Highborn get.' All that woe-is-me crap. Figures why you think you can just vandalize property and get away with it. Hands behind your back, missy."

Akane cocked a brow. "Really?" she said with a dry laugh. "I kicked over a fucking trash can and a mindless automaton."

The policeman wasn't going to engage in a back-and-forth. "Turn around and put your hands behind your back. *Now.*"

Akane's heart skipped a beat. "But—"

The policeman's frown deepened. "Turn around, you little brat, and put your damn hands behind your back! I'm not gonna say it again!"

Fear stiffened Akane's shoulders. Shaking, she complied.

Cold metal clamped around her wrists, locking her arms in place.

"Hey, that's a little *too* tight," she said, teeth clenched so hard her jaw hurt. The policeman jammed the muzzle of his firearm against her spine. "What the—?"

"Quiet, nadir." The policeman glanced around conspiratorially. The coast was clear. Absolutely no one else was around. "There are enough immigrants on Eden. We don't need any more of you obnoxious pissants here."

Aghast, Akane became a bundle of nerves.

The policeman thought, *Whiners like you are the reason brave men and women are being gunned down in some idiotic civil war.*

Just as his finger slipped into the trigger well, a vicious roundhouse kick slammed into the back of his skull. He lost his grip on the pistol, and it clattered to the ground along with his shades.

His feet floundered, fighting to recover balance. As he massaged the back of his throbbing head, he turned around—red-faced. "Who the hell—?"

Standing before him was a woman in her late twenties who had an ocher complexion, complemented by a long braid of caramel blond-streaked hair. Ready to beat him down if necessary, she shot him a stare that screamed: Back the fuck away from Akane, or else.

The broad-shouldered amazon of a woman towered over the dirty cop, who was a head shorter. Her running shorts exposed a pair of athlete's legs, and her sports bra showed off her sculpted abs and solid arms. It was glaringly obvious she kept herself in tip-top shape.

The policeman's head still ached as he closed in on Akane's fearless rescuer. "Lady, I'm gonna make you regret messin' with me."

His threat was meant to intimidate the woman. It didn't. Not by a long shot. She stood firm—an immovable object—and didn't even bat an eyelid. She knew she could take the asshole, not out of hubris, but out of *skill.*

Just as the policeman was about to throw a punch her way, she swiveled her hips and spun into a second roundhouse. The kick autographed his forehead with a nasty red gash and dropped him before he could make his move, putting him to sleep.

Akane was impressed. This woman was fast. She was powerful. She hit with explosive force. She was lightning and thunder, and her physique was something fierce, stout and strong. And it was appealing to the eye, feminine curves blatantly noticeable. Who the hell was this good Samaritan?

That takes care of him, the woman thought.

Relief washed away the tension in Akane's muscles. "Th-thank you." Her voice strained for strength.

The woman knelt and searched the policeman's pocket for the cuffs' key fob. *Got it.* She touched the fob to the cuffs' transceiver.

Metal clacked to the ground. Akane was free.

The woman then tossed the fob aside. "Are you okay, girl?"

"Um, yeah, thanks to you." Akane rubbed and flexed her sore wrists. Her gaze dropped to the policeman's crumpled form. "You throw a helluva kick." She tilted her head back up at her tall, athletically built rescuer. "My name's Akane, by the way."

An eccentric face of blended ethnicity gave Akane a kindhearted smile. "I'm Simone Conyers. Sergeant Simone Conyers."

"Sergeant? Are you a policewoman?"

"No, CDF. Luckily, I frequent this construction zone on my jogging route."

"Thank goodness."

"Is there anything I can do? Maybe take you home?" Simone glared at the unconscious policeman. She had nothing but disdain for him. "After I make sure this disgrace of a human being gets locked away, of course."

Akane stood in embarrassed silence. "I, um, don't have a home," she admitted. "I've just been lodging at different places for weeks or months at a time while trying to get on my feet. No luck yet." Moisture welled in her eyes. "I don't know what I'm gonna do. My credits won't last forever, and—"

Simone gently settled a hand on Akane's shoulder. "I'm an immigrant too. It was difficult for me at first. You can stay with me."

Akane stared at Simone as if she couldn't believe what she had heard. "Re-really?" she stuttered.

"Of course." Simone took Akane into her muscled arms and held her.

"Thank you, Simone," Akane squeaked out. She was glad to have a permanent home on Eden.

The warmth and safety of Simone's embrace instantly neutralized all the fear, anxiety, and uncertainty that had been eclipsing Akane's hope and morale day by day.

Simone unfolded her arms. "It's no problem. You're a fellow immigrant. Now I'm going to contact the authorities. When they get here, I'll give my witness statement, and they'll lock up this piece of garbage. Why don't you sit down until they arrive?"

Akane nodded. "Yeah, sounds good." She walked over to a stack of phyocrete blocks and sat down, taking a load off.

Simone knelt beside the policeman and peeled back the cuff of his left sleeve, uncovering a distinct tattoo of a winged skull and crossbones. Her expression grew rigid, fury burning in her oak-brown eyes. *A Purist. I knew it.*

• • •

WEEKS LATER

Inside Simone's penthouse residence, Akane—dressed in jeans and a dark blue top—sat browsing social media on the holographic interface of her wristcom. She was waiting for Simone to return from a shopping trip so they could go out for dinner.

The wristcom chirped. MESSAGE FROM SKYLAR flashed across the interface. Akane jumped from the sofa, smiling. She was relieved to finally hear from her friend. She knew Skylar had been having a rough time. That's why she'd been ghosting her, Jacobi, and Desmond for the past three days, ignoring all their calls and texts, making them worry.

Akane eagerly opened the message.

Skylar: Akane, I wanted to say farewell.

Despair ripped the smile off Akane's face, and heartache accumulated in her chest. *What?*

Skylar: You were right all along. This world doesn't take kindly to us immigrants. It'll never accept us. I tried. I really tried. But I can't go on anymore.

Akane: What are you talking about?

Skylar: I can't live like this.

Akane's trembling fingers dialed Skylar's number. The wristcom rang. *Come on, Skylar, answer.* Akane's body quivered, her chest tightened, and tears filled her eyes. Skylar refused to pick up.

Skylar: Goodbye, girlfriend. And thank you. Love you a bunch.

Akane: Skylar, what are you saying? Where are you?

No answer. A sick feeling swelled up inside Akane.

Akane: Skylar?

Thunder roared, lightning flashed, and the gray sky unleashed a flood, sheets of rain beating the windowpanes.

For five minutes, Akane paced back and forth, gnawed her nails intermittently, and kept trying to reach Skylar. The iciness spreading through her veins served as a warning that something terrible had happened.

In today's cyber-enhanced world, news traveled fast. It didn't take long for the headlines to go viral: YOUNG WOMAN LEAPS OFF ROOF OF APARTMENT COMPLEX.

57

The headlines wrecked Akane. Bereft, she collapsed to her knees. The neighbors could most likely hear the heart-wrenching shriek that came from her throat. Sobbing and wailing, she hammered the floor until her knuckles were red.

Just as Akane had salvaged herself, standing to her feet, the front door opened, and Simone entered. She was clad in a yellow water-repellent trench coat and a black bell-bottom jumpsuit. Worry registered on her face. "Akane, what's wrong?" She dropped her shopping carryalls, and purchases of clothes and cosmetics tumbled out from them.

Akane kicked over the coffee table. "I hate this world! I *fucking* hate it!"

Simone peeled off her coat. She then hurried to Akane and gripped her biceps. "Akane, what's going on?"

Akane squirmed. "Let me go!"

Simone shook her dramatically. "Akane, stop it! Tell me what happened!"

"Get away from me!" Akane tore herself from Simone and sat against the wall, tucking her knees to her chest.

Simone sat down next to her. "Akane, please tell me what's wrong."

"What isn't?" Every muscle in Akane's face convulsed. Anger, disgust, and grief shaped her expression. "Skylar managed to grind her way to an okay life. She got a secretary gig. In her spare time, she was working on her singing career and dabbling in modeling.

"She was trying to make things happen, but a couple of stupid bitch-ass Highborn kept harassing her at the office *just* because she was an immigrant. When she sent her demos to promoters and studio owners, they were impressed. They said 'I love your voice.' But when they found out she was an immigrant, they sent her packing." Akane hugged her knees.

As Skylar's hopes and dreams were being obliterated, Akane had watched her joy wither over time, until she became a shell of her former self. The glimmer her eyes once held had faded.

Akane said, "She sent me a goodbye message today. Said I was right all along." She whimpered, tears soaking into the front of her shirt. Constant harassment, relentless cyberbullying, and rejection from society had pushed Skylar over the edge. "Saw it on the news. She leapt off her six-story apartment complex."

Akane remembered Skylar's relentless optimism. She had always been a motivational person, a true morale booster. She had dreams of becoming a star, and now she was just a mess of shattered bones, her beauty splattered across some street.

"I'm sorry," was all Simone could manage. Sorrow clenched her heart.

Akane broke out in sobs. "As for me, I got another rejection. That's the fourth university I applied to." She wiped her eyes with her forearm. "The truth is that I'm being blackballed, aren't I? And it's because I'm an immigrant." Emotions spiraling, she cried out, "Skylar was shunned for what? Being a human being who had no say where she was born? How could any sane person believe that's fair?"

Simone said, "It's not. But too many people believe in AEGIS's blueprint for humanity and want to ostracize immigrants from society. They're intent on preserving the Commonwealth's current social structure." *We can thank AEGIS's creators—Cyrus Kline, Jagr Vlcek, and Atticus Hancroft—for the oppression we immigrants have to deal with.*

Akane's brow creased in anger. "There are too few of us in these major circles of influence, government and whatnot." She shook her head. "We're told we, too, can make it, just like any other Edenite, but that's a buncha crap. We've been sold a pipe dream.

In reality, we immigrants don't have a snowball's chance in hell of achieving real prosperity."

Simone smiled. "We *do* have a chance. Oviereya Amaechi is one of us, a colony immigrant, and look at her: She's a chairwoman and the Chancellor of the Supreme Judiciary. Then there's Arson Scott, who became a beloved war hero, respected captain, and recipient of the Commonwealth Meritorious Service Medal."

Akane scoffed. "Yeah, I keep hearing that, and it's getting old." She was tired of such redundant platitudes. "So two people made it big. Great. That's cool and all, but what about the rest of us? Are we all just gonna forever be desk jockeys and hirelings at golem factories?" Wryly, she added, "Hooray, next-level slavehood. A step up from being a resource harvester."

"It's true we're underrepresented. It's true we're being denied economic opportunities, merely because AEGIS didn't select us for Eden citizenship. You and I aren't supposed to be even breathing the same air as the 'upper echelon' of the New Humanity. But a lot of us immigrants are fighting to upset the balance of power.

"I was determined to make sergeant, no matter the pushback, so I could do my part in diversifying the CDF's leadership.

"You see, we can either embrace the spirit of subservience or the spirit of rebellion. I choose the latter. From within the military and political system, I play my part in transforming this biased society. I won't allow my lineage to be disgraced, or my future bloodline to be trapped in an endless cycle of disrespect and marginalization."

Akane said, "You keep mentioning you volunteer for some group trying to turn things around. So, is it like a nonprofit or something? Can I join? And what exactly do you guys do? If it's not totally on the up-and-up, don't worry. I used to do a lotta black-market dealing back in Sector 07."

Simone replied, "We're involved in a lot of social-impact initiatives, but that's not something you need to be concerned about right now." *Who knows, maybe she has what it takes to be an asset to us.*

"Well, I've been thinking about something," Akane said, changing the subject. "Since my aspirations for attending a university keep getting flushed down the toilet, I wanna join the CDF."

Surprised, Simone was wordless for a moment. "Really?"

"Yeah, I wanna do what you do. I wanna be a Guardian in the ETF and go after the Commonwealth's 'most wanted.' And I wanna be on *your* team. What's it called again? Vanguard Alpha?"

"Joining the CDF isn't a bad move, but I don't have the influence to guarantee your assignment, Akane."

"C'mon, you don't have *any* connections?"

Simone curled a finger around her chin, contemplating names in her mind. "Well, I just *might* be able to pull a few strings."

"Awesome, so when are we going to the enlistment station?"

Night had fallen. The rain had lessened to a drizzle, pitter-pattering against the windows.

Simone sat at the desk in her living room. The lights were off, and she was dressed for bed in a filmy backless nightie.

The faint glow from her laptop's net browser cast a soft light over the pronounced exoticism of her features.

After taking a sip of warm tea, she darted her fingers across the keypad. The text that came onscreen said ENTER ENCRYPTION KEY.

She typed a numerical code.

The screen flashed:

Resist oppression

Initiate change

Stop violence against immigrants

Engage in activism

An icon appeared—a raised fist bordered by a circle. Inside the lower half of the circle was a single word: **R I S E**.

She was now logged into the encrypted portal.

BEGIN CHAT WITH SAM GUTHRIE blinked onto the screen. She dragged the cursor to ACCEPT and clicked the touchpad.

> Chat Stream <

SAM: Report.

SIMONE: I like her. *Smiley Emoji*

SAM: Where's the kid now?

SIMONE: Asleep in her room. I want to bring her in. Reminds me of myself. And she's whip-smart.

SAM: That's nice, but does she have what it takes to champion the cause and be an agent of disruption?

SIMONE: She's still a work in progress, but she's been on-planet long enough to taste the bitter struggle immigrants face. Actually, she never deluded herself with romanticized illusions of Eden or the central government's promises. Real down-to-earth girl.

SAM: Being down-to-earth doesn't qualify her to join us.

SIMONE: She was facing hard times when I found her. Her friend committed suicide today. She's been hit with discrimination at every turn. She's full of anger, ready to act. Her blood is boiling. She's been emboldened to fight for equality. Immigrants who've been pushed to the edge like her are ripe. She fits the profile. And she's enlisting tomorrow. We need more recruits with military training.

SAM: Not convinced yet. *Thumbs-down Emoji* If her heart is soft, she won't be mentally equipped to handle everything we might ask of her. Let's revisit this conversation after she gets back from BCT, if she survives it.

SIMONE: Roger.

Simone drank more tea. *She'll survive it.*

"Hey, what are you up to?" Akane asked, jarring Simone out of her thoughts. She edged closer, in yellow-polka-dot white pajamas and flip-flops.

Simone's mouth froze in a partial gape, and her heart thudded.

She slapped the laptop shut and spun around in her swivel chair. Nervously, she brushed stray strands of hair back into place and clamped a hand over her pounding heart. "Akane, you startled me. I didn't even hear you walk up." Had Akane seen the screen?

"Yeah, so what are you working on at this time of night?" Akane took a veggie chip from her snack bag and munched on it.

No, Akane hadn't seen the private chat log. Simone was sure of it. Close call. Regaining her composure, she said, "Just . . . nothing important, really."

"Oh, okay." Akane stuck another chip into her mouth. "Well, I can't get back to sleep," she said, chewing. "I'm gonna watch some TV for a while, if that's cool with you."

"Yeah, that's fine. Knock yourself out." Simone stood, tugging down the hem of her rucked-up nightie. She scooped up her laptop, tucking it under her arm, and headed to her room. "Good night, Akane."

Akane raised two fingers, forming the peace symbol in response.

Simone disappeared from Akane's view. *You've got what it takes to be one of us, Sugimori. I'm right about you. I know it in my gut. We'll show you how to turn all that pain into power, into transformative action. You'll become a weapon for the cause, like me.*

Akane sat on the sofa, channel surfing. She saw a commercial for a Mercedes Gardner concert at Starlight Colosseum and couldn't help but think of Skylar.

The impulse to cry arose, and Akane rubbed her eyes.

She missed her friend's buoyant nature, her unwavering positive attitude. *Life fucking sucks sometimes.*

CHAPTER TWO

Star Palace
Shipyard

The *Nightingale*, a class-A space vessel, had crew cabins and a galley to support in-ship living for when Vanguard Alpha was assigned a long-distance mission. And it had a state-of-the-art weapons package that allowed it to hold its own in battle.

Vanguard Alpha had assembled in the *Nightingale's* conference room. The war table they stood around projected a 3-D topographical map that provided them a detailed lay of the land. Graphs suspended above the display presented data on regional climate, land elevation, wildlife species, and more.

A goateed black man had the floor. He was Lieutenant Carl Breckenridge, Vanguard Alpha's field leader.

Akane sauntered up to Randy's side, stood on her tiptoes, and whispered into his ear, "Remember, watch out for Shaffer." She scowled at the douchebag. "Chances are he's even a ringleader."

Randy silently bobbed his chin. Whether or not Paul was a Purist, he had intended to keep his defenses up when around him.

Carl jabbed his pointing stick at the red cubical vector graphic in the middle of the display. He spoke with an air of command, going over the avenue of approach. "We'll land twenty-three miles from the compound, where they're holding the slaves." Which was on planet Randarex. "Three weeks ago, Defense Force Intelligence intercepted one of these traffickers' ships and rescued thirteen abductees.

"Three of the women were from Eden; the others were from undocumented worlds. Intel can't guarantee whether the compound we're about to raid has Commonwealth abductees or not, but there's a very good chance. Even if there are no human abductees, the women from those outer worlds still need to be rescued from these dirtbags and returned safely to their families."

Bridging the linguistic barriers of outerworld slaves and locating their unmapped homeworlds was a difficult undertaking. Situations like this often resulted in displaced young women. Queen Pappalonie had been granting rescued slaves from outer worlds asylum on Taramassia until the Commonwealth could identify and locate where they came from.

Carl said, "Once the *Nightingale* lands, we'll make our approach on hoverbikes, staying inside the compound's surveillance blind spot. After a quick recon, we'll cloak and enter the rear access."

Sergeant Jenny Pines, an albino woman of European descent in her early thirties, raised her alabaster hand. "Question: What kinda heat are they packing?" she asked, voice noticeably accented.

"Unknown," Carl replied. "We'll find out when we get there. Any more questions, people?"

He got nothing but silence.

Nope, Akane thought. *Basically: go in; bang, bang, bang; rescue captives; head back to Eden; and then relax until we get our next marching orders.*

Carl continued, after giving everyone ample time to speak up. "Alright, no questions, then." He tapped a glyph on the war table's touchpad with his finger. The holographic map dissolved into pixels and dissipated. "Ten mikes prior to landing dirtside, you're to be shelled and locked n' loaded. Clear?"

"Yes, Sir," Vanguard Alpha replied in unison.

"Good. You're all dismissed." Everyone turned to head out. "Except you, Specialist Scott. I need a word with you."

Paul snickered as he left.

Randy grunted.

He marched up to Carl. *Okay, here comes the scolding.*

The door hissed shut.

Carl's brow furrowed. "Specialist Scott, what in the world were you thinking, starting a damn slugfest with a noncom (noncommissioned officer)?"

Fuming, Randy disregarded deference. "You're barking up the wrong tree! Shaffer's the one who provoked *me!*" he made clear, jerking a thumb at himself. "So put him in your hot seat!"

"You were the one who tried to sucker punch him, Scott, throwing the first blow." According to witnesses.

"This is absurd. I have a mission to prep for." Randy pivoted and began stomping away.

"I didn't dismiss you yet, Specialist."

Randy stopped, but he kept his back to Carl. The last thing he needed right now was a write-up for being recalcitrant.

He was seething, his lips pressed tightly together. Why'd he have to get a bad rep because of some immigrant-hating asshole?

He gave Carl more backtalk. "I have nothing else to say, Sir. Now I need to go prep for the mission. You can chew me out more after it's over. Sound good?"

"I'm not your enemy, Scott. I fought alongside your father."

Why am I not surprised.

"I'm actually rooting for you, my friend's son, to go far in the CDF. We need good soldiers like you. I just don't want to see you self-sabotage your career, so keep that temper of yours in check. If someone's messing with you, report it to me. There's no need to play the tough guy and take matters into your own hands like you did last night." That incident had gotten Carl a chewing-out session of his own from Narvaez. "Understood?"

"Understood, Sir."

"Look, I've got mad respect for you. Fighting in the Battle of the Quad wasn't nothing. Just don't go getting into scrapes with any more Guardians. You feel me, Specialist?"

"No guarantees," Randy said defiantly and walked out.

Carl shook his head and exhaled an irate breath.

The anchors securing the *Nightingale* disengaged. The shipyard door yawned open, splitting apart along a horizontal seam. A runway with marker lights extended into the starry wilderness of space.

"Vanguard Alpha, you are clear for takeoff," said a man over the shipyard's speaker system.

With pre-liftoff checks complete, the *Nightingale's* helmsman engaged the engine. Plasma thrusters flared as the ship rolled across the runway and glided into space.

Accelerating, it headed outsystem.

• • •

Planet Randarex

Stacie Spencer—now one of the richest women in the Commonwealth since becoming the sole proprietor of her parents' enterprise—had gone on a PR campaign across the interview circuit. She needed to reassure her parents' noncriminal business clientele that she had no knowledge of their web of illegal commerce. She vowed to end all unlawful domestic and intergalactic ventures. And she promised herself she would use her family's fortune for just causes, not merely for profligate spending.

But Stacie refused to stand by while the other family heads continued their parents' criminal legacies. To thwart them, she assembled a four-person tactical combat team.

The team was officially registered as a bona fide bounty-hunting entity. Bounty chasers supplemented the CDF's task forces in apprehending malefactors, both intergalactic and human, who disrupted the Commonwealth's peace and safety. But the registration was a front, a clever smokescreen. As bounty chasers, Stacie's team could legally purchase arms and remain off Defense Force Intelligence's radar.

In truth, Stacie's mission was one of vigilantism. So if caught red-handed, the team would face serious consequences. But they were willing to take the risk.

Her dedicated crew included both familiar and new faces. Jason Mansford, who had led First Squad of Lima Company's Fourth Platoon, served as the team's second-in-command. Eli Manson, another former comrade, brought expertise in hacking and demolitions. Ryoko Nahara, the third ex-Guardian on the team, had also fought alongside First Squad. Lastly, there was DeShaun Watkis, a young friend of Jason's with four planetary-impact missions under his belt.

Stacie and her team were on Randarex because her intel had confirmed that the trafficking operation, the same one the CDF was tracking, was the work of Damien Sykes.

Since chasers weren't allowed to have mechsuits, she equipped her team with the best threat-reduction body armor and combat smartgear money could buy.

Their featureless helmets' visor was capable of visual magnification, infrared vision, heat-signature tracing, and a slew of other functions. The rest of their gear had more nifty features, including an emitter on their belts that could generate a holographic camouflage field.

Stacie dropped to one knee, lowering herself into the concealment of overgrown weeds and thick foliage. She punched a black-gloved fist skyward, commanding her team to follow suit. They quickly complied, kneeling in unison.

As a former Guardian who'd worked her butt off to earn the mantle of Warrior Extraordinaire, Stacie got a thrill out of being back in the field. When she wasn't wining and dining, hitting her personal gym, shopping, or indulging in leisure activities, this was where she preferred to be—with her team going after bad guys, not stuck in boardrooms or business meetings. It was exhausting having to playact the sophistication and savoir faire expected of an entrepreneur of her supposed stature. She was "modern-day royalty," after all.

"Businesswoman" just wasn't her forte, at least not yet. She didn't possess her parents' entrepreneurial acumen, and being thrust into the driver's seat of a financial empire was no cakewalk. She was learning on the job, so to speak. But this job, here on Randarex, she knew how to do well.

Stacie aimed her visored gaze at the traffickers' secluded compound, which consisted of a large, dull, windowless building and a scattering of small prefabs.

She magnified her optics by blinking three times. As she meticulously scanned for defense systems, she caught sight of a man with a rifle slung over his shoulder. He was dressed in dirty pants and a muscle shirt.

The man was taking a frightened young human woman—wearing jeans, a tank top, and boots—to the corroding entrance door of the main facility.

"Move faster!" he barked, giving her a one-handed shove.

The captive's feet scrambled for stability.

At the door, the man punched in a code on the access panel. Bolts and latches clacked. The door screeched open.

A stoutly built figure in tactical pants and a black tank top stood in the doorway. Stacie blinked twice, triggering her visor to freeze-frame a close-up of the hairless man's rugged mug. If eyes were indeed the window into the soul, his were the eyes of a stone-cold killer, a killer whose rap sheet included just about every criminal offense imaginable.

That has to be the lieutenant of this operation, Jacob Kilbourne, Stacie concluded. Her intel had given her the lowdown on him. He was every bit a scumbag.

Her helmet's sensor scans detected combat mods inside his body for strength, healing, and speed. And there were endoskeletal plates inside his chest, to repel bullets.

"She the last of the merchandise?" Jacob asked his henchman.

"Yeah. All the broads have been off-loaded."

The captive sobbed.

"Let's toss her in the pen with the rest and get some chow," Jacob said. He snared the woman's wrist in an ironclad grip and dragged her into the building. "C'mon, get in here."

The door lowered as the two traffickers and the captive disappeared from Stacie's vision.

Abject disgust filled Stacie's face. *Women uprooted from their homelands and treated like animals in a menagerie. If we find proof this operation belongs to Sykes, that smarmy bastard's toast; he'll never get the chance to run for CE.*

There were plenty of words Stacie could use to describe Damien: narcissist, prick, playboy, delusional, cunning, hotheaded, arrogant. She preferred "run-of-the-mill asshole."

He deserves to be in jail. Better yet, he deserves to be six feet under for what he did to Cassie. Outrage sizzled within Stacie.

She recalled the bruises on Cassie McCanns' face that awful night. Yep, Damien was a run-of-the-mill asshole, and that was putting it mildly.

She shook her head, forcing away the bitter memories.

Oddly enough, Cassie had just returned to Eden after completing an offworld assignment for her employer. She'd left without telling Stacie, and hadn't let her know she was back, either. It had been two years since they'd last seen each other. Two whole years!

Stacie figured Cassie never mentioned her assignment because she'd been furious, and still was. After all, she was the one who'd introduced Cassie to Damien.

Well, she intended to make it up to Cassie by putting Damien Sykes where he belonged—behind bars. She just needed evidence to connect him to this trafficking racket.

"Okay, people," she said, "we're going in. This should be an easy op. Just ten hostiles with energy weapons. No powered combatwear or any heavy artillery. We need to take one of these creeps alive, though." *Unfortunately.*

Jason took up a position right next to her. "Hey," he said in a hushed tone.

Stacie flipped her visor up so that it rested atop her helmet. "Yeah? *Question?*" she whispered back, clearly exasperated and not eager to delay the team's advance.

Jason lifted his own visor. "You sure your informant's reliable? We don't want to go in biting off more than we can chew because of faulty intel."

"Beltasia Corbezeus isn't exactly an angel, but she's an information broker who takes pride in her rep. She's got high standards. She wants to maintain her clientele and keep her revenue stream flowing. That doesn't happen by being a slouch."

"How'd you find this Narphaisian info broker?"

"I found out she did some sleuthing for my parents. She got them intel on rival interstellar operations. I got in touch with her to do some sleuthing for me, *okay?*" Stacie's "gee whiz" expression told Jason he should drop this conversation.

But Jason wasn't done. "So she works both sides of the fence, good or bad, and has no real morals?"

Stacie shrugged, palms up. "Yeah, well, sometimes you've gotta make uncomfortable alliances to get things done."

Jason didn't trust easily, particularly when it came to shady businesspeople. "Let me get this straight." He had a challenge on the tip of his tongue.

OMG, Stacie thought. Couldn't he just roll with the plan?

"We're supposed to wager our lives on the intel of some . . . freelance mercenary info collector?"

Jason's protests were irritating Stacie. Still, she knew his caution came from experience. As a former CDF squad leader, he understood that when soldiers' lives were on the line, the wrong decision could lead straight to the morgue.

"*Someone* has to rescue those slaves," Stacie said.

"You could've just informed the CDF and let them handle it."

"And have Defense Force Intelligence breathing down my neck, wondering why I'm *illegally* waging a personal war on intergalactic crime instead of chasing bounties like we're supposed to?" Stacie shook her head. "No thanks. I'd rather not end up staring out the bars of an orbital prison. Besides, the only person I trust to take down the Seven Elite is *me*. Who knows who they've bought? Anyone could be in their back pocket."

Preparing to move out, she flipped her visor back down.

Jason sighed in resignation and lowered his visor. "Okay, fine, let's get this over with." In his command voice, he said, "Chameleon mode, people."

Each team member tapped their belt, activating a cloaking field. The camo protocols adapted to the green-and-earthy tones of the forest.

Everyone rose from their crouched positions.

"As planned, we're going in from the rear," Stacie said. "First, we take out the back-door security cam."

She removed the microdrone attached to her belt and set it on the ground. She guided it into the air using the control keys on her bracer. Times like this, she wished she were in a Shell, utilizing neural-control interface. With her resources, connections, and credits, she could've had her own mechanized combatwear built. But the Commonwealth Government didn't allow any private entity to rival the CDF's power.

The drone's video feed appeared in Stacie's optics. She aligned the crosshairs of her targeting reticle on the security camera mounted above the back door. Target locked, she triggered the drone's microblaster. A narrow beam of energy shot out, scrapping the camera.

Stacie recalled the drone and reattached it to her belt. "Okay, let's move."

The team hustled down a hill. Underbrush crunched beneath their boots as they circled to the rear of the building.

Inside the traffickers' main facility, a man with a red mohawk sat at a control console. He told Jacob, "The back-door camera feed just died. I'll go check—"

Jacob cut him off. "No, no need." He grinned sharply. "Our visitors have likely arrived." His voice rose as he said, "Everyone, pause what you're doing! Let's get ready to welcome our guests! You know what to do!"

Around him, bodies moved in a hurry.

Eli connected three color-coded cables from his bracer to the back door's interface ports. He went through the rigmarole of code-hacking to bypass the security lock. After two tense minutes, he heard the satisfying click he'd been waiting for. "Eureka."

Moving as one, the team advanced down a wide, dark, grungy corridor.

They cleared an empty room to the left, then another to the right. A few paces ahead, the hallway opened into a large square space packed with cages, some containing women from the Commonwealth, others filled with women from multiple worlds. Most appeared between eighteen and twenty-five, the traffickers' ideal age range. Some bore bruises and contusions. All were visibly distraught.

Stacie spotted the woman she had seen outside.

The team spread out into the slave hold, their footsteps cautious and measured.

The lights mounted to their rifles sliced the darkness.

From the cages came desperate pleas for help.

Relief overcame a human woman when she saw the team. "Please, get us out of here." Tears clustered in her hazel eyes.

Eli pressed a finger to his lips. "*Shhh*. We're going to get all of you out. But first, we need to take care of your abductors, okay?"

The woman nodded.

A single door in the center of the far wall led to the facility's main room. Eli, acting as breach man, placed a charge on it. He stepped back and tapped his bracer's touchpad, triggering the detonation.

The blast blew the door outward. Rifles at the ready, the chasers fanned out into a cavernous, warehouse-like enclosure housing shipping containers of munitions and a few combat vehicles, items that would fetch a high price from planetary warlords, despots, and tyrants.

"Nobody move!" Stacie shouted.

Jacob clapped in mock applause, one henchman standing to his right and one to his left, all three clad in protective gear.

Each of Jacob's men had an arm around the neck of a captive, using them as human shields.

The gagged women mumbled.

"The jig's up!" Jacob had a lupine smile on his face. "Welcome to our humble abode!" He was completely unruffled.

A subtle tremor ran up Jason's spine. *They were expecting us. Not good.*

Loud footfalls thudded across the metal grate-floor of the catwalk connecting two upper-level platforms.

The team angled their heads upward.

Two traffickers in exoframes stood on the catwalk. They aimed their wrist-mounted guns down at the team. One of the mechanical chassis, painted crimson, had a white number one on its shoulder; the other, painted blue, had a number two. Exo-One and Exo-Two.

Stacie and her crew were in a hairy situation.

Jason didn't like the odds the team was up against. *Damn, funneled right into a deathtrap. And so much for these guys not having any powered combatwear. And I count over ten of them.* His HUD tallied twenty hostiles, and there could be more. *Fucking faulty intel.*

A lime-green woman with reptilian eyes emerged from behind Jacob, cackling wickedly—the wily Beltasia Corbezeus.

She wore a purple legless getup, which exposed the dark green dalmatian-like spots on her arms and legs. Her thigh-high boots had numerous buckled straps and a scabbard each, sheathing knives. The leathery brown belt fastened around her waist holstered an energy gun.

Stacie yearned to tear Beltasia apart. *Double-crossing bitch sold us out.*

The hands-free translator around Beltasia's neck echoed her words in the humans' language. "Don't be so angry. I'm an information broker." After getting Stacie the intel she needed, Beltasia sold Jacob the details he needed to foil today's foray—the date and time. A devious grin widened her green cheeks. "Couldn't resist the opportunity to get double paid."

Two-timing charlatan. Stacie trained her rifle on the deceiver. "Any special words for your obituary?"

Jacob leveled a handgun at Stacie. "Whoa now, let's not get trigger-happy here!"

Stacie ignored his warning, her hands shaking as she kept her aim locked on Beltasia.

Jason directed a chastising frown at Stacie and slapped her rifle's muzzle downward. "We're in no position to resist. They'd pick us off before we can even blink."

"Listen to your friend," Beltasia said smugly. She faced Jacob. "Now, Mr. Kilbourne, all I need is my compensation and I'll be on my merry way. Nice doing business with you."

"Of course."

Jacob's handgun flashed. Beltasia went down, a geyser of blue pulp exploding from her chest. That was her compensation, for ratting the traffickers out in the first place.

Jacob realigned his weapon, making it clear to Stacie and her team that they'd be next if they resisted. "Hands up!"

Jason's eyes, still fixed on Stacie, narrowed further. He couldn't understand what she was hesitating about. Surrender was the only option that would keep the team alive, at least for a while. "We've got no choice. Those exoframes have the high ground. One move and we're dead."

"Ten seconds is all you got!" Jacob shouted. "We already have one cadaver to clean up." He glanced down at Beltasia's body. "Spare us the trouble of having five more." He began counting.

"Your call, boss lady," Eli said to Stacie. "I say we take 'em."

Jacob counted to five.

Stacie froze. Surrendering was the last thing she wanted. And if they did surrender, wouldn't they be as good as dead anyway? *We could make a run for it. No, what am I thinking? We'd get knocked off in a heartbeat.*

"Three seconds left!" Jacob held up three fingers.

Sweat slid down Jason's face. He gritted his teeth and muttered angrily, "Stacie, give the fucking order to surrender."

"One!" Jacob shouted.

Stacie threw her arms up. "Okay, fine! We give up!" *This way, maybe we can pull off an escape. Maybe.*

"Hang 'em up!" Jacob ordered his men.

Ryoko spun and made a break for the exit. *Outta here.*

One of the exoframes above unleashed a devastating energy blast that tore open her back. Red splotches and bits of flesh violently splattered over the walls and floor. Her body lay, the massive hole burned into it still smoldering.

Jason shook his head. *Stupid.*

The traffickers moved in and took the chasers into captivity.

Outside, Vanguard Alpha stood on a nearby hilltop under a dense canopy of green-leafed branches. From their vantage point, they had a clear view of the compound.

Carl had deployed an aerial microdrone and sent it into the building. His AI Combat Assistant—the Oracle—handled the flight path, weaving the drone between lanes of shipping containers, crates, and parked vehicles. "Stand by, people. I'm sharing my visuals . . . now."

The ACCEPT FEED prompt flashed on everyone's HUD. They accepted.

The drone's visual relay showed Stacie and her team, their arms held aloft by chains.

"Who are they?" Carl wondered aloud.

Randy flinched. Eyes agape, he looked nonplussed. "Stacie?" he blurted. *What the heck are you doing here?*

"You know her?" Akane asked. Recognition clicked. Since taking over her parents' enterprise, Stacie had been in the limelight more than ever. "Wait, isn't that Stacie Spencer? Who's she to you?"

The evocative sight of Stacie's face conjured up a wave of memories for Randy: a kiss, a nature walk, laughter and joy. "We served together. And she's my ex." The reminiscence of their naked bodies making tactile confessions of love zinged from his implant to every nerve ending inside him.

"Your ex? What happened? What'd she do?"

"More like *what did I do.*"

Randy recalled Stacie's fury when she discovered his coupling with Kesley Whittaker: *"Not only have you joined the enemy, but you sleep with them too! You betrayed your duty, but you also betrayed **me**! **Me**, Randy, the woman who dragged you out of your emotional withdrawal from society! The woman who broke you out of . . . being a loner! The woman who made you smile time after time since your mother's death by the very people you now ally yourself with!"*

Then he remembered how Stacie had censured him after her parents' execution by Reza's kill squads: *"And you—who I let touch me, make love to me—helped put this murdering piece of garbage in power, who just sent his bozos to my family's doorstep to murder them. Damn you, Randal Scott."*

Shaking off the memories that were keeping him from staying focused, Randy said to Akane, "But this isn't story time. Eyes on the mission."

Paul queried his CPU for an ID on Stacie:

Name: Stacie Lynette Spencer
Chaser agency registration: 5-EL0519
Position: Lead Chaser

"She's the leader of a bounty-hunter agency," Paul notified everyone. "But she's trespassing. Chasers aren't cleared to be in X-Quadrant. It's all ETF-campaign jurisdiction. She and her team are facing fines and potential imprisonment." *What a dumbass. The lady's got a net worth in the millions but wants to play space cowgirl and flirt with danger.* He shook his head in ridicule.

Randy rushed to Stacie's defense. "Maybe she and her team were just pursuing a bounty and had to pass through," he suggested.

Paul said, "If that were the case, she should've requested transit authorization. Permission isn't optional, Scott."

Carl's baritone voice ended the chatter. "Okay, it's time to get moving. Forget the back entrance. New plan of attack. We're blowing a doorway into the west wall. And with no abductees in the line of fire, we can cut loose."

"No abductees in the line of fire?" Randy spat. "Don't those chasers count?"

Carl replied, "Yeah, try not to hit the chasers with friendly fire. That's a no-brainer. I was more worried about innocent women being in the line of fire than a bunch of chasers who just made themselves felons by breaking the law. Now let's stop wasting time.

"Randy, Akane, Paul, and Sam, you're with me. Jenny, Mark, Dan, and Jay, sweep those outbuildings and get any captives you find to the *Nightingale.*

"To be on the safe side, we'll maintain radio silence and communicate using C-comms only. Activate stealth mode."

The Shells cloaked.

Carl said Vanguard Alpha's motto. "Let's bring the thunder."

The team split off.

Inside the main facility, Stacie and her crew were lined up in a row, hands suspended above their heads by chains that hung from the ceiling. Their body armor and smartgear had been stripped from their uniforms.

Jacob grabbed Stacie's jaw, his fingers digging into bone. "Alright, just who the hell are you guys? You're definitely not CDF."

"Oh, we're just tourists," Stacie quipped. "I love a good safari, you know?"

Jacob answered Stacie's witticism with a vicious slap.

On the catwalk overlooking the ground floor, the two exoframe operators, now dismounted from their machines, watched the scene unfold. They laughed and took swigs of alcohol from metal flasks.

Jason, who was next to Stacie, glared at Jacob. He wanted to tear the creep's head off.

Stacie stayed tough. She refused to show Jacob even the slightest hint of pain. She wouldn't give him the satisfaction.

"Again, who are you people?" Jacob demanded.

"We're just a bunch of sightseers," Stacie replied, her slapped cheek still throbbing.

You think you're funny, don'tcha? Jacob slammed a punch into Stacie's gut, knocking the air from her lungs. She wheezed and coughed. "Don't toy with me, bitch."

Jason struggled to contain his anger, but it finally burst forth in a loud shout. "Hey, leave her alone, asshole!"

"Shut the fuck up!" Jacob fired back. "You'll get your beating soon enough."

An earsplitting explosion announced Vanguard Alpha's arrival, blasting a hole in the left wall and slinging debris everywhere.

Jacob tensed. "What in the name of—?" He didn't wait to find out who or what was coming. He hightailed it behind a container and unslung his energy rifle.

His men scattered for cover too, weapons in hand.

Vanguard Alpha appeared in the opening, their black-and-gunmetal forms exuding an air of dominance.

They dodged an onslaught of blasts from traffickers who'd taken up defensive positions behind crates, containers, vehicles—anything that could serve as cover.

On the catwalk, the exoframe operators wore panic on their faces. They were about to go up against Shells, arguably the most lethal mechanized combatwear in the Interplanetary Union—

wearable armaments of immense killing power.

They scrambled back into their exoframes' cradles, inserting their arms and legs into the interior armature's control brackets. Securing mechanisms clacked, locking them in. Metal parts clinked. The machines came alive with electronic whirs. Pistons hissed.

Sensory scans mapped their muscular signals, translating them into movements for the exoframes' modular limbs.

The operators fired their wrist weapons at Vanguard Alpha, autobursts vibrating the metal chassis.

Noisy shooting filled the air.

Bullets from Vanguard Alpha's rifles pierced containers. Traffickers' energy blasts ruptured metal drums, coating the floor in a yellow-green chemical ooze.

Now that the CDF had come to the rescue, Jason's jittery nerves stilled. Then he remembered that he'd just broken the law. But he and the rest of the team had known what they were getting into when they hung up their BDUs to fight Stacie's personal war. And they were getting paid handsomely to do so. *Well, better to be detained by the CDF than these maniacs,* he thought. Hopefully, the CDF would go easy on the team—though it didn't have a track record of leniency—or maybe Stacie had an ace up her sleeve.

"Stacie, hang on!" Randy shouted over the weapons fire.

Stacie frowned. *Randal.*

<<*Randy, Akane, Paul, take the exos,*>> Carl ordered over the C-comm. His rifle shot a conflux of bullets. <<*Sam and I will deal with these thugs.*>>

<<*Gotcha,*>> Randy said. A blast struck his shoulder, jolting him back a step. *Damn it.* He located the shooter and fired a three-round burst. The enemy snapped backward against a wall in a spray of blood, then slid down its surface, smearing it with red streaks.

That takes care of him.

Randy turned his attention to the threat above. He docked his rifle, summoned his plasma saber, and power-leapt, exploding into the air. Exo-One fired energy blasts from its shoulder mounts. Missed shots blew holes in the ceiling. Debris rained down. One lucky blast caught Randy in the chest midair, and he plummeted to the floor.

His HUD blacked out, then rebooted.

A diagnostic check reported negligible damage. All vital components were fully operational.

Even though his Shell's shock inhibitors absorbed the brunt of the fall, he got a good taste of the impact. His body ached because of it.

Akane craned her head in his direction. "Randy!"

A plasma beam belched from the barrel protruding from Exo-Two's front panel, aimed at Akane.

Her Oracle triggered her barrier shield just in time.

The vortex of energy swirling around Akane ballooned outward into a protective dome, blocking Exo-Two's high-powered beam. Then the shield shrank until it vanished.

"Hey, keep your head in the game, dollface!" Paul shouted as he reached back for his rifle. "Let's not worry about Scott right now!"

A missile deployed from Exo-Two, homing in on Akane. Quick to react, she vaulted onto an elevator platform docked at the second level. But the missile adjusted course, tracking her.

Frantic warnings lit up her HUD. *Shit. Smart missile.* Threat-detection systems highlighted the projectile in a glowing yellow circle.

The Shell's CPU fed her real-time data on its speed and estimated time to impact.

Her Oracle responded to the incoming threat. "Countermeasure applied." The AI triggered the Shell's EMP defense.

The missile reversed course and smashed into Exo-Two, detonating in a red-orange explosion that tore away chunks of metal and killed the operator inside.

The wrecked exoframe tumbled over the guardrail, bounced off metal containers, and crashed to the floor. Damaged electronics fizzed and crackled.

One goon down, Akane thought.

Gun compartments on Exo-One sprang open. A rapid-fire volley of bullets hammered Paul's Shell. The Kryoplaste held strong, remaining unbreached.

Enough of this shit. Time to put the peashooter away. Paul locked his rifle to his back. A recess on his thigh opened, delivering his handgun. He removed it from the securing clips and returned fire, muzzle disgorging sizzling energy blasts.

Akane dropped beside Paul in a crouch, one hand slapping the floor. Just being near the suspected Purist, and being called dollface, made her cringe. Still, she unholstered her handgun and fired alongside him.

A frontal force field generated by the exo repelled their blasts.

Paul fumed. *Oh, great, a defensive shield.*

Suddenly, Randy descended from above. He landed behind Exo-One and activated his right-wrist plasma saber.

Alerts went off on the operator's HUD. He whirled around to face Randy, blasts from the energy guns below still lancing toward him.

<<*Cease fire. I got him,*>> Randy said to Akane and Paul.

He raised his arm for an overhead slash, but as he brought the blade down, the operator captured his wrist in the exoframe's skeletal metal fingers.

"Not today," the operator snarled.

The exoframe's arm shrieked under the strain of holding back Randy's blade.

Struggling to counter the Shell's strength, the operator sweated profusely. "Damn it."

At the speed of thought, a second saber flared from Randy's opposite wrist. He drew back his fist and drove the blade straight through the exoframe's chest plating, into the man inside.

Sparks erupted.

The operator howled as the blade burrowed into him. His exoframe had now become his coffin.

Randy powered down both sabers.

The exoframe teetered.

Randy hopped back as it thunked onto the catwalk floor.

The power gauge on Randy's readout showed that using both plasma sabers had drained an entire unit of energy. He, like all Guardians, hoped that the development of the M-X03 would solve plasma weaponry's excessive power consumption, a problem that made good old-fashioned lead still necessary.

The M-X03 was set to incorporate technology from the Reldaldri mechsuits now in CDF possession, so it would definitely have flight capability. Randy couldn't wait to test the new model.

Jacob had been detained by Carl and Sam. The rest of the traffickers lay dead or mortally wounded.

One barely-alive trafficker coughed, choking on his own blood.

Sam went up to him and finished him off with a kill shot to the head. *No mercy for the wicked,* he thought. Blood pooled around the corpse.

Randy hopped down from the catwalk, landing near Akane and Paul.

"You alright, Randy?" Akane asked. She sealed away her handgun. "That fall you took must've been a doozy."

"I'm fine. Now come on, let's free those chasers." He had Stacie on his brain and was eager to make sure she was okay.

Paul held out an arm to stop him. "Just hold up one friggin' minute, Specialist Scott. These chasers violated Commonwealth law, *remember*? Let's leave them hanging until we're ready to detain them."

"Yeah, mellow out," Akane said to Randy. "We've got a bunch of slaves that need our help. The chasers can sit tight for now."

"Right," he muttered in reluctant agreement.

Carl walked over to Stacie. His faceplate slid away. "Stacie Lynette Spencer, you and your team are now in CDF custody for contravening Commonwealth law. Do you understand?"

Blah, blah, blah, Stacie thought. "Uh-huh," she said to Carl, sounding completely unworried.

She seemed nonchalant, Jason observed. Maybe Stacie *did* have connections that could get them out of this mess. He hoped she did, anyway.

<<*Breckenridge to Pines, status report,*>> Carl transmitted.

<<*We've recovered ten captives and are bringing them to the Nightingale for aid,*>> Jenny replied.

<<*Good work.*>> "Randy, Akane, Paul, sweep this place for captives," Carl ordered aloud.

"There *are* captives here," Jason said. He tilted his head toward the slave hold. "They're down that way."

Carl glanced at the blown-in door. "You heard the man. Move it."

Akane, Randy, and Paul took off.

"Thanks," Carl said to Jason.

"Hey, I was a Guardian too. We're all on the same side here."

"Maybe so, but you don't break the law. Righteousness is what a Guardian stands for. You should've remembered that."

"We were just trying to help the slaves, that's all." Jason's face grew somber at the thought of Ryoko. "Hey, one of our teammates was killed. Her body needs to—"

"We got it," Carl interrupted. "We'll find out where they took her body and get it cryofrozen for transport back to Eden."

"Thank you."

Carl walked off, shaking his head. *Sloppy-ass chasers.* He made his way over to Sam, who had Jacob on his knees with his wrists pinioned behind his back.

Jacob watched Carl approach. He contemplated when to make his move.

"Alright, on your feet," Sam said. "You're being taken into CDF custody."

Jacob hadn't planned on going anywhere. *Now!* he told himself. The strength-enhancing mods in his arms broke the cuffs. In a flash, he leapt up, pulled a disc-shaped mine from his belt, and clamped it to Sam's chest. Then he bolted.

Sam recoiled. "What the—?" An explosion detonated in front of his face, blasting him to the floor.

Stacie and her crew looked stunned, hearts pounding.

Jacob thought the distraction would be enough for him to get away. He made a beeline for the hole Vanguard Alpha had blown in the wall.

Carl aimed his wrist gun and fired an energy blast. "Oh, no you don't."

Jacob's blood spurted like red liquid projectiles.

He was finished.

Sam pushed himself up. A lattice of damaged circuitry flickered beneath the jagged metal of his semidemolished chest plate. His

HUD read: DAMAGE SEVERE.

"Are you injured?" Carl asked.

Sam removed his helmet. "I'm fine. But my Shell's going to need serious repairs."

"That can be arranged. We can even get you another Shell. We can't get you another life."

Sam smiled.

Randy stepped out of the slave hold. "Everything okay in here? We heard the explosion."

"Everything's fine, Scott," Carl replied. "How are the captives?"

"They're okay."

"Good, let's hurry and get them to the ship."

• • •

Randy, Akane, and Jenny were docking their Shells in the *Nightingale's* arms vault.

Randy shut the glass door of his Shell's recharging pod.

Akane appeared at his side and clapped him on the back. "Hey, mission complete, and the captives are gonna be A-okay." Physically, anyway. "C'mon, kick it with me in the galley for some R&R."

Randy held her optimistic gaze. "Not now," he said, declining her offer. His expression was serious, and his voice was stern, mind on Stacie. He peeled his eyes away from Akane. "I'm going to go view the chasers' interrogation."

Akane cocked her head. "'Kay. Catch you later, then."

Randy watched her leave out the vault hatch. *We'll definitely talk soon, Akane. I want those answers you owe me, after all.* He'd have plenty of time to get those answers, since Vanguard Alpha was on downtime for the next two weeks per duty rotation.

"Scott," Jenny said, her accent thick, an accent which had hints of Scottish, Finnish, or maybe even Australian origins. It was clearly a blended accent from one of the New Humanity's assimilated cultures.

Randy spun to her as she came closer.

She had her sleeve unzipped a few inches past her clavicles to cool off, exposing a strip of skin. "You like her, eh?" she asked.

Randy's brows lifted. "Akane? Yeah, she's cool, but I'm not champing at the bit to get her into the bedroom, if *that's* what you're implying."

Jenny undid her hair ribbon. Whorls of reddish-brown tresses tumbled free, framing her face. "So yer interest is strictly professional, huh?"

"And personal, I guess. But in the platonic sense."

Jenny clicked her tongue. Then she shook her head skeptically. "She's a beaut, and you two seem to be getting close. But alright, if you say so.

"By the way, you seem tense lately. I'm guessing it's got something to do with Guardians giving you hell because you fought for the Coalition. Am I right?"

"Well, yeah. Safe to say, my military career hasn't been so great since the Battle of the Quad."

"Just pay me a visit anytime you wanna blow off some steam," Jenny said flirtatiously. She winked before turning to leave.

Her sleeve—snug against her curves—explicitly highlighted the contours of her shapely backside, stoking Randy's libido.

Unlike the militaries of Earth Era, the CDF allowed Guardians to engage in sexual activity while on active duty. And Jenny had just given Randy the green light for a sleepover.

At the hatchway, she looked back at him, those pretty aquamarine-blue eyes of hers sparkling. "I hope you take me up on my offer." She walked out, deliberately swaying her hips in an exaggerated fashion.

The hatch closed, taking Jenny's lovely posterior out of view, much to Randy's disappointment. Her invitation was tempting, especially since most Highborn women gave him the cold shoulder, treating it like blasphemy to sleep with a so-called traitor.

Being an ex-Coalition fighter came with so many downsides: ridicule from fellow Guardians, judgment from society, and women ignoring him, even though they wouldn't have before.

Still, none of that mattered right now. What did matter was Stacie's future, and at the moment, it seemed pretty damn bleak.

• • •

Paul had brought Stacie to the *Nightingale's* interrogation room. She was the chasers' leader, so it made sense to start with her.

Frowning, he said, "Fess up."

Stacie sat in a chair behind a metal table, wrists shackled, her hair loose and disheveled from its bun. She remained unfazed by Paul's imposing, musclebound presence. "I told you, those traffickers captured us while we were en route to—"

Paul slammed a fist into the table. Her defiance was shredding what little patience he had left. "Maybe you're suffering from rich-twit syndrome and think you can weasel your way out of this, but I *guarantee* you that's not gonna happen. Now tell me the truth, or that photogenic face of yours is gonna need surgery to fix all the—"

Stacie interrupted him. "Sergeant, I guarantee you my *photogenic* face will remain untouched." She angled her head at the surveillance camera in the upper corner of the room, a subtle reminder that they were being recorded. Brimming with confidence, she added, "And so will every limb on my photogenic body, assuming you want to keep your job with the CDF." She kicked her heels up on the table.

Arrogant bitch. Paul swiped her feet off the table. "Enough posturing!" He swore that if Carl weren't watching outside, he'd give her face a makeover. "No connections you've got are gonna insulate you from this blunder."

"How do you know that? You got my personal-friends list or something?"

Stacie's chutzpah was unraveling Paul's composure. He was about to blow a gasket. "Shut up!"

In the corridor outside the door, Randy and Carl were watching the interrogation on a wall screen.

"He's not making any progress," Randy said, stating the obvious. Stacie was a hard nut to crack, trained by the CDF itself to resist interrogation. "Let me try. We served together. She might talk to a familiar face."

"It's worth a shot, I guess."

"One request, though."

"What?"

"Cut the camera." Which meant both video and audio.

"I can't do that."

"Then just the audio. It'll help me gain her trust."

Carl silently evaluated Randy's request. The regs said both the audio and video had to be on for all interrogations, but he conceded. "Alright, Scott, I'll cut the audio." He pressed the intercom button on the wall panel. "Shaffer, I need you for a sec."

Paul glowered at Stacie. "Saved by the bell. Lucky you."

She casually plopped her boots back on the table. *Sorry, no dice, baby.* "Toodles," she said in a chirpy, over-the-top pitch, waving one of her shackled hands.

Paul growled and keyed the door's release code. *You're a tough one, Spencer, but everyone breaks eventually.*

Once outside, he grumbled to Carl, "She's such a fucking irritant." Frustrated, he ran a hand over his silver-blond flattop.

Carl said, "Let Scott give it a shot. He's got a rapport with her, might get something out of her."

Paul glared at Randy, his eyes hard. "Go ahead, have at her, Mr. Big-Shot Hero."

Feelings for Stacie, engendered by thoughts of the past, crept up on Randy. He entered the interrogation room, and the door sealed behind him.

Carl got in Paul's face. "'Dollface?'" he snapped, referencing the sexist slur Paul had called Akane. She'd reported the unprofessional conduct to him. "'Mr. Big-shot Hero?' You need to watch your mouth and act like the professional you're supposed to be. I know all that training didn't leak out of your fucking brain. So straighten up, you feel me? Or *I'll* straighten you up. And if I have to, I *guaran-damn-tee* you won't like it." Carl had zero tolerance for boorish behavior.

"I gotcha, boss," Paul replied, but he didn't sound sincere.

Carl knew Paul wasn't really sorry. "I hope so."

Paul pivoted and walked away. "Hopefully Scott has better luck with her." *I'd prefer to work that dumbass dishwater-blond over till she begs me to stop. Maybe even inject some pain analeptics into her vessels. That'd loosen her lips.*

Inside the interrogation room, Randy stood across from Stacie. Her sculpted features and piercing cobalt eyes intoxicated his mind, evoking old lovey-dovey feelings. "It's been a while, Stace," he said gently.

Amused, Stacie arched an eyebrow. She slid her boots off the table. "Really? They sent you?" She tut-tutted, entertained by the absurdity of him thinking she'd ever divulge anything to him.

Randy kept his poker face and tuned out the rising emotions. As he pulled back the chair in front of the table, the fixture on the underside of its seat slid along the floor track.

He sat down and scooted the chair forward. "The audio's off. They can't hear. It's just you and me. You already know you're neck-deep in trouble because you traveled into territory off-limits to chasers."

"Whoops."

"This isn't the time for jokes. You need to talk. What are you doing in X-Quadrant?"

Hurt hearts didn't mend quickly, and the proof was on Stacie's face. "Go fuck your rebel playmate."

Randy couldn't fault her for still being upset. "I apologized for my . . . infidelity. Like I told you, it's not something I planned on happening."

"Apology not accepted," Stacie snapped.

"I tried flowers and candy."

With notorious Spencer cruelty in her tone, Stacie said, "And I *trashed* them with joy."

"You sound like your mother." A woman Randy had never met in person, only spiritually through his and Stacie's Link.

Stacie grunted. To her, that was a big snub. Being likened to her mother was basically calling her a bitch. But the truth was undeniable—she *had* picked up some of her mother's traits. Like mother, like daughter. "Why don't you leave me alone and go stick your dick in that redheaded bimbo of yours."

"Kesley and I aren't together anymore. We never really were." Their relationship turned out to be one of convince, not genuine affection, just a lengthy hookup.

"So was her heart on lease like mine? Did you cheat on her too?"

Randy was losing focus on his task: questioning Stacie. "Damn it, Stace, what do you want me to do? What can I do to make it up to you?"

"Too bad you can't '*make it up*' to my parents. Because they're no longer *alive*," she said, rubbing their murder in his face.

"First you hate your parents, then you don't, then you do again. Make up your mind, Stace."

Stacie's parents, especially her mother, had been overly hard on her, but she'd also experienced many beautiful moments with them. "I wanted them to change. To understand me. To cut ties with whatever illegal crap they were into. I wanted them to leave the Eight. I never wanted them *murdered*."

"Reza killed them, not me," Randy said, defensive. "And it would've happened whether I was involved in Hammer Fall or not. You *know* that."

"That doesn't make it any easier to accept that my boyfriend helped put their murderer in power."

"Reza pulled the wool over the Coalition's eyes. There's a judicial system meant to deal with criminals; he deemed himself above it. But I tried to rectify my part in his government takeover. I'm the one who shot him, remember?"

"You should've done it sooner. Then my parents might still be alive."

Randy opened his mouth to argue, then stopped. "You know what? Enough of this." *I'm totally off track here.* He forced himself to refocus. "What are you doing in X-Quadrant? Maybe I can help you get out of this ditch you dug."

"I don't want your help, Randal."

"Dial back the attitude. This is serious, Stace. You could face jail time."

Stacie shifted in her chair, bringing her cuffed hands behind her head. "Sounds comfy." Having nothing more to say, she stared at Randy in silence, waiting for him to leave.

"Forget this." Randy had had enough of Stacie's irreverent

attitude. He rose from his chair and withdrew from the conversation. He might as well have been talking to a brick wall. As he headed for the door, he said, "I hope you don't get locked away, Stace. I really mean that."

"I won't. I have connections to people in high, *high* places, if you know what I mean."

Randy realized who she was talking about. It had slipped his mind that Oviereya Amaechi, the Chief of the Commonwealth, had helped raise Stacie as a child, something few people knew. He was one of them. Stacie was like a daughter to Oviereya, and Oviereya was like a second mother to Stacie, a mother way more cherished than her biological one.

Randy left.

Stacie remained motionless. Seeing her ex after all these months stirred up ghosts of sweet memories. A fleeting pinprick of Cerebral-Attachment Syndrome pulsed. *No, thanks. No nostalgia for me,* she told her cerebral implant. *I'm not interested in a relapse.*

She quickly banished the memories. She'd considered an implant cleanse once or twice, but the potential neurological side effects were too risky: reduced short-term memory, temporary motor impairments, difficulty Linking. Anyway, being the one hurt, not the one who did the hurting, she had beaten Cerebral-Attachment Syndrome more quickly than Randy had. There was no need to take any drastic measures in her healing process.

She leaned back. All she wanted now was to get home and soak in a long, relaxing bath. She needed it after the enervating day she'd just had.

• • •

In the corridor, Paul and Akane crossed paths, walking toward each other from opposite directions.

As Paul edged closer, Akane's features darkened. Try as she

might, she couldn't hold back the tide of rage rising within her. "You know you're gonna bite the dust for murdering her. If I could, I'd cap your ass right now."

Paul smirked, enjoying her discomfort. He planted a hand on her head and ruffled her scruffy hair like she was some misbehaving mutt. "I don't have a clue what you're talking about, kiddo."

Akane slapped his hand away. "Bug off, creep. Stay outta my orbit."

Paul departed, his unsettling laughter echoing throughout the corridor. The sound of his boots clacking the floor grew fainter as he moved farther away from Akane.

The corners of Akane's mouth twitched. She wanted to gouge out Paul's eyeballs. *Purist filth. You're just a dead man walking, Shaffer. A dead man walking.* She flexed her fingers into the shape of a gun and pretended to fire. *One day, for her.*

INTERLUDE TWO

DURING MARTIAL LAW IN COLONIES ONE, FOUR, AND SIX

Planet Eden

Akane and Simone stood on the rooftop of Simone's residential complex, admiring the breathtaking view of the city as the sun dipped below the horizon.

Simone's cornrows were tied back into a thick flowing stream. She wore a purple one-piece pretzel swimsuit, while Akane wore a dark blue bikini top with matching shorts.

Around the massive communal pool, men and women in swimwear mingled, chatting and laughing. One at a time, attractive people of all skin colors somersaulted off the diving board.

"Geronimo!" a heavily tattooed man shouted before cannonballing into the water.

Simone leaned forward, resting her forearms on the waist-high safety wall. She gazed out at the awe-inspiring panorama of high-rises and skyscrapers. She loved coming up here; it always helped clear her mind.

Ignoring the slight pang in her head from being chipped with a cerebral implant at the enlistment processing station today, Akane glanced around at the rambunctious activity.

Eden being a judgment-free society, bare-chested women lounged poolside and couples shamelessly made out in the open. No behavior was taboo; nothing was forbidden, unlike in NeoJapan. When troubles were nearly nonexistent and people could overdose on bliss, why would anyone care about the affairs of Satellite One, another planet, regardless of its inhabitants being fellow human beings?

Simone turned from the cityscape and looked at Akane, who was massaging her temples again. "Stop doing that." She laughed. "That won't help."

"Yeah, I know. Just an impulse. My head should stop feeling weird soon, huh?"

"Yes," Simone assured her.

To complete her ascension to neohuman, Akane had undergone not only chipping but genetic metamorphosis at the enlistment processing station. "Well, physically I feel . . . superfantastic."

"I remember my conversion. Now you've got expedited healing, heightened reflexes, boosted immunity and stamina, youth longevity—"

"Wait, so does that mean I'm gonna look eighteen for the next fifteen years or something?"

"The anti-aging spurt kicks in at different ages for different people. For you, maybe around twenty-five."

"Okay. Good to know."

A soothing warm breeze graced their faces.

"You ready for your first day at the Academy tomorrow?"

Simone asked.

Enthusiasm lit Akane's face. "You know it!"

"I'm glad to hear that. And with Desmond starting too, you'll have a friend there to watch your back."

"Definitely a plus."

Simone was delighted to see Akane happy. She had come so far in adapting to life on Eden. When she first arrived, she couldn't even operate a gamecom pad, let alone a wristcom—tech that was entirely foreign to her. But she and her friends had brought themselves up to speed. Akane's indestructible resolve reminded Simone of herself when she first arrived.

After a thoughtful pause, Simone said, "Akane, I want you to join me in mental communion. It's not easy for me to say this, but your company has meant a lot to me. It would be an honor to be your first Link."

Akane instinctively stepped back, palms extended in a reflexive "no thanks" gesture. "Let's hold off on that." Even after the psychological-safety and proper-consent classes, Linking still wasn't something she'd normalized. "I'm not sure I want someone poking around in my head, or if I want to be poking around in someone else's."

"You've got it all wrong, Akane. Human beings share feelings, thoughts, and experiences through words. We build bonds by sharing time, sharing beds, sharing life. Linking is next-level sharing, next-level love."

Simone's disarming smile—the smile of the woman who had saved Akane from a Purist cop, cared for her, and guided her— offered reassurance. It told Akane her mind and memories would be safe, encouraging her to Link.

"Come on, Akane," Simone said. "Don't miss out on this part of the human experience, this part of the New Humanity."

Akane mulled it over in silence. Did she really want to skip out on Linking forever? Her first Link would be a major milestone, and she might as well share it with someone who truly cared about her. "Oh, what the hell. Sure, let's do this."

Simone forwarded the Link request, pinging Akane's implant.

It seemed so simple, Akane observed, almost as easy as saying hello or shaking someone's hand.

She accepted the request. Then the marriage of minds began, thought convergence initiated.

<Akane, can you hear me?> came Simone's garbled voice from inside Akane's mind. Then it sharpened, sounding clearer. *<Akane, can you hear me?>*

<I can,> Akane responded.

<You and I are a lot alike, you know? Who we are today was forged by similar hardships. See for yourself.>

Akane felt her consciousness detach from her body. She found herself standing within a nebulous cerebral construct, an environment Simone had manifested. Its purpose was to help Akane navigate Simone's memories.

All sorts of colorful patterns undulated in the skies of the dreamscape.

In this ethereal space, Akane appeared as a ghost-like figure.

A row of doors materialized, one after another. Each was a portal into a fragment of Simone's past.

<Go on.> Simone's disembodied voice reverberated from all directions.

The door farthest to the left glowed.

Akane stepped inside it . . .

In Colony Six, twenty-year-old Simone sloshed through mud.

She raced toward her destination as fast as humanly possible, her yellow raincoat whipping in the wind. *Please still be there.*

She huffed, oxygen rushing in and out of her lungs.

Lightning split the murky sky. Thunder growled. A deluge of rain hammered the ground.

As her foot plunged into a pothole brimming with rainwater, her leg folded. She fell hands-first into the soggy earth. *Damn it.* She scrambled to her feet and pushed forward, half-stumbling, boots caked in mud.

Up ahead, she saw the dull-silver crescent-shaped freight shuttle, beckoning her to come. It was time to leave this life behind. She'd heard so much about Eden. She had dreamt of this day.

A large-chested man in his forties with a Bandholz beard stood outside the shuttle. "You're late, woman! Come on! Everyone's waiting on your keister so we can take off!" Rain drizzled off his shaved scalp.

She'd made it. Thank goodness they hadn't left. "Th-thank you for waiting. Dax, right?"

"Yeah, that's me." Getting straight to the point, Dax said, "Got your ID?"

Simone could hardly catch her breath. "Yeah," she panted.

"Well, don't just stand there, show me."

Thunder boomed.

Simone reached into the inner pocket of her raincoat. Her shaky hand pulled out a plastic card, almost dropping it.

Dax snatched the bootleg registration card and examined it. "Kasim's definitely a pro Counterfeiter. This looks legit." He glanced at the ID again: C-ZERO-THREE-THREE-EIGHT. The "C" stood for "colony," marking Simone as an immigrant, a lottery beneficiary. "Kasim couldn't make you a nonimmigrant

ID?"

Simone shrugged. "He said it'd raise more red flags in a background scan."

Dax gave the forged ID back to her. "Okay." His feet left big shoeprints in the mud as he went to the cargo-hold door. Gripping the manual crank, he began to twist.

The door spooled upward. Inside the hold were three men and one woman with black-market IDs. They sat among unmarked crates and containers, on a metal floor coated with motes of dust and debris from countless cargo runs.

"Get in," Dax told Simone. He was smuggling them all to Eden.

Simone climbed inside.

A gust of wind whooshed into the hold, carrying droplets of rain. Thunder crackled.

Grunting, Dax twisted the crank again, and the cargo-hold door unspooled, sealing the travelers inside.

The faint red glow from the overhead lights bathed the dark interior.

Simone settled next to the woman, who wore a red hijab and a decorative dress. She had olive skin and long, curly raven hair, and she was in her twenties.

Simone turned to her. "Hi, I'm Simone."

The woman smiled. "Khadija."

They shook hands.

Sitting against the rear wall, the three men chatted, speaking in a Slavic language. They sounded excited and full of hope.

As the engines growled to full power, the cargo hold rattled.

Simone toppled sideways. "*Omph*!" She righted herself and rubbed her elbow, which had struck the floor.

Khadija rested a hand on Simone's back. "Are you okay?" Her

words were slightly stilted, English being her second language.

"I'm good."

The shuttle ascended into the howling tempest, rain crashing against its metal body. Then it left Satellite One, rocketing into space.

"So, which province do you intend to live in?" Khadija asked, her words deliberately spaced for proper enunciation.

"I'm not really sure. I don't exactly have a plan."

Khadija retrieved a handheld device from the pouch on her belt. "Here, let me show you some viable options for us immigrants." She pressed a button, and the four-by-four screen displayed a two-dimensional map. Eden's continent was divided into region states, and those were further divided into provinces, collections of cities and towns.

She tapped a region state, magnifying it. "This is Region State Six." She tapped it again. "And this is Province Eight of Region State Six. People say it's one of Eden's most immigrant-friendly provinces. But that's because many of the First live there."

The First were the earliest colony immigrants transported to Eden. In the early years of humanity's reset, before the lottery's inception, the central government had needed laborers to accelerate Eden's development. Therefore, the Parliament and the Chief Executive imported several million colonists to do the work. These individuals were thoroughly vetted, deemed the best of an "inferior crop."

In addition to monetary compensation, the government promised them Eden citizenship at the conclusion of their service, a move that sparked controversy among original Edenites. It was the first time AEGIS's blueprint for humanity had been compromised.

Although they were living better than on Satellite One, these first immigrants found themselves relegated to the bottom of Eden's labor market, and the government withheld their genetic upgrade. Financial constraints and other excuses were provided as reasons. In truth, the government didn't want immigrants to prosper on par with original Edenites. Not to mention, government officials wanted to stay in favor with their voter base.

Even though they were at the bottom of Eden's socioeconomic ladder, the First still enjoyed a life better than what they had on Satellite One. Some of them even amassed considerable wealth and used it to support loved ones back home.

A number of wealthy First established relief nonprofits to aid colonists. Others, less fortunate, turned to the criminal underworld, engaging in intergalactic trafficking and other illicit activity.

"Do you know if there's a way to link up with them?" Simone asked. "The First."

"I don't, but I'm sure we can find one. However, not all immigrants—First or lottery beneficiaries—will help us."

"What do you mean? Aren't we all in this together?"

Khadija shook her head regretfully. "Some immigrants are snooty. They think they're on the same level as original Edenites, the people chosen by AEGIS to reign dominion over Eden. They believe they've risen to greatness and avoid associating with new immigrants.

"They fear compromising their success, their societal status. They want to stay in the upper echelon's good graces and are afraid that associating with new immigrants might jeopardize that. These *social climbers* have forgotten where they came from. It's shameful."

The two young women continued getting to know each other.

Simone, as a newly minted Guardian, had often found herself sitting alone at mess-hall tables. When she was deployed on planetary-impact missions, feelings of isolation and loneliness often gripped her. She had few true friends in her platoon. Most of her comrades were nonimmigrants and kept their distance, holding fast to the wrongful beliefs instilled in them by AEGIS—that they were the superior breed of human and the CDF was their domain.

After transferring to the ETF, Simone met Sam Guthrie and Jamie Lister, two people who became real friends.

Akane approached another door in the dreamscape. A shield of light blocked her from entering. When she turned left, more shields blinked over other doors. These memories were being firewalled, blocked from her cerebral implant. They were things Simone didn't want her to see yet, or that she had to earn the right to access.

Akane opened her eyes and left the dreamscape, returning her consciousness to the physical plane. She batted her thin-lashed eyelids, blinking sparkles from her vision.

Simone opened her eyes too.

Linking turned out to be not so weird for Akane after all. "Cool."

Simone fake-punched her shoulder. "See? That wasn't so bad."

A group of attractive guys walked past, heading for the rooftop exit. They directed a flurry of wolf whistles and catcalls at Akane and Simone.

"Did you see the phat ass on that tall brown chick?" one of them said, referring to Simone.

"Yeah," another responded. "Fucking amazing."

The thong tucked between Simone's thick, meaty ass cheeks

left nothing to the imagination.

Simone laughed at the men's compliments.

"I can't blame 'em for wilding out over you," Akane said, pointing at her. "That's a bodacious figure you've got there. Total badassery."

Simone definitely had a body that warranted stares—every muscle chiseled, every curve perfectly shaped.

"I think some of those eyes were on you, Akane."

Akane's brows shot up in mock hilarity. "Nah, I don't think so."

"Why's that?"

"Because 'killer bod with curves' trumps 'petite Japanese chick.'" Simone exemplified power and allure, not her.

Simone said earnestly, "*Ridiculous*, Akane." She gently took her friend's chin between her thumb and forefinger. "You're a gorgeous young woman. Don't believe otherwise."

Akane's face warmed. "Uh, well, thanks. I appreciate the—"

And then the unexpected happened.

Unspoken feelings and pent-up impulses, intensified by Linking, bubbled up inside Simone. She gripped Akane's shoulders, leaned in, and pressed her lips to hers.

Simone's hands slid to Akane's waist as she drove the kiss deeper.

Flabbergasted, Akane lurched back, unsticking her lips from Simone's.

An awkward pause stretched between them. Neither woman knew what to say.

Simone scratched the back of her head and stuttered, "I . . . I'm sorry. Was that not okay?"

Akane, just as nervous, toyed with her bangs. "Oh, no, it's okay. That just . . . caught me off guard. Kinda sudden, you know?"

She swallowed. "Anyway, I did like it. I mean, I'm into guys and gals, so—" She trailed off, unsure where the conversation was going.

"Akane!" someone shouted, breaking the tension.

Akane jumped at the sound of the familiar voice. "Jacobi!" Desmond stood beside him. "Des!"

Desmond went up to Akane, cool-guy shades on. "Simone invited us over to celebrate your first day at BCT tomorrow. Mine too."

He opened his arms for a hug, and Akane launched herself into his embrace.

They held each other for a long, sentimental eight seconds before letting go.

Jacobi edged closer. "It's been a while, Akane." His face flushed—he still had a crush on her.

"Good to see you too, J. Good to see both of you guys," Akane replied warmly.

"It's a shame about Skylar. I wish she were here with us." Jacobi's chin hung, and his shoulders slumped.

Desmond stepped between them and flung an arm over each of their shoulders. "Yeah, it's a bummer that Skylar isn't here anymore, but she wouldn't want us sulking day in and day out, right? Now come on, let's get wet!"

Akane punched a fist skyward. "Hell yeah!"

"You guys have fun," Simone said. "I'll head down and get supper ready." She walked toward the rooftop exit, silently chastising herself. *What was I thinking, lip-locking with Akane? Stupid me.*

Akane shimmied out of her shorts, revealing a high-waisted bikini bottom. "Des, Jacobi, come on!" she called out, running to the pool.

Jacobi momentarily lost his train of thought, distracted by Akane's beauty: pretty eyes, angular cheekbones, and a lean figure. Despite the amount of near-naked women around, his eyes were only on her.

Desmond elbowed him. "Still in love, huh?"

"Oh, just shut up, man. I'm dating someone, anyway. And it's going well."

"She's probably some plain Jane you ain't even into. Stop being a wimp and work up the courage to tell Akane you like her."

"Des—"

"Come on!" Akane hollered from the poolside, interrupting Jacobi. She dove into the water.

"Let's go, man," Desmond said. He and Jacobi dashed to the pool.

As the last glimmers of daylight faded, night crept over the city.

Simone lay awake in bed. Outside her window, the night sky glittered with stars.

Tomorrow, Akane would start her first day at the Academy. Simone would miss her. Not having Akane's presence for three months would leave a void in her life. She'd grown used to her company, *needed* it.

Simone rolled onto her side, restless.

She loved Akane a lot. Akane had become her best friend, and she wanted to protect her. And one day, she wanted Akane to know the part of her life that she'd kept firewalled from her in the dreamscape, the part of her life that was RISE.

A soft knock tapped twice on the door.

"It's open."

Akane stepped in, dressed in a spaghetti-strap camisole and a pair of skimpy panties.

Simone's eyes followed her as she approached the bed. "Akane, what is it? Are you having jitters about your first day at BCT? It's only natural to—" Akane crawled onto the bed. One strap of her camisole slipped precariously down her shoulder. Simone's heart rate went up. "Akane, what—?"

<Simone, I'm great. Chill the fuck out.> Akane's eyes made her intent unmistakable. She wanted to show her appreciation for Simone's love and support through physical intimacy. *<Like I said earlier, I'm down with what happened between us.>* Her lips moved closer to Simone's, a hairbreadth away from a kiss. *<And I'd like more.>*

Before long, their nightclothes and underthings were on the floor.

The electrifying sensations flowing between their Linked minds, as they consummated their friendship, amplified every touch and kiss. Euphoria slammed into Akane as Simone's lips explored her body, titillating her in the most intimate of places.

Naked flesh pressed against naked flesh, and the desperate whimpers of the women morphed into fervent moans.

The feeling that overwhelmed Akane was indescribable. Bones trembling, lungs expelling shallow gasps, she reached her first climax of the night—one of many to come.

• • •

FIVE WEEKS INTO BASIC COMBAT TRAINING

Satellite Two
Boot Camp

Cadets stood at parade rest in the torrid heat, lined up outside their company HQ in tight formation—sleep-deprived, muscles sore from rigorous training. Their battledress clung to them, soaked with sweat.

Bleak and barren, the obsidian landscape surrounding them offered little to admire, save for the mesas and volcanic mountains in the distance.

A drill sergeant stood in front of the formation, stern-faced. "Colony insurrectionists are the *sole* cause of this war that's killing our comrades. Fueled by Independent Movement ideology and Arman Reza's liberation philosophy, these dissidents seek to subvert authority and establish a republic independent of the Commonwealth. Which is treason! Their aim is to sow chaos and defy the rule of law."

Cadet Desmond Castillo, bold to a fault, spoke up. "You're wrong!"

The drill sergeant locked his eyes on him. "What did you just say, boy?"

"*Des*," Akane hissed. She yanked his shoulder. "Calm down, or you'll end up in remedial re-education."

Akane had backbone; she wasn't one to silence herself. But Simone had warned her to never challenge the drill sergeants, no matter how crass or offensive their remarks. Speaking up might feel righteous, but it could brand her as an Independent Movement sympathizer—and get her killed.

"I can't ignore this guy's bullshit any longer, Akane," Desmond said. Hard-nosed, he continued to challenge the drill sergeant. "Yeah, it's technically treason for a colony to separate from the Commonwealth. But the government pushed the citizens of colonies One, Four, and Six into rebellion. Armed dissidence, ya know? I realize peace has to be restored, but that won't happen if we keep painting the Coalition as bad guys. We need to—"

Quickly and fluidly, the sergeant drew his pistol.

A shot rang out.

The bullet struck Desmond square in the forehead. He collapsed instantly, blood spraying the reddish-brown earth.

Akane gasped, and her heart froze inside her chest.

Cadets chilled to the core quivered. Color drained from faces scared witless.

The sergeant holstered his weapon. "Independent Movement sympathizing is a behavioral sign of an insider threat, so Cadet Castillo had to be put down. I suggest the rest of you think twice before following in his footsteps, unless you want to be removed from service as well."

Akane could hardly believe her eyes. *A Guardian killing a comrade for exercising free speech? Insane.* She hadn't expected even the most anti-immigrant drill sergeants to be *this* brazen.

What none of the cadets could see was the drill sergeant's skull-and-crossbones tattoo, the mark of the Purists. *It's our job to purge the CDF's ranks of these deficiencies, these unchosen. Gotta keep the military pure,* the sergeant thought.

• • •

MONTHS AFTER BCT

Planet Kendaldras

Simone said over the C-comm, <<*Alright, Private Sugimori, it's game time. This is only your third field mission as a member of Vanguard Alpha. Don't screw up your shining record now.*>>

<<*Relax, Sarge, I got this,*>> Akane replied.

<<*You'd better not botch it, Private.*>>

Yada yada, Akane thought.

Simone was Akane's friend, but out in the field, she was still her superior.

The enemy would be on high alert. Over the past few days, CDF task forces had hit five of their bases in a coordinated offensive. The final six were going down tonight. Vanguard Alpha's mission in this joint operation was to destroy this base deep in the forests of Kendaldras.

A pang of sadness rippled through Akane. *I wish Desmond could see me in action.* Shaking off the emotion, she activated her Shell's stealth cloak. *Time to get to work.* Her jumper struts launched her into the air, catapulting her over a fence of laser bands.

She landed in a crouch and then stood to full height. *Easy.* She jogged toward the east side of the building. Though she was in stealth-cloak mode, she'd still have to be tactful in her approach. Stealth cloaks did a good job of camouflaging a Guardian but didn't make them a hundred percent invisible, and there was the telltale rustling of grass with each step of a mechboot.

<<*This is Shaffer. Charge set,*>> Paul transmitted over the C-comm.

<<*Same here,*>> said Simone. <<*Akane?*>>

Akane replied, <<*I'm just about—*>> Energy blasts streaked past her, one zipping over her shoulder. "Fuck!" The hairs on the back of her neck rose. <<*Enemy engagement! I'm taking fire!*>>

Two Kendaldrak charged straight at her, their forearms locked into cylindrical energy blasters. They wore thick, scaly armor with high collars. Skintight hoods concealed their hairless heads, and glowing goggles covered their eyes.

Akane unholstered the rifle from her back and returned fire. *How in the universe can they see me while I'm cloaked? It has to be those bizarre goggles. Must be made of some gnarly tech.* A blast struck her shoulder, chipping away fragments of Kryoplaste. *Sonuva—!* She gritted her teeth and emptied three rounds into the attacker who hit her, taking him out. Then she gunned down the second Kendaldrak. *Ha, eat lead!*

Pumped full of bullets, he lay on the ground, convulsing and gurgling on the green blood upwelling from his mouth.

A strobe light coming from the guard tower scoured the darkness, sweeping for intruders. Voices shouted in a language unintelligible to the human ear. The firefight had drawn more hostiles.

Akane's Shell auto-translated the voices that were getting nearer. "Find and kill all intruders," one said.

More Kendaldrak were closing in on her position.

Moving fast, she docked her rifle and slapped a charge onto the building. <<*Charge set,*>> she let the team know. She spun around and made tracks, augmented strides carrying her away from danger.

A foot chase ensued, hostiles racing after her. Spears of energy flew by. *Damn, that was close.*

Flanked by gunfire, she swung her arm sideways while running, wrist gun spitting plasma blasts. The agile figures behind her dodged and discharged blue-white bolts from their arm cannons.

Akane jumped back over the laser fence and took off. Missed shots from her pursuers sliced the air, their glare lighting up her armored frame. <<*Akane here. I'm clear! Blow the sucker!*>> She maxed her run speed, kicking up a rooster tail of grass and dirt.

More shots came her way, and then a grandiose mushroom cloud of smoke and fire thundered into the starlit sky.

Akane skidded to a stop and whirled around, chest heaving. The enemy base was now a smoldering wreck. *Fuck yeah!* She smiled triumphantly as embers snowed like scorched confetti.

A fort of steel prefabs had been set up as a forward operating base for the task forces assembled for the operation. With all eleven enemy bases taken out, the Guardians of the joint force celebrated. They were in their sleeves, enjoying the moment.

"We secured five thousand weapons," Sam said to Simone. "You know the drill. Cook the books and make sure De'Angelo smuggles at least a thousand to the Coalition."

"Roger," Simone replied. After taking a moment to give it some thought, she said, "You know, I think it's time we bring Akane in."

"I know she's your bestie, and she handles herself well in the field, but that doesn't mean she'll cut the mustard."

"Let's find out."

Sam paused, considering. "Okay, do it. But feed her info in small doses. Bring her in slowly. No need to overdo it."

Simone bobbed her head. *Welcome to RISE, Akane.*

At a nearby table, Paul, Mark, and Dan chatted, nonalcoholic drinks in hand.

Mark glared at Akane, who was holding a cup and talking to another female Guardian. "Ugh, another damn immigrant." He downed a third of his drink. "These pissants don't belong in the CDF with us, AEGIS's chosen. They think they're as good as us, but they ain't. You can put sugar on shit, but it's still shit." *And that's exactly what these insolent immigrants are,* he thought. Hatred wrinkled his brow.

Paul smirked wickedly. "Well, by the end of tonight, there'll be one less of these *curs* in Vanguard Alpha."

"You about to pull something?" Dan asked.

Paul nodded. "Damn right. We've gotta do our duty, don't we?"

The three men laughed.

Mark raised his drink. "Amen to that, brother."

"For the purity of the republic," Paul said.

Mark and Dan repeated the Purist motto in unison: "For the purity of the republic."

Akane was with Simone, inventorying confiscated firearms stacked on pallets inside the trailer of a BUS.

Akane said, "That's it for me." She clipped a datapad to her belt.

"Good," Simone replied. She then segued into the long-awaited talk she wanted to have. "By the way, you mentioned wanting to know more about the activist group I'm part of. You even asked if you could join."

"Yeah, I remember."

"Jay and Sam are members too. We've all been watching you grow into the woman you are today, and we think you'd make a great addition to the group. We're called RISE. Our goal is to get more immigrants into those power circles you and I always talk about. We're a secret group, though. No one outside of us knows we exist. That's to protect our members.

"I'd like to bring you in, but there's a vetting process. It's nothing you can't handle. So . . . are you interested?"

"You fucking bet I am!" Akane said without hesitation. "Anything you're a part of, I wanna be too!"

"The final call isn't mine to make," Simone let her know. "But you're a high-speed Guardian. I'm confident you'll ace the initiation process."

"So what's next? What do I have to do?"

"I'll fill you in once I wrap up here. It'll be a quick talk. Should only take about thirty minutes."

"Okay."

"Great, I won't be much longer." Hands on Akane's shoulders, Simone leaned in and planted a kiss on her lips.

Akane and Simone weren't lovers, but they were friends with benefits, which made for an unorthodox mentor-mentee relationship when out in the field. Simone had once suggested they stop being physically intimate, but Akane wanted to keep it going. To her, there was nothing wrong with fooling around every now and then, especially when she was feeling horny.

Simone pulled her lips away. "We'll meet by the riverside. Sound good?"

"Sounds good to me, Sarge." Akane's voice turned sultry. "And I think we should celebrate tonight's victory . . . if you know what I mean."

Simone matched her tone. "Sure."

They'd have to be more careful this time. During another joint mission on Planet Bazular, they had decided to engage in a little leisure-time sex in their tent, and their naked silhouettes had put on an unintended show for a few Guardians. They were embarrassed, even though the CDF permitted sexual activity on active duty.

Before Akane left the BUS, Simone gave her a friendly pat on the rear. *She'll make it,* she thought as Akane walked out of sight.

She finished logging her batch of weapons after twenty minutes and stepped out into the tranquil stillness of the night. Turning left, she walked along the lengthy trailer of the BUS.

The sinister eyes of a man crouched in the bushes tracked Simone. When he saw his opportunity, he snuck up behind her.

Just as Simone was about to clear the trailer's concealment, a gloved hand clamped over her mouth.

She let out muffled cries, eyes wide with fright.

The attacker clicked the knife hilt he held. An energy blade flared to life, and he drove it into Simone's back, cutting through flesh, muscle, and bone.

When he pulled the blade out of her, she collapsed, a charred, smoking hole in her chest. As she gasped for breath, he leaned down and said, "Enjoy the afterlife, immigrant bitch. Your plucky little gal pal is next."

Simone recognized the man's voice. "Sh-Shaffer." Her eyes closed, and Paul dashed off into the night.

Akane had become concerned. Simone hadn't shown up at their meeting spot, and their Link was unresponsive. A mounting sense of dread frazzling her nerves, she returned to the BUS, worry blanketing her face. When she saw her friend lying deathly still, a knot twisted in her gut, and her knees buckled. The bloodcurdling scream she released jolted Guardians from their sleep.

All the Guardians were now awake and alert. Search teams had been dispatched to comb the forested terrain for Simone's killer.

Sam sat at one of the bench-tables with Jay. "No one saw who did it," Sam said. "The commander thinks one of the Kendaldrak must've come for some payback. He figures that maybe some were outside the explosion's radius, but we both know that theory's bullshit."

"Yeah," Jay agreed. "My guess is it was a Purist. Could've been someone from our team or one of the other task forces. They were probably watching Simone, just waiting for the right moment." He looked over at Akane, who sat two tables away, crying into her palms. "What about her?"

"Simone wanted her to join us. We should honor that." Sam stood and gestured for Jay to follow. "It's the least we can do."

They went to Akane's table and sat across from her on the opposite bench.

"Hey," Sam said gently, "we know you're hurting, but did Simone ever mention what she, Jay, and I are involved in?"

Akane sniffled and lifted her head, meeting their eyes. Grief jammed her throat, and she could hardly see through the sheen of tears. "Yeah. She said you're part of some activist group called RISE."

"That's right," Jay replied. "We can't prove anything yet, but we don't think it was a Kendaldrak who killed Simone. Our hunch is it was a Purist."

Sam elaborated. "Basically, a member of an immigrant-hating extremist group. Just like RISE, they're a secret; no one knows they exist. They're infiltrating the highest levels of government, the CDF, and law enforcement. Their sole objective is to ensure immigrants remain powerless and to keep colonists a bunch of labor slaves. The group we're a part of counteracts them."

Akane made a vow to her heart: The Purist who murdered Simone would suffer a fate worse than death. "I want in. I wanna find the butcher who murdered my friend. I want revenge." Her voice dropped to a low and gritty timbre. "I'm gonna kill this creep, whoever they are." Her expression was a foretoken of what awaited Simone's killer, and it was going to be painful, bloody, and messy.

The same yearning for vengeance stirred within Sam. "We want justice too. And we *will* find that bastard."

"We'll fill you in more tomorrow," Jay said. "When we get back to Eden, you'll meet the rest of the group."

CHAPTER THREE

ONE DAY AFTER VANGUARD ALPHA'S RETURN TO EDEN

Planet Eden
Chief Executive's Manor

Chief Amaechi stood facing the window behind her desk, hands clasped behind her back. She wore a purple pencil skirt that had gold decorative accents. A matching suit jacket with padded shoulders and dark heels completed the executive ensemble.

She stared at the mob of vindictive protesters corralled outside the manor's gate. They were shouting for retribution, demanding that Coalition fighters be held accountable for crimes against the Commonwealth. Hand-written signs said "Death to the Chief," and that wasn't even the worst of them.

The aftershocks of the Battle of the Quad had injected a fresh dose of venom into the New Humanity.

Oviereya wondered, Was this continuum of hate incurable? Could people not rise beyond it? Was peaceful coexistence a

Sisyphean task? As mankind transcended into the New Humanity, it had apparently dragged along Earth Era's deficiencies.

Outside, the cries and curses of protesters filled the air. A cordon of EPAs in riot gear stood stationed at the gate, ready to subdue any aggressors.

Oviereya asked herself "Am I good enough? Can I do this?"

A male EPA in a dark suit came into the office. "Madam Chief, your guest has arrived."

"Send her in." Oviereya's voice mirrored her morose mood.

The EPA left. After five seconds, Stacie entered, dressed in a crisp turquoise blouse tucked into khaki pants. As she walked forward, the carpet muted her heels.

Oviereya remained at the window, gazing at the protesters. "Hello, Stacie," she said, greeting the young woman who was like a daughter to her, and whom she had just saved from being locked away in an orbital prison.

Stacie moved further into the office and paused. "It's been a while since we've talked." She attempted to access their Link. There was no response from Oviereya's implant. "I see you've terminated our Link." She'd expected as much, but it still stung— just a touch.

"Of course. I'm Chief Executive now. Even with my implant's firewalls, I can't risk the *slightest* leak of the confidential information I'm entrusted with." As long as Oviereya was Chief Executive, she had to end all Linked interpersonal connections, nuptial Links excepted. It pained her to relinquish such a crucial aspect of life.

Stacie went up to the executive desk. "So, what's it like at the top? Must be incredible, making history as the first immigrant to become Chief Executive, even if it happened by default."

Oviereya felt her heart fall. "Honestly? It's cold at the top. I wanted to be a changemaker. I wanted to pave the way for unity and equality among all the Commonwealth's peoples—original Edenites, colonists, and immigrants. But now—"—her voice dimmed, as though all hope had been drained from her spirit —"immigrants are protesting all over Eden, outraged by the surge in hate crimes. Meanwhile, nonimmigrant Edenites are furious. They want every Coalition fighter punished. Some of those vengeful souls are gathered outside my window right now.

"I've spent many sleepless nights trying to find a way forward. But I've realized this problem can't be solved by me alone. It cuts across cultural and ideological lines. I can't wave a magic wand and make the hate go away. Only society, united, can end this us-versus-them mentality. Yet the Chief is always held responsible for the Commonwealth's unresolved issues."

"I'm worried about you," Stacie said. "I don't need a Link to see how stressed out you are."

Oviereya's face, still turned toward the window, betrayed her exhaustion. "It comes with the territory, I guess. But enough about me. Let's talk about you. What were you doing in X-Quadrant? Why are you putting your future at risk?"

"I'm dismantling the Seven's operations." The need to take down the Seven Elite vibrated in Stacie's chest.

"And why are you doing that?"

"I don't know the full extent of my parents' wrongdoings." Stacie wondered why they had resorted to such despicable actions. "Maybe they were only involved in the lesser offenses—bribery, racketeering, money laundering, extortion—instead of the more heinous ones like human trafficking, murder, or drug smuggling. But I can't say for sure. I'm still combing through databases, trying to uncover the truth—and root the evil out of Spencer Enterprises.

"What I *do* know is my parents never protested the crimes the other families were involved in. Of course they didn't. The Eight were all one big happy criminal conglomerate. Going after the Seven is my way of making amends for my parents' sins. Okay?"

"If you want to make amends," Oviereya said, "don't break the law. Donate to charitable causes or try philanthropy."

"I'm already doing all that. *And* I'm taking down the Seven."

Oviereya spun around, her long ebony locs whipping the air. Her strong features steeled.

By the pointed look on Oviereya's face, Stacie knew she was about to be scolded, albeit out of nothing but love.

"Let me make one thing clear: The Seven is not your concern." Oviereya wished Stacie weren't so stubborn. "Word is your recklessness even led to a young woman being killed."

Stacie bit her lower lip, Ryoko's death tugging at her soul. "I feel for her family. But that wasn't on me. She ignored orders."

A muscle in Oviereya's jaw twitched. "I beg to differ. And if you execute another unlawful mission, don't expect me to save you. As much as I love you, I'm not your get-out-of-jail-free card. I despise when the powerful or wealthy escape consequences because of their connections. It goes against my principles. I refuse to partake in such injustice. So this was a onetime deal."

"I know," Stacie said humbly. "I'm grateful you helped me out. But the seven family heads have kept their parents' criminal empires alive. So what am I supposed to do? Leave everything to the CDF and law enforcement? They've failed for *years* to bring them down. Someone has to do something. And I believe the trafficking outfit the CDF recently busted is tied to Damien Sykes, *your* opponent in next year's election."

Oviereya narrowed her eyes. "Do you have proof?"

Stacie was a little embarrassed, to say the least. She wasn't the type to talk a big game and not back it up. "Well, it's nothing concrete, but—"

"Just turn over what you know to the CDF, Stacie, and let them handle it from here," Oviereya interrupted. "I've already ensured that you and your team won't face any charges. But if you keep going after Damien and the rest of the Seven and get caught again, don't expect me to bail you out. I won't be your crutch. I'm not willing to risk my reputation as Chief Executive, not even for you." The Office was bigger than their relationship.

Stacie intended to go after Damien until he was dead or behind bars, for Cassie. "I can get to Damien in ways the CDF can't, and —"

"Damien is already being investigated by Defense Force Intelligence," Oviereya revealed. "But not for trafficking. Still, whatever you have, even if it seems insubstantial, could help DFI build a case."

"Okay, so what *is* he being investigated for, then, if not trafficking?" Stacie asked, genuinely curious.

"He may be involved in a domestic extremist group. Whether he's a financial backer or a figure of authority is still unclear, but there's strong evidence tying him to them."

Stacie pushed for additional information. "Tell me more about this group Damien's involved with."

"The group launched a virulent movement aimed at keeping Eden free from colonist integration, preserving the Commonwealth's class system, and halting progress for immigrants. None of that is illegal, but they may be violating laws in the process. Damien could be connected to those violations.

"The members of the group call themselves Purists. Since its inception, other Purist groups have formed, but the one Damien is involved with is the original and the largest. That's all I can tell you. The rest is need-to-know."

"I can get close to Damien, *really* close," Stacie insisted. "I can get him to confess his involvement in this . . . cult, or whatever it is. I can find out what they're up to. And maybe I can even tie Damien to the trafficking operation."

"Why are you so adamant about taking down Sykes? It's more than just because he's one of the Seven, isn't it? Does this have anything to do with Cassie McCanns?"

Memories of Cassie's bruised body unsettled Stacie's mind. She blinked them away. "Yes. She *never* would've gotten hurt if I hadn't introduced them to each other."

Stacie and Damien had once been casually involved, until her mother caught wind of their relationship. The rules were clear: No two children of the Eight were allowed to be in an intimate relationship of any kind. Intermarriage and the merging of family empires were strictly forbidden. Forced to end their relationship, Stacie moved on to other lovers. But, being the headstrong and rebellious woman she was, she continued seeing Damien in secret from time to time.

Eventually, she introduced him to a friend, Cassie McCanns. The two hit it off, but Cassie soon discovered Damien had other girlfriends. He'd told Cassie she was his one and only—his paramour, as he liked to say. It was a lie.

The night Cassie found out about Damien's other bedfellows, a heated argument erupted between them. Though she claimed she was done with him, Damien's charm kept luring her back to him. Then the abuse began. At first, he claimed it was an accident, a single slap. But he turned out to be a serial abuser. He manipulated Cassie into a cycle of psychological and physical torment.

Cassie had encountered a side of Damien that Stacie hadn't, but had inklings of. A controlling, possessive, and dangerous side. Stacie ultimately convinced Cassie he'd never change and urged her to press charges. But the charges never stuck. Damien had bought off the jury. He was a son of the Eight, after all, virtually impervious to the justice system. In the aftermath, Cassie's physical wounds healed, but the mental scars lingered.

"I can use his attraction to me to my advantage," Stacie said.

"Realistically, how close do you think he'd actually let you get?" Oviereya asked. "After you accused him of abuse and helped take him to trial, don't you think he'll be suspicious if you suddenly try to rekindle your relationship with him?"

"I know him. It won't be hard to make him believe I'm eager to crawl back into his arms. He thinks his power, wealth, and new political spotlight can rope in any woman, no matter how much of a self-absorbed jerk he is. That megalomaniac would love to get his grubby mitts back on me. He's *never* stopped trying."

Even after the rigged trial that cleared his name, Damien continued to sporadically message her over the years.

Stacie said, "All I have to do is give him the impression I've come around, that I'm drawn to his new status. He'll think his efforts finally paid off, that I've come to my senses now that he's in the public eye. People like him, Madam Chief, are obsessive control freaks. They think they can hurt a woman and then win her back with their mind games, fake charm, and manipulation tactics. I know his type all too well.

"And I'm sorry to be blunt, but he thinks with his dick way too much to let a woman he's desperate to reclaim slip through his fingers. I've got that narcissist pegged.

"So here's what I'm proposing: Let me go undercover for the CDF as a confidential informant. You know how much taking down Damien means to me."

Stacie remembered the digital tabloids Damien had paid to smear Cassie after the trial: COUNTRYSIDE BUMPKIN

FAKES ABUSE TO STEAL MONEY FROM THE SYKES FAMILY.

Stacie imagined how humiliated Cassie must have felt. It was no surprise Cassie had cut off all contact with her. Stacie was certain Cassie blamed her for introducing her to a monster.

Oviereya sighed, taking in Stacie's fiery expression. "Stacie, I don't know." She didn't want to put Stacie in harm's way.

"Come on, this wouldn't be the first time a chaser worked with the CDF on a contract basis." The CDF had a history of outsourcing high-risk, cloak-and-dagger missions to chasers when they needed to deny involvement and sweep things under the rug.

Oviereya thought over the proposition for a long moment. "General Conlan, Chief of Defense Force Intelligence, will be in touch," she said at last. "I'll defer to his judgment. So your involvement in this investigation isn't guaranteed. If Conlan approves, you do exactly what he says. Understood?" Her tone left no room for debate.

Stacie tipped her chin. "Gotcha. Conlan gets full carte blanche."

"Go now."

Three steps from the door, Stacie paused and turned around. "Oviereya, please take it easy. Don't burn yourself out."

"Thank you, Stacie. I'll be fine."

"Hey, do you ever miss Mom and Dad?"

"I do."

"It's crazy, isn't it? After all the wrong they did, after all the pain Mom caused me, I still get choked up when I think about them."

"Well, they loved you," Oviereya said softly. "And I know she was hard on you, but your mother absolutely *adored* you, her little baby girl. She was an imperfect mother, no doubt, but she wanted what she thought was best for you—to be the family's successor. A successful one."

Tears rose in Stacie's eyes, and she swallowed. "Now look what you've done, got me all teary-eyed."

"We simply love those who loved us, even if their love was flawed."

Flawed love, huh? Stacie thought. That sounded like her mother's kind of love. "Yeah, we do," she said. Just as she was almost out the door, she paused again. "Hey, Oviereya, don't worry, you're doing an outstanding job. You're not some pseudo-Chief. You're the real deal."

"What makes you think I need a pep talk, young lady?"

"You might be older and wiser than me, but we shared a Link for *years*. You can't fake it with me. All that doubt is just antiquated second-class programming still running in the back of your mind. You're a kick-ass Chief. Don't let anyone tell you otherwise. You hear me?"

Oviereya's spirits lifted, and her self-doubt dissolved, snuffed out by a wave of confidence. "You know me too well. Thank you, Stacie."

"What are friends for?" Stacie exited the office.

Oviereya faced the window, gazing pensively at the protesters. The crowd had grown. The Commonwealth was a mixed bag of ideologies. Not all nonimmigrant Edenites were dead set against colony advancement. Not all anti-reformists were Purists. Some held biases; others were simply misinformed, but they weren't Purists. Also, not all colonists and immigrants were saints. There were dangerous extremists among them.

She wondered what she could do to bring the Commonwealth's fractured society together. How was she supposed to win the upcoming election?

Conspiracy theories claimed she had colluded with the Coalition to steal the Chief Executive seat. Others claimed that, if elected next year, she'd alter Eden's demographics to a fifty-fifty split by replacing half of all nonimmigrants with colonists. Misinformation campaigns were feeding Eden citizens lies, such as that she planned to phase out all planetary-impact missions.

Oviereya supported the CDF being an interventionist force, but not contract mercenaries. The power to save lives and make the universe a better place should be used responsibly. She was only canceling the shady missions, the ones launched for government profit—for blood money. They were missions that had the CDF backing the wrong side or supporting genocide, leaving behind war-shattered communities. Such missions wouldn't bode well with the Union if they found out about them.

An EPA burst into the office without knocking. "Madam Chief, there's been a bomb threat from one of the protesters. We're taking you to the bunker."

"Let's go." Oviereya left with the agent.

• • •

On the heels of a successful rescue mission, Randy, Akane, Sam, and Jay went to a club for a nighttime celebration.

Randy, Sam, and Jay sat around a table with drinks. Akane was on the dance floor, gyrating to the pulsing techno beat. Her sexy party-girl outfit included a tube top, a miniskirt that barely reached her thighs, and sheer thigh-high stockings clipped to garter belts. She never missed a chance to make a fashion statement.

Sam said to Randy and Jay, "According to the report, all the women from the Commonwealth that trafficking ring abducted were colonists."

There was no shortage of disgust in Jay's expression. "Maybe that operation belonged to some Purist fat cat."

"It wouldn't be the first," Sam replied. "There's no way to tell for sure. Sometimes these trafficking rings target colonists because Eden's defenses are tougher to bypass, though not impossible if you've got the right criminal infrastructure."

Randy didn't seem to be listening. His mind was on Akane as his eyes followed her across the dance floor, through a sea of partying nightlifers.

She had painted her face white like a Geisha's, red winged eyeliner framed her eyes, and she had written Japanese characters on her arms in V-ink.

A woman danced near Akane, her appearance snagging Randy's attention. The excessive piercings decorating her face, the glimmer bracelets hanging from her wrists, and the colorful bead-lights festooned on her skirt made her stand out. To Randy, she looked like a dancing ornament. He didn't quite understand this neo-dress-up club culture that had emerged within the past couple of years. Outfits ranged from tame to utterly outrageous.

As his eyes stayed locked on Akane, who was lost in the rhythm, Randy found himself wondering about her. He wanted to know more about her past. She seemed to be growing on him by the day.

Sam took a swig of his drink and laughed at Randy's entranced look. "She's quite the dancer, huh?"

"Seems so." Randy watched her twerk. She was a quintessential hipster, always on top of contemporary fashion. And apparently, she followed all the latest club trends.

Jay said, "Don't let her size and easygoing demeanor fool you. She'll go full beast mode if you mess with her or her friends."

Akane moved under the florescent light show of colorful circles and blinking lasers that illuminated the dance floor. A young fair-skinned man posted up in a corner was checking her out. He was attractive, about five-eight, and in his early twenties. The aura of mystery Akane exuded—her face painted white and eyelids tipped with vivid red wings—held his gaze. It was now or never. He asked her to dance. She accepted.

"It's nice to see her happy," Sam said.

He closed his eyes, remembering the emotional toll Simone's death had taken on Akane. Depression and sadness had nearly swallowed her mind and soul, fitful night-long laments making it hard for her to sleep sometimes.

A heartfelt smile for Akane appeared on Sam's face. "It's taken her a long time to rebound from the funk she was in, a lot of fortitude to arrive at this place of happiness. It wasn't easy for her to get past the hurt, the hurt that crushed her." *A big thanks to the entire RISE organization too,* he thought.

Randy said, "Akane mentioned these Purists you guys keep talking about murdered someone close to her. Is that what you mean by 'getting past the hurt'?"

Sam nodded. "Yeah."

Reflexively, Randy winced in sympathy. *I know that kind of pain.* It was a pain that never truly stayed buried. He thought about the tragic accident that claimed his mother's life and made his father a widower. "Was she Linked with this person when they were killed?"

"No. Not to my knowledge."

Thank goodness for that. "So, what exactly happened?"

"That'd be her story to tell."

Randy changed the subject. "She mentioned some kind of shadow war going on between these Purist groups and an opposition force. Are you guys and Akane part of that force? And what exactly is it you do?"

"Answer to question one: yes. The answer to question two is . . .

complicated."

"I'm listening." Randy's brows furrowed. "And *no* dodging." His irritation with cryptic bullshit had reached its peak.

"We're basically a small, privately funded organization of social activists, Scott. That's all. Even with Oviereya as Chief, there need to be people on the ground fighting for colony and immigrant equality. She's not the supreme authority of the Commonwealth. Anti-reformist Parliament members do everything they can to obstruct her efforts."

"You activists got a name?"

"We're called RISE. We engage in political and social activism. We provide forums and safe spaces for marginalized immigrants to speak their minds, to express their pain. We help immigrants find employment and fight discrimination. We use media channels to debunk superstitions about colonists and push back against bigotry. We spread awareness about political candidates who actually intend to make a difference, and we hold them accountable. We also lobby for causes that support colonists. Purists basically do the exact opposite."

"Who started Purism?" Randy asked.

Sam replied, "The twisted mind behind Purism goes by the name Quinn. No one's ever seen his face. No one's even heard his real voice. He only appears in vids as a shadow, speaking through voice-anonymizing software.

"His identity remains a mystery. Quinn probably isn't even his real name. Sometime after Reza started calling for colony equality and preaching his liberation philosophy, Quinn emerged and started a counter-movement. He became a figure just as enigmatic and influential as Reza, except on the opposite side of the ideological battle.

"Quinn began releasing his vids over the dark net, urging

people to 'not let the republic be contaminated by Independent Movement sympathizers and reformists.' He called his devout followers Purists, claiming they were knights fighting to uphold AEGIS's design for humanity. He warned that dismantling that design would bring suffering to families. Fearful, paranoid sycophants bought into his manipulation.

"Quinn founded the first and largest Purist organization, the Brotherhood for Humanity's Salvation.

"Many extremists rallied around the Purist cause and formed their own groups. The White Knights of the Republic, the Black Wolves, and the Justice Society are just three of many. But they all revere the man who started it all, Quinn. Anything the Brotherhood or Quinn puts out, they follow.

"Through coercion, Purists have deterred immigrants in multiple communities from voting. Progressionist politicians, under duress from Purists, have rescinded their support for reform legislation after their families were threatened. And honestly, I can't blame them for backing out. When your loved ones' lives are on the line, what the hell do you do?

"RISE existed long before the Brotherhood for Humanity's Salvation, and I can tell you, we've never seen a more dangerous group of colony and immigrant haters than this. It was the Brotherhood who recently published the identities of Coalition fighters on the net, marking them for death. That was a directive from Quinn.

"And we believe Damien Sykes, a man who could become the Commonwealth's next Chief, is involved with the Brotherhood."

"These Purists sound like a dangerous bunch," Randy said. "But I have to say, I'm not too worried about ex-Coalition fighters. They all live on Satellite One, except maybe CDF defectors like me. What are the odds of Purists, or lone wolves under their influence, or any extremist, getting to Satellite One? Traveling to the planet isn't exactly like catching an air-cab to your local supermarket."

"Well, don't underestimate the ambitious mind of a determined fanatic. Some of these people can be pretty resourceful, and you never know what connections they have." Sam took a sip of his drink. "I know you're skeptical about RISE. We all were at first—me, Jay, and Akane—when we got approached. That's why I've given Akane permission to take you to our sanctuary tomorrow, so you can see what we're about firsthand."

Randy flicked up a brow. "Permitted?"

"I'm one of RISE's leaders," Sam revealed. "We're cautious about who we let into our house, just like you wouldn't let just anyone walk through your front door or be around your family. We want immigrants to feel safe, and stay safe, under our umbrella. Purists would love for some sellout to reveal our location. We can't afford weak links in the chain. You know what I mean?

"But you seem okay, Scott. You seem trustworthy. Go with Akane tomorrow. At the very least, you'll know of a place to escape to if you ever need to get away from all the crap you've been catching, just for doing the right thing. Just for liberating the colonies."

"I'm not promising you anything, like I'll join or something," Randy warned, dispelling any preconceived notions or clandestine motives.

Going head-to-head with Randy's assertiveness, Sam shot back, a subtle edge in his tone. "I didn't ask you for any commitments, now did I?"

Randy mulled over Sam's offer. A place to escape to sounded good to him, but he'd keep his guard up. "Okay, I'll go check you guys out tomorrow with Akane. It couldn't hurt."

"Good."

Randy got up from the table. "Gotta take a leak." He walked away, following the mens' restroom icon on the wall.

"Is this wise?" Jay asked Sam.

"It's just the first step, Jay. This doesn't mean he's got my endorsement yet. But Scott *is* good people."

"That doesn't mean he's *good* for us."

"It's not like we're taking him deep." Sam took another swallow of his drink. "Akane thinks he's a suitable candidate, and he trusts her. So let's see where things go." *Right now, he feels alone, isolated. People have turned against him. If there was ever a time Randal Scott would be open to joining RISE, it's now.*

As Randy left the club to head home—while Sam, Jay, and Akane kept partying—he heard someone shout, "Hey, you!"

He twisted around. Three men were stalking toward him. The one who'd shouted had arms covered in tattoos and wore his long dark hair in a ponytail.

"Yeah, what?" Randy said with a bite, defenses up.

"I know you. You're Randal Scott." The tattooed man sounded like he had an axe to grind with Randy.

"So what's it to you?"

"You Coalition filth killed my brother during the Battle of the Quad."

Randy extended an open palm, gesturing for the man and his friends to maintain their distance. "I'm not happy about Guardians being killed. The Coalition didn't want anyone to die. But it was a war, a truly senseless war, and in war, people die. There was never any fairy-tale scenario where equality was going to happen without bloodshed. I'm sorry for your loss, I really am."

"Your 'sorry' doesn't mean a damn thing!" The tattooed man

swung a fist at Randy, but he sidestepped the attack.

"I don't want to fight you. And fighting me won't bring your brother back." Sympathy was killing Randy on the inside.

The tattooed man stared daggers at him. "Maybe not, but beating the tar out of one of you Coalition punks will make me feel a hell of a lot better!"

The three men spread out around Randy like predators circling prey, cutting off his path to his flyer. With no choice but to fight, he squared off, sizing them up. In front, the tattooed man who had a score to settle. To the left, a guy with a spiky green hairdo. To the right, the tallest and most jacked of the three, a man practically built like a tank.

The guy with the green hair came at Randy, fist raised. Randy kicked him in the back of the knee, collapsing a joint and sending him falling face-first to the phyocrete.

The tattooed man lunged next. Randy ducked under his punch and shot upward, driving the heel of his palm into the underside of the man's jaw.

Three against one, Randy's attackers overpowered him.

The shredded guy caught Randy in a choke hold from behind.

Randy planted an elbow into the man's ribs. The brute recoiled, his square-jawed face contorting from the impact. But then he cinched the hold tighter, crushing Randy's throat. He was a freak of nature, insanely strong.

Shit, Randy thought.

The tattooed guy drove a fist of vengeance into Randy's gut, causing air to explode from his lungs.

A follow-up punch cracked Randy in the jaw.

Just then, Jay, Sam, and Akane exited the club, laughing and talking, until they spotted Randy being assaulted.

"Hey!" Sam shouted. "I'm Sergeant Sam Guthrie of the

Commonwealth Defense Force! Leave that Guardian alone, or I'm calling the authorities!"

The green-haired guy said, "Hey, no need to go down for this piece of trash. We roughed him up good, though."

The tattooed man clenched Randy's jaw. "You're lucky. I don't see how scum like you can look yourself in the mirror." He spat in Randy's face. "Come on, let's get out of here."

The muscleman who had Randy in a choke hold released him.

Randy dropped, knees and hands smacking the phyocrete.

His three attackers walked off.

Akane ran to Randy and crouched beside him. "Hey, are you okay?"

He groaned and forced himself upright, body aching, a thin rivulet of blood trickling from his mouth.

Akane rose with him.

"No need to worry. I'll be fine, Akane." Randy felt like he'd just been hit by a freight ship.

"Maybe you should get checked out by a doctor."

Randy spat blood onto the ground. "No. I said I'm fine."

Jay said, "Hey, if you need anything, champ, let us know."

Randy rubbed his throbbing jaw. "Yeah, thanks, but I'll be okay. I've taken worse." He squared his shoulders, kept his head high, and set off for his sports cruiser, one arm clutching his ribs. Even breathing proved to be a challenge, much less walking.

Akane followed. "Randy, I can come with you if—"

What he wanted right now was to be alone. "I don't need a babysitter, Akane. I'm a big boy. What part of 'I'll be okay' don't you get?"

Akane refused to back off. "You might be okay physically, but it just helps to have someone to talk to, you know?" Randy made a face, reiterating his wish to be alone. "Just 'cause I'm nineteen doesn't mean I'm inept at comforting somebody when they're down in the dumps," Akane stated, dismissing any idea that her age made her incapable of consoling him, if that was what he thought.

I never said you were. The frustration on Randy's face slackened. Akane was just trying to be a good friend, that's all. He pulled her into a side hug and rid his tone of irritation. "Thanks, but I'm good." There was no need to be mad at her. "I'll see you tomorrow for our trip."

He climbed into his sports cruiser, revved the engine, and lifted off for home.

The departing flyer kicked up a gust that sent Akane's wavy hair fluttering. She was disappointed that Randy had rejected her offer. She could relate. She understood what it was like to feel alone. To feel shunned. To feel like an outcast. Didn't he see that?

She'd bounced back from plenty of hard knocks in life, perhaps tougher tribulations than the ones he'd faced. He was born in a colony but raised on Eden, after all. He was essentially a Highborn, and it's not like he had a world of life experience on her. He was twenty-two years old, just three years older than her.

See you tomorrow, Randy. She cared about him, more than he knew. All she wanted was to be there for him.

Jay wrapped an arm around her shoulder. "I know you're worried about him. The guy'll be okay. He's Randal Scott. Let's head home and get some rest."

Akane, Jay, and Sam walked to the flyer they had carpooled in.

• • •

Randy had activated the autopilot.

He sat hunched forward, elbows on his thighs, fingers laced. His beating outside the club haunted him. *Is this my life for the foreseeable future?*

He thought about Paul's offhand insults, the whispered slights from Guardians who loathed him, and the delaying of his rank promotion, the screwing of his career. What was next? Another beatdown tomorrow? Was it only a matter of time before someone tried to put a bullet in his head? Would he have to spend every waking hour watching his back?

It felt like him against the world. And even someone as strong-willed as he could only take so much. The emotional toll of being branded a traitor by comrades and society was wearing him down.

He knew being a Coalition fighter would come with burdens after the war. But his expectation was that change would accompany them. One would think the animosity toward colonists would've subsided now that net filters were no longer suppressing the truth. Streamers, bloggers, and citizen reporters of Satellite One were free to expose their suffering. But Edenites seemed to cling to the same redundant responses:

"What did you expect? We're still recovering from two wars, a financial meltdown, and an ongoing debt crisis. You don't start a civil war and kill people. You wait until things get better, until the government can offer more aid. You colony folks need to calm down."

"The Commonwealth was trying to help you people, until you rebelled. Maybe the colonies would've seen more progress if you hadn't gone off the rails and started a war. *Duh.*"

"Come on, you're not starving. Sure, the colonies aren't like Eden, but there aren't enough resources right now to make both planets paradise. Hard decisions had to be made, and AEGIS made them. If you just hang in there, things will improve."

When would society finally recognize that colonists, as well as immigrants, deserved true prosperity?

Emotionally drained, Randy needed to confide in someone. Minutes ago, he thought solitude was what he needed, but he was wrong. He didn't need to be an island right now.

He tapped a few numbers on the control console, and the comms signal, routed through outer-space net orbiters, reached Satellite One.

The head and shoulders of Sariah Manard projected across the flyer's windshield. She sat in a modest bedroom, wearing a nightgown. "Whoa, Randy, what happened to you?" She could easily tell from his face he'd been beaten.

Randy managed a weak smile, the resonance of Sariah's lovely, sonorous voice taking the edge off. It felt good to see her.

At first, he'd been uncomfortable with his father getting involved with someone new, but, if anyone, Sariah was a good choice. She actually reminded him of his mom in some ways. Like Kathleen, she was a strong woman who had a kind soul.

"I got my ass kicked, that's what happened," he replied.

"No kidding. By who?"

Randy bypassed the details and got straight to the reason for his call. "I just need to speak to my father real quick. Is he around?"

Sariah nodded. "Arson, your son's on comms," she called, moving off-screen.

Arson's manly face, beard neatly trimmed, slid into view.

Shirtless, he sat down in a chair and rubbed his tired eyes. "Son, it's late, what——?" He paused as the injuries on Randy's face registered. "What happened? *Who did this?*"

"I got ganged up on, Dad, by some Coalition haters. But that's not even the worst of it. Feels like every Guardian's against me just because I sided with the Coalition."

Arson reached over and grabbed a shirt, pulling it over his hairy chest. "I figured things would be rough for you in the CDF," he said, buttoning up the shirt. "I can relate, to some extent." He was a veteran of war and of society's prejudice. "When I enlisted, it seemed every one of my comrades was against me because I was an immigrant, because only those chosen by AEGIS to inhabit Eden belonged in the 'prestigious' CDF. They kept snubbing me, talking trash behind my back. But I was able to win them over, earn their respect and gain acceptance.

"I ignored disparaging insults, stayed the course, and proved my critics wrong. I became someone Guardians admired, original Edenite and immigrant alike. But that was a different time. Believe it or not, a less hostile time. Once the RUC formed and the Three-Week War started, the discrimination toward immigrants spiked. It went from a one to a five. Hell, I imagine it's at a ten nowadays."

Randy said, "I didn't think everything would be all hunky-dory after the Battle of the Quad, but—"

"I know," Arson cut in, years of hard-earned wisdom at play. "You thought Eden's people would finally understand why young Guardians like you defected, why they joined the Coalition, now that the colonies' full calamity has been exposed. You thought things would start to get better. But they haven't. Not yet. And truth is, they might get worse before they do.

"Edenites are furious that Guardians died at the Coalition's hands. They don't see the whole picture. It's not like we had a choice. The Coalition had an ethos. It had *morals*. We ran first, fought last, and only killed if our backs were against the wall. And colonists didn't cause the New Humanity's civil war. The

141

Commonwealth Government's failure to address their suffering was the impetus.

"The natural response to inequality is to take a stand against it, even if that means taking up arms. It's been that way since Earth Era, since time immemorial."

Arson gave a grim look and continued. "The Coalition won, but the war isn't over. A civil war is still being waged, a war of hearts and minds, of ideologies. You'd think by now people would understand the circumstances that pushed colonies One, Four, and Six to rebel."

"So what the heck do we do?" Randy asked.

"I wish I knew. Edenites aren't going to unlearn years of an indoctrinated supremacist mindset in just two or three months. I don't have an answer, Son.

"By the way, how are you holding up? Still having nightmares?"

"Yeah," Randy sighed. "The lives I took, of both Coalition rebels and Guardians, still weigh on me. Trauma's a beast."

"You know, there are support groups you can go to. I've started one here in my zone for former Coalition fighters. You could—"

"I'll think about it, Dad."

"Okay, you're a grown man, Randy. I won't tell you what to do. I just wanted to put that out there. Is there anything you need from me? Is there *anything* I can do?"

"I'll be fine, Dad, and I appreciate the talk."

"Are you sure?"

"Positive."

"Well, if you ever do need anything, don't hesitate to reach out. I'm always here to talk, no matter the time."

"Thanks, Dad. By the way, have you ever heard of an immigrant activist group called RISE?"

"Doesn't ring a bell. During the civil war, many antigovernment resistance groups formed, some ultraextreme, like the People's Revolutionary Party of Colony Four. Most of them have dissolved. Maybe RISE is one of the few still in operation. Do you think they're dangerous or something?"

"I don't know. I want to learn more about them. Secret organizations usually have secrets to hide, and if RISE has any, I'd like to know what they are."

"Tell you what, I'll check with some of my old Coalition buddies and see what turns up."

"I appreciate that."

"Okay, I'll keep you updated."

"Awesome. Oh, Lieutenant Carl Breckenridge says hello."

A memory made Arson brighten. "Tell him I said hello back."

"Will do. Good night, Dad."

"Same."

The video transmission ended.

The air lane Randy was traveling brought him to the Quad, reawakening the horror once again: explosions cratering the Parliament Building's yard, a storm of energy blasts and bullets hitting Coalition rebels and Guardians.

Randy shook his head, trying to fight away the uncomfortable memories.

Akane had been right. Talking to his dad had helped, but it would help even more to have someone *physically* with him tonight. He needed someone to drink with, confide in, laugh with. He used to depend on Stacie to realign his emotional compass when it was off-kilter. She knew how to pry him out of his reticence. She was someone he could lean on, talk about his feelings to without judgment, and cuddle with at night during disconcerting moments like this.

He needed companionship right now. There was no point in

pretending otherwise. But who could he turn to?

He thought about it and figured, Why not? He set a new course, and the flyer shifted air lanes.

• • •

After five knocks, Jenny Pines opened the door of her apartment. She wore a slinky red nightie that was so short it revealed a smidgen of her backside. "Randy! You look a mess!"

Randy stood with his hands in his pockets. As much as he tried to front, he couldn't hide how low he felt. "It's just a few bruises. They'll heal by morning."

"Well, even looking like a train wreck, you're still a handsome bloke, Randal Scott."

That actually drew a laugh from him, his first in a while. And it felt good. He couldn't remember the last time he had laughed. "Thanks. You said you were going to visit family up north during our off-duty weeks. I took a gamble and hoped you hadn't left yet. I just . . . need some company right now. You mind if I—?"

"Nah, not at all," Jenny said coolly. "What're teammates for? Make yerself at home, luv. I'll pour us some drinks."

"Thanks, Sergeant Pines, I'd like that."

"Hey, none of that 'sergeant' stuff. Call me Jenny, or Jen, whichever you prefer."

"Thanks, Jen."

"Do you like whiskey?"

"To tell you the truth, anything sounds good right about now." Randy stepped inside.

Randy and Jenny quickly dispensed with the formalities, shedding all their clothes in the bedroom.

Jenny lay on her back as Randy leaned over her, admiring her smooth pale skin and full, round breasts.

His lips brushed her neck, sucked on her standing nipples, and continued their journey downward, dropping delicate kisses along her naked body.

Dying to satiate his urges, Randy opened her legs wide and rubbed the length of his shaft against her clit, warming her up. Heat seared her cheeks, and her mind spun with anticipation.

Randy pushed a full thrust into the crease between her lovely, thick thighs, stuffing every inch of his cock into her.

She gasped as she felt him stretching her, filling her completely.

Randy's head snapped back as he savored the feeling of her walls sheathing him.

Struck by euphoria, Jenny tensed up and shut her eyes, gripping the bedsheets. The sibilant sound rushing from her lips morphed into a breathy moan.

Randy began moving at a leisurely pace, taking his time. Then, in a burst of adrenaline, he sped up, repeatedly slamming his loins against hers.

His steely erection speared her again, again, and again—tirelessly, ferociously. Each palliative thrust brought him some temporary relief from his frustrations. Sex was the best remedy he could ask for tonight.

Taking a break, they lay next to each other.

Randy stared out the window to his right, moonlight casting its glow on him and the beautiful woman beside him.

Jenny turned to him, nuzzling his neck. "What are you thinking about, Scott?"

Randy's personal crisis bedeviled his mind. "This unending cycle of animosity. Am I going to be fending off haters for the rest of my life?"

Jenny snuggled in closer, her body warm against his side.

Randy's heart pounded.

Jenny swept a hand through his hair. "Listen to me, Scott." Her whisper-soft voice sent a tingle prickling over Randy's flesh. "This animosity won't last forever. *Nothing* does. I don't know when, I don't know how, but humanity *will* pull it together. And don't let yer detractors get to you. Don't let 'em break you down.

"You're Arson Scott's son. You're the guy who took out Arman Reza and ended his menace, with your pop's help, of course. You're the reason Chief Amaechi, the first colony-born Chief, is leading the Commonwealth. And yer legacy ain't done being written yet.

"And don't think all Guardians hate you. I was born n' bred right here on Eden. I'm Highborn."

Randy laid a thank-you kiss on her cheek. "Thanks, Jen. I needed to hear that." He sat up. "I should probably get going. I have to meet Akane tomorrow to—"

Jenny pulled him back down onto the bed. "You're not going anywhere, Specialist. That was just a warm-up. I ain't done fuckin' you." This dishy young man had shown up at her doorstep, later stripping naked in her bedroom and putting his gym-goer's bod on full display. He had enticed her with his faultless physique and impressive dangling man-parts. He wasn't about to leave so easily.

"I just assumed—"

Before Randy could finish, Jenny shifted on top of him, straddling his gorgeous sculpted torso. She pressed her hands flat against his firm chest. "You're staying the whole night, and that's not a request; that's an order, Specialist."

Randy's body thrummed with desire.

His hands traced the small of Jenny's back before sliding down to cup the globes of her ass. He squeezed them ravenously, his fingers sinking into her creamy porcelain flesh.

Jenny rose slightly, escaping his grasp, and then descended onto his upstanding erection. She jerked her hips back and forth with wild abandon, gripping the headboard for leverage.

The faster she moved, the more the bed shook and creaked. "If I'm too much for you, just say 'Mayday.'" She locked her thighs around his hips and kept fucking herself on him. Her walls clenched his girth, and her clit rubbed against his pubic bone with every downward grind. Sliding up and down his cock, she impaled herself repeatedly. He was as hard and straight as a rod of Kryoplaste—much to her satisfaction.

Randy clung to her waist and rammed himself into her, matching her pace. As he bucked his hips, his eyes stayed fixed on her luscious breasts jiggling above him.

For a moment, his mind wandered to tomorrow's meeting with Akane. What was in store for him at RISE's base? Suddenly, Jenny tightened her walls around his cock, and all thoughts of tomorrow vanished in a haze of lust. Right now, his sole focus was on one thing: pleasure. Which was exactly what he needed tonight.

INTERLUDE THREE

Planet Eden

Sam, Jay, and Akane were in a ground car, cruising down a scenic roadway.

From the back seat, a restless Akane said, "Are we almost there yet?"

"Almost," Sam replied from behind the wheel. Jay sat in the passenger seat beside him.

Through her earbuds, Akane listened to one of her favorite jams—a catchy neo-flow techno-pop tune—as she watched trees, green plains, mountain ranges, and colorful flowers go by. She wore a pink top, jean shorts that had suspenders, and white sneakers. *There's nothing out here . . . but I guess that's the point.*

The car turned onto a narrow access road and pulled up to a gate. Sam held out a remote control, pressed a button, and the gate slid open, granting the car entry to the road beyond.

RISE HQ sat in a remote clearing, surrounded by forest. Sam slowed the car to a stop in the outdoor parking lot of the expansive two-story building. Several other vehicles were parked there too.

Akane examined the building. *This is a pretty big place.*

Sam turned off the car's engine. "Welcome to RISE HQ."

Everyone got out of the car.

Akane shut off her music and tucked her earbuds into her pocket.

The trio entered the building's ground floor. Inside, there were cubicles, communal rec areas, and shared workspaces. The place looked makeshift but had a homey feel to it.

People milled about, chatting and laughing.

Akane swept her gaze across the numerous computer stations in the room. "What's all this?"

"Our operations center," Sam replied. "It's come a long way since we first got it off the ground."

Machines hummed, their algorithms scanning the net for electronic communications from Purists and other extremists who posed threats to the immigrant community.

"What exactly does it do?" Akane asked.

Sam explained, "It searches the net for traffic from anti-immigrant extremist groups, especially Purists, allowing us to thwart their schemes. It also helps us identify government officials who want to undermine equality. Sometimes we're even able to seize financial assets from wealthy businessmen who support immigrant oppression, redirecting them to benefit RISE or the Coalition.

"We've stopped plots by Purist groups to bomb immigrant homes or gun immigrants down in cold blood. These are coordinated attacks happening right under the authorities' noses, because protecting immigrants isn't their priority, especially now that there's a civil war raging on our homeworld. Someone has to keep our people safe. That someone is us, RISE."

"Cool." Akane was A-okay with that.

Sam addressed the room. "Hey, everyone, this is Akane! She'll be joining us!"

Handshakes and hugs bombarded Akane.

"Welcome!" exclaimed a young woman.

"Wassup?" said an umber-skinned man in a gray hoodie, seated at a nearby workstation. "Name's Zeke," he added.

"Nice to meet you," Akane said.

The generous greetings continued, hands waving, voices offering hellos.

Akane felt good—felt wanted, felt like she belonged.

Sam made a hand gesture. "Akane, let me show you around."

Akane finished her conversation with a woman and followed Sam. He brought her to the legal aid office, the community hub where immigrants came to socialize, and the upstairs rooms that provided homeless immigrants shelter until RISE could help them get on their feet. Then he took her outside.

Akane saw men and women engaged in marksmanship drills, laser lights from practice guns shooting holographic targets. Several other RISE members sparred in hand-to-hand combat exercises.

A feeling of unease gathered in Akane's chest as she wondered what was going on out here. "So, what's this, a . . . paramilitary or something?"

"It's protection. We're at war, and sometimes we have to defend ourselves." Sam patted Akane's back. "Don't worry, we're not some insane militia trying to take over Eden."

Now that Akane's concerns had been put to rest, the unease in her chest went away. "Well, that's a relief."

"Now, I'm not going to front," Sam said. "Sometimes we have to put people down, because the law can't, or won't. But they're always bad people. *Like Simone's killer.* Like the Purists I mentioned, the ones who want to bomb innocent immigrants' homes. Do you have a problem with that, Akane?"

Akane's thoughts spiraled back to the miserable night she saw Simone's lifeless body. A sense of duty stiffened her spine.

Not only did she feel guiltless about killing bigots who subjugated her people like chattel, she felt it was her duty to remove such people from society, by death if necessary. Yeah, she preferred death for them, actually. To hell with prison. "Nah, I don't have a problem with that. If you guys are putting down savages like Simone's killer, it's all fine n' dandy with me. It's no different from taking out bad guys as Guardians of the ETF, right?"

Sam nodded. "Glad to hear it. We need more people with military experience. We were thinking you could help train recruits, maybe start with basic self-defense for newcomers."

"Sounds superb. I wanna help however I can. I wanna fight for equality, like Simone did. I'm all in." *This is it, Skylar—my ikigai.* With a drive born from a need to help others, Akane had worked the black markets of her home colony, and now she was here, joining RISE. She should've realized it sooner: Her ikigai was to protect, to liberate, to fight for equality. A humdrum life wasn't for her, not with her restless, rebellious spirit.

"There's one more thing I want to show you," Sam said.

He led her down into an underground phyocrete bunker.

The overhead lights clicked on.

Seven Shells stood in docking pods: six M-X02s—four male models, two female—and a lone M-X01.

Akane's eyes lit up. "Whoa, Shells?" she exclaimed. "How the fuck did RISE get ahold of CDF property?"

"We fudged some inventory numbers and altered a few shipping logs. Seven was all we could get. Any more would've

151

raised alarms.

"We've overridden credentialed authentication, so anyone can access these Shells. We also disabled signature tracing to prevent any Nerve Center from tracking them. That means no C-comms, audio transmit/receive functionality, or Nerve Center software updates. However, the weapons package is fully installed and operational."

To address any moral qualms Akane might have, he added, "Now, you might think that's stealing, but believe me, the Defense Department has more than enough funding to manufacture war machines. They can replace seven Shells. We just need to be ready in case Purists or any other anti-immigrant group decides to come for us. These Shells are strictly for protection."

Akane released a dry chuckle. "Well, stealing a little from our oppressive government is no biggie to me. I've been bucking their system since I was sixteen, dealing in the black markets of my home colony."

"You're truly RISE material, Akane. Simone would be proud. Come on, let's head inside and grab some chow. There's more I want to talk to you about."

CHAPTER FOUR

Cornerstone Park: Elysian fields of colorful flowers, well-manicured grass, and turquoise trees.

Stacie Spencer stood atop a footbridge spanning a lake, her wide-brimmed sun hat shielding her from the sun's rays. The strappy yellow dress she wore flowed freely around the arcs of her hips, its pleated hem riding high on her thighs, drawing attention to her attractive legs. The outfit was custom-forged by her personal stylist. She hadn't dressed up *just* for Damien, though. Stacie often wore her sexuality on her sleeve, and she made no apologies for it.

"Has your prince arrived yet?" Jason asked over her wristcom.

"No, but he'll show. Even on short notice, he wouldn't pass up seeing me. He's probably just running a little late."

General Conlan, initially reluctant, had ultimately approved Stacie's plan to assist Defense Force Intelligence as an undercover informant. He also signed off on her request to let her team run point on the operation. They'd gather intel and evidence, reporting directly to him.

Having a chaser go undercover had its perks. If the plan backfired and Stacie was caught meddling in Damien's affairs, the

CDF could plausibly deny any involvement, not that framing a chaser appealed to Conlan; Stacie was simply DFI's "in." And if at any point he thought she was in real jeopardy, he'd pull the plug on the operation.

Stacie watched a flashy limo roll into the distant parking lot. *Yep, that's him,* she thought. She told Jason, "He's here. Maintain radio silence until you hear from me."

"Okay, be careful, and if you need anything, just comm me."

"I'll be fine, Jason."

She adjusted her dress, making sure the hidden wireless microphone was secure.

From the back of the limo, Damien appraised Stacie's appearance. Drop-dead gorgeous, she was definitely something to gawk at. *She must have to beat them off with a stick. It's a wonder she's gone unclaimed for this long.* He said to his driver, Jasmine, with zest, "There she is. More stunning than ever."

Jasmine replied, "Don't you find it odd that she's entertaining face time with you after ignoring you for years?"

"Attention addicts like her run at the beck and call of the limelight. They crave the alpha male, he who elevates their status. That would be *me*, the man who's going to win next year's election. Power lures women like honey attracts bees."

"Bees, sir?"

"Brush up on your Earth Era Insecta," Damien said in a berating manner, as if Jasmine were a complete dullard. That was his usual modus operandi, making people feel small, weak, or stupid whenever he got the chance.

"Will do, sir," Jasmine said obediently. All she cared about was her pay.

Damien straightened his tie.

Jasmine asked, "What is it you see in Ms. Spencer, besides her physical attributes?"

"The bylaws and prehistoric traditions of the Eight, which our parents created, expect us, their children, to conform and uphold the institution's sanctity. Stacie Spencer is like me, restless and uncontrollable. She has a contumacious spirit.

"It was that spirit that led to our surreptitious romance, one unapproved by our organization's bylaws. That same spirit drove her to do something no other child of the Eight has done, enlist in the Defense Force. And my spirit has called me to defy the bylaws and throw my hat in for the Chief Executiveship. I am a lion, and she is a lioness. In Stacie Spencer, I see my counterpart. We're cut from the same cloth.

"There is no shortage of contenders for my attention. Not at all. But they're just pets—ephemera. Good for bed, but not much else. The flavor of the week, you might say. They don't intrigue me like Stacie Spencer does, and I seek a queen. Dare I tarnish my family name by letting the inadequate take a permanent seat at my side, especially if they're to be the First Lady of the Commonwealth. That answer your question, Jazzy?"

"It does, sir. I imagine a rebellious woman like Stacie Spencer might be a tad difficult to deal with."

"And that is the challenge, the thrill of the pursuit," Damien said, invigoration inundating every word. "It takes an apex predator like me to tame an exotic creature."

He got out of the limo and shut the door. Checking his reflection in the window, he straightened his white blazer and smoothed back his slick hair with a practiced sweep of his hand. Satisfied, he made his way toward the bridge, where his princess awaited.

Stacie watched him saunter down the cobblestone walkway. He had an arrogant stride and a charming but smarmy expression on his face. And he radiated an aura of untouchability. He acted like he owned the universe. A high IQ, sharp business acumen, natural charisma, and looks that had helped him finesse the pants off countless women ensured his confidence was always sky-high.

Triumph consumed his features as he closed the distance between him and his erstwhile lover. In his mind, he'd finally won her back. She'd come to her senses, realized he was innocent of Cassie's accusations. The anger had finally blown over. She was no longer the silly girl who'd once walked out of his life. Victory.

Nerves kicked in for Stacie. *Here we go.*

Damien's hungry gaze roved over her. A woman like Stacie was his Achilles' heel—flawless skin, sculpted legs, a slim waistline, and curves to boot.

Stacie waved dramatically. "Damien!" she said in a bubbly, high-pitched tone, her delivery just a tad over the top. She was playacting like her former self, which put knots in her stomach.

Damien joined her on the bridge. "Stacie, long time, no see." He edged closer.

Stacie kept hamming it up, pretending to be ecstatic about seeing him. "Indeed! I've been a busy girl."

"So I hear—protecting the Commonwealth, fighting in the Battle of the Quad against Coalition invaders." He leaned in, took Stacie's hand, and kissed it. Then he straightened his six-foot-two frame. "It's good to see you, my dear. I've missed you."

"I've missed you as well, Damien." Stacie was cringing inside.

"Oh, pardon my manners." Damien caressed her jaw, then wound threads of her hair between his fingers. "I was so captivated by your succulent beauty that I forgot to ask, How have you been since those Coalition *bastards* murdered our parents?"

Stacie pretended a sigh. "It's . . . been a challenge."

"Yes, of course." Damien thought about his father. "It has been a challenge for me as well, losing the man who taught me everything I know, the man who made me strong. The news of Amaechi letting the Coalition off the hook enraged me, just like it enraged the other children of the Eight. Someone needs to set things right, and that person will be me. And if you ever need a shoulder to lean on, I'm here for you."

"Thank you, Damien. I appreciate that." *I don't need anything from you, you deranged sociopath.*

Damien braced his forearms against the bridge's balustrade. "Crazy, isn't it? Our parents' empires now belonging to us. We knew we'd eventually take the reins, but not this soon, and not like this."

"No, definitely not like this." Stacie sounded genuine, thinking of her parents.

"No, but we mustn't let what they built for us—" Damien's wristcom chirped. "Excuse me for a moment." He walked a few feet away and spoke into his wristcom.

Stacie couldn't hear the man on the other end.

"You mean now?" Damien shouted furiously, drawing the eyes of passersby.

There it was, Stacie thought. That uncontrollable anger, the Damien that could emerge at the flip of a switch.

A voice babbled urgently from the other end of Damien's wristcom.

"Alright, fine!" Damien snapped. He headed back over to Stacie, mumbling.

"Bad news?" Stacie asked.

"My deepest apologies. I have matters that require hands-on attention."

"No worries." Stacie manufactured a smile. "Shall we resume tonight?" she asked eagerly, giving the impression that she was yearning for more quality time.

Damien returned the smile. "You read my mind. I'm actually hosting a fundraiser at one of my estates tonight. You know the deal: mix and mingle, solidify support, rub elbows." His wanton hands slid around Stacie's waist and dragged her closer. "It would be an absolute pleasure if you accompanied me."

His palms sank into the fabric of her dress, indulging in the feel of her comely figure, which had been refined by CDF training and power workouts since he'd last slept with her. As he recalled, she used to love it when he touched her, when he took her into his arms.

"Of course. It sounds like fun." Skin crawling, Stacie wanted to kick Damien in the teeth.

He kissed her jaw. "I'll have a driver swing by your place to escort you."

"Until then." *Now take your hands off me, you filthy creep.*

Damien released Stacie and made his way back to the limo.

Once he was out of view, Stacie exhaled. She felt like she was going to barf. *What the hell was wrong with me, getting involved with someone like him?* Old, naive Stacie had definitely left the building. Her taste in men had evolved. It was different back then, before she matured—before Randal Scott, a caliber of man she hadn't experienced prior to meeting him.

Stacie said into her wristcom, "The meeting got cut short."

"What happened?" From the sound of his noisy surroundings, Jason was around a bunch of people.

"He had some kind of business emergency to tend to. Running a financial empire, unexpected stuff happens all the time, believe me. But he invited me to some shindig tonight. I'm going. I need to butter him up more, then see if I can get a confession out of him, to connect him to the trafficking and show all the people he's no different from his parents." *And to finally get justice for Cassie.*

"Be careful."

"Always. I'll keep you posted."

• • •

Akane was at the wheel of her spiffy yellow convertible, with Randy sitting beside her. They were headed to RISE HQ.

"Curious," Randy began, wind ruffling his short, wavy hair, "what are the qualifications for joining RISE, besides being an immigrant?"

"Everyone's screened and vetted before they're allowed to become a member," Akane answered, not giving a direct answer.

"Screened and vetted how?"

"Dude, you ask *too* many questions. That's not even something you need to be concerned about right now."

More evasiveness, Randy thought.

Akane pulled into RISE HQ's parking lot. "We're here." She was excited for Randy. "C'mon."

They got out, and Akane led the way forward.

Birds perched in treetops chirped.

"How many members does RISE have?" Randy asked.

"*Mmm,* 'bout seventy-three of us live here; others live off-base, and we've got an extensive network of supporters."

They went into the building.

A man with thick facial hair in his early forties looked at Akane like he'd just seen a ghost. He was practically brawn stacked on brawn and wore a blue denim vest, red shirt, and jeans. "Well, well, if it isn't Akane Sugimori! Haven't seen you in a while! What's the deal? You don't love us no more?"

Akane shrugged. "Yeah, well, y'know, apprehending evildoers throughout the cosmos doesn't always leave your favorite girl here with a lotta time to make house visits."

The man approached her and gave her a hearty pat on the back. "Yeah, I know. I'm just messin' with you. Good to see you. Damn good."

"Ditto."

Zeke waved. "Akane, wassup?"

"Nothing beyond the usual," she replied.

"It seems like you're quite popular here," Randy commented.

Akane knew there was nothing preferential about her treatment. "Nah, we're just all family."

Randy observed his surroundings. Busy men and women sat at workstations, fingers dancing across keyboards. Others stood in pairs, holding touchscreen tablets and discussing subjects of importance. "There's a lot of activity going on." Randy's mind kicked into analytical mode.

"Yeah, of course. Election day's near. We're social activists."

All of this equipment gave Randy the impression that more than just election-day business was happening in this room.

A blur of multiple voices said, " . . . Canvassers deployed . . . Donations up by ten percent . . . New ads posted . . . Caught some Purist chatter on the dark net . . ."

A man in his mid-twenties with blue hair, buzzed short on one side and long on the other, walked up to Akane and her guest. "Who do we have here, a newcomer?" It didn't take long for him to recognize who the "newcomer" was. "Oh, shit, you're Randal Scott!" He craned his head sideways. "Everyone, it's Randal frickin' Scott, Arson's son!"

RISE members greeted Randy.

A bum-rush of handshakes wore out his arm.

Akane recalled her first time coming to RISE HQ, a heartwarming experience. Watching Randy receive the same reception made her happy inside.

A mocha-skinned woman in a tawny button-down shirt and jeans—black-and-brown hair arranged in a braided faux-hawk—hurried down a set of metal stairs to the ground floor. "Hey, close your mouths!" she commanded. Everyone fell quiet. The woman now owned the room. "Quinn's broadcasting on the dark net! Bring up the audio feed now!"

Randy assumed she held a leadership role.

A short-haired brunette woman struck several keys on her computer console.

The loudspeakers blasted Quinn's altered, artificial-sounding voice. "To all my Purist brothers and sisters, the next special election is two days away. During the last one, Ron Burchardt, a reformist, won, but only because of interference from RISE. For the purity of the republic, we cannot afford any more electoral losses in this war. Every immigrant that votes could tip the scale.

"Next election day, ensure as many as possible do not cast a ballot."

The transmission ended.

Anger flooded Akane's veins. *Damn, first Quinn's directive to hunt down ex–Coalition fighters and now a directive to stop immigrants from voting.* Fire burned beneath her skin.

The woman with the faux-hawk anchored her hands on her hips, her rigid stance exuding authority. "You heard that, everyone. The Brotherhood is serious. We're now on heightened alert for predominantly immigrant communities. Expect spikes in violence. We have to ensure immigrants exercise their right to vote without incident. I know we can't cover all communities, but we can cover some. I'll need volunteers for voting-station guards, patrolmen, and vehicular escorts."

Akane and several others raised their hands courageously.

"Good," the woman said. "Khalid, Umer, Wes, make sure all

volunteers get an assignment."

The three men responded in unison: "Yes, ma'am."

Everyone returned to business as usual.

The woman strode up to Randy and Akane. "Akane, it's nice to see you around. ETF treating you well?"

"Can't complain," she replied.

"Good. I really appreciate what you, Sam, and Jay do. You guys help hold it down in the CDF for us immigrants, calling out mistreatment, guiding new immigrant Guardians when you can." The woman turned to Randy. "Randal Scott, it's great to meet you. I was told you'd be here today." She clasped his hand. Her grip was strong and confident, just like her voice and even the gaze in her chestnut eyes. "Janice LaCroix, head of RISE operations."

By Randy's estimation, she was in her early thirties. He shook her hand and then glanced around. "So this equipment lets you guys monitor the net for Purist traffic, I assume."

"It does, and it serves other functions."

Sam approached. "I'm glad you made it, Scott. I wasn't sure if you'd change your mind and decide not to come."

"Well, I'm here."

Jay walked up next. "Randy, good to see you, champ."

Being so close to Jay's family, Janice spoke to Jay in a way that wasn't just friendly but familial. She might as well be a blood relative. "Jamie, it's been a while. How's the wife and child?"

"Nicole and Zola are doing well," he replied. "And Zola's loving fifth grade."

"Good to hear that. Tell them both I said hello."

Randy felt a genuine sense of togetherness here. These people truly cared about each other. They acted like kin.

"Most of us are heading to the mess hall," Sam said. "Randy, Jay, Akane, why don't we go too?"

Randy's stomach rumbled. He could use a bite. "Sounds good."

"It's this way," Akane said cheerfully. "Just follow me." Randy trailed behind her.

Well, she's certainly happy he's here, Sam thought. *Let's see if he disappoints or eventually joins.*

Randy and Akane crossed a hallway.

Janice leaned into Sam's ear and whispered, "In forty-five minutes, Code Red meeting."

Sam's eyes widened. Code Red meant something major was about to go down. "Does this have anything to do with the Coalition fighters' identities being publicized online or Quinn's announcement just now?"

Janice shook her head. No, this meeting was about something else. Something big. "You'll find out in forty-five minutes. Go eat." She offered no further details and walked away.

The discontented expression on Sam's face made it obvious that he didn't like being kept in the dark.

Randy and Akane sat at a far-off dining nook in the mess hall.

"So, do you still see that apparition of your mom?" Akane asked.

Randy sipped his tangy citrine-colored drink. "No, not since I made amends with Dad."

"I don't know. It seems kinda nice keeping a piece of a loved one's essence with you after they're gone."

"That's kind of what Linking does anyway, without the ghosts," Randy said, thinking of Stacie.

"Well, you've got a point there." Akane's own experiences with Simone were forever diarized within her cerebral implant.

Randy hesitated. Then, haltingly, he asked, "So, who was the

163

person special to you who was killed?" He hoped he wasn't sticking his nose where it didn't belong.

"She was a Guardian—a sergeant—in Vanguard Alpha, and a member of RISE too. Her name was Simone Conyers. She saved my life from a Purist prig, a cop actually, who was gonna shoot me just because I'm an immigrant. After that, she took me in, let me stay with her.

"Her dream of diversifying CDF leadership inspired me to enlist. I loved her. She was a true-blue friend. And she's no longer alive because a gutless Purist coward murdered her, knifing her in the back. We believe it was Paul Shaffer. He might even be a member of the Brotherhood."

"Shaffer? Do you have proof he killed Simone?"

Akane's countenance changed to something darker, something murderous. "Enough to convince *me*." She didn't have the slightest doubt. But it wasn't a hundred percent confirmed that Simone's killer was Paul, which was why Sam wouldn't let Akane kill him, *yet*. However, she believed Paul was guilty. "We think he and his posse, Dan and Mark, are making careers as Guardians while advancing Purist causes as civilians."

A man urgently said, "Hey, yo, turn that up!"

The crawl at the bottom of a live newscast on a wall screen read: BREAKING NEWS: ACTIVE SHOOTER GUNS DOWN THREE EX-COALITION FIGHTERS INSIDE COLONY ONE.

Behind the serving counter, a chef grabbed a remote and increased the volume.

Onscreen were a male and female anchor, both dressed in professional attire.

The man said, "Our own Gisele Lockhart was in Colony One covering the Colony Restoration Initiative's progress when murder and mayhem erupted in Zone 12 of Sector 05, just ten minutes ago."

"Gisele, take it from here," said the female anchor.

Gisele's live feed streamed grainy at first, net orbiters across the Commonwealth adjusting to stabilize resolution. White noise faded. Distortion lessened. Behind Gisele, three dead men lay riddled with bullets as colony authorities, reinstated following the end of martial law, sectioned off the grisly crime scene with yellow caution tape.

A stunned crowd had gathered around the massacre.

Gisele said, "Just moments ago, my camera crew and I heard gunfire coming from this area." Her two-person crew operated twin hovercams using remotes. "According to eyewitnesses, a van pulled up, and a man dressed in black stepped out and opened fire on the crowd using a high-powered automatic weapon.

"Although other civilians were injured, it appears the gunman specifically targeted the three men who are now deceased." First responders zipped the bodies into black bags. "We've been told the victims were former Coalition fighters.

"We have a witness to this brutal massacre here with me now." The hovercams shifted to a teen with a ruddy complexion. She had pink pigtail braids and wore a white shirt, hoodie, and slim-fit jeans. "Tiffany, can you tell us exactly what you saw?"

"It . . . it was just like you said," the sixteen-year-old stated. "This van came barreling through really, really fast. It nearly ran everyone over." She made frantic gestures, swinging her arms. "Then this guy dressed in black jumped out and started shooting at the three guys. The shooter yelled something . . . something like 'For the purity of the republic,' I think."

Akane punched her right palm. "It's just as we feared. Purists, or lone-wolf extremists influenced by their preposterous ideology, have finally gotten to Satellite One. They're acting on the Brotherhood's . . . on Quinn's directive to get payback for Operation Hammer Fall. You can bet there'll be copycats, like it's open season on ex-Coalition fighters. *Motherfuckers.*"

"Terrible," a man in the serving line said solemnly.

Concern clouded Randy's eyes. His father was arguably the most notable of all former Coalition fighters. That put a bull's-eye on his back. Having been attacked outside the club, Randy had already gotten a taste of the violence against ex-Coalition fighters. Would he or his father be the next target for some group of gun-toting maniacs?

Inside Akane, a storm of hate, revulsion, and rage brewed. She wished she could vent her spleen by tearing the balls off those fucking murderers. "No doubt, come election day, crazies are gonna act on Quinn's other directive too: stopping the immigrant vote. Like Janice said, we can expect an uptick in violence in immigrant communities."

A muscle tensing in his jaw, Sam approached Randy and Akane's table as the newscast continued. A young man followed close behind. "Randy, I'm sorry, but your visit's going to have to be cut short," Sam said. Forty-five minutes had passed. It was time for Janice's meeting.

"Why? What's up?" Akane asked. Sam leaned over and whispered "Code Red" into her ear. Her brows perked. "Oh, shit," she blurted, bolting to her feet.

What's with all the secret whispering? Randy wondered.

Sam jerked a thumb over his shoulder at the young man behind him. "Randy, Jeshua here is going to take you back home. Sorry."

Randy wasn't going to budge so easily. "Care to fill me in?"

"Some of us have an emergency meeting, and the operational tempo around here is about to kick into high gear."

"Are Purists about to pull something you guys know about?" Randy asked, trying to sleuth out the truth.

"I'm afraid I can't tell you what's going on. But no visitors are allowed right now."

Randy stood and shot Sam a hard-eyed glare, a reminder that he wasn't sold on RISE just yet.

Randy and Jeshua set off for the exit.

Sam rounded up eleven other RISE members from the mess hall. They knew what this was about. Janice had summoned them. Leaving their interrupted meals behind, they rose and left with Sam.

In the strategy room, twenty-seven men and women joined Sam, Akane, and Jay. These were RISE's solutioners, an ad hoc kill team.

Janice LaCroix, head of operations, was the founding council's organizational overseer. By day, she worked as an assistant office manager at a golem manufacturing company.

She said, "First of all, I want to thank every one of you for volunteering to be part of RISE's Strike Team. Solutioners aren't deployed often. Killing is messy, and we don't want to get on the radar of DFI or the authorities. We're not trying to go public, but tonight, you're being called to action.

"Damien Sykes is throwing a soirée tonight, and you're crashing it. The council has designated him a critical threat, and we have the chance to rid the Commonwealth of him."

Sam shook his head in disapproval, eyes fierce. He had a protest on the tip of his tongue but held it.

Janice said, "Sykes winning the Chief Executiveship would be a disaster for both colonists and immigrants. Our hackers accessed his guest registry and conducted a data pull. At least ten of his guests are confirmed Purists. The rest likely support colonist and immigrant oppression, but we can't confirm that, or if they're Purists.

"The confirmed Purists are to be eliminated. But Damien Sykes is the priority target. Once he's eliminated, you exfil. And you will use nonlethal force on all security personnel and anyone else who isn't a Purist. Understood?"

"Understood," everyone replied together.

"Good. Be geared up and ready to roll out by nineteen-hundred hours."

The solutioners filed out.

Sam went up to Janice. "I need a quick word with you." This mission wasn't sitting well with him.

While leaving, Jay said to Akane, "This double life is gonna wear me out. You would think we'd be able to get some rest before we're rotated in for our next ETF assignment. *Sheesh.*"

"There's plenty of time for beauty sleep." Akane was ready for action. "This is big. This is our chance to knock off Damien Sykes."

The sliding door shut. Sam and Janice were now alone.

Sam spoke in an even, measured tone. "I don't like this, not one bit. Pulling risky stunts like this attracts investigations from the authorities and Defense Force Intelligence. That's why we don't do drive-bys like that hit squad today. We stay off the radar as much as possible.

"Shoot, we'll rig elections, even resort to blackmail to keep Purists and immigrant haters out of power, but this? There's just too many ways this op could go awry. What was the council thinking?"

Janice boosted herself into a sitting position on the desk, fingers clasping the edge. "The council deemed Sykes a critical threat, Sam."

"Yeah, you said that already."

"And that's why you solutioners are being deployed."

"So we're acting irrationally out of fear? There are other ways to keep Sykes from winning the election. This is reckless."

"We've assassinated people before," Janice said matter-of-factly, stating a simple truth.

"And I don't mourn those assholes, but those ops were more discreet—poisonings, car bombs, arranged accidents. And those targets were small fry compared to Damien Sykes.

"Think about it, if we take out a big fish like him in an open assault on one of his estates, anti-reformists won't hesitate to weaponize it. They'll spin it as an attack by an immigrant or colony extremist group. That could ignite a level of colonist/immigrant hatred we haven't seen before, full-blown chaos in the streets."

Janice replied, "I know this is drastic. I know we risk exposure. Yeah, it could all go sideways, and killing Sykes might be the spark that lights an inferno. But I'm just the messenger."

"The council's on Satellite One. You're their eyes and ears on the ground. You're leading the charge here on Eden. You've got clout. Maybe they'll listen to—"

"I already tried, Sam," Janice interrupted. "They're not listening to me."

Sam mumbled something angry under his breath.

"We're at war. Our enemies murdered Coalition heroes today. Eliminating Sykes would serve as payback. It'll show the Purists that we can get to them too."

"This is a fucking terrible idea."

"You're in command of the Strike Team, Sam. We've only got one shot at this, so make sure it goes smoothly."

Sam sighed. "Yes, ma'am." He left.

• • •

A long limousine pulled up to Damien's mansion, one of several mansions he owned.

Damien waited outside in a wrinkle-free white suit. On his finger gleamed a gold ring engraved with the Sykes-family signet: a palm holding the world.

One of the limo's doors opened. Stacie exited, dressed to the nines in a strapless sequined halter dress that hugged her in all the right places.

Shiny gemstones adorned her neck and wrists. Turquoise eye shadow that matched her dress highlighted her eyes. And just to keep up appearances, she wore a ring bearing her family signet.

Her wispy blond hair bounced on her bare shoulders as she strutted toward Damien.

Even from a distance, her infectious aura seemed to envelop him. *Well, well, the belle of the evening has arrived.* Self-satisfaction entered his eyes. He knew that if he held out, she would come back to him. Most women always did.

Stacie saw that the fenced-off perimeter was well-guarded. The place was crawling with security, men in suits patrolling every edge of the property.

"Be careful," Jason's voice said from her earrings. Stacie had insisted her team sit this one out, but Jason had talked her into letting them tag along. They stayed close to the mansion in a van, just in case she needed backup. "If you need us, we're here."

"I'll be fine." Stacie flounced up to Damien and twirled, showing off the dazzling scintillating dress. "You like?" she asked with exaggerated cheer.

"Yes, quite the fetching outfit." Chivalrous, he invited her to take his arm. "Come, my dear."

She hooked her arm around his.

A doorman opened one of the tall gilded double doors, and they went inside, into the tasteful decor.

People of status sat at circular tables draped in white linen, laughing and chatting. At the wine bar, a server in formal wear mixed drinks for a small group, while white-shirted chefs wheeled carts filled with exquisite dishes.

"Damien," someone called out.

A commanding older man, wearing a dapper black suit and a ruffled cravat, approached Damien and Stacie. Stacie recognized the face but couldn't place it. She assumed she'd seen the man on the Academy's wall of distinguished service members.

"I just wanted to say that you are *exactly* the kind of Chief the Commonwealth needs right now." The man raised his champagne glass in honor of Damien.

Recognition dawned on Stacie. He was Malcolm Horowitz, a retired CDF colonel and a U.S. serviceman during Earth Era.

"What this Chief has permitted turns my stomach, allowing treasonists to go unpunished. *Despicable*," Malcolm said. "She's even fighting to strip NCOs and officers of the authority to execute insider threats on judgment alone." He scoffed. "This woman's menace needs to be stopped."

Damien intended to do exactly that, defeat Oviereya in the coming election. "Thank you. I trust I have your support."

"Indeed, you do. Well, enough of my rambling. It'd be rude of me to keep you from this fine lady." He stepped off to leave Damien and Stacie to themselves. "May you win the election."

Damien asked Stacie, "Shall I get us drinks?"

"Yes, please do."

Damien went to the wine bar.

As Stacie waited for him to come back, guests greeted her. She recognized CDF service members, politicians, scions of immense wealth, and industry leaders from fields ranging from science to engineering. But there was an air of entitlement and superiority about them that sent a cringey feeling worming its way through her, a feeling reminiscent of the one she'd gotten at many Eight Elite gatherings and Highborn parties, except worse. These people reeked of arrogance.

Damien returned with two glasses of wine.

Okay, time to get down to business, Stacie thought.

Damien handed one of the glasses to her.

She held it high for a toast, pretending to be Team Sykes. "To your victory next year." The rims of their glasses clinked, and they drank. Now it was time for her to get some answers. "Damien, dear, have you ever heard of Purism or Purists?"

Caught off guard mid-sip, Damien coughed and cleared his throat. "What's it to you?" Caution underscored his tone.

"Is that a 'yes'?"

"You answer first," he replied, words clipped.

Stacie downed more of her wine. She followed the script she'd rehearsed a thousand times in her mind. "Running my parents' empire, I've heard whispers about . . . some radical cult. I think some of my parents' business clients might be involved with these weirdos."

Damien lifted a quizzical brow. "And you thought to ask me because—?"

Stacie knew Damien was no fool and that she had to be careful. She replied smoothly, "Because I have no one else to ask. Ever since leaving the Eight to spread my wings, I'm not exactly popular with the other family heads.

"And I'm trying to keep the authorities out of my hair. If I've got carryover clientele from my parents involved in some psycho cult, I need to know." She hoped he was buying it. "You're a smart guy," she added, flattering him, "and you seem to know a lot." Then she hit him with the thought of losing her, like he had just screwed up. "But if you're going to be up in arms over me asking a simple fucking question, I can just go home." She slammed her glass onto the table. It tipped over, spilling red wine across the white linen.

She spun around, to leave Damien without a date.

He grabbed her wrist. "No need to storm off, my dear." He set his glass down and curled an arm around her waist. "Stay. It'd be a shame for you to have gotten all dressed up for nothing."

"Then give me a fucking answer, or I'm out of here," Stacie said demandingly.

"Quite the negotiator, aren't you?"

"Got it from Mom." Stacie tapped her foot and crossed her arms, sending Damien a look that said "go on, start talking."

"You drive a hard bargain." Damien decided to provide Stacie an answer. "Purism isn't a cult. It's a religion. And its followers aren't weirdos. Christians believe in Christ. Muslims in Allah. Purists believe in the science and technology that birthed the New Humanity, the work of Cyrus Kline, Jagr Vlcek, and Atticus Hancroft.

"AEGIS purged the New Humanity of deficiencies and qualified us, Eden's chosen caretakers, to be the helmsmen of the Union's human community. This jewel we call home wasn't big enough for all of mankind, and we were selected to be here." Selected based on social ranking, health, life expectancy, IQ, education, and more unfair determinants. "How would you feel if someone were just *handed* the title of Warrior Extraordinaire, when you clearly *earned* it? We, Eden's chosen, went through a process too."

So these Purist dweebs are a bunch of stuck-up, sanctimonious pro-

caste separatists, Stacie thought.

Damien said, "The purity of AEGIS's grand design for a better mankind has been jeopardized by reformist initiatives and legislative tokenism like the immigration lottery. At its core, Purist activism is about preserving AEGIS's framework. Tampering with or defiling that framework will only lead humanity to repeat its own destruction. I, for one, don't want to see that happen.

"It is the misguided—Coalition and Independent Movement sympathizers—who have continued to defile the system. Such foolish mooks plunged the Commonwealth into civil war, proving AEGIS right, that they are not fit to be among us here on Eden.

"These low-level thinkers have shown they belong where they are, as resource harvesters. And that's not a bad thing. But can you imagine people like that, people who simply cannot grasp why the system must remain as it is, gaining influence in Eden's government or military? They are not on par with us, as determined by their value coefficients."

Stacie was quailing on the inside.

Damien said, "Purists are fighting, nonviolently, to keep Eden's bloodline from contamination by the impurities of the inferior class. If Chief Amaechi prevails, the Commonwealth will be doomed.

"Nadir, those who didn't cut the mustard to be here, do have a place in our society, as resource harvesters. That is where they are best suited to contribute to humanity. No one wants to see them perish, be killed, or live unsuccessful lives. These unfortunate people just don't know what's best for them. Purism is about protecting them from themselves just as much as it is about protecting us Edenites." *Even if violence is necessary to prove a point.*

It was exactly the kind of snobbish blather Stacie had expected to hear from Damien. "I see, and who started this so-called religion?"

"That, my dear, no one knows. A mysterious figure calling himself Quinn began preaching the truisms of Purist ideology over the net. Call him a counterpart to Arman Reza, if you will.

"Purism caught fire after the Three-Week War. Chat forums and virtual networks clung to Quinn's doctrine. Then Purist groups formed, unaffiliated, yet aligned. All peers. You won't see them making public statements, though, especially with Amaechi in office. But they're harmless. In our society, you're free to believe what you want, right?"

Stacie was well aware that this was a free republic, but she was also aware that sometimes people used their beliefs to justify harming others. "True. And are you a *follower* of this religion? You seem to know an awful lot about it."

Damien threw his head back, letting out a duplicitous laugh. "I'm simply an academic."

Stacie didn't believe him one bit.

"Mr. Sykes," came a male voice unmistakable to Stacie. The man emerged from a huddle of guests.

Stacie's pulse quickened. *Paul Shaffer?* Why was he here?

"Stacie," Damien said, "meet Sergeant Paul Shaffer."

"Oh, we've met before," she replied. She remembered how infuriated Paul was when she refused to tell him anything about her business in X-Quadrant.

"Then I'm assuming you two know each other from the CDF. From a mission, perhaps?"

"You could say that."

"Well, Sergeant Shaffer is one of *many* Guardians supporting me and has been an asset to my campaign." Damien sounded proud of the number of service members backing him.

Paul recalled Stacie's obnoxious attitude during the

interrogation. *Bitch.* Irritation crawled over him, but he maintained his poise. "I wish you were in office now, Mr. Sykes, and not that soft reformist, Amaechi."

Stacie grimaced. That "soft reformist" was her friend—and a mother figure.

"I wish I were too, Sergeant," Damien said. "But by next year, I will be. You can bank on that."

Paul gave a subtle nod and then gestured with his chin, signaling that he and Damien needed to speak privately.

Damien turned to Stacie. "I need to speak with the sergeant for a moment. Business stuff."

Stacie was glad to get a break from these two creeps. "Sure. I'll be at the wine bar." She kissed Damien on the cheek, then walked off, flashing Paul a smirk. *Loser.*

Once Stacie was out of earshot, Paul said, "First, I just wanna say if I had known that trafficking operation was your outfit, boss, I would've—"

Damien flicked his wrist, dismissing the matter. "Don't worry about it, Sergeant. You weren't supposed to know. None of those traffickers knew I was behind the operation either. And even if you *had* known, you'd have had no choice but to comply with your orders. Everything's fine. The CDF has nothing that traces back to me."

"Thanks. By the way, that dame's one of the chasers who tried to compromise your operation. It can't be a coincidence that she's here, worming her way into your good graces."

"Thank you for letting me know, Sergeant. I appreciate your concern. You're one of my finest lieutenants and a prime role model for our young Purist neophytes. But Stacie Spencer is completely oblivious to my involvement in the trafficking industry. Don't worry about her."

"If you say so, boss."

"Go enjoy yourself, Sergeant." Damien nudged Paul's shoulder with a chummy fist bump.

Paul wandered off. One thing he enjoyed about working for Damien was how well he treated his subordinates. He took good care of them.

A young man spoke into a handheld mic. "Ladies and gentlemen, may I have your attention?" He stood atop the landing of a red-carpeted staircase, looking sharp in pressed pants, a dress shirt, bow tie, and waistcoat.

Conversations stopped. A few people murmured. What was this about?

The man said, "Please give a warm welcome to Mr. Sykes' special keynote speaker—" There was a long pause. Everyone waited anxiously. "—Doctor Atticus Hancroft!"

Gasps and reverent whispers of shock and excitement filled the room.

At the wine bar, Stacie recoiled. *Atticus Hancroft? **The** Atticus Hancroft?* He was the last living creator of AEGIS, and one of Eden's first-ark settlers. At his age, the man rarely made public appearances.

In a sumptuous black suit, Atticus emerged from a door behind the announcer. Wrinkles and crow's feet lined his timeworn face, deep grooves furrowed his forehead, and his hair was thinning and gray. Though elderly, he appeared to be in good health. He didn't seem weak or fragile.

Damien was confident that if any guests tonight had lingering doubts about supporting him, and were considering throwing their weight behind other candidates, having Atticus in his corner would change their minds. Independent Movement antagonists and people outraged by Coalition fighters being let off the hook respected Atticus.

Atticus took the mic from the announcer. "Distinguished ladies and gentlemen," he began, "I am proud to say I've known Damien Sykes for quite some time. He is an extraordinary businessman, a brilliant thinker, and a natural leader.

"I know he will make an outstanding Chief Executive. Like me, he understands our republic is being endangered by reformists and extremists who seek to compromise the balance—the harmony —that keeps our society thriving.

"Humanity had brought itself to the brink of extinction but survived and forged the Commonwealth, with the help of the Union and other worlds beyond the Union's borders.

"AEGIS laid the foundation for the New Humanity. But the state of our republic is in jeopardy. Independent Movement proponents. Terrorists like the Coalition. Pro-reform politicians. Radicals. These people have one agenda: to destroy our republic. We now have a de facto Chief, a woman who openly champions their destructive ideals. She cannot win next year's election.

"I call on you to vote for Damien Sykes. A vote for Sykes is a vote for the right path. It is a vote to keep Eden free from those unfit to be here, those better suited to the role they currently occupy. Save our republic." He delivered his endorsement masterfully.

The audience gave him a standing ovation.

Stacie, however, was creeped out by the mad genius's speech. Sure, she loved attention and had lived a rarefied life, but never had she believed that any segment of humanity was inferior, defective, or undeserving of a shot at prosperity.

She understood that Eden's real estate wasn't big enough for all of humanity. Tough choices had to be made. Still, she wanted the government's promise to the colonists honored, the promise that their world would be an "Eden" too. And yes, when she was a Guardian, she had believed the colony rebellion was unjustified, like most Edenites did.

Damien greeted his VIP with a perfunctory half bow. *<Thank you for coming. You have my sincerest gratitude,>* he said to Atticus, their Link transmitting his voice.

<Think nothing of it, Damien. You've always been my prize disciple.> Atticus placed a hand on the wildcard's shoulder. *<You are on the cusp of fulfilling what I believe is your destiny. Someone must step up to maintain the taxonomy of humanity.>* He glanced over at Stacie. *<That's the late Patrick and Darlene Spencer's daughter, isn't it?>*

<She is.>

<Careful, Damien, don't let your penchant for pretty women distract you from your campaign.>

<Don't worry, it won't.>

<Very well. I must go now.>

<Thank you again, sir.>

With pride, Atticus said the Purist motto. *<For the purity of the republic.>*

<Yes, for the purity of the republic.>

While Atticus was on his way out, several guests stopped him for handshakes and comments on his speech.

Outside, Atticus got into his limo and departed.

As the vehicle sped away from the mansion, five armored cargo vans raced past in the opposite direction, their fronts retrofitted with heavy battering rams. The grooves on Atticus's forehead deepened. His intuition told him those vans, heading straight for Damien's estate, spelled trouble.

179

Sam, Akane, Jay, and five other solutioners, dressed in dark fatigues, sat on two benches inside the rear hold of one of the vans. In just a few minutes, they'd don their balaclavas and crash Damien's fundraiser.

Jay held up a double-barreled handgun, which was the primary weapon for the mission. He executed a quick functions check. "Sweet," he said, admiring the craftsmanship.

The gun was programmed to go lethal only for the Purists logged into its CPU, a measure to help the Strike Team avoid dispatching the wrong people. One of the barrels dispersed nonlethal taser rounds; the other, lethal rounds. But even with that safety feature, the team needed to be careful.

Akane examined the weapon, its smart-grip auto-customizing to the size of her fingers. *I wonder how Janice scored these Tarzekian weapons.*

Jay shifted his head toward Sam. The Strike Team's leader was a reserved man, but this was quiet even for him. "You haven't said a word. Something bothering you?"

Sam exhaled a hiss of air from his nose. "It's just that . . . this could turn into a clusterfuck really fast."

"We got this. Don't worry."

On edge, Sam didn't share Jay's optimism.

Damien's wristcom buzzed. Its message-notification light blinked. He tapped the device's centerpiece, and a message from Atticus swelled into view in a text bubble, warning him of the approaching threat. His face tightened into a scowl. *Damn it.* It had to be RISE.

Stacie glided over from the bar, her third glass of wine in hand. "How did you get Atticus Hancroft to back you?"

"I met him at one of his seminars and have been under his tutelage."

"Tutelage for what?"

Damien knew they needed to leave the mansion fast. "Right now, we should—"

Gunfire crackled outside.

Pandemonium broke out in the mansion.

Damien brought his wristcom to his mouth. "Wallace, report. What the hell's going on?"

His Chief Watch Officer replied, gunfire thundering in the background, "Perimeter breach. A coupla vans just crashed the gate. It has to be RISE, sir."

"Shit." *Solutioners, RISE's hit men.* Damien knew solutioners weren't deployed often. RISE usually kept a low profile. Did they fear his candidacy that much? He considered this attack a badge of honor.

More gunfire roared, closer to the mansion this time.

The front doors exploded inward. Solutioners rushed forward. Interior security drew firearms from the shoulder holsters beneath their suit jackets and fired.

Damien overturned a table and ducked, dragging Stacie down beside him. He reached into his jacket and produced a collapsible handgun. Extendable and flip-out components clacked. Then he was wielding a full-length weapon.

"Stay down," he told Stacie. He sprang up, squeezed the trigger three times, and stooped back down. "When we get the chance, we need to make a break for the stairwell and get to the car park on the roof. Follow my lead."

A barrage of rounds from solutioners and security pounded the room.

Guests screamed and fled in all directions.

A solutioner spotted Damien out of the corner of his eye. "Primary target acquired!" He fired at Damien, gun bucking in his hand. Bullets chipped splinters off the table Damien and Stacie were using as cover.

A stray bullet caught a guest in the side. The once-elegant function had become a shooting gallery.

Paul sheltered himself behind a pillar. He leaned around the tall white fluted column and leveled Damien's attacker with three shots, protecting his and his cohort's ticket to promised central-government positions.

Akane saw Paul. *Shaffer's here? He wasn't on the guest list.* The death of Simone plagued her mind again. *This is my chance to kill him.* Thoughts of revenge were inescapable.

She didn't care that Paul hadn't been officially confirmed as Simone's killer. In her heart, she knew it was him. He was going to pay tonight.

She switched to lethal rounds and exploded into motion, charging toward Paul while shooting wildly.

Amid the chaos, ornaments, glassware, and expensive things shattered.

A bullet from Akane's gun struck Paul's pillar. *Shit,* he thought, flinching. His eyes flitted sideways, to the petite angry woman coming for his life. He pointed his weapon at her and cut loose, firing off a rapid succession of shots.

Akane twisted out of Paul's line of fire, dove, and rolled over her shoulder, coming up in a crouch behind a long buffet credenza. Paul didn't let up, still determined to take her out.

Akane popped up and tapped the device on her wrist. An energy buckler crackled to life. It flickered as Paul's bullets crashed into it. With her shooting hand, Akane returned fire.

Paul sprayed more bullets in her direction.

She started to move closer, but a bullet out of nowhere wounded her shoulder, derailing her momentum. Her face contorted behind her mask from the pain. She found the shooter and blasted a taser round at him. The paralyzing shock incapacitated him instantly.

Akane looked back to where Paul had been, but he was gone. She scanned the storm of gunfire. *Shit. Where the hell did he go?* He wouldn't just abandon Damien. He had to still be out there, fighting.

Stacie and Damien, still taking cover behind the overturned table, waited for the right moment to escape to the stairwell.

Stacie's heart thundered in her chest. "I don't suppose you have another gun?"

"Afraid not," Damien said. They had to get to the stairwell. It was now or never. "Let's go!" He jumped up and ran, Stacie staying close behind him.

As they made their getaway, he triggered his gun, shooting bullets across the room. His shoulder rammed the stairwell door's push bar, and they retreated inside.

The door fell shut behind them, muffling the firefight.

Stacie struggled to keep pace with Damien, her heels hindering her climb up the staircase.

A solutioner shoved open the swinging doors of the second-floor landing. He reached for the gun holstered on his hip, but before he could draw, Damien sent three rounds into his bullet-resistant vest. The impact pitched the solutioner backward through the doors he'd just entered from.

They've infiltrated upper floors too, Damien thought. *They're trying to cut off all exits.* He hoped they hadn't reached the car park yet.

Damien and Stacie ascended the zigzagging flight of stairs. Footsteps clattered behind them, nearing rapidly. Solutioners were in hot pursuit.

Damien and Stacie reached the rooftop. A dozen luxury flyers sat on the landing terrace, their glossy hulls gleaming under floodlights.

Damien grabbed Stacie's arm and guided her to a sleek mauve two-seater. "Come on." He keyed his wristcom, and the flip-up canopy clicked open. "Ladies first. Get in."

He didn't have to tell Stacie twice. Chest burning from labored breaths, she leapt into the passenger seat.

The rooftop door whooshed open. Sam Guthrie stormed through, Jay at his side.

"Damien Sykes!" Sam shouted, raising his weapon.

Damien fired first.

One bullet caught Jay in the leg. He collapsed, clutching the wound. "Damn it!" he cried out.

Sam retaliated, firing back.

Damien quickly tossed his gun into the flyer and jumped behind the controls. A bullet grazed his shoulder, staining his suit with blood. He hit a button on the dashboard. The canopy snapped shut, and a light flashed from red to green.

Sam's bullets pinged off the armored flyer as it lifted into the night sky.

In the distance, sirens wailed. Blue-to-red strobes from approaching police flyers flashed in the night. Someone had called the authorities.

Not good, Sam thought.

Over his wristcom, a solutioner said, "Time to vamoose, Sam. Authorities inbound."

"Roger." Sam knelt, dragged Jay's arm over his shoulder, and helped him to his feet. "Let's get that wound taken care of and get you back to Nicole and Zola."

Jay grunted in pain as he limped, step by step, to the exit with Sam.

Inside the flyer, Stacie said, "Damien, are you okay?" She would've preferred the bullet had hit him in the head.

"The wound's superficial. Nothing to worry about. I'll be fine," he replied, sounding frustrated. He was livid that his fundraiser had ended in chaos.

He retrieved the gun from the floor, collapsed it, and slid it into a compartment underneath the dashboard.

"I heard your security guy mention RISE," Stacie said. "Who the heck are they?"

"They're a pro-reform extremist group. A violent one. They obviously attacked me because they fear my candidacy." Damien couldn't wait to burn RISE to the ground. He just needed to find their base.

Stacie wanted to press him for more information. She knew he was holding back. But there was no need to push. Not yet. Pressuring him now might arouse suspicion and jeopardize her mission, or even get her killed. It was better to take things slow.

The flyer decelerated as it approached the three-floor house sitting on one of Damien's ultraexpensive properties.

The property's defense system cleared the flyer to land inside the gate, on the lawn.

"I'm sure the authorities will want to question me and others who survived the attack," Damien said. "They'll probably pay me a visit tomorrow. I'm sorry the night had to end in such disarray."

"Hey, at least we're alive. And despite dodging bullets, I had a good time." Not really. Not by a long shot. In fact, the longer she spent with Damien, the more she felt like puking.

"I enjoyed your company as well, as I always have." He leaned in, his mouth finding hers. Then his lips trailed down to her clavicle.

Stacie fought to keep the disgust off her face and twisted away. *Yuck.* "Sorry, I'm just not in the mood tonight. I'm a little exhausted after all the, you know, shooting."

"Of course, I understand. Shall we reconvene tomorrow, perhaps? Lunch?"

"I'll clear my schedule."

"Excellent. Take one of my flyers home. I have quite the selection in—"

"I'll just take an air-cab. I'll be fine." Stace didn't want to use anything that belonged to her friend's abuser. The thought of doing so was abhorrent.

"As you wish."

They stepped out. Damien pressed a button on his wristcom to open the gate for Stacie, then went inside his house.

Stacie called an air-cab using her wristcom. The moment it landed, she hurriedly climbed in and headed home.

Damien removed his suit jacket and shirt, tossing them on the floor. After he spoke a voice command, one of his medical-service golems approached and initiated treatment for his wound. Microbots deployed from the interior storage of the golem's midsection and got to work, applying medical unguent to the nicked skin before suturing it.

Once the microbots finished, the golem called them back.

Damien made his way to his Feng Shui-inspired study, impeccably decorated with opulent white furnishings. Bone-tired, he slumped into an armchair.

He brought up his wristcom's interface and dialed a number.

A hologram of Atticus's face materialized. "Damien, are you alright? The attack on your estate is all over the news."

"I'm fine, sir."

"RISE, I assume."

"Yes, the ever-present thorn in our side."

"Be careful. This assassination attempt means they fear you. They're becoming more brazen."

"It appears so, but I'm not surprised. My chances of winning the election keep improving. I owe that to you and your teachings. They've guided me, transformed me. Being chosen to Link with you—the *founder* of Purism—and absorb your knowledge and mindset is an honor."

Atticus was the mystery instigator, the anomaly known as Quinn, the leader of the Brotherhood for Humanity's Salvation. To him, influence was the ultimate power. And as Quinn, he had clearly influenced many Edenites.

"Think nothing of it," Atticus said. "I simply recognized your potential and sought to elevate it. Now rest. The authorities will be knocking at your door tomorrow."

"Yes, and I am prepared."

"Well, I bid you a good night, friend." The video transmission ended.

For Damien, being called a friend by the founder of Purism was awesome.

The mind's eye of Atticus Hancroft had awakened him to the "perceived" dangers facing the New Humanity. Atticus's teachings had edified his life and given it purpose. He had become infused with a desire to change society. The interpolation of immigrants would end with him, and he'd continue to implement AEGIS's blueprint for humanity. He'd ensure the unworthy never gained power.

Like Stacie, he had sought a higher calling. She had joined the CDF to escape her gilded cage, desperate to be more than just the "princess" of the Spencer family. Speaking of . . .

He tapped his wristcom. Images of Stacie floated above it. Microdrones had captured them during the fundraiser without her knowledge.

Damien glued his gaze to her, tracing her curves. He wetted his lips with his tongue, eager to possess her. To him, she was the epitome of physical excellence—solid, statuesque, and well-developed. This woman had hit some genetic jackpot, he thought. He was mentally gushing over her perfection.

He unzipped and reached inside his pants.

The memory of the first time he'd made love to Stacie rushed back. He had thrust into her until she nearly came undone, her fingers knotted in his hair, her hips arching against him. He ached for the feel of her bare skin. It was like warm satin stretched over sinewy muscle.

The more he reminisced, the more his erection strained against his palm. He kept stroking himself, his grip tightening. Before long, he was spilling cum into his clenched fist.

His father had instilled in him the belief that anything could be his. He simply had to take it. And he had declared that Stacie Lynette Spencer would be his.

• • •

Rain pummeled the awning of the restaurant's outdoor seating area. A chestnut-blond woman sat with Stacie at a table for two. She was Cassie McCanns: young, demure, and susceptible to manipulation. Damien Sykes had taken advantage of her easily.

"Enough," Stacie said. An angry wave of her hand sliced the air. Even with the makeup, the bruising on Cassie's face was still evident.

"It ends today."

Cassie replied, "He—"

"Won't change. You know that." Stacie was tired of Cassie glossing over Damien's behavior.

Cassie sat silently, her mind replaying good times: flowers waiting on her doorstep, thoughtful gifts, pampering, surprise visits to her workplace, planet-hopping vacations. Who would want to give all that up?

Damien was a charmer. He knew how to win a woman's heart, how to romance her.

But the arguments, when they happened, were severe. And during them, Cassie paid the price. She made him do it, made him hit her, Damien would say.

"Stacie, I—" Cassie began, her youthful, innocent face reflecting hesitation.

"Come on, let's go after him. We can press charges. I'll foot the bill for everything."

Cassie's chin dropped. "Stacie, you know—"

When Cassie raised her head, Stacie found herself staring at a mirror image of her own face.

*Doppelganger Stacie's features contorted, becoming a sinister mask. **"You're right, it's all your fault! You're incompetent! You couldn't see past his facade and delivered me into the hands of a demented monster! You're responsible for these bruises and all of my mental scars!"***

Everything began dissolving into a dark glob.

Stacie, still in the air-cab, gasped, awakening from the bad dream. *It was my fault. I ignored the signs of who . . . what he was.*

She sighed. Tomorrow, she'd debrief with Conlan, and they'd plan their next move. *I'm going to make up for it, Cassie. I'm going to get him, for you.*

• • •

Randy was up watching newscasts on his TV. The firefight at Damien's estate was the top headline and was trending across the net. His gut told him that his shortened visit to RISE HQ, the important meeting Sam had mentioned, and tonight's attack were all connected. But that was just speculation, for now. He'd have to unearth the truth. And he swore he would.

His father had already checked in with some ex-Coalition fighters. He hadn't found out anything about RISE yet but planned to follow up on another lead tomorrow.

Randy wondered, *What really is RISE? Some kind of social-justice vigilante outfit, taking the law into their own hands? What are you involved with, Akane?*

INTERLUDE FOUR

A metal door swung open, slamming against the wall. Akane, Sam, and Jay walked into the compact space.

A disheveled-looking man sat in a lone chair, hands restrained behind his back and mouth gagged.

He mumbled fearfully.

"Wh-what's this?" Akane asked, her voice shaky. She had no idea she was about to carry out an execution.

"Your final test, Akane," Sam said. "Jay, proceed."

Jay screwed a silencer onto the end of a pistol, then extended the weapon to Akane grip-first.

Akane hesitated to accept it. "What's that for?"

"Just take it. It'll be okay," Jay said coaxingly.

Akane's trembling fingers settled into the grip's ridges.

Sam glared at the captive like he wanted to kill him himself. "This man is one of the Highborn who kept harassing Skylar at her job. He's one of the bullies who pushed her over the edge. Now, you might be thinking bullying and harassment aren't punishable by death, but this asshole needs to pay for the way he treated her. Skylar reported him to upper management, and they ignored her complaints because she was an immigrant. That's right, isn't it?"

Akane recalled Skylar's stories of the harassment she endured at work. It was so disgusting. "Yeah, that's what she told me." Her shoulders sagged as she stared solemnly at the floor.

Sam gripped the man's chin. "Because management wasn't going to do a damn thing, you just kept getting bolder and started playing a little game of touch and grab, didn't you?" Sam looked back at Akane. "That's what Skylar said, right?"

"Yeah," she replied, her voice heavy with sadness.

"Go on, Akane, finish him. Make him pay," Jay said.

Working up the nerve to kill the man wasn't easy for Akane. *This shouldn't be so hard, but it is. Why?* "I . . . I just don't—" The pistol rattled in her trembling hand.

Piss saturated the man's pants as he mumbled a plea for mercy he didn't deserve.

Sam could hardly wait for him to die. "Do it, Akane. Erase this son of a bitch from existence." Akane's finger tentatively hovered over the trigger. "I bet you're thinking: He didn't murder anyone, and he's not like Simone's killer. But if we let him go, he'll just find another immigrant woman to harass. He's a waste of air."

Tears streamed down Akane's cheeks. Memories of a joyful Skylar blinked through her mind. She remembered Skylar's enthusiasm: *"Me? I'm destined for **stardom**."*

"Do it!" Jay shouted.

Internally, Sam rooted for Akane to take this last step. "Prove you can do what needs to be done to our enemies."

He'd been in Akane's position before, when he first joined RISE. He'd wondered if a man not formally sentenced should die by his hand. But RISE needed warriors, men and women willing to take justice into their own hands when the system failed. He became what immigrants and colonists needed him to be: both shield and axe—the shield that kept harm at bay and the axe that severed the heads of those who meant them harm. Law be damned.

Akane lowered the pistol. She just couldn't do it.

Sam exhaled, more disappointed than angry. "It's okay," he said understandingly. "This isn't a disqualifier. It just means you're not ready for the harder jobs. I just hope that when we find Simone's killer, you don't balk."

Disgust for those who were prejudiced against immigrants surged within Akane. She yanked the trigger twice. Two muted pops went off, and blood and brain matter slathered the walls and floor. The man's dead body slumped forward.

That's for Skylar. Tears kept flowing from Akane's eyes.

"Good job," Sam said. "Simone would've been proud."

Red rivulets ran down the blood-smeared walls.

"Here, I got it." Jay took the pistol from Akane.

She was grappling with her first illegal kill. Was it justice or murder? Maybe murder was justice sometimes.

Sam knew better than to waste guilt on scum. "Don't second-guess yourself. You did the right thing."

Akane dipped her chin in a resolute nod and fixed her gaze on the lifeless body. *This isn't what we wanna do, but sometimes it's necessary to ensure our safety.*

She had completed the vetting process. She was now a full-fledged member of RISE.

CHAPTER FIVE

Stacie stood in Conlan's office, finishing her debrief about last night. "That's it, Sir. But with the way Damien spoke about these Purists, he has to be involved with them."

"All just conjecture."

"Yeah, I know, no substantial evidence yet. But I'll get some."

"Be careful. Continue to exercise extreme caution. If you ask too many questions too fast, that might tip him off."

"Yes, Sir. Anything on this RISE organization yet?"

"Cyber Intel uncovered some ramblings on chat forums, people claiming they're part of RISE and declaring it the new Coalition." Conlan steepled his fingers, flesh meeting the metal of his cybernetic prosthetic. Then he closed his eyes in contemplation. Purists? RISE? What was going on in the Commonwealth?

"I'm meeting Damien today for an outing. I'll squeeze more info out of him about these Purists and RISE. And I'll eventually get a confession out of him about his trafficking operation."

"Be careful."

"Yes, Sir."

Stacie was about to leave until Conlan said, "Have you talked to Randal lately?"

Annoyance painted Stacie's face. "Why, Sir?"

"I know he misses you. At the graduation banquet, you two seemed like such a wonderful couple. He told me what sparked the breakup, but how long are you going to stay mad at him for one moral folly? Give him a chance to make things right."

"With all due respect, Sir, I'm not interested in talking about Randal Scott. He and I are done. *Finito*."

"I see. I'm still rooting for you two, though."

"Can I go now?"

Conlan knew when to leave well enough alone and dropped the topic of Randal Scott. "Yes, you're dismissed." He shifted his eyes to his computer screen, and Stacie departed.

• • •

Satellite One
Colony Four

Arson and Sariah drove up outside a tavern in a rickety car. A Coalition buddy of Arson's was supposed to meet him there and share what he knew about RISE. Arson intended to make good on his promise to Randy and uncover what he could about the secretive organization.

Sitting in the front passenger seat, Arson said to Sariah, "I'm going in. Keep an eye on the vehicle behind us." A black van had followed them. Its occupants thought they were unnoticed, but they were wrong. "The moment someone moves, let me know."

"Will do."

Arson kissed Sariah's cheek. "Thanks. I won't be long."

After exiting the car, he approached the tavern, opened a pair of barn-style doors, and entered a room full of raucous, jawing patrons.

195

Men flirted with waitresses. People cheered and booed uproariously while watching a game of field hockey on a big screen. Cue sticks clacked against billiard balls. Bottles were raised to mouths. The scent of smoldering cigarettes and alcohol was potent.

Arson scanned the boisterous crowd for his Coalition friend, Sergei Gurin, former commander of the Gurin Faction.

Sergei, seated at one of the booth-tables, spotted Arson.

Sergei's attire was simple: olive-green shirt, tan cargo pants, black boots, and a wool overcoat. In front of him sat a half-finished mug of amber liquid. He smiled at Arson, a man he greatly respected. Despite becoming a lottery beneficiary and living in Eden's opulence, Arson had never forgotten his roots. He had betrayed the CDF to fight for the Coalition.

Some lottery beneficiaries forgot where they came from after getting a taste of paradise. They had "made it." But Arson Scott still considered Satellite One home. Even now, exonerated of war crimes and allowed to return to Eden, he remained in this outdated colony to support restoration efforts and help people rebuild their lives after months of military rule. Arson Scott wasn't the type to rest on his laurels.

Sergei lifted a hand, waving Arson over.

"Sergei, good to see you," Arson said, approaching the table.

"Come, sit," the Russian replied merrily. Arson settled into the seat across from him. "It's been a while, Arson."

"It has."

Sergei reminisced. "Do you remember that time we were supposed to take out that convoy of Shells and the charges didn't go off?" He shook with laughter. "*Phew*, I thought we were dead for sure."

A sequence of events spiraled through Arson's recollection: crackling gunfire, energy blasts, grenades exploding. "But we gunned our way out of that situation and got the job done, *without* killing a single Guardian," he said proudly. "We might have sent a few to the infirmary, though."

"Yes, I'm lucky to have fought alongside you."

"Same. And the Coalition's efforts paid off, just like we hoped."

"Thanks to Operation Hammer Fall. It must've been a *glorious* day, the Battle of the Quad."

"I wouldn't call it glorious. We just did what had to be done. Unfortunately, there were Guardians we couldn't avoid killing."

"That wasn't our fault." Sergei had not only fought for the Coalition, but for the RUC in the Three-Week War as well. He remembered homes and buildings being carpet-bombed into ash and rubble. "The government started the conflict. We simply fought back. They could've let Colonies One, Four, and Six have their independence. Even the Union leaders concluded those colonies were justified in breaking away from the Commonwealth."

"Yeah, and now with Amaechi in office, things are getting better. Construction's ramping up. Old, beat-to-hell MHUs are being retired. Plans are in the works for the colonies' first university. Finally, steps are being taken to close the chasm between the prosperous and the marginalized."

Sergei took a gulp of his drink. "Sad to say, my friend, but this progress won't last. Amaechi became Chief by default, next in line after that madman Gould's death. She's just a temp, a placeholder until the winner of the upcoming election takes over. And that winner, unfortunately, won't be her.

"We colony citizens and our immigrant brothers and sisters on Eden are the minority. Conformist Edenites, who want to preserve their monopoly on prosperity, will outvote us. Sure, some nonimmigrants who have common sense will vote for Amaechi, but they are few.

"In this new era of colonist and immigrant hate—and anger toward former Coalition fighters—most Edenites are going to vote for someone other than Amaechi. Maybe it'll be that lunatic Damien Sykes, or even a centrist. But it's going to be someone aligned with their values, someone who gives them what they want.

"That candidate, whoever they are, might even annul Amaechi's ruling absolving all Coalition fighters of war crimes." A humorless laugh escaped Sergei. "Just think about that. By this time next year, you and I could be playing holo table-games in some maximum-security orbital prison.

"And not even all colony citizens are on the same page. The people of colonies Two, Three, and Five never joined the RUC, and they opposed the Coalition's formation. They were fine jumping through hoops, negotiating endlessly, and slogging through red tape, enacting change at a snail's pace. They saw the Coalition's rebellion as a setback that worsened relations between the colonies and the central government.

"But those of us who fought with the RUC and the Coalition had sense. We chose to accelerate change. We didn't just stand by hoping for it, or sit around praying for divine intervention. We said 'no more lying down.'" Sergei's voice rose. "We're the ones responsible for the progress happening today!"

Heads turned toward Sergei, his volume far too loud.

Arson made a calming gesture, signaling Sergei to keep it down and be mindful of the other patrons. "I won't say you're wrong. But I'm hopeful. I'm hopeful Amaechi will win next year's election."

Sergei scoffed. "*Bah*, even with the net filters down, even now that we colonists can expose how horribly we've been treated, Edenites still turn their noses up at us, believing themselves superior. I guarantee you, Arson, a storm is on the horizon.

Perhaps another war."

Exhausted from fighting, Arson wanted no more war. "I pray you're wrong, Sergei. It's been good chatting, but I need to get down to business. I can't keep Sariah waiting outside forever."

"Ah, yes, your new . . . lady friend."

"Let's cut to the chase. You said you could tell me about this RISE organization. Who are they?"

"Our best hope."

Arson frowned, growing impatient. His tone stiffened. "I'm going to need more than that."

"We're a pro-reform activist group," Sergei supplied.

A question played across Arson's features. "We?"

"I have been a member since the first year of its inception. You should join too, my friend."

Arson's eyes narrowed. "So, is RISE some product of the Independent Movement, or some entity formed during martial law? And what exactly does RISE do?"

"Firstly, RISE formed well before the Three-Week War. Initially, its mission was to raise awareness about the colonies' deteriorating conditions, advocate for equality, and get more immigrants into the CDF, the government, and positions of power.

"After the Three-Week War ended and martial law was imposed on colonies One, Four, and Six, RISE's mission broadened. It began fighting for increased funding for Assisted Living Centers and supporting the Coalition. In short, we do what needs to be done to make reform a reality. In the election between Ron Burchardt and Todd Sieger, Burchardt won because of RISE."

That news jolted Arson. "What do you mean?"

Sergei replied, "We hacked a voter database here and there,

bribed a couple of people. Sprinkle in some blackmail and a few threats, and then . . . *voilà*: Burchardt wins. Not by much, not by a landslide, but just enough to make it look like a legitimate upset victory. Though, of course, the authorities are investigating."

Arson snarled derisively. Manipulating election results went against his principles.

Sergei said, "Oh, don't be so surprised, Scott. Did you actually think a pro-reform candidate like Ron Burchardt had a real chance in this era of colonist and immigrant hate? Come on. Someone has to even the playing field in these elections."

"We'll never know if Burchardt could've won legitimately, will we? Sometimes miracles happen. Believe in people, Sergei."

Sergei rolled his eyes. "We colonists tried *believing* for years, and where did it get us? Nowhere. That's why the RUC formed."

Arson's disdain for election fraud creased his forehead. "Tampering with elections is wrong, and illegal."

"Amaechi's fairy-tale Chief Executiveship doesn't stand a chance of lasting without RISE." Sergei was convinced that RISE's tactics were necessary. "You should join us, my friend. We've become the new Coalition. But you won't have to worry about guerrilla warfare, *unavoidable* shootouts, or leading hit-and-run attacks on CDF bases and arms contractors. RISE's fight is different. Our tactics aren't like the Coalition's. We're a liberation force working behind the scenes, not fighting on the front lines of a battlefield.

"We're making plans to swing as many of the special elections as we can in our favor. We could use you on our side, the great Arson Scott. We'd benefit from your input, your leadership."

This was a "no" for Arson. He refused to involve himself in anything unethical. If RISE's connection to rigged elections was discovered, it would only further demonize colonists and immigrants, fueling public hatred and almost certainly ensuring Oviereya's defeat in next year's election.

But Arson couldn't keep openly criticizing Sergei and RISE. He needed to play along, to infiltrate the organization and find a way to shut it down. Though he doubted RISE could stay hidden from Defense Force Intelligence and the police forever, the sooner it was dismantled, the better.

Trying not to sound too gung-ho just yet, Arson said, "I . . . I don't know. I mean, you're not totally wrong about our chances in these elections."

"Of course not. And Tristan Gelano is one of the three founders, the shot-callers who are our council, if that means anything to you. And you know Tris is smart. She won't let RISE or its members get exposed, including you, if you join. Assuming that's what you're worried about, you'll be safe."

"Tristan? Our mining colleague?"

Sergei chuckled. "Yes. What other Tristans do we know?"

From inside the car, Sariah saw three men leave the van behind her. They wore masks, dark clothing, and long trench coats.

Sariah brought her handheld comm-set to her mouth. "Arson, movement headed in your direction."

Arson heard Sariah's warning in his earpiece and told her to stay put. Instincts screaming at him to get his weapon out, he reached into his trench coat. "Three guys tailed us," he told Sergei, drawing a handgun. "Whoever they are, they're about to make a move."

Sergei also pulled a handgun from his coat. "I am not a violent man. But as we used to say in the Coalition: When violence comes to you, violence begets violence."

"I suggest everyone take cover!" Arson shouted. "Things are about to get messy!"

The barn doors swung wide as the three men charged in, their automatic weapons spraying bullets all around.

"For the purity of the republic!" one of them shouted.

People screamed in horror.

Arson and Sergei scattered in different directions, slipping between patrons fleeing to the nearest exits. But many didn't get far, cut down by a barrage of wild gunfire.

"Arson Scott, you're a dead man!" one gunman yelled.

These three Purists were after Arson, and killing colonist scum who had caused the civil war was just a bonus.

The bartender reached under the counter and grabbed a shotgun. "Bastards!" The double barrels exploded in a loud blast, but the rounds missed. His targets were still standing.

One of the Purists fired his submachine gun at the bartender. Bullets riddled him, and his blood flecked the counter.

A woman hiding under a table sobbed.

Sergei avenged the bartender by pumping a flurry of bullets into his killer's back.

One of the remaining two Purists turned his weapon on Sergei. The other chased after Arson, who'd sprinted out an exit, hoping to divide the Purists and draw them away from the bar patrons.

A bullet nicked Sergei, flaying skin from his shoulder. "Damn it!" He sprinted for the bar counter as bullets peppered the wall parallel to him.

He jumped behind the counter, feet landing beside the dead bartender, and ducked.

The Purist continued firing madly.

Splinters of wood shot up from the counter and cascaded over Sergei. He sprang to his feet, shot four rounds, and ducked again. *Damn, didn't get him.* He rose and fired a short burst. Still no success. He dropped back into a crouch as more gunfire from his attacker pierced the air.

The Purist's gun finally ran empty; the dry, mechanical clicking of a depleted chamber betrayed his vulnerability. He reached into his coat for a new clip.

Sergei seized the moment. He popped up and triggered a couple of shots.

One bullet punched through the Purist's arm. He howled and lost his grip on his gun. Now unarmed, it was over for him.

Sergei adjusted his aim and squeezed the trigger—once, twice, three times—ending the murderer's rampage.

The smell of spent rounds hung in the air.

Sergei released an unsteady exhalation.

Out back, Arson crouched behind the tavern's dumpster as bullets slammed into it and the brick wall behind him. He peeked over the edge and fired.

His target went down, hot lead drilling holes into him. As soon as the body dropped, Arson sprinted back inside.

"Sergei!" Arson shouted, reentering the tavern.

"Arson, are you alright?"

"Yeah."

Sariah rushed inside, gun in hand. Arson had told her to stay put, but she couldn't sit around in the car any longer, and she'd never been one to stay out of the action anyway.

"Holy shit." Her eyes swept over the crumpled mess of dead patrons.

"I'm assuming you're Sariah," Sergei said.

"I am."

"Good to meet another fellow Coalition fighter."

"Who were these guys?" Sariah asked Sergei.

"Purists. A thorn in the side of immigrants and colonists." Upon checking their bodies, he found Purist tattoos on one's neck and the other's wrist. And one of them had shouted the Purist motto—that was a pretty dead giveaway. "Somehow, they've expanded their movement to Satellite One."

Sariah found the word "Purists" deeply disturbing. "What the fuck are Purists?"

Sergei explained, "They're an extremist group of immigrant haters, driven by the belief that AEGIS declared part of humanity superior. Their toxic ideology, Purism, has influenced government leaders, Guardians, police—you name it. Some Purist groups are methodical and organized; others are just gun-crazy maniacs, like the ones who attacked this tavern."

"Any idea how many groups there are?" Arson asked.

"Over a dozen," Sergei replied. "We suspect Damien Sykes is involved with the biggest one, the original group that spawned all the copycats. It's called the Brotherhood for Humanity's Salvation. Damien might even be its leader. One thing's certain, he *is* a Purist. And if he wins the Chief Executiveship, it'll be the ultimate Purist power grab. That cannot happen."

Sariah said, "I can believe he's one of these *Purists* alright, with the rubbish that comes out of his mouth. So, who founded Purism?"

"A man calling himself Quinn," Sergei replied. "Quinn could be one man or more. Quinn could even be a woman."

Arson's inflamed eyes roamed the devastated tavern. Shot-up men and women lay sprawled across the floor. The Purists had come for him, but they didn't have to involve innocents.

They were acting on Quinn's—Atticus's—call to action: to take out Coalition fighters.

Sergei's heart wept for the dead. "You see, this is why RISE exists—to stop killings like this, to counter the Purists' political power plays, to make equality a reality. Join us, both of you."

Arson's thoughts whirled.

Police sirens grew closer.

• • •

Randy sat at his desk in his condo, videoconferencing with Arson through a laptop.

"I've heard about these Purists," Randy said. "It was the three RISE members who befriended me that filled me in." He hadn't told Arson their names, or that they were Guardians of Vanguard Alpha. Sam, Jay, and Akane were actually good people trying to look after him. It didn't feel right to rat them out.

"Well, Sergei arranged a meeting with this council for me tomorrow," Arson said. "I'm playing along to get closer. As pissed as I am about what happened at the tavern, and about the three ex-Coalition fighters who got gunned down, RISE still isn't good for the Commonwealth. What they've done, interfering in the election process, is illegal.

"Yeah, they've got good intentions. They're not scumbags like Purists are, but wrong is wrong. Both RISE and Purists have to be stopped. They both violate the law to advance their agendas. Purists do it to maintain the unfair status quo. RISE does it to achieve equality."

"So you meet with this council, and then what? Take them out?" Randy asked.

"I wouldn't rule it out entirely. I'll do whatever's necessary to protect the Commonwealth. But it's not my place to decide people's punishment for their wrongs. I'm not Arman Reza.

"What I'm going to do is meet with the council to uncover their plan for compromising the upcoming elections, then contact Conlan so Defense Force Intelligence can take further action. He's the one person we both know would listen to us."

A dear family friend, Conlan was one of the few people within the CDF who still respected Arson. Conlan had respected him even when Arson was fighting for the Coalition, because Conlan understood the civil war wasn't black and white, but gray.

Arson said, "But Conlan won't commit DFI's resources unless we come to him with something solid, not hearsay or theories or some 'this person told me that' nonsense.

"I'm not happy about taking down a well-intentioned activist organization. I even know one of the council members, Tristan. It's a shame RISE couldn't stick to *legal* activism. Apparently, they've decided that going outside the law and resorting to extreme measures is the best way to help immigrants and colonists, the best way to bring about social change. That makes them extremists. That makes them dangerous.

"I want true reformists and Amaechi to hold power, but the legal way. There are no such things as 'good extremist groups' and 'bad extremist groups.' It doesn't matter what their intentions are.

"We need to gather as much info as we can before going to Conlan. We need to know how large RISE really is. It could have multiple bases.

"The council operates things from Satellite One, according to what Sergei told me. We need to know who's leading the charge for them on Eden. Even if DFI took the council into custody, there might be someone on the ground to assume command."

Randy said, "That person could be this woman named Janice LaCroix. She mentioned she was the head of operations. From what I've seen, though, RISE has only one central base here on Eden, the place I was taken to. But you're right; we don't know that for *certain*. They might have several branches. If the Defense Force takes out that one base, there could be others."

"Okay, so do what you can to learn more on your end, and I'll do the same on mine. Just keep letting your three friends believe they can recruit you. Let them keep trying to reel you in."

"'Superspy' isn't part of my skill set," Randy joked. "The Academy didn't cover that."

"Same here, but we'll make do."

"So, I guess we're working together."

"Yep, and just a warning: This RISE member you told me about—the female, whoever she is—could be very dangerous. Extremist groups like RISE take advantage of the hurt and the weak. They catch them at the right time—when they're emotionally vulnerable, when they're down and out—and then offer them a place, a home, a family, a *mission*. That's how they earn their victims' allegiance.

"I'm simply suggesting she might be radicalized to the point where she can't comprehend that RISE, however well-intentioned they are, is detrimental to her, immigrants, and the Commonwealth. I'm not saying it's her fault. Our exclusionary society breeds extremist activist organizations like RISE and makes marginalized immigrants susceptible to radicalization."

Randy stood up for RISE, saying, "Yeah, but all in all, RISE just believes they're doing the right thing, the necessary thing. They don't see themselves as *radicalizing* anyone, just enlisting people who are willing to fight for equality and *want* to."

"No matter how just or right they think they are, *they're not.*"

Arson cautioned his son, adding, "Be careful around this girl."

"Let me worry about her."

"Alright, fine. I'll be in touch, Son." The screen went blank.

Election fraud? Blackmail? All for immigrant and colony equality, huh? Akane was a Guardian moonlighting as a RISE member, and Sam and Jay were partners in crime, was that it? *What have you gotten yourself into, Akane?*

• • •

Damien waited for Stacie at a two-person table shaded by a wide umbrella.

She approached in a red top that clung to her braless breasts, its low neckline drawing attention to her décolletage. Perfectly fitted jeans and red heels completed the outfit.

As she swayed her denim-clad hips, she slipped into character —old Stacie.

Damien questioned her intentions. Was she really interested in him or more so the information he could provide her? He thought about what Paul had said. Was this some sort of subterfuge?

Damien might've been head over heels for her, but he wasn't a dimwit. If Stacie was putting on a charade, who was she working for? The CDF, her former employer?

Every step Stacie took projected confidence and sexual prowess. Reaching the table, she sat down in the chair facing Damien and hooked a leg over a knee. "How's the shoulder?"

"Fine."

"So, tell me more about RISE," Stacie said, sounding enthusiastic.

"Why do you want to know more about RISE?" Damien's voice carried an undercurrent of distrust.

Stacie gave him the answer she had prepared. "I was a sergeant in the CDF. I fought a war to defend our republic from the

Coalition. The Coalition killed my parents. Now Coalition-lite has taken aim at me—*me*, the daughter of Patrick and Darlene Spencer. I need to know as much as I can about these people to defend myself.

"They were after you, you say, but it certainly didn't matter to them that I was in the crossfire, and they may come after me next. I need to protect Spencer Enterprises. I need to make these people pay. It'd be blasphemy for me to let them get away with nearly killing me.

"My mom and dad taught me that no one, and I mean no one, fucks with the Spencer family. They made sure that anyone who did never did again, gave them the scare of their life. So quit playing, Damien. Tell me about RISE. Trust is the foundation for all personal relationships. You want me to trust you, right? How else can we . . . take things further?"

Damien went back and forth with himself, unsure if he should believe her answer. "Well said, my dear. I understand your concern about these people, and as you said, we must trust each other." Maybe she was being sincere, he thought. "What I know is that three people lead RISE: Tristan Gelano, Franco DeFalco, and Julian Hurst. They are RISE's council.

"They're headquartered somewhere in Colony Four, I believe. They do well at keeping their whereabouts undisclosed. I've got people working to pinpoint their location. The gun-toting ruffians who attacked my estate were solutioners, RISE's Strike Team.

"RISE must have a base here on Eden, a place where they run their vigilante operations."

Stacie said, "So this council runs things from Satellite One, and their lackeys on Eden carry out their orders."

"Yes. I will find RISE's Eden base and make them pay for their assault on my estate. You better believe it."

"These Purists, you know more about them than you've been letting on. Spill it. Are you affiliated with them?" Stacie hoped that, at last, she would get some answers, her earrings capturing every word. "I want to trust you, Damien, but you have to let me in."

Damien lounged back in his chair, thinking. "Okay. I'll give you your answers tomorrow tonight. You'll be joining me to watch the election results come in. I'll tell you more then."

"Where are we going?"

"You'll find out tomorrow night. Like you said, trust is the foundation of all relationships. You trust me, don't you?"

"Yes, Damien, I do." *Never in a trillion years.*

"Well, let's just leave it at that for now and enjoy ourselves, shall we?"

"Fine by me." At least she had more information on RISE she could report to Conlan in the meantime. Defense Force Intelligence was a powerful entity. They were better equipped to locate this council than Damien. The CDF had jurisdiction on Satellite One that he didn't have and could go anywhere. They could even lock down entire sectors while searching for this council, this supposed threat to Commonwealth law and order.

Stacie flagged down a server golem to place her order. After it logged her meal and moved on, she asked Damien, "Did the authorities have any luck identifying any of the solutioners?"

"No. All those solutioners hid behind masks, and the event floor was too contaminated to extract DNA from any who might have bled. But the authorities weren't aware of the skirmish on the roof, nor did I inform them about it." He preferred that he and his Purist legion take care of RISE. "My forensics specialist extracted DNA from the blood of the one I shot." The memory of his bullet striking Jay flashed in his mind, and he smirked. "Paul Shaffer has a connection inside law enforcement who will get him a match. Once they do, I'll wring the location of RISE's base out of that solutioner."

"Vengeance is a dish best served cold, they say," Stacie said.

"Indeed."

• • •

THE NEXT DAY

Colony Four

Mid-morning, Sergei and Arson were in a two-door flatbed cargo truck, traveling an unpaved, uneven road. Through the truck's windows, they saw Guardians—mobilized by CDF Command due to Conlan's intel from Stacie—questioning pedestrians, shopkeepers, and outdoor vendors.

Sergei struggled to steady the racing thoughts clawing at his focus. The CDF had deployed an army of Guardians to the colony, and word was that they were asking about Tristan Gelano, Franco DeFalco, and Julian Hurst. Somehow the CDF had gotten tipped off about RISE's council, about the *entire* organization. Now they were in hunting mode.

The CDF was committed to eliminating domestic threats to the Commonwealth, and RISE had made the list, after attacking CDF service members, government officials, scientists, and business leaders at Damien's fundraiser.

Throngs of Guardians in black-and-gray camo, swarming the street, gave Sergei flashbacks of military rule. *Damn, who could've told them about the council?*

Perturbed colony citizens watched as Guardians spilled out of BUSs and flooded their zone, reminding them of a time of raids and arrests, reawakening old mental wounds.

Arson hung his head out the open window and glanced at the side mirror, conducting another routine check for tails as the truck rumbled past firebombed buildings—ruins of the Three-Week War. A handful of vehicles traveled the same pitted road.

"Anyone following us?" Sergei asked as the truck went under a crumbling overpass.

"I don't think so." Arson wondered how the CDF had gotten wind of RISE. It was ironic that the CDF and he were trying to track down the council at the same time, but it seemed he'd get to them first.

Deserted shops, now dwellings for squatters, lined a Disaster Area, their signs cracked, windows shattered, and interiors looted by desperate souls. Bomb craters, felled trees, and mounds of rubble filled the strip of land.

As the truck left the Disaster Area, Arson shook his head. *Thank goodness we've got Oviereya in office working on restoration.* Jared Kerner didn't do much of anything.

The drive lasted twenty-five more minutes before Arson and Sergei arrived at an Assistance Living Center.

The council's here? Arson thought.

"Come," Sergei said, getting out of the truck.

A female service worker in a gray tracksuit leaned against a cistern tank, a cigarette dangling from her lips. Early forties. Wild dark orange hair. Cerulean eyes. Willowy frame. Thin face.

"Alexandria!" Sergei called out joyfully.

The woman took the cigarette between two fingers and pulled it from her lips, exhaling a plume of smoke into the air. "Sergei, what're you doin' here?" she asked, her drawl pronounced. "It's not your usual day."

"I know." Big and strong, he wrapped her in a crushing hug and then released her.

"What's with all these dang Guardians trawlin' around our colony?"

"They suspect something. What exactly, I don't know."

"Do you think they found out about RISE?"

"That's my hypothesis. But I have a meeting with the council. And I brought a guest."

Alexandria took a good look at the man with Sergei. "Oh, man, Arson Scott."

Arson shook her hand. "A friend of Sergei's, I assume."

"Yeah, he and I go way back." She flicked the cigarette onto the ground and crushed it under her heel. "Come on in."

All three headed into the center.

"Sergei!" shouted a seven-year-old boy.

Sergei patted him on the head. "Good to see you too, Lynx. Now go play."

The orphaned boy ran outside.

Alexandria said, "Hopefully, these kids will have a proper home and parents again soon."

"Oviereya's going to make that happen," Arson assured her.

"If she's in office long enough," Alexandria added.

Sergei didn't want to waste another second on chitchat. "Follow me, Arson. The council awaits."

They left Alexandria behind.

Sergei led Arson into the center's refectory. They arrived at a set of stairs that descended into a basement storage room filled with wooden crates, well-stocked shelves of supplies and nonperishable food, two dormant emergency power generators, a pegboard of tools, and miscellaneous equipment.

Motion-sensor lights buzzed on as Sergei and Arson reached the bottom of the stairs.

Sergei flipped open the housing of a wall-mounted access panel and yanked a lever downward. A hidden entrance rumbled open. "Beyond here is RISE's Satellite One operations hub."

Arson stepped in behind Sergei. The door shut. How clever of the council to use an Assistance Living Center as a front for their operations hub after martial law was declared. Assistance Living Centers had been designated safety zones, off-limits from Guardian search and seizure unless the CDF had direct evidence of insurgent activity. That had been Jared Kerner's mandate. At least the man had some kind of value system.

Inside the operations hub, machines and computers hummed. Men and women sat at various workstations and in cubicles, staying in contact with RISE's Eden headquarters.

So, this is the council's safe house, Arson thought.

A woman—late forties, asymmetrical haircut, black shirt and tawny corduroy pants—was speaking with a technician, her expression serious. But when she noticed Sergei and Arson, her demeanor shifted. "You've arrived," she said, facing them. Leaving the technician, she walked over, her smile bright. "So good to see you, Arson."

Arson nodded. "You as well, Tristan." They hugged. "I was told there are three of you."

"My colleagues are not here. They're out with family. Those quarries, though . . . *whew* . . . they nearly killed us. I was happy for you when you obtained Eden citizenship and left with Kathleen. I knew you'd become something special."

"Thank you." Arson wished Tristan weren't involved in RISE. She was such a good person. Maybe he could convince her and the rest of the council to change.

"So, Sergei has told you about RISE and the work we do," Tristan said.

"Yeah."

"What do you think? Will you join us, even if just as a consultant? Your expertise would be greatly valued."

"Tristan, I don't know. Interfering in the free election process? I'm sure RISE does a lot of good, but you have to do it clean."

Tristan wasn't fond of breaking the law, but she believed it had to be done. "I wish we could. But reformists have only a slim chance of winning elections. Voters who support the oppressors outnumber colonists and immigrants. Society has conditioned their minds to fear change, and the natural response to change you fear is to fight it, just like the natural response to inequality.

"Outvoted, we'll never get the reform we need in our republic's government by playing fair. That means we have no choice but to play dirty, but we're doing it for the right reasons. RISE will stop tampering with elections once things are made better, made right.

"Purists. Anti-reformist politicians. Spin doctors. Pundits. They are all against us, Arson. We must prevail against overwhelming odds, and we need to use unfavorable methods to do so."

Arson's lips tightened.

A small warning chime sounded.

"What's that? What's going on?" Arson asked, dropping the conversation.

A man at a monitor replied, "Alarms have been triggered. Guardians are in the building."

Sergei stepped onto the operations dais and went to the man's side. He planted his palms on the computer panel and leaned over the soundless, grainy black-and-white feed on the monitor. Cameras showed a dozen Guardians. Alexandria was engaged in a heated exchange with one of them, a female Guardian who appeared to be in charge.

The shouting match between Alexandria and the Guardian in

charge (GIC) intensified.

Alexandria made a move for something in her pocket. A weapon? Maybe. The GIC ordered her to keep her hands visible. She didn't comply. A male Guardian reacted, taking no chances. His weapon discharged. Blood doused the floor. Alexandria fell down, alive but bleeding from the leg. In a fit of anger, two service workers jumped the Guardian who shot her. Chaos ensued as a fight broke out between Guardians and service workers.

Bellicose Guardians tased their attackers with shock batons, subduing them and trying to prevent the situation from escalating further. For now, they were holding back from using lethal force.

The GIC fired two shots into the ceiling with her rifle to defuse the situation. Everyone froze. Then she shouted something. A frightened young man raised his arms and mouthed a response. The GIC and two lower-enlisted male Guardians followed him out of the room, while the rest stayed behind to secure the area and tend to Alexandria. The fight was over, with no casualties.

Sergei looked up from the monitor. "I think he's taking them here."

The technician at the computer panel clicked over to another feed, hallway camera four. Onscreen, the young man—held at gunpoint—was leading the three Guardians forward.

"Quickly, initiate deletion protocol," Tristan ordered.

Technicians' fingers flew across keyboards. Numbers, letters, and symbols flickered rapidly on monitors as machinery whirred and beeped.

The hidden entrance door slid open. The three Guardians entered, marching the young man into the room.

His face bore the weight of remorse, and his shoulders slumped in shame. He was disappointed in himself for giving in to fear and leading the Guardians to the council's safe house.

"It's okay, Chris," Tristan said.

"No one move!" the GIC shouted. Everyone raised their hands. "I'm Sergeant First Class Ryleigh MacRae." She recognized Tristan's face from the reference picture that had been provided. "You, identify yourself."

Tristan replied calmly, despite the tension of the moment. "My name is Tristan Gelano."

"You're coming with us for questioning," Ryleigh told her.

Tristan whispered to Arson and Sergei, who stood behind her, "Don't worry. I seriously doubt they have anything incriminating on me, and all evidence of RISE has just been wiped. Once I'm released from CDF custody, I'll contact the rest of the council, and we'll reach out to both of you."

Ryleigh's rifle clacked as she leveled it at Tristan. "Hey, no talking. Get over here, now!"

Tristan moved forward. One of the lower-enlisted Guardians grabbed her bicep and took her away.

Contempt saturated Ryleigh's expression as she confronted Arson. "Arson Scott. It doesn't surprise me you're involved in this somehow. Once a traitor, always a traitor."

"Involved in what? Volunteering at an Assistance Living Center?" Arson said, feigning innocence.

Ryleigh chuckled. "I doubt this secret room full of high-end tech is part of normal center operations. Now all of you, move. And don't try anything stupid."

She and her subordinate marched the group through the hidden entrance, ready to open fire if anyone resisted.

Once upstairs, Ryleigh ordered Tristan to sit on a stool. She obeyed. Ryleigh pulled up a stool of her own and began to browbeat Tristan with pointed questions and accusations, to intimidate her into confessing her involvement in RISE.

At this point, all the CDF had on RISE were the unfounded claims Damien Sykes had shared with Stacie, which was that Tristan Gelano, Franco DeFalco, and Julian Hurst had set up a shadow vigilante organization on Eden and were leading it from Satellite One. That wouldn't be enough to detain Tristan for long.

Ryleigh continued grilling Tristan, but Tristan didn't let the pressure loosen her tongue. She denied any connection to RISE.

Arson stood silently in a corner, waiting for his interrogation to start. The CDF getting this close, despite having no solid evidence, meant Defense Force Intelligence was on their game, he thought. He didn't think he'd have to this soon, but it was time for him to call in backup. He'd bring Conlan into the loop, updating him on what he and Randy had uncovered about RISE.

As Arson waited for Ryleigh to finish with Tristan, he wondered how Randy was doing on his end.

• • •

Randy's thoughts were on his dad as he walked from his parked sports cruiser toward Akane's dome-shaped home. Arson had missed their scheduled check-in, but he was a tough son of a gun, a war hero and former Defense Force captain. Arson could take care of himself.

Randy paused at Akane's door for a long, contemplative moment. He was fed up with the prevarication from her, Sam, and Jay—their half-truths and cryptic answers. He was tired of only getting bits and pieces of information about RISE, only what *they* wanted him to know.

His brow furrowed as he recalled what Sergei had told Arson about RISE's unlawful social-justice tactics.

Randy was supposed to keep playing along, maintain RISE's trust, and gather intel about their plans for the upcoming elections.

But like he'd told his dad, "superspy" wasn't part of Guardian training. He just wanted straight answers. He wanted Akane to be forthcoming with him.

No, he wouldn't bungle the mission; he had more sense than that. But getting deeper into RISE didn't mean he had to be indirect with Akane. Avoidance wasn't his style.

He'd demand real answers from Akane, and then he'd go on temporizing, pretending he was still feeling RISE out. In reality, they never stood a chance of recruiting him.

Randy—steamed—pounded on Akane's door unannounced. Questions about RISE had been nagging him, testing his self-control.

After checking the external viewer, Akane slid the door partially open. She wore an oversized T-shirt, its wide, drooping neckline half-exposing her shoulders. Her freshly shampooed hair was wet and uncombed. She'd just rushed out of the shower. "Randy, what the fuck, man? I thought it was the cops or something."

Astute as usual, Randy eyed the bandage on her shoulder. He was sure that injury was from the attack on Damien's estate. He felt deceived.

"How'd you get that injury?" he accosted Akane, his emotions getting the better of him.

"How'd you get those lousy manners?" Akane slammed the door in his face.

Randy knocked loudly three times. He continued to falter in his choice of words, still coming off way too abrasive. "Akane, open up! I'm serious here!"

Akane cracked the door and poked her head out. "War hero or not, that's not a hall pass to just show up at my doorstep unannounced. My mom taught me that's rude," she said, cranky.

"Yeah, dumb move. I'm sorry," Randy apologized.

The door banged shut again.

He knocked gently. This time he spoke without the pushiness. "Hey, can I come in? I just want to talk."

From behind the door, Akane replied, "*Uhhhh*, well, you're just gonna have to wait outside until I'm dressed."

"How long will that be?"

"You'll have to wait there and see. Oh, well."

Damn it, Randy thought. He needed to calm down and get his emotions in check. He didn't have to be passive while trying to get answers from Akane, but he couldn't be quick to temper either. Nobody wanted to talk to a hothead.

He readjusted his attitude, practicing emotional discipline.

After circling in place for an extended period, he heard the door open. Akane slouched against the frame, her right elbow resting on the paneling, her left hand on her hip. Her hair was still uncombed, but she was fully dressed this time, wearing a different shirt and baggy cargo shorts that sat low on her hips. "Come on in, and don't bring any bad mojo with you."

"Thanks. Sorry for showing up unannounced." Randy stepped into Akane's tidy abode. With the scent of burning incense permeating the air, he immediately felt a sense of zen.

The ultramodern design of the house featured walls made of phyroplastek, some of which had containment alcoves. At the center of the space was a communal area, elevated on a circular step-up dais. Within this area were an Oriental-style love seat, two armchairs, and a coffee table positioned beneath a chandelier. A mini-gym, enclosed by plexiglass, contained weight equipment and a punching bag. In the left corner of the house, next to the arched window, there was a bed that could be lowered into the floor. A standard kitchenette with a four-person dining table completed the setup.

Randy's eyes explored the cozy space. *Nice.*

Akane pointed at the shoe rack. "Leave your kicks at the door."

Randy took off his sneakers and set them down on the rack. "So, what happened to your shoulder?"

"You a detective now?" Akane said, visibly annoyed. "Since you're dying to know: I fell hover-boarding." Randy didn't believe her. "Don't worry, no one's ever died from a minor bruise."

They walked farther inside.

"Incoming stream from parents," the home's virtual assistant alerted Akane.

"Put them on holoscreen." A rectangular holoscreen expanded beside Akane in midair. "[Mom, Dad, how's it going?]" A smile blossomed on her face.

"[We are just calling to check up on you,]" Akari said.

Benjiro followed with, "[Yes, how have you been?]"

"[I'm good, guys,]" Akane replied. "[Just been busy *taking down* bad guys across the universe.]" She struck the air with a punch-kick combo. "[*Hi-yah!*]" Her parents laughed. "[Hey, I promise to call you back. I have company.]"

"[Well, we don't want to interrupt, then,]" Benjiro remarked.

"[See you later. Love you.]"

Akane ordered her virtual assistant to end the stream, and the holoscreen disappeared.

She sat on the love seat and crisscrossed her ankles.

Randy lowered himself beside her. "When's the last time you saw them in person?"

"Since I first left Satellite One. During the Three-Week War, net connectivity and long-range comms got disrupted in my home sector. For the longest time, my parents had to travel outside the sector to get a signal to me. Since Oviereya took office, the communications grid has been fully restored."

"How'd they take you joining the CDF?"

"It scared them at first. Mom especially freaked out. It took her a while to come around, but she did. They both support my decision now, especially with the credits I send home."

Randy heard a meow and tilted his head downward. "A cat?"

"Yeah, genetically engineered to mimic the real deal. Her name's Bubbles."

The cat rubbed against Randy's leg. He leaned over and patted its gray pelt.

Akane said, "Do you ever wonder what happened to all the animal lifeforms we left on Earth during the exodus? Maybe they're all like . . . mutants now or something."

That made Randy laugh, but his expression quickly turned serious. He remembered why he was there: to get answers about RISE.

Akane got up. "Let's move over to the kitchen." They took seats at the dining table. "Sushi? Made it myself."

"Never had it."

"There's a first time for everything."

Randy popped sushi into his mouth. *There's no need to wait. Just get down to it.* After chewing and swallowing, he said, "I'm not going to play games. I'm just gonna get to the point. My dad got in touch with a Coalition buddy of his, who told him what RISE does. He said their tactics aren't always lawful, even though they're for good causes."

This was unexpected for Akane, Randy learning this much about RISE without *her* telling him. But she stayed relaxed. "Does that bother you?" she asked, chewing on sushi.

"It does. I'm a Guardian, and righteousness is what we're supposed to stand for. I need you to come clean with me, Akane.

No half-truths. None of this shifty bullshit. It was RISE who attacked Damien's estate to kill him, wasn't it?"

"Is that what your dad told you?" Akane asked coolly.

"No, that's my hypothesis. Now tell me, Has RISE played judge, jury, and executioner for other people they deem bad guys? What other unethical actions have you guys taken in the name of equality?"

Akane wanted to bring Randy into the fold, like Simone brought her in. She was supposed to ease him into the organization, guide him slowly day by day, like Sam and Jay did for her. She had thought Randal Scott—one of the liberators of the colonies, a former Coalition fighter, the son of Arson Scott— would surely be on board with joining RISE.

Her hopes had been high. She had thought that Randy just needed to learn about all the good RISE was doing for immigrants, for *his* people, and then he'd surely want to be involved in such an impactful social-activist organization.

Maybe she *had* let her affections blind her. The vetting process was supposed to weed out prospects who weren't compatible with RISE. Had Randy failed the test?

Maybe his values were just too uncompromisable for him to be down with RISE's tactics. But then again, maybe he just needed some more persuading for his thinking to be converted to "the RISE mindset."

"Finish your meal," Akane said after a long, thoughtful pause. "Then we're headed out."

Randy's brows quirked. "What? Where are you taking me?"

"Leefside Grove, a town in Precinct Twelve. Before you go casting judgment on RISE's ethics, you need to get the full picture. Plus, I volunteered to be a voter-station watchguard today, at the east Leefside voting station. I could use the company, and depending on how crazy these Purists get, I might need some backup too. So heads up, it's gonna be a long day."

Randy would use the time to talk some sense into her. "Okay, fine." *Whatever it is you're gonna show me, Akane, doesn't mean my mind's gonna change about RISE. Wrong is wrong. Period.*

As Akane shoved down another bite of sushi, Randy took notice of the framed photo atop a table. In the picture, Akane had her arm around another young woman, who was blond, bright-eyed, and full of health and cheer. Both were flashing their pearly whites. Randy could tell they were close. "Who's she? If you don't mind me asking."

Akane washed down the sushi with tea. She squeezed her eyes shut, attempting to ward off grief's clutches. "Her name was Skylar Grace. She was my friend, one of the three lottery beneficiaries I made the journey to Eden with."

She laughed at her old more pessimistic self. "Skylar got on my damn nerves at first, but she grew on me. We became good friends." Her voice cracked, throat constricting. "She was beautiful, inside and out." A lone tear drizzled down her cheek.

Randy bit his lip, staring into her sad eyes, eyes that held a story of pain.

Akane cleared her throat. "She loved Mercedes Gardner and wanted to be a singer just like her. She had big dreams, man, like all of us immigrants." She rubbed her eyes and swallowed, battling the torturous ache in her heart. "But she's dead."

"What happened?"

"Marginalization. Harassment. Bullying. That's what happened. There were even a couple of Highborn at her workplace who kept messing with her. One of them, a man, got too bold. He started physically messing with her. Management didn't do jack. To them, Skylar was just an immigrant bitch overreacting and trying to make trouble, trying to garner sympathy."

Akane's next words came out like broken glass. "She couldn't take all the unfair treatment that society had dumped on her. So she threw herself off a building."

Damn. The sentiment on Randy's face was one of remorse. "I'm . . . sorry, Akane," he bemoaned.

Her harrowing tale went on. "Another of my day ones, Desmond, enlisted the same time I did. We went to BCT together. I made it; he didn't. A drill sergeant was berating the Coalition, berating the colony revolution. Desmond wasn't the type to withhold his opinions. He challenged the drill sergeant. For that, for being an 'Independent Movement sympathizer,' he was dishonorably discharged with a bullet to the head."

Randy cringed, gritting his teeth. *Geez.*

Akane wasn't done. "After that, someone killed my best friend, my kindred spirit, Simone." Admiration for her bestie filled her. "She was the baddest bitch I knew. No doubt her murderer was Paul Shaffer, her own comrade and a Purist bigot. Loss after loss, I had to battle depression. I had up days and down days."

Randy shifted in his chair, his body language hinting at his discomfort with all of Akane's losses.

"Jay and Sam introduced me to RISE." Akane owed the organization more than she could easily express. "There, I found a safe place for immigrants, a place where I didn't have to worry about being degraded or demeaned, and I found family. RISE saved me, Randy. If it weren't for them, I might've given up on life, like Skylar."

Randy rested his chin between his thumb and index finger and quietly processed Akane's life story. He didn't know what to say.

Akane said, "So, when you go accusing RISE of wrongdoing, think about all the good they've done. That includes saving my life and the lives of other immigrants.

"When we get to Leefside, you'll get a good sample of the impact RISE has had on the immigrant community of Eden. Then you can make your judgment." She stood, walked to one of the wall alcoves, and grabbed two pistols. Then she offered one of the pistols to Randy. "Here. These are dangerous times. You might need it."

After the assault outside the club, Randy would've been a fool not to accept the weapon. He got up from the table and took it.

Akane put on some shoes and went to the door. "Shall we?"

Randy retrieved his shoes from the rack. "Let's go."

• • •

In Akane's convertible, Randy and Akane cruised Leefside Grove —a rustic town in every sense.

The car passed supermarkets, shops, clothing outlets, and strip malls.

A sign in front of a building under construction read: EARTH ERA MUSEUM COMING SOON TO LEEFSIDE.

Akane turned onto another street. "As you know, most of the government municipalities of region states are anti-reformist. RISE has played a major role in helping immigrants gain an economic foothold here in Leefside. Many of the establishments you're seeing now are owned by immigrants. The oppressors used to own them, but over the past few years, immigrants have bought them out. You know how that happened? RISE."

"How'd RISE get the funds?" A note of accusation crept into Randy's tone. "Did they steal it from the government?"

"Yeah," Akane admitted. "And RISE also got some endowments and did fundraising too."

They drove into a suburban community where subdivisions sprawled for miles.

Children played joyfully on brilliant green lawns.

Akane said, "This is an immigrant community, and a lot of the First live here."

"First? You're referring to the first immigrants, right?"

"Yeah." Akane pulled over and parked beside a row of nice homes. She opened her door and stepped out. "Come on, we're taking a little walk."

Randy got out and followed.

Akane strolled forward on the sidewalk. "Mr. and Mrs. Feller live in that house over there." She pointed to a single-floor brick home that had a square patio. "They're immigrants."

A seven-year-old boy played in the front yard. Once he saw Akane, he ran onto the sidewalk, beaming. "What are you doing here, Akane?"

Akane stooped and wrapped him in a hug. "Just passing through, Ryan. Go play now." The boy darted back to the lawn. Akane said to Randy, "Funny how AEGIS's 'chosen ones' don't consider immigrant children Highborn." They were often referred to as Lowborn, another slur like "nadir." "Ryan was on the brink of death three months ago. His family couldn't afford the heart mods to save him. You know who paid for them? RISE."

The thought of parents nearly burying their child stirred something deep inside Randy. *So young to be on death's doorstep.*

Akane said, "RISE raised money and redirected some funds from our government oppressors. Better that money help immigrants live than pay for military proliferation or wasteful government programs."

Randy kept his thoughts to himself, disagreeing with RISE's actions but choosing not to dispute Akane.

"There's a family about three blocks from here," Akane went on. "They were attacked by some immigrant-hating Highborn who

227

claimed the beatdown was self-defense.

"RISE covered their legal fees, and the attackers got what they deserved, jail time. Not as much time as an immigrant would've gotten if the roles had been reversed, but still a win." She pointed down the street, at a grayish octagonal building. "That foundry used to be owned by a nonimmigrant. Now it belongs to a young immigrant entrepreneur. RISE helped him buy out the previous owner. Immigrant hiring at that foundry has gone up since then.

"RISE is deeply involved in the prosperity of immigrant communities all over Eden, not just this one. If RISE didn't exist, the immigrants of Leefside, and other towns like it in this province, wouldn't have had all the success they've had.

"If it weren't for us, a child would've died, and assaulters would've gotten away with their crime. RISE even ran voter registration drives to help Amaechi win her seat in the Parliament, back when many immigrants thought voting was useless, thought their vote wouldn't make a difference.

"Do you see now, Randy? Do you see why RISE is necessary?" She hoped for a shift in his perspective.

Randy remained silent, dissecting everything Akane had said and shown him. RISE had done so much good. But at the same time, RISE had committed illegal acts—crimes.

Akane continued advocating for RISE's existence. "There are millions of immigrants on Eden, and I'd say about eighty percent have never received their genetic metamorphosis or a cerebral implant, and not by choice. That's the government barring them from neohuman conversion. And the excuses are always the same: a lack of funding, CDF enlistees come first, a program is in the works to make it happen. *Blah, blah, blah.*"

Something happened to Akane's voice—a rush of sympathy entered it. "Immigrants who go underground to get enhancements become vulnerable to fraudulent black-market dealers. A lot of bootleg cerebral mods are hazardous to their health. People end up damaging their brains or getting stuck with mods that offer inadequate Linking capabilities.

"Immigrants just want what's theirs. They want to be part of the New Humanity. Who knows, maybe the discrimination regarding genetic metamorphosis will finally change with Amaechi in office. That'd be thanks to you Coalition fighters."

Randy appeared torn. Akane had exposed him to an uglier side of Eden, a side RISE was fighting to change. Even so, some of the tactics used to achieve that change were still wrong.

"What's on your mind, Randy? What are you thinking right now?" Akane asked after the silence stretched too long.

"To tell you the truth, I don't know what to think at the moment," Randy answered evenly.

"That's fine. No pressure." Akane knew arm-twisting wouldn't get him to join RISE. "Come on, I've gotta get to the voting station. RISE already has two guys there, Hank and Vaughn. I'm joining them. It's just a ten-minute drive from here."

Randy and Akane headed back to the convertible.

The car breezed past more homes on the way to Leefside's east voting station.

On the local net radio, a female broadcaster said, "This just in: A young immigrant man, early twenties, was found bludgeoned in an alleyway. He's being transported to a hospital in critical condition. It's believed he was the victim of what appears to be increasing violence against immigrants on this election day."

"That's exactly why RISE members are out in Leefside today, to keep people safe," Akane commented.

"Keeping people safe is the authorities' responsibility," Randy said as Akane lowered the radio's volume.

"Well, from what I just heard, they're not doing a bang-up job. Sounds like they could use a little help."

A black van traveling in the opposite lane honked a hello, and Akane waved.

Randy knew his intuition was right, but he sought confirmation from Akane. "RISE?"

"Yeah. We've got teams patrolling Leefside neighborhoods to protect immigrants, and volunteers like me pulling security at voting stations that need it. Think of us as . . . neighborhood guard dogs today."

There was a burning question on Randy's mind, one he'd been avoiding. He tossed hesitation to the wind and spoke. "Tell me, Akane, have you killed for RISE?"

Akane's silence was all the confirmation Randy needed. She was trying to conceal the truth behind a veneer of stoicism.

"Akane, tell me the truth," Randy pressed. "Don't bullshit me."

Randy had already learned more about RISE than he was supposed to at this stage of vetting. Akane concluded there was no need to tiptoe around the truth. "Yeah," she admitted. "I got even with the uppity Highborn bastard who was sexually harassing Skylar."

Randy's face conveyed everything—he rejected her revenge killing. "Vigilante justice? That's okay with you?"

Akane's features set. "That asshole had been having his merry way with her. Come on, are you gonna feel sorry for a piece of shit?"

Randy, opposed to vigilantism, didn't answer, restraining his anger. Then, after a beat, he said, "Since you suspect Shaffer killed Simone, are you planning to murder him too, like you did Skylar's harasser?" He fought the urge to shout. He was aching to grab Akane and shake some sense into her.

Akane stayed focused on the road, enjoying the feel of the wind ruffling her hair. She replied, "As soon as Sam gives me the green light, you betcha." Her admission was rife with satisfaction. She didn't have a second thought about killing Paul.

Randy suppressed a grunt and shook his head. If Paul was a murderer, and it wouldn't surprise Randy if he was, it was still wrong to kill him. Paul, who'd thrown numerous verbal jabs, was no friend of his. But the law was the law.

Randy understood the soul-searing craving for vengeance, though. Not too long ago, he'd wanted to eliminate his father. However, the law had deemed his father a terrorist at the time.

He had to talk Akane out of killing Paul and get her out of RISE.

Speaking of his father—he still couldn't reach him. Had something happened at the council headquarters, where his friend Sergei had taken him? *Dad, I hope you're alright.*

• • •

Arson Scott sat on the bench of a detention cell inside a BUS parked outside the raided Assistance Living Center. He'd survived a round of intense questioning by Ryleigh MacRae and was waiting to make his one courtesy call, to contact Conlan.

He heard the cell door click open, and Ryleigh stomped in.

She shoved a tablet at him. "Here, make your call."

Arson snatched the tablet from her hand, giving her the same unpleasant attitude. "Thanks."

She jerked her chin up and crossed her arms over her chest.

Arson poked at the tablet's touchscreen, and Conlan's image wobbled into view.

"Arson?" Conlan said.

Surprise registered on Ryleigh's face when she heard Conlan's voice. Arson had a direct line to the Chief of Defense Force

Intelligence?

"Hey, old friend, I'm in a bit of a snag," Arson said. "The CDF's after RISE, I assume. And I'm also assuming, as Chief of Defense Force Intelligence, you know what RISE is *and* know about the raid that just happened."

"How do you know about RISE, and where are you?" Conlan asked.

"I was at the raided safe house of RISE's council. I'm currently being detained inside a cell in a BUS." Arson angled the tablet's front-facing camera so that Conlan could see Ryleigh. "Before we talk any further, just so you know, we've got company."

"Give us thirty minutes alone," Conlan ordered Ryleigh. "When we're done, release him."

She stumbled over her words, flabbergasted. "Y-yes, Sir." She exited the cell, giving them privacy.

Conlan said, "Now that it's just you and me, let's talk."

• • •

Randy and Akane arrived at the voting station, located in another predominantly immigrant community in Leefside, and got out of the car. Simply dressed townspeople trickled in and out.

A light-complexioned woman with chin-length flaxen hair called out Akane's name, delighted to see her. She was thinly built and wore a shirt, blue jeans, a denim vest, and boots.

Akane said to Randy, "This is Johanna Wright. She's a RISE supporter and a friend of mine. She's the voter administrator for this station. It was Simone who introduced us." She winced, haunted again by the mental image of Simone's lifeless body lying in the grass.

"Yeah, Simone was a sweetheart," Johanna said. "Man, the three of us had some good times." She squeezed Akane's shoulder. "I know you miss her, kiddo. I do too."

"You and I aren't the only ones. She touched a lot of lives."

"Yes, she did."

"Hank and Vaughn are inside already, right?" Akane asked, changing the subject.

"Yeah, and I'm glad they're here. They've already chased off two shady characters today." Johanna made a face. "I heard on net radio that a man was bludgeoned in an alleyway. Something's really gotten the crazies riled up today."

Akane knew that was because of Quinn's directive, his call to action. "Don't worry, we'll keep this center safe."

Johanna pressed a hand over her heart in gratitude. "Yes, thank goodness for RISE." She craned her head toward Randy. "It's good to meet you, Randal Scott."

Randy nodded. "Likewise. Are you an immigrant as well?"

"No, I was born right here on Eden." She took both of Randy's hands in hers. "But I'm a woman of faith. God wants all His people to prosper in this star nation He's blessed us with, despite our vices, which led to the annihilation of humanity's birthplace."

Suddenly, the loudening growl of an engine startled them. A customized van, built like a tank and nearly twice the size of a standard van, was on a collision course with *them*. Military-grade armor encased its body, and it had massive steamroller wheels.

In a spasm of panic, Akane drew the handgun tucked between her belt and pants. "What in the ever-loving fuck?" Impulse screamed at her to take out the driver. The gun kicked in her hand as she fired at the windshield. Each bullet struck and ricocheted off the bulletproof glass. With the pedal to the metal, the driver increased the van's speed, intent on running her over.

Fear rendered Akane immobile.

"Akane, what the fuck are you waiting for? Move!" Randy shouted as he darted out of the way.

Akane unfroze and hurled herself out of the van's path, rolling across the ground. Johanna dodged left and ran, the van narrowly missing her.

The driver jerked the steering wheel right and slammed the brakes. The van's wheels screeched as it swerved in a semicircle, the driver coming for Johanna. There was blood rage in his eyes; he was hellbent on turning her into roadkill.

Terrified, Johanna moved her legs faster.

"Johanna!" Akane screamed.

The driver stomped the gas, and the van crushed Johanna, her bones crunching and blood gushing out from underneath the steamroller wheels. She was this maniac's first victim of the day, and he wouldn't stop with her.

Akane shrieked, "No!" Seeing Johanna get mushed numbed her to the core.

The driver veered off in a new direction.

Randy grimaced, uncertain what this lunatic would do next.

Out for immigrant blood, the driver floored the gas pedal, crashing the van through the station's doors.

Voters screamed and scattered.

The driver braked hard, bringing the van to a screeching halt. Then he climbed out, a deadly automatic weapon in his hands.

Akane shakily rose to her feet. Her elbows and forearms were chafed, her shirt had been dirtied, and her eyes were wet with grief. "Johanna!" she cried, still reeling from the death of her friend.

Machine-gun fire roared from inside the station. Sharp pops from handguns followed, Hank and Vaughn shooting back at the attacker. They were in a desperate fight to protect innocent voters —immigrant voters.

Randy snatched his gun from his belt. "I'm going in! You stay put! Wait for the authorities!"

"But those are immigrants in there, my people. I can't—"

"Just stay here, Akane!" Randy knew she was too shaken to be of any help.

He dashed through the opening the van had made. The station's now-twisted metal doors lay on the floor, and rebar protruded from the damaged wall. He sprinted right up next to the van, which appeared almost unscathed due to its military-grade armor.

Damn, he'd entered a gory nightmare—bullet-riddled bodies lying on the floor, human viscera strewn everywhere. The sight was brutal to bear, even for a soldier like him.

Randy spotted two dead men with handguns beside them. They were Hank and Vaughn.

Some survivors had barricaded themselves inside rooms, while others had hidden in utility closets, hoping the attacker would just go away.

Randy tensed as a man in makeshift riot gear, cobbled together from scraps of metal, rounded the corner. It was the attacker, finished with his sweep of the station. He was big and heavyset. And he had a balding scalp and a long, scraggly beard that hung from beneath his metal mask.

Randy raised his gun in a two-handed grip and emptied half a clip, *blam* after *blam*.

The bullets pinged off the attacker's improvised armor system.

I have to stop this guy, Randy thought.

The attacker raked his weapon back and forth as its rotating barrel thundered, filling the air with bullets. He was like a one-man firing squad.

Randy ran to the rear of the van, debris crunching under his feet. "I'm a Guardian! Put the fucking weapon down!"

The gun's barrel whined to a stop, hissing smoke. "Naw, I don't think so!" the attacker yelled back, then unleashed another fusillade, keeping Randy pinned behind the van.

"Why'd you do this?" Randy's voice barely carried over the metallic ping of bullets ricocheting off the van's reinforced exterior.

The attacker released the trigger of his weapon and replied, "These immigrants will put reformists in power. They'll put *Amaechi* back in power. She's working with them, you see. It's all one big conspiracy. Once reelected, she's gonna deport half of us nonimmigrants, trade us out for colonists. I'm not letting that happen to my family! No way, man!"

Randy ground his teeth. *This guy's fucking delusional.* Sweat dripped down his forehead. This was the result of outlandish smear propaganda about Amaechi, propaganda put out by Quinn and the Brotherhood. *I have to take this guy down and save whoever's still alive.*

Randy played his gambit and dove sideways, firing a string of bullets. Two of his shots struck home—one in the unprotected sliver of the attacker's midsection and another in his leg—just as Randy's shoulder hit the floor.

The attacker was now down.

Randy rose, shoulder aching, and walked up to him. "You're finished! The authorities—"

"A White Knight of the Republic never *ever* gives in!"

One of the Purist groups Sam mentioned, Randy thought. *Wait, what the hell's he—?* The White Knight yanked a cord on his belt. A series of beeps warned Randy to get the hell out of there. *Shit, a bomb!*

Just then, a woman and her seven-year-old daughter crept out of a locked room. "Is . . . it safe to come out?" the woman asked.

Randy screamed, "Run! Get out of here, now! There's a bomb!" He took off toward the exit.

The beeping accelerated. The bomb was seconds from blowing.

Randy glanced over his shoulder. The mother and daughter were too far from the exit. They weren't going to make it.

He dashed out of the building. Glancing over his shoulder again, he saw the mother and daughter gasping for breath.

The girl tripped.

Her mother pulled her up. "Come on, sweetie, we need to—"

A plasma explosion devoured the building's interior, sending shock waves in all directions. Windowpanes burst into fragments.

The force of the blast slung Randy off his feet.

Ejecta shot into the air and cascaded down.

"Randy!" Akane cried, shrouded in a cloud of smoke and debris. Her ears rang. Did Randy make it? Or had the blast claimed him? Her pounding heart battered her chest.

The roof, structurally compromised, collapsed. Akane jumped at the harsh, resounding crash.

Slowly, the smoke started to clear, and Akane's ears stopped ringing. She saw Randy rise within the haze, unsteady but alive.

She ran to him and threw herself into his arms. He drew her close, both of them covered in soot and sweat.

"I'm glad you're okay," Akane said with shallow breaths. Her heart relaxed, returning to a normal beat.

"There was a . . . mother and child." Randy had fought in the civil war, so he'd seen plenty of death as a first-year Guardian. But never—*never*—had he been witness to a child's life being extinguished. "That kid couldn't have been older than seven or eight." He could hardly keep his voice working. "I . . . couldn't stop him." His hands curled into fists. He kept seeing the girl's face— her wide, innocent eyes; her freckled cheeks; her cute pug nose. "That son of a bitch had an explosive ordnance on him. I had him down. Maybe if I'd just been quicker, shot him in the throat or something, then—"

"Don't do this to yourself. *Don't* wallow in shame." Akane pulled Randy against her, arms squeezing his clammy back. "What that punk-ass bitch did isn't your fault."

"I can't help but think—" Could he have done something differently? The answer was no.

"It's okay, Randy. It's okay," Akane said softly. "We're not on a battlefield, but this is a war. And unfortunately, we can't save everyone, just like no one could save those three ex-Coalition fighters."

"That doesn't make it any easier." Sorrow laced every one of Randy's words.

"I know. But be at peace with the fact that you did everything you could."

They held each other in a long, tender moment as fire crackled in their ears and sirens approached.

What an election day.

Police land and aerial vehicles arrived at the scene.

Randy said, the sorrow in his voice thickening, "We should go, but I guess we need to give statements to the authorities first."

"Yeah." Akane's tone was equally heavy. *Everyone killed today was an immigrant like me. Why?* Tears threatened to spill from her eyes. "After we leave, I don't wanna be alone."

Randy's next words emerged as a croak. "Me neither."

"Then let's keep each other company, go back to my place and watch the election results come in." Akane fought to suppress the pain born from the deaths of Johanna and a mother and her child. But the dam broke. Tears carved tracks into the ash on her cheeks. "Whaddya say?"

"Yeah, I'd like that." Randy valued Akane's friendship above all else right now.

• • •

Stacie sat in the back of a ground limo beside Damien. She wore white pants and a red top that had one strap resting over her right shoulder.

Because Damien still wasn't ready to trust her with the location of their destination, he had blindfolded her.

"Are we almost there yet?" she asked, for what seemed like the hundredth time to Damien.

"Ten more minutes," he replied.

"You know, not being blindfolded would be nice. It's kind of irritating."

"Sorry, dear. One of many lessons my father taught me was to err on the side of caution. I'm responsible for the safety of others and cannot jeopardize their well-being. You'll understand better once we arrive at our destination."

"You talk about your dad a lot, but I never hear much about your mom. What's the deal?"

A tense silence dragged before Damien answered. "Let's not toy with each other. We both know our parents bypassed the law to amass their fortunes, no matter what we tell the government or the media. The files released by the Coalition barely scratched the surface of what they were involved in. The more my mother learned about my father's dealings, the more uncomfortable she became. So she abandoned us."

"I see."

The news played on a screen lowered from the ceiling.

The anchorman said, "We now have more information about the sadistic attack at a Leefside voting station, where an active shooter gunned down several immigrants and then detonated an explosive. It's being reported that a Guardian was on the scene. He ran into the building to stop the murderer and succeeded in neutralizing him, but couldn't prevent him from triggering the bomb. The Guardian's name is Randal Scott, and he—"

Randy? Stacie thought, tuning out the anchorman. That sounded like him, him and his heart of heroism. He'd always believed he had a moral obligation to help people, to save lives. It was one of the qualities she'd found most attractive about him.

The anchorman said, "Despite the attack, immigrant voters continued to go to the polls. Earlier today, not long after the attack, Chief Executive Amaechi made this statement."

On the replay, Oviereya denounced the terrorist attack. "Tragedy has befallen a community. The attack on the voting station today in Leefside was a despicable, heinous act by a heartless coward. Perhaps not as horrific, but you will hear about other outbreaks of violence against immigrants that also occurred today. These are nothing more than fear tactics from small-minded people who want to disrupt our election process. I urge all immigrants not to be discouraged. Do not let the fearmongers win. Continue to exercise your right to vote." The replay ended.

Stacie stifled her disdain. She couldn't show it, not with Damien, a Purist, right beside her.

"All polls have closed," said the anchorman, "and now the vote count is well underway."

Damien watched the vote count fluctuate.

The screen showed young political newcomer Tim MacGowan, a reformist, neck and neck with anti-reformist Warrick Radaker. Damien needed as many anti-reformists in Parliament as possible so he could implement his and Atticus's agendas with ease.

He hoped tonight would be a victory for anti-reformists, especially after all the work the Brotherhood had put in by hacking voter databases to purge immigrants from them, making immigrants ineligible to vote. Not to mention, Brotherhood street teams had made threatening calls to immigrant homes, warning them not to vote; roughed up immigrants who were on their way to the polls; and blackmailed region state leaders into closing voting stations in immigrant communities so it would be harder for immigrants to exercise their rights.

Stacie felt the vehicle swerve onto another street and jerk to a stop.

An adenoidal male voice said, "Mr. Sykes, good evening, sir."

A security guard, Stacie figured. Her ears continued to paint a visual picture. Clacking noises—had to be locks. A shushing sound and some rattling—that was a gate opening.

After five minutes, the limo stopped again.

"You may remove the blindfold now," Damien said.

Stacie took it off. They had arrived at a windowless gray building surrounded by a phyocrete wall.

"Where are we?" The lenses on Stacie's pupils were recording visuals for documentation, and her stud earrings were capturing audio. DFI really provided the coolest spy tech, she thought.

"We're at the compound of the Brotherhood for Humanity's Salvation. The Brotherhood is the first and largest Purist organization. Quinn started it."

"How are you connected to all this?"

"I was bestowed the honor of being Headmaster by Quinn himself," Damien revealed.

"So that means you know who Quinn is?"

"Yes, but that's not something I can disclose to you. I'm sure you understand."

"And you Purists are just activists upholding AEGIS's grand design for humanity? And you guys do everything in accordance with Commonwealth law?"

"Of course," Damien lied. "Now come, let's go inside."

Stacie and Damien approached the dark, intimidating structure.

Stacie was already getting eerie vibes from this place. An utterly cold feeling chilled her veins.

At the double doors, which bore the Purist emblem, two men stood chatting. When they saw Damien, they quickly stiffened and saluted.

"Good to see you, Headmaster," one of them remarked.

"Relax," Damien said.

The other man opened the door for Damien and Stacie, and they went into the building's vestibule.

"We'll be going to my personal suite, where we can watch the election in private," Damien told Stacie, "but I have to check on some of the men first."

Being trapped in a room with Damien was a total no-go for Stacie. *Okay, take it easy. You can finesse your way out of this.*

They moved down a hall and entered a room full of unsavory characters, Purists holding an election watch party.

"It's Headmaster Sykes!" a man said as he saw Damien and Stacie come in. It was Paul Shaffer. "Everyone, hush up!"

The loud, cheerful chatter died. Someone muted the screen's audio.

Every eye homed in on Damien. Postures straightened.

Damien didn't condone the tactics of the rogue White Knight who'd attacked the east Leefside voting station. Crashing through a building with a souped-up van and mowing down a mass of people wasn't his style. To him, that kind of violent barbarism, for the sake of killing a few immigrants, was senseless, and it brought the meddlesome attention of the authorities. Damien preferred to play his cards smarter—more cleverly, more craftily, more subtly. Nevertheless, he wouldn't waste the opportunity to talk up Purists and their cause.

"I won't be long," Damien said. Everyone listened attentively. "Today, a brother—a member of the White Knights—took his own life, fearful of the future state of our republic."

He must be talking about the guy who blew himself up at the voting station, Stacie thought. *So the White Knights are a Purist group.*

Damien carried on with dramatic flair. "I don't condone death by one's own hand. You Purists are far too important to lose. Blame the reformists and Amaechi for our brother's demise today.

"What drives a man to take such violent action? What drives him to sacrifice his life in the name of Purism? The answer: desperation. Desperation to save himself and his family from a daunting fate—being deported to Satellite One if Amaechi were to win the next election. Desperation to preserve our republic as it is, as it was meant to be. Though I don't condone his actions, he died a hero, a hero for our republic."

Hearing Damien dote on a sicko disgusted Stacie. *That murdering piece of filth was no hero.*

Cheers filled the room.

"Please," Damien said, "continue the party."

Someone unmuted the screen. Conversations resumed.

Paul expressed his praise to Damien face-to-face. "That was a good speech, Mr. Sykes."

Damien slid an arm around Stacie. "I understand you and Paul have had a bit of a confrontational encounter."

Paul pretended he was over it. "It's water under the bridge for me."

"I hope the same goes for you," Damien said to Stacie, hinting that her coexisting with Paul wasn't optional.

She clicked her tongue, still pissed. "All in the past."

"Good." Damien unwrapped his arm from around Stacie. "Paul

is actually the Brotherhood's Chief Enforcer, when he's not busy with his duties in the ETF. I'd hate for there to be any ill will between the two of you. You might be seeing more of each other."

Paul stepped closer to Damien. "Boss, I got something I need to talk to you about."

Damien turned to Stacie. "Wait in the hall for me."

She silently left the room and stood just outside the door.

Damien and Paul isolated themselves from the others in a corner. "Sergeant, if this is about Stacie again—"

"Nah, I've got nothing else to say about her, though I still think it's a big mistake letting her get close to you. But you're the boss. What you want, you get."

"So what is it?"

"My contact in law enforcement was able to match the DNA of that solutioner you shot on the roof."

"Don't keep me waiting, Sergeant."

"His name is Jamie Lister. I serve with the guy in Vanguard Alpha. My contact also pulled his address."

A menacing smile hooked the corners of Damien's mouth. "Excellent. Take Mark and Dan and beat RISE's location out of him. But not tonight. Handle it tomorrow. For now, enjoy the party."

"Thanks, Mr. Sykes." Paul returned to his brothers.

Damien rubbed his hands together eagerly. Now, back to Stacie.

Outside the door, Stacie stood with her arms crossed, nerves worsening. She had to finish up and get out of here. She'd already planted a micro audio transmitter in Damien's limo tonight, and she'd planted one in the flyer she and Damien had used to escape the fundraiser. Also, she had pretended to drop her purse to conceal a tracker beneath the limo before getting in and being blindfolded. That tracker would lead Defense Force Intelligence straight here.

She intended to plant one or two more transmitters in Damien's suite before hightailing it home. This place, and these Purists, were making the hair on the back of her neck bristle.

Damien left the room. "Let us continue to my suite, so we may have some privacy."

"About time," Stacie said flirtatiously, pretending to play right into his arms.

They entered an elevator and rode two floors up. After exiting, they walked down a hall and went into Damien's suite.

The room was about eight-hundred square feet and featured expensive carpet, a comfortable L-shaped couch, armchairs, a love seat, wall art, and a Jacuzzi.

Stacie's instincts told her to hurry.

A muted screen, nearly the size of the entire wall, streamed election coverage.

Stacie wandered around the room. "Wow, nice spread." She discreetly slipped her hand under a table and planted one of her listening devices. "So, Damien, I know the Sykes family has utilized the trafficking industry to build their fortune, and I was wondering if you might give me some guidance on how I, too, could break into the industry."

"Is that so? Who told you we were involved in trafficking?"

"Oh, just . . . a few of my company's executives who did business with your parents."

"We can talk business another time."

Darn, she was aiming for a confession. Well, it was worth a try.

Damien loomed over her. "End stream," he commanded the suite's virtual assistant. The megascreen winked off. "I didn't bring you here just to watch the election or talk business. I brought you

245

here so we could be alone and indulge in each other, like old times. If I recall, you loved our physical escapades."

Yes, Stacie remembered the assignations filled with copious drunken sex and endorphin-boosting drugs. The thought sickened her now.

Damien leaned in, nuzzling her neck with his lips. He was eager to satisfy his lust.

Bluh. Stacie chewed the inside of her cheek. "Um, Damien, sweetheart—" She jerked away and unintentionally backed herself against a wall. "I . . . need to leave, I'm afraid. I'm sorry. Business, you know?"

Damien wasn't buying her excuse for needing to leave. "Really?" he said skeptically. "I'm sure it can wait." He pasted his lips to hers and thrust his tongue into her mouth.

Stacie slid sideways along the wall, escaping Damien. "I'd love to stay, but I—"

A vein pulsed in Damien's temple. Feeling toyed with, he lost his patience and punched the wall. "What the fuck is your game, Spencer?"

There it was, Stacie thought, that uncontrollable anger that always emerged when someone deprived him of his wants, defied him, or challenged him. His father had raised him to be a spoiled punk kid.

Damien's gaze bore into her. "You've been asking a ton of questions. And for someone who supposedly wants to pick up where we left off, you seem mighty evasive."

Stacie snickered. "What's my *game*? *Ha*, I assure you—"

Damien gripped her throat and pushed the back of her head against the wall. He wished he could rip the truth out of her.

Cassie McCanns' bruised face flickered in Stacie's mind.

"Who are you working for?" Damien demanded.

The wrath vibrating in his fingertips suffused Stacie with fear. *Gotta think fast.* Her manufactured straight-faced expression lent no hint of dishonesty. "Working for?" She laughed, rolling her eyes like his accusation was completely ludicrous. "*Puh-leeze.* I do the bidding of no one. Why would I? I'm the queen of Spencer Enterprises. All I do is on my *own* accord, Damien."

Not believing her, Damien let go of her throat and frisked the sides of her midriff. "Are you wearing a listening transceiver?" He dug his hands into the side and rear pockets of her pants, searching for micro devices.

Get your filthy hands off me. "A listening device? What, you think I'm a . . . spy or something?" Stacie said sarcastically.

"I take no chances, woman. I'd have to be a fool. So I guess we'll find out, won't we? And there's only one way to do that." A strip search. "Disrobe, *now.* And that's not a request. It's not like I haven't seen you naked before."

Fuck you to hell. Stacie needed to sedate his hotheadedness and get out of here. She'd hate herself for this, but . . . "Damien, relax, you're getting all spooked for nothing." Framing his face in her hands, she pressed her lips to his, offering up her moist tongue— like she was still into him.

The anger stiffening Damien's features disappeared. He kissed her back with barbaric intensity, his hands splaying across her rear end in a greedy, self-serving way. He was lusting to dominate her.

Stacie broke the kiss. She had permitted enough. "Sweetie, I promise, tomorrow night we'll continue this, and it'll be very rewarding," she said in a playful, seductive timbre. "I'll even wear the red teddy you liked *soooo* much." She sounded too saccharine that time, almost fake. "But I need to go. Now please be a gentleman and escort me out of here."

Damien remained wary. Maybe Paul was right. Maybe her

trying to disrupt his trafficking operation and then suddenly reconnecting with him wasn't a coincidence. "Fine." He'd have someone monitor her. If she were up to something, he'd uncover it. "I'm excited about what tomorrow night will bring. Don't go back on your word and disappoint me."

"I wouldn't dream of it." She'd cancel on the asshole tomorrow.

She and Damien exited the suite. Once outside the building, he blindfolded her again and had one of his men drive her home.

• • •

Three hours into the election-night coverage, Randy sat on the love seat in Akane's home, watching candidates' vote percentages rise and fall, while Akane showered. What a roller coaster of an election. It was impossible to tell who was going to win. Every race was a toss-up.

Randy once again contemplated what he should do about RISE. He was supposed to be working with his father to dig up more dirt on them and whatever interference they might be planning for the next round of special elections.

Technically, RISE was an extremist organization. They'd meddled with the democratic process, stolen government funds, and assassinated people they deemed deserving of death. But those people were men like Damien Sykes, or the deranged bastard who blew up a little girl today. RISE did illegal things for good causes, but still, wrong was wrong. Illegal was illegal. And Randy was a Guardian, sworn to protect the Commonwealth from all enemies, foreign and domestic. That included organizations like RISE and the Brotherhood.

RISE was flouting the law, but they were also advancing social justice for immigrants and colonists. That was where the dilemma came in for Randy.

He hadn't told his dad where RISE's base was. But when the

time came to contact Conlan, as planned, he'd be asked to reveal its location. And if he did, what would happen to Sam and Jay? Both had wives and children. And what would happen to Akane?

She was his friend, someone who had treated him with kindness since he returned to the CDF a pariah. And today, they had grieved together, bearing witness to a cold-blooded act of violence.

Randy wondered: What do you do when someone you care about, someone you love, is on the wrong side of the law? He struggled between his feelings and his duty.

Done with her shower, Akane—wrapped in a pink robe—emerged from the bathroom. "How's the election going?"

Randy tapped the remote control, cutting off the wall-mounted screen. "Truth is, it'll be sometime tomorrow before we know who the victors are." He pushed himself up from the love seat and approached Akane, halting at a measured distance. "Are you going to be okay?"

Memories of Johanna removed Akane from the present. She cast them out of her head and closed the distance between her and Randy some more. "It's not fair. It never is, though."

Randy gazed into her sad eyes, unsure of what to say. He moved closer and settled his hands on her shoulders.

The care and compassion in his touch set Akane's blood ablaze.

Would he . . . *could* he reveal RISE's location to his father and Conlan when the time came? Could he break Akane's heart, destroy what was essentially her family here on Eden? RISE was full of people she knew and loved.

Randy said, "We can't bring the dead back. All we can do is mourn, celebrate their life, and keep them alive in our hearts and minds. They might be gone, but they'll *never* be forgotten." He thought of his mother.

"Yeah, it's tough, though."

"I know." Randy continued holding Akane by the shoulders and leaned in dangerously close, the minuscule space between their lips shrinking. A voracious look flickered in his eyes, impossible to hide.

Damn it, he wasn't trying to get emotionally entangled with another woman right now, he reminded himself. And Akane, still unpersuaded to leave RISE, was a member of what was considered an extremist group. She had committed murder, destroyed private property, and aided in an attempted political assassination. And she intended to kill a Guardian, Paul Shaffer. That was basically premeditated murder. Nevertheless—staring into her pretty eyes, emotions swirling, sex cravings running wild—he just couldn't . . .

Randy continued to fail at keeping a platonic distance. Noses touching, their lips were now just shy of a kiss.

The logical part of Randy's mind urged him to walk away and go home. According to CDF Code of Military Justice 3-12, the consequences for a Guardian who willingly associates with criminals, extremists, and domestic terrorists were dishonorable discharge and prison time. But Akane's lips were right there, daring him to kiss her. And under that robe, she had on nothing but a pair of panties, if anything.

Akane shut her eyes and sighed. "Well . . . I guess you've gotta go." Her tone implied she didn't want him to leave. "Um, maybe I'll see you to-"

Before Akane could finish, Randy grabbed her waist and pulled her flush against him. He fastened his lips to hers, finally breaking the boundary of friendship. Enough bullshit.

A wave of arousal colored Akane's cheeks.

Fueled by adrenaline, Randy kissed her more urgently, sucking on her lower lip, intertwining his tongue with hers.

Down below, he felt himself getting hard.

Akane leaned into the kiss, elation prickling her flesh.

Randy finally detached his lips from hers and withdrew his hands from her waist.

They stared at each other, breaths bated, hearts racing. Their eyes spoke volumes. No words were needed. They both knew where the night was headed.

Their lips met again, hungrier this time, and their tongues danced in each other's mouths.

Randy couldn't fight his desires any longer. He needed to feel Akane's body—skin to skin. There was no way this night ended without both of them naked and his hips between her thighs.

He worked quickly to unknot her cloth belt, thirsting to plug his burgeoning erection into her.

The belt slipped loose, falling to the floor.

Akane shrugged the robe off her shoulders. She stood clad in her silk panties, her small cute breasts and trim waist exposed.

Randy grasped her lean, limber frame and pulled her in once more, his member pressing against her through his pants—a sample of what was to come.

They moved recklessly around the room while kissing, exchanging tongues and sharing saliva.

In their frenzy, they bumped into a table. Something fell off of it and thunked to the floor. Neither cared.

Randy's hands roamed over Akane's body, clutching her hips, sliding up her thighs, cupping her backside. He committed every detail of her to memory.

She wished he would just take his damn clothes off already and get down to business. She wanted to fuck.

Their lips clashed as euphoria electrified Randy's veins. At this point, going home to reconsider getting deeper involved with an "extremist" was utterly impossible.

Akane's implant alerted her to a Link request from Randy, which she accepted. The synchronized drumbeat of their hearts reverberated in their ears and souls. Passion infused every touch and kiss. Their psychically connected minds confirmed their shared desire for one another.

In a psychedelic blur of fevered kisses, touching, and stumbling, Akane ended up seated on one of her tables.

Randy tore her panties down her legs, leaving her completely naked, except for the pinstriped socks on her feet. Then he dropped his pants and boxers in one motion.

Akane got turned on by the sight of his hardness.

Bracing herself for what she'd been yearning for, she clasped the table's edges and parted her legs. Eagerly, Randy tucked the head of his rigid cock into the slit between them. She inhaled sharply, her heart pounding. Holding her by the waist, Randy pushed his hips forward, gradually stretching her folds. Her entrance was a tight fit, and needless to say, he liked it.

She lay back on her elbows, taking him in.

Once he was completely rooted inside her, he paused for a moment, allowing her to adjust to his size. Then he drove into her, his rhythm unyielding.

Her entire body came alive, waves of euphoria bombarding it.

Randy threw all his strength into each thrust, consumed by his desire for this beautiful young woman. He loved her symmetrical facial features, her sylphlike body, and the satisfying tightness between her thighs.

With their minds Linked, they crashed through the intimacy threshold, sensations and emotions merging into an all-encompassing force that stimulated every fiber of their being.

A dizzying wave of ecstasy struck Akane, nearly making her

faint, and Randy felt every pulse of it due to their Link. Invigorated by it, he instinctively accelerated his pace, each spear of his cock into Akane rattling the table.

The smacking of skin against skin filled the air, mingling with Randy's grunts and Akane's whimpers.

Overcome by an insatiable hunger, Randy pulled Akane up from the table to her feet. He cradled her buttocks and hoisted her up. She wrapped her legs around his waist and her arms around his neck, anchoring their bodies together. She was ready for whatever he had in mind.

Pressing her back against the wall, Randy slid into her again.

The friction, the heat, the sound of their bodies colliding—it all exhilarated him. His thrusts became more forceful, more dominating. Each one was a confession of how badly he'd been wanting to fuck Akane.

She silently cursed as she felt his aroused cock expand further and widen even more inside her.

Eventually, Randy set her down, and their lovemaking transitioned to the bed.

Randy held Akane's wrists against the mattress, his gaze traveling slowly over her body. She was slight, a stark contrast to his usual preference, yet he found himself increasingly attracted to her. He lowered his mouth to her skin, trailing savage kisses downward.

Her body arched instantly at the touch of his lips. He continued his intimate exploration, and when his mouth reached the place where Akane wanted him the most, she gasped, her face flushing.

His lips made wet noises. Akane's palms flew to her hair, her fingers tangling in the strands. She didn't know what to do with herself. Randy was *undeniably* talented.

They rolled across the bed, positions shifting. Sometimes their kisses were tender, other times fierce. When Randy moved above Akane again, she reached down and guided his cock to her entrance—both of them wanting the same thing as he entered her once more.

She felt him sliding back and forth inside her, the pleasure almost torturous.

As they continued surrendering to each other, their Link laid bare their feelings—preventing them from hiding, suppressing, or denying them—even as they wrestled with whether, or how, to speak them aloud.

Randy was thankful for Akane's warmhearted welcome on his first day as a member of Vanguard Alpha, appreciative of her warnings about Purists, and grateful for her companionship, which had lessened the loneliness of being branded a "treasonist." Then there was his fear of losing her when the White Knight who had attacked the voting station nearly ran her down.

Akane had been concerned about Randy's well-being, his life, since day one. She refused to let him—one of her heroes and a fellow immigrant—fall victim to some Purist, like Desmond and Simone had. Love had been the root of her constant worry and warnings, and when the voting station exploded, her heart stopped. She was terrified she'd lost him.

A wondrous, spellbinding hurricane of white-hot psychosomatic stimulation engulfed their Linked minds as a naked exchange of feelings and emotions began, the mental amplifying the physical.

Randy sat back on his heels, pulling Akane onto his lap and thrusting upward into her.

Their Link allowed him to experience her trials firsthand: the sorrow of leaving her parents; the devastation of losing Skylar,

Desmond, and Simone; the horror of watching Johanna get run down, powerless to stop it. He wished he could tear away every layer of her pain.

He held her in place, fingertips kneading her back in a silent show of affection. For Akane, his touch was like emotional acupuncture—soothing, centering.

Giving herself to him, body and soul, felt therapeutic. She knew Randy couldn't erase her pain, but he could help numb it. Sex would be her anesthetic.

Bucking atop his lap in time with his thrusts, Akane said, <*Fuck me harder. Give it to me. Rock my fucking world.*>

Committed to doing just that, Randy dipped his face into her chest and kept drilling into her while suckling her stone-stiff nipples, causing her to moan in pure exaltation.

Akane tightened her arms around Randy's solid torso, hands bunching the gorgeous muscles of his back. He jerked her naked body closer, fucking her nonstop.

A cry of ecstasy tore from her throat, spurring him on.

In one smooth movement, he guided her onto her back, never letting their bodies part. He continued burrowing into her without pause, each thrust stealing her breath.

The bed frame groaned and shuddered.

A pressure swelled in Randy's groin, demanding release, but somehow, he held it at bay.

As the stroking of Akane's insides intensified to something beyond feral—beyond words—an overwhelming orgasm threatened to split her in half.

Randy considered the consequences of continuing without protection, but it was a struggle for him to pull out. He was too absorbed in the experience, both emotionally and physically, and didn't want to stop.

Somehow, he slowed his pace, fighting to regain control. But using cerebral communication, Akane assured him that she'd taken a contraceptive capsule before her shower, just in case they were intimate that night.

Freed by that knowledge, he hooked her legs over his shoulders and leaned forward, folding her lithe body in half. Holding back had been killing him.

Abandoning all restraint, he jackhammered into her with a barrage of uncontrollable, wild thrusts. Every carnal instinct, lustful desire, and primal urge to fuck Akane surged forth within him.

Akane's breath hitched, words failing her as she yielded to his onslaught. Her nipples stood erect, rock-hard and hypersensitive.

As she was being fucked out of her wits, she said, *< That's right, let me be your healthy addiction tonight. >*

Randy thought about Code of Military Justice 3-12. Every spear of his cock became a vehement protest against it. Whether or not she was regarded as a dangerous extremist, he wouldn't rue the night he got into bed with this spirited teenager from NeoJapan.

The pressure building in his groin reached its peak. Groaning a guttural sound, he surrendered, his release detonating inside Akane as his entire body trembled from the intensity of it.

Satisfied, relieved, he pulled out and rested beside her.

Akane blew a puff into her bangs and inhaled to regulate her breathing, postcoital tingles dancing across her flesh. After such a dreadful day, fantastic sex was exactly what she needed.

Still hungry for more, she straddled Randy's midriff and plunged into his lasting erection, which was soaked in cum.

She knew he still harbored feelings for his ex, but after she worked her magic tonight, he'd be saying "Stacie who?"

She rocked her hips fervently. Responding in kind, Randy

arched his body. His hands found the curve of her back, then journeyed lower, gripping her ass cheeks as he rose to meet each of her fearsome movements.

Akane massaged her breast, thumb circling the nipple. Eyes half-closed, she gyrated her hips like an exotic dancer, wringing a desperate sound from deep in Randy's throat. Sweat glistening on her skin, body moving sinuously, she looked like a sexy mirage made flesh.

She moved faster now, her muscles working overtime as she set a frantic pace. Randy's fingers struggled to maintain their grip before he finally tightened them, hanging on to her ass. She had a lot to get out of her system, and her sex drive wasn't waning anytime soon.

Arousal coursed through her. "Fuck," she panted, her head falling back.

She bent over and nipped Randy's shoulder, tasting him. He folded his arms around her so intensely—flattening her against him—that she felt them dig into her bones. Shuddering, he climaxed again.

They both came to a stop, Akane lying on top of him, her head pressed against his chest. She savored the feel of his defined body as she regained her breath, the ridges of his hard muscles pleasing to her skin.

<*Thank you,*> she said.

His hands caressed her.

She had had sex with several men and women, but tonight was by far the best she'd ever had. She felt like the luckiest nineteen-year-old woman in the Commonwealth.

Randy could stay like this forever, Akane's warm bare form draped over him. He placed one hand on the small of her back and the other on her backside. Then he claimed her mouth. He wanted her. Her flesh. Her bones. *All* of her.

He eased himself back into her while she remained facedown atop him, his hips now perfectly nestled between her thighs. As her body rose and fell, matching the motion of his loins, she expelled a contented moan that ignited sparks in his core.

In the throes of passion, Randy thrust into her at a tempo that was almost criminal. He couldn't bring himself to stop. Soon, another sobering release from him creamed her insides some more. Every nerve ending in her body screamed, threatening to burst. Then there was a pause, a moment of quiet stillness, a brief respite for them both.

Throughout the night, Randy and Akane explored each other's bodies in a hypnotic indulgence neither would forget.

But even as their lovemaking continued, Randy's mind returned to the question that troubled him: When the time came, could he disclose RISE's location to his father and Conlan, knowing it would break Akane's heart?

FINAL INTERLUDE

AFTER THE BATTLE OF THE QUAD

Planet Eden

Expedition Task Forces Headquarters
(Vanguard Alpha's Area of Operations (AO))

"No fucking way!" Akane said to Sam. "Are you pulling my leg, man?"

"You know me. I don't kid around," he replied.

"So lemme get this straight. Randal Scott, Arson Scott's son, is joining Vanguard Alpha *today?*"

"Yep."

"We've *gotta* convince him to join RISE. Just think about it, one of the liberators of the colonies joining us? He'd be a tremendous asset."

"Whoa, take a step back," Jay said. "We don't recruit prematurely. We have to find out if he's truly a fit for us, colony hero or not."

The doors to Vanguard Alpha's AO slid open as Randy stepped through, dressed in neat, well-pressed battledress.

It was his first day on assignment, his first day as a member of the ETF. He didn't know what to expect from Vanguard Alpha. So far, every Guardian he'd met since returning to the CDF had treated him like crap.

Akane snapped her eyes toward Vanguard Alpha's newest member, staring at him like he was some mythical hero. She skipped over to him excitedly, a warm greeting written on her face. "Welcome to Vanguard Alpha!" She smiled from ear to ear. "I'm Akane."

Randy smiled back at the bright angular face in front of him. "Thanks. You know what? You're the first Guardian to say anything even remotely polite since I returned to the CDF from my leave of absence."

"'Cause you were a rebel, right? Well, I'm an immigrant. I've had my fair share of being ostracized, so I know how you feel."

It's good to be around someone who does, Randy thought.

"But hey, heads-up, we've got some dicks on the team." Paul Shaffer, Dan Maddox, and Mark MaCallum, to be exact.

Randy expected as much. "Not surprised."

Akane hooked her arm around Randy's, and he gave an awkward glance at the overly flirty gesture.

"C'mon," she said, "you need to report to Lieutenant Breckenridge to finish in-processing, right?"

"Uh, yeah, that's right."

"Lemme escort you to his office," she insisted.

"Um, okay. Thanks."

They walked right past Sam and Jay without so much as a hello, Akane clearly wanting Randy all to herself for now.

A pair of doors hissed open to a corridor.

"So, where are you from?" Randy asked, making small talk.

Akane was psyched to be conversing with Randal Scott.

"Colony Three," she replied. "You were born in Colony Four, right? That's where your dad's from."

"Yeah, that's right. But I was a baby when my parents brought me to Eden. I'm an immigrant, I guess, but not really. I grew up among Highborn."

A few chatting Guardians in battledress passed them.

Akane said, "So you were privileged compared to us lottery beneficiaries, but you didn't grow up with a privileged mindset, did you?"

"Well, not every Highborn does. But my dad was an immigrant, a lucky lottery beneficiary like you. Over the years, he told me stories about how people looked down on him because AEGIS didn't choose his bloodline. He became an Edenite by luck of the draw, which still made him a 'nadir.'

"Despite facing bias, he taught me to respect everyone—colonist, immigrant, nonimmigrant. This included people harboring a skewed view of society, people who endorse systemic inequalities. My dad said they weren't always to blame for their beliefs. They were products of their upbringing.

"During my school years, I befriended a lot of Highborn. Many of them didn't even know I was the son of an immigrant. And believe me, I heard plenty of arrogant talk from my so-called friends. Not all of them, but enough.

"I could never understand why anyone would think they were superior to another human being just because of where AEGIS assigned them to live. My dad was an immigrant, after all, and he was one of the most awesome people I knew.

"As I got older, formed my own opinions about society, and studied Earth Era history, I started to think the requisites for Eden citizenship were unfair. But I also understood that some sort of selection process was necessary to divide humanity between its new planetary habitats. I thought maybe the requisites used were just the best option at the time, a time when humanity was on the brink of extinction.

"How else do you divide up Earth's remaining people between two planets, when only one offers the best chance of survival? I certainly didn't have any better ideas. Like everyone else, I believed the government would eventually elevate the colonies, give them what we had on Eden.

"When the Three-Week War started, I thought the insurrectionists were traitors, just like most Edenites did. I saw them as impatient complainers who couldn't wait for the Commonwealth to recover from the Phazharian and Bhalkran wars and obtain the resources to fix the colonies.

"But after the CDF won the Three-Week War and the Coalition formed, I went to Satellite One for the first time, as a new Guardian. I was ready to carry out the oath I had taken to defend the Commonwealth. I even believed my mission to eliminate my father, who'd defected, was just."

Akane said, "And when you got to Satellite One and saw how bad things really were, how people were still suffering after years of empty promises, you realized the truth and joined the right side."

"Yeah," Randy said. "With some help. A rebel named Kesley Whittaker and my father opened my eyes. But switching sides wasn't a straightforward decision. I went back and forth with myself for a while. Eventually, I saw joining the Coalition for Operation Hammer Fall as the right thing to do." Then, in a hero voice that came naturally to Randy—a voice that left Akane thirsty for osculation—he said, "My dad always told me to do what I believe is right. Right in my heart. And I guess that's what I did."

Akane was getting goose bumps just being near this man, the good kind of goose bumps. There was something about the way he carried himself that had her gushing over him. He had an air of valor about him. And then there was that handsome face. He practically exuded virility.

Akane felt the chest-rattling urge to drag him off to a supply closet and conduct her own in-processing procedure, no clothes allowed.

She envisioned them together in the bedroom. Oh, yes, she had made up her mind: Come hell or high water, she was going to engage in Linked copulation with Randal Scott. Sooner or later.

Up ahead were the doors to Lieutenant Breckenridge's office.

"That's it, the lieutenant's office." Akane paused, a little nervous. "Hey, um . . . you wanna grab some chow later? Maybe keep getting to know each other?"

"Yeah, that'd be great, Private Sugimori."

"Cool." Butterflies fluttered in Akane's stomach.

Randy liked Akane so far. She was small in stature but packed with personality. Maybe they'd become good friends.

As Akane was leaving, she stopped. "Hey, Randy?"

"Yeah?"

"I'm glad you joined the Coalition to help free the colonies from oppression. I'm glad you followed your heart. Thank you for doing 'the right thing.'" With that, she walked away.

Randy went toward Breckenridge's office. "Thank you, Akane," he subvocalized.

CHAPTER SIX

Randy, fresh from his morning shower and shirtless in a pair of jeans, sat on Akane's bed. As Akane was finishing up her shower, he stared at the text message he had received from Arson five minutes ago, holowords hovering above his wristcom. It laid out everything that had happened. The CDF had raided the council's safe house while Arson was meeting with Tristan Gelano, and they took him into custody for questioning. He used his one courtesy call to contact Conlan and fill him in on what he and Randy were doing—infiltrating RISE, which they believed to be a threat to the Commonwealth.

Conlan informed Arson that he'd learned about RISE from none other than Randy's ex, Stacie Spencer, who was apparently working with DFI on a covert investigation into Damien Sykes, a Purist. So Stacie, Conlan, and the duo of Randy and Arson were all pursuing the same objective. What a strange twist of fate. The message concluded with the next course of action: The four of them would hold a videoconference in five hours and make a plan to take down both RISE and the Brotherhood.

Randy knew Arson and Conlan would ask him to provide the

location of RISE's base. He pondered what he should do.

Akane emerged from the shower, her lissome figure nude, and walked to the closet to get dressed.

She was barely seventeen when she snuck away from home and had sex with a man for the first time. It was an experience filling to the soul. However, last night had surpassed that and all her other intimate encounters.

Looking over at Randy, she grinned. She had never been a vain woman, but she had to give herself some credit for being the first Asian woman Randal Scott had ever fucked. She wasn't even his usual type, but she had learned that "killer bod with curves" didn't always overshadow "petite Japanese chick." Must be her magnetic personality.

Noticing Randy seemed distant, she asked, "Randy, somethin' up?" She tugged a pair of underwear up her hips. There was no response from Randy. "Randy? *Yoo-hoo,*" she said after a pause, fastening the front clasp of her bra.

Randy kept glancing at her, unsure what to say. He opted for, "I'm fine." An obvious lie.

What was he supposed to do, keep the location of RISE's base a secret from Conlan and his father while continuing with business as usual in Vanguard Alpha? Was he supposed to just pretend that Akane wasn't involved in a vigilante social-justice organization?

Ever scrupulous, he rested his elbows on his thighs and interlaced his fingers, deep in thought.

Akane felt fur brush her leg and heard a meow. She leaned over and gave Bubbles a good-morning pat.

Randy remained silent, fidgeting. He stole another glance at Akane. She looked enticing—slim figure with ribs faintly visible beneath smooth skin, exotic eyes, adorable smile. His mind took him back to last night, the two of them lost in a world of pleasure.

It had been beautiful.

Clad in her white cotton lingerie, Akane joined Randy on the bed and sat against the headboard. "Well, you don't seem *fine*." She glided her fingers over his shoulder and pressed a kiss to his cheek. "What's up?"

He stared into her eyes thoughtfully, wondering how he could convince her to leave RISE. Acting on impulse, he answered her kiss with one of his own, pecking her lips.

In an instantaneous reaction, she began necking him.

Randy eased her down onto the mattress, stretched her out, and unsnapped the front clasp of her bra. He gathered her hands above her head, holding her wrists down, and kissed her along her breastbone, neck, and jaw.

He didn't want to attend the four-way conference today. Staying in bed with Akane and having endless sex sounded far better. This whole Brotherhood-versus-RISE secret war was something he'd rather ignore. He was tired of ultraists singing the praises of dead men like Cornelius Gould and Arman Reza, keeping their spirit alive in the name of some imagined "greater good."

The rise and fall of Akane's small bare chest quickened, a thrill traveling down her spine. "Damn. Wanna go again? I'm always down for—"

Randy interrupted her. "Listen, Akane." He kissed her lips. Suppressing his desire for her was challenging, especially since he'd already halfway undressed her. "I need to be honest with you." He combed his fingers through her tousled hair. "In a few hours, my father and Chief of Defense Force Intelligence Michael Conlan are going to ask me where RISE's base is."

Worry tautened Akane's forehead. "Are you gonna snitch on us?"

"No." The word snapped from Randy's mouth, rigid and definitive.

Akane's face took on a distrustful frown. She was unsure whether to believe Randy. "You'd better not." She knew he was a man who often lived and died by his values. Would he go against them to keep RISE's base a secret when the Chief of Defense Force Intelligence and his own father asked for its location?

Cogently, Randy said, "I won't reveal where RISE's base is, Akane."

"Promise me. *Promise* me I have your word." She needed to hear the right answer.

After three heartbeats of silence, and an impatient grunt from Akane, Randy finally replied, "You have my word." He stroked her rib cage in a gesture of devotion.

If there was one thing Akane was sure of, it was Randy's feelings for her. Last night, as they made love, their Link had shown her those feelings were strong. She knew that Randy giving up RISE's location would wound his soul.

"I'm glad you decided to do the right thing." A pause. "Uh, so, are you gonna let me up or finish stripping me naked?"

Slow to leave Akane's side, Randy let his eyes linger on her breasts. Caught in the jaws of arousal, he sucked on Akane's nipples. Right now, he wanted nothing more than to stay.

Because of the intimacy of mental communion, Randy had formed a strong emotional bond with Akane. She was the first lover he'd Linked with since Stacie, once again experiencing the ultimate connection with a woman.

Knowing he needed to go, he stopped just short of removing Akane's panties. One more second and they would've been on the floor. "I'd better get going." He gave Akane's nipples another suck apiece before pulling on a tank top.

Akane sat up and refastened her bra. "Am I gonna see you later tonight?" She hoped he'd say yes.

"Um, I'm not sure. I might be busy tonight."

Akane walked Randy to the door, still unsure of what he would do. His guarantees hadn't been enough to alleviate her concerns.

After Randy left, Akane flopped back onto her bed. Bubbles jumped up and perched beside her.

As she rubbed the cat's soft fur, she thought, *Don't go back on your word, Randy.* She could only hope that his feelings for her, the magic they'd shared last night, the bond their Link had deepened, and his reluctance to disappoint her would be enough to keep him from revealing RISE's location.

• • •

At home, Randy had been pacing back and forth in a straight line for the past three minutes, waiting for the four-way powwow to start. Indecision gnawed at him. His thoughts seesawed between giving up RISE's location and keeping it to himself. A choice of this magnitude wasn't easy.

His father's words held his conscience hostage: *"There are no such things as 'good extremist groups' and 'bad extremist groups.'"*

Is there? Randy questioned. *No, what am I saying?* A lawbreaker was a lawbreaker. What to do? Give RISE's location to Conlan? Betray Akane?

Randy's mind drifted back to earlier this morning . . .

The blinds filtered the sun's light as he and Akane awoke from an orgasmic high, the room still thick with the scent of sex. They lay next to each other, stark naked, sharing their innermost thoughts through their Link. Akane whispered seductive things in Japanese, enthralling him. In an endless cycle of kissing and caressing, they continued to unmask their feelings, waves of exhilaration propelling them forward . . .

Randy snapped himself out of the memory. He'd given Akane his word he wouldn't reveal RISE's location, but he still hadn't decided what to do. He was trying to find a middle ground, some way to keep his word without breaking his commitment to the mission. *What's the answer here?* His internal conflict raged on.

He thought about the terror he and Akane had endured at the voting station, how that moment had bonded them. His cerebral implant's inscription of their intimate night rekindled the warmth he'd felt from her naked body draped over his.

Her heartbeat echoed in his mind like an endless rhythm. The thrill of her lips working their magic on him down below, in an act of fellatio that felt surprisingly experienced for a nineteen-year-old, engulfed his senses that instant.

"What do I do?" he said aloud. Should he give up RISE's base?

His home's virtual assistant made an announcement. "Reminder, meeting in one minute."

Randy composed himself. *Okay, Scott, get it together. Just . . . do what's right in your heart.*

He sat at his desk, clicked on his computer, and joined the videoconference.

His screen split into two windows. One showed Arson from the shoulders up; the other showed the same of Conlan.

"It's good to see you, Randy," Conlan said warmly. It had been two months since they last saw each other, following the end of the civil war.

"You as well, General," Randy replied.

A third window appeared as Stacie joined the conference.

Wearing a sleeveless white turtleneck blouse beneath a red blazer, she sat in a brown armchair in her home office. The polished filigree brooch on the blazer caught the light in the room, shining brilliantly.

Behind her, a display of trophies and awards from Cadwell Institute of Higher Learning covered the wall: track, swimming, zero-G fencing, and racket puck. Among them was a plaque marking one of her highest honors, Warrior Extraordinaire.

From the outside, Stacie might have seemed like a prissy princess, but she had deliberately taken on rigorous challenges to transcend that image. She had even defied her parents by enlisting in the CDF instead of being groomed to succeed them.

"Hey, everyone," Stacie said.

Seeing his ex brought back old feelings and a wave of nostalgia for Randy.

Conlan kicked off the meeting. "Let's start by piecing together how we got to this point. Before we begin, please note that by participating in this conference, you've agreed to keep everything discussed here strictly confidential. I'll need verbal confirmation from each of you." Everyone gave their assent. "Good," Conlan continued. "Chief Amaechi was the one who recommended Stacie for this assignment. Since Damien Sykes is one of the Seven Elite, Stacie is familiar with him, as her family was once part of the conglomerate."

Stacie interjected, unabashed about her past, "Basically, Damien and I had a thing. Just to clarify."

"Right," Conlan said. "Apparently, Damien is still infatuated with Stacie. That's why I recruited her to go undercover for DFI. I knew she could leverage their past relationship to get close to him and help us investigate his ties to a dangerous extremist movement called Purism. Its followers call themselves Purists, and we've confirmed that Damien is the Headmaster of the first and largest Purist group, the Brotherhood for Humanity's Salvation.

"Stacie gained Damien's trust and worked her way into his good graces. She and her team of chasers have been collecting intel and reporting directly to me. During a fundraiser hosted by Damien, the two of them were attacked by a group of masked, armed assailants. Damien revealed to Stacie that the attackers were members of an organization called RISE. They are another extremist group, one fighting for immigrant and colony equality. But regardless of how righteous their cause may seem, they pose a threat to peace, stability, and the rule of law.

"Stacie's report was the first time I'd heard of RISE, and I immediately tasked my intelligence teams with investigating them. They uncovered very little. Stacie later learned from Damien that RISE is led by a three-person council based in Colony Four.

"With that information, the CDF deployed a force to hunt down the council. A team of Guardians traced them to an Assistance Living Center, where they maintained a hidden safe house. Only one member was present at the time, Tristan Gelano. The Guardians took her in for questioning. With nothing substantial to hold her on, they eventually released her. However, they also took my friend Arson Scott into custody at the center. Arson, maybe you can take it from here for a bit."

Arson said, "Randy is keeping their identities to himself for now, but a few days ago, he was approached by three RISE members. They saw someone society had mistreated for being a former Coalition fighter and tried to recruit him. Randy asked me if I'd ever heard of RISE. I hadn't, so I reached out to an old Coalition buddy to see what I could dig up.

"It turns out he's been a member of RISE for quite some time, since the organization's first year in operation. He told me about

Purists and the Brotherhood. He wanted me to join RISE and took me to the council's safe house at the Assistance Living Center so they could try to persuade me and dispel my skepticism.

"Randy and I set out to gather as much concrete evidence as possible so we'd have something solid to bring to Conlan—facts, not just conjecture. Then the CDF could take action to shut down RISE. It was while I was meeting with Tristan Gelano that the CDF raided the Assistance Living Center and took both of us into custody.

"I used my one courtesy call to contact Conlan. I told him everything, and that's when we realized we were all on the same mission: stopping RISE, the Brotherhood, and all Purist groups. None of them have a place in the Commonwealth."

Conlan said, "Stacie, anything you'd like to add?"

Stacie nodded. "Damien took me to the Brotherhood's compound last night. He had me blindfolded, so I didn't see the route we took to get there. But that place made my skin itch. The way these Purists think is insane.

"Fortunately, I planted a tracker on the limo we took to the compound. I also wore a listening device whenever I was around Damien, so DFI's been recording everything. And I planted a few bugs in key locations."

Randy knew that going undercover for DFI was risky, yet Stacie had embraced the danger when she could've simply been enjoying her new fortune. He respected her for that, just as he respected her for enlisting.

His heart ached from the thought of the pain he had caused her.

Stacie said, "During my interactions with Damien, I confirmed that he's the Brotherhood's Headmaster, the guy directly under Quinn."

Arson felt uneasy seeing Stacie again. The only other time they had met was when Randy had detained her in the Parliament Building during Operation Hammer Fall. "How's your cover?" he asked her, worried for her safety.

"Well, Damien has obviously become suspicious. During my jog this morning, I noticed someone following me. The same guy's been lurking outside my place, probably thinking he's gone unnoticed. He's gotta be one of Damien's goons.

"Oh, and Randy, Paul Shaffer was at the compound, a member of your task force."

Figures, Paul's with the Brotherhood, Randy thought.

Conlan took over the conversation. "DFI has reviewed hours of audio surveillance. There's enough evidence to charge the Brotherhood with multiple crimes against immigrants. We even have a recording of Damien admitting to trafficking. The CDF will raid his estates while he's at his rally tomorrow and move to apprehend him afterward. The CDF will also be executing a raid on the Brotherhood's compound.

"Arson says Tristan Gelano will eventually reach out to him. When that happens, he will lead us to the council, and we'll take them into custody." Conlan shifted his attention to Randy's window. "Randy, I understand your three talent scouts brought you to RISE's base here on Eden."

This was it. Randy had to decide. "Yeah."

"Good. We can raid RISE's base and shut down their operation."

Randy thought about all the good RISE had done. He thought about Sam and Jay. He thought about Akane. His expression exposed his ambivalence toward revealing RISE's location. "These people aren't bad. RISE is just trying to make the Commonwealth better. Whatever action we take, we can't harm them."

273

Conlan had a duty to fulfill. To him, no matter how good RISE's intentions were, they had to go. "Randy, RISE interfered with our elections, according to Arson's friend Sergei and Stacie's intel. They also took justice into their own hands when they tried to assassinate Damien Sykes—the target of *my* investigation. Who knows how many other people they've killed?

"And I'm not shedding tears for people like Damien, but the justice system, not vigilantes, decides a person's fate. The Commonwealth doesn't need RISE or the Brotherhood, or any other Purist gang. They're poison to our society. They indoctrinate susceptible minds with their ideology and manipulate people into supporting their cause."

"After I give you the location, then what?" Randy's features became stony. "The CDF sends in the troops?"

"Yes," Conlan replied. "We need to confiscate any data they have, find out how much damage they've done to our election infrastructure, and uncover whether anyone inside the government's institutions is secretly aligned with them. But if they surrender peacefully, no harm will come to them. We're not planning to kick down the door and start shooting everyone, Randy."

Randy's jaw muscles tensed, his hesitation showing.

"Randy," Arson said, "I understand that some of these people have convinced you they're your friends, but—"

"They *are* friends, Dad," Randy shot back.

"You need to find some new friends, then," Stacie said matter-of-factly.

Randy ignored her and went on. "They aren't bad people. That's all I'm trying to say."

"Maybe you're right," Arson said. "But the Coalition fought the Battle of the Quad to give colonists a voice and expose the injustice they've suffered. And, sure, some Edenites have changed their mindset. But let's be real, no one expected an instant paradigm shift after the war. Societal transformation takes time. It's an incremental process. And groups like RISE and the Brotherhood aren't part of the solution; they're roadblocks."

Randy gnashed his teeth.

Conlan's demeanor softened. "Randy, give us the location, son."

Chin down, Randy wondered what to do. He didn't want to betray RISE. He didn't want to betray Akane. She had trusted him —*him*, one of her heroes.

He remembered the smiles and handshakes of the RISE members who had welcomed him.

Stacie noticed the apprehension in Randy's eyes. She could tell he was torn between his duty and his desire to protect people he had, for some reason, come to care about. Randy, though imperfect like anyone, had a heart of gold. That was one of the qualities that had drawn her to him. He always wanted to do right by people, by humanity. And once, he had treated her like the most precious thing in existence.

For the first time since their breakup, Stacie spoke to Randy kindly. "Randy, come on." His eyes clung to her. "I know this decision is tearing you up. I can tell you care about these three RISE members who you've been in touch with. And maybe they aren't bad people, but you swore an oath to protect the Commonwealth from all enemies, foreign and domestic. I know that oath means something to you. So what's it going to be? Are you loyal to your duty, or are you loyal to RISE?"

Stacie's words struck a chord within Randy, evaporating the uncertainty enveloping his mind.

• • •

It was nighttime. Dressed in a long-sleeved moisture-wicking shirt and jogging pants, Jay pulled into his driveway in a ground vehicle. He'd just returned from a run in the park.

He immediately noticed the house's lights were off. Nicole and their daughter, Zola, were usually still awake at this hour.

He got out and inspected the front door for any signs of forced entry. Nothing. But that didn't rule out the possibility that someone had hacked the biometric lock. And he was unable to access his Link with Nicole. Maybe she was just asleep.

He pressed his palm to the biometric reader on the door. It zipped open, and he stepped into the living room, which was steeped in darkness and chillingly quiet.

"Lights on," he said. The house's virtual assistant didn't respond. "Nicole. Zola," he called out. His unseeing eyes scanned the room. The knot of worry in his chest built into an agonizing, heart-stopping pressure.

Suddenly, something metallic clinked to the floor near his feet. A sensory-debilitating gas dispersed into the air, and he sagged into unconsciousness.

Jay groaned awake, eyes squinting against dim light. He sat in a chair, wrists zip-tied behind his back. He was in the basement. In front of him, a blurry figure slowly came into focus. It was Nicole. She, too, was bound to a chair, her wrists pinioned behind her.

Standing beside her was Paul Shaffer, the man responsible for her bloody nose, bruised face, and split lip.

Jay's eyes stung with tears at the unbearable sight of his battered wife. "Nicole!"

Paul unsheathed a dagger from his belt and hovered it near Nicole's vulnerable throat.

From behind Jay, Mark MaCallum and Dan Maddox came down the stairs, entering the basement. All three Brotherhood Purists were in plain clothes.

"Hello, Jamie," Paul said. A crooked smirk hitched the corners of his lips as he pressed the tip of the dagger to Nicole's neck.

"Shaffer, you hurt my wife, and for that, I'll—"

Paul cut him off. "You're not in a position to do anything, Specialist. And we know you're with RISE."

A pop-out microblade extended from the ejector cartridge inside Jay's left sleeve, and he began sawing at the zip tie. He figured the blade would come in handy if some Purist punks got the drop on him. He just needed to stall long enough to free himself.

"Tell us where RISE HQ is, or wifey gets a set of brand-new scars," Paul threatened.

Nicole said to her husband, *<Jamie, don't tell them anything, you hear me?>*

<Where's Zola?>

<With her cousin, at my sister's place, for a sleepover. We need to—>

"Hey!" Paul shouted. "No mind-talk while we're around!"

Jay ignored him. *<I have a knife on me. I'm cutting myself free right now. We just need to keep them yapping until—>*

Paul dragged the dagger across Nicole's neck with just enough pressure to break her skin and put fear in her eyes.

Jay trembled, their Link forcing him to share in her pain.

"I told you, no Linked conversations while we're here!" Paul held the bloodied dagger up to his face. "I suggest you listen, or I'll do to both of you what I did to Sergeant Conyers."

"I knew it was you who killed Simone," Jay said. He continued to work at the zip tie with his microblade.

"Where's RISE HQ, Jamie? I'm not kidding around, as you can

see."

"Listen to him, pissant," Dan said. "Cooperate, or die."

Unadulterated hatred contorted Nicole's visage. "Why don't you just shut the hell up, bigot?"

"Now that wasn't very classy." Paul pressed the dagger's tip into Nicole's shoulder, deep enough to draw blood. "I suggest you watch your mouth, or you'll be needing prosthetic replacements for all your limbs."

Nicole winced as a trickle of blood raced down her brown flesh. Jay clamped his teeth, battling the pain he felt in his shoulder too.

Nicole said to Jay, voice quivering, "Don't tell them a- anything."

Paul grinned. "I think it's time for your facial, *Nicole*." He laid the flat of the dagger's steel against her cheek.

A gamut of emotions raided Jay's mind. "No!" He couldn't watch his wife be tortured any longer. He yielded and gave up the coordinates to RISE's base.

"Smart man," Paul sneered.

Nicole glared at her husband. *<Jay?>*

<I had no choice.>

"Thanks for your help," Mark told Jay. He pulled a handgun from behind his back. "Congratulations, you win a quick death. It's better than the slow option, trust me. Though, I have to admit, the slow option's way more fun."

"No, not yet," Paul ordered. "We keep him alive until we verify those coordinates."

"Right," Mark replied, "that makes sense. We can't take this shit stain's word at face value."

Paul said, "I'll take the others and check out the location. If it's legit, you can finish 'em both off. If Jamie lied? Torture part two begins."

As Paul headed upstairs, Jay frowned. Paul was reneging on his promise to let Nicole go if the coordinates weren't fake.

Moments later, the roar of Paul's flyer taking off reverberated from somewhere nearby.

Mark said to Dan, "Let's see what they've got in the fridge."

"I'd say 'don't go anywhere,' but it's not like you can," Dan teased Jay and Nicole.

Mark and Dan left the basement.

They returned after grabbing a bite.

Dan smiled diabolically. "Alright, Shaffer's confirmed—" Nicole remained restrained, but Jay was nowhere in sight. Dan reached for the pistol on his hip. "Where'd—?" A crowbar slammed into the back of his skull, killing him instantly.

Mark spun around, eyes wide. Jay let out a hair-raising scream and swung the crowbar again, bashing in Mark's head.

After Mark's body dropped, Jay breathed hard. He let go of the blood-stained crowbar, and it clattered to the floor. Then he cut the zip tie binding Nicole's wrists.

As they embraced, Nicole sobbed into his shoulder.

Jay said, "Let's get you fixed up. Then we need to get you to your sister's place. The Brotherhood knows I'm with RISE. We can't stay here."

Jay helped Nicole up the stairs.

• • •

Randy knocked on Akane's door. No answer. He knocked again, louder this time. Only the chirping of nocturnal insects answered. "Come on, Akane, open up."

Lights flicked on inside. The front door slid open. Akane—dressed in a mesh negligee that revealed a tantalizing glimpse of her pretty lingerie—poked her head out. "Randy!" she said, surprised but pleased. "Wasn't expecting a pop-in, but come inside!"

He entered, his steps timorous. He wasn't sure how to break the news. The door hissed shut behind him. "Akane, I—" She kissed him, stealing the words from his mouth. "Akane—" he tried again.

Another enticing kiss smothered the rest of his words. Akane obviously didn't want to talk right now.

Randy gently pushed her away. Under normal circumstances, he wouldn't refuse her advances. He'd love nothing more than to get back in bed with her, but that wasn't why he came. "There's something I need to tell you."

Impulsive and hormonal, Akane gave him another kiss, this one fiercer. "Tell me later, 'kay? Take your fucking clothes off." Clearly a command, not a request. She reached to unfasten his pants.

Temptation was staring Randy in the face, but he stayed firm. He moved Akane's hands away. "No, it's important."

Akane released an impatient sigh. "Fine. What is it?"

"I—"

Randy's hesitation gave Akane pause. "Randy, just tell me."

It took much effort for Randy to get the words out. "I . . . gave RISE's location to DFI."

Akane's mood soured. "Are you fucking bullshitting me right now?"

"I *had* to, Akane," Randy insisted.

Akane tightened her fists until her nails bit into her palms, disappointment swelling in her chest. "I trusted you. And after everything we experienced yesterday . . . and did last night, you turn my family in to DFI?" She felt betrayed, having given Randy access to her mind and body. "Damn you!" She shoved him hard.

He stumbled but caught his balance. "Stop, Akane." He kept

his cool in the face of her aggression.

Memories of last night flooded Akane's mind: Randy's hands cradling her face as they kissed, her breathless gasps, his lips and tongue devouring her between her thighs. "So, that's how it is? Fuck me and then sell us out, huh?" She shoved him again, forcefully. "Was that the plan?" Acid invaded her veins. "*Motherfucker!*" Her fists became hammers as she whaled on his chest. "Traitor!" Angry tears reddened the white of her eyes.

Randy grabbed her wrists, trying to restrain her. "Cut it out, Akane!"

Furious, she fought to break free. "Let me the hell go!" She tried to kick his knee but missed, and her slipper went flying to the other side of the room.

Her implant replayed more memories of last night, their bodies drawn to each other like magnets.

She flung her arms upward, but Randy held on to her wrists. Her mind raced with thoughts of the CDF rounding up all her friends. "*Motherfu-*" Randy attempted to pull her into a comforting embrace, but she resisted, jerking back. "I said—"—she grunted —"let go!"

Akane saw Randy as someone who'd just harmed her family, siccing Defense Force dogs on them.

They collided with a table. Something crashed to the floor. Furniture overturned. Bubbles scurried under the bed, hiding.

Randy lifted Akane over his shoulder. Her legs flailed in the air, and she let loose bilingual curses. He set her down in a supine position on the bed, pinning her wrists to the mattress.

She wiggled and squirmed. "Son of a—!"

"Stop it. *Now.*"

"—bitch!" she finished through clenched teeth.

"Please, Akane, enough," Randy pled, eyes searching hers. He hoped the worst of her fury had passed.

Akane calmed her breathing, perspiration glistening her brow.

"Stop fighting me," Randy urged. "I'm not your enemy."

"Right now, it sure feels like you are."

"I'm sorry, but I had to do it."

"Just get off me," Akane said in a less hostile tone, settling down.

"Fine, but don't attack me again." Randy let go of her and got off the bed, his clothes rumpled and damp.

Akane got off the bed too, strands of hair plastered to her forehead and the hem of her negligee riding up.

Randy knew that, after Johanna's death and the attack at the voting station, Akane was already devastated. He had expected her to get pissed off once he told her he'd given up RISE's base. He thought he could soften the blow by explaining himself in person. Maybe even Link with her to prove his sincerity. He hadn't intended to spark a fight.

Akane straightened her negligee's hem. "So, did you know you were gonna betray me before or after the panties came off?"

"You know I didn't plot to sleep with you and then betray you," Randy replied. "You *know* that's not me."

Akane snarled under her breath.

"The CDF doesn't know you're with RISE," Randy said. "You can still move forward with your career as a Guardian." He tentatively reached for her shoulder, hoping to comfort her and show her everything would be okay.

Akane stepped back, out of reach. "Don't touch me! My mom always said that's a privilege. One you don't have anymore."

"Listen, you can still fight for immigrant equality, the *right* way, the legal way. But RISE is history."

Akane ground her teeth. Sam and Jay had been right all along.

Randal Scott didn't fit the mold of a RISE member. Now the CDF was going to raid RISE HQ because of her. Because she'd convinced Sam to let her bring Randy into the fold. "I can't believe this! Why?" She whipped her arms out wide in anger. "Why'd you betray us? You promised you wouldn't!"

RISE was helping immigrants. Randy hadn't wanted to end the organization. "I'm sorry, Akane. It's not like it was an easy decision. But RISE has broken the law. As a Guardian, I can't just turn a blind eye."

Akane nibbled on her bottom lip. Why couldn't he understand? "Everything we do is to fight this oppressive system."

"So the end justifies the means?"

Akane snorted. "It's not like the CDF has been the universe's do-gooders all the time."

"I'm not here to debate morality."

"Just get the hell outta my home."

Randy needed Akane to listen. "There's still time to warn everyone before—"

Akane's wristcom chirped, receiving a message. *What's this?* Akane accessed the message. It was from Jay. She read it. Her heart skipped, and the color drained from her face.

Randy took a step closer. "What is it?"

"Why do you care, sellout?"

"Just tell me."

"HQ's about to be attacked."

"What? The CDF isn't moving in until—"

"No, not by the CDF. By the Brotherhood."

"How the hell did they find RISE?"

Akane summarized Jay's message. "Long story short, Paul and his bitch boys, Mark and Dan, paid Jay and Nicole a visit." She rushed over to her closet. "They roughed up Nicole and forced Jay to give up RISE's location. Jay took care of Mark and Dan, though. He's on his way to HQ now. He already tried contacting Sam but had no luck. Most people are asleep at this hour."

"I'm coming to help."

Akane scoffed. "*Pfft*, whatever." She shook her head. Forgiveness wasn't on the table right now.

She stripped off the negligee and threw on jeans and a shirt.

Randy reached out to her through their Link, hoping the sincerity of his emotions—the weight of his decision to surrender RISE's location—would curb her outrage. *<Akane, you know I'm serious when I say it wasn't an easy decision, right?>* His thoughts were pleading for understanding.

<Stay outta my mind.> Akane disconnected their Link. She then grabbed a pistol from a wall alcove. "I'm outta here." She ran out the door, shoes still unlaced.

"Wait up!"

Akane hopped into her flyer, parked in the driveway, and took off.

Randy sprinted to the lay-by where his sports cruiser sat and jumped inside. He stabbed the ignition button. The start-up sequence engaged, electronics hummed to life, and the flyer zoomed into the night sky.

Akane was already far ahead.

Randy tried to reach his father over the comms. Nothing. Next, he dialed Conlan's number. Nothing. *Damn it.* He keyed in another contact. Five chirps rang out from the dashboard. *Come on, Stace.*

On the seventh chirp, a holo expanded over the windshield. Stacie, groggy and rubbing sleep from her eyes, appeared in a diaphanous fuchsia-colored chemise. "Randy, it's late. What is it?" she asked, speaking into her wristcom's visual interface. Randy's grave expression sobered her instantly.

"The Brotherhood's attacking RISE HQ," Randy said. Stacie sat upright. "I know it's late, but try to get in touch with Conlan. Call him a *million* times if you have to."

"Wait, where are you going?"

"I'm headed to RISE HQ now."

"To do what?"

"Whatever I can."

"Hey, be careful. The Brotherhood's . . . fucking crazy."

"Thanks, Stace." It felt good, him and Stacie being on the same team. It felt good not arguing about the past. "See if you can get in touch with Conlan."

Stacie nodded. The holo shrank and blinked away.

• • •

An army of Brotherhood Purists, clad in nondescript tactical gear, converged on RISE HQ, led by Paul Shaffer. They stood atop a grassy elevation.

Finally, tonight we rid the Commonwealth of these nuisances. Paul used his binoculars to scope out the perimeter. *No defense system that I can see. Easy.* He hand-signaled one of his soldiers.

The broad-bodied man nodded and set a rocket launcher on his shoulder. He put RISE HQ in his launcher's crosshairs and pulled the trigger. A flaming rocket blew open the eastern side of the building.

Frantic alarms went off inside.

Janice launched herself out of bed. The first theory that came to mind was that the unthinkable had happened: Purists, most likely the Brotherhood, had found RISE HQ. She quickly swapped her nightclothes for pants, a shirt, and a pair of boots.

She hit the intercom button on the wall module. "All bodies, arm yourselves! We are under assault!" She grabbed the handgun on her nightstand.

Trained solutioner or not, everyone was going into battle.

Faint gunfire echoed beyond her walls.

Holding her gun in a two-handed grip, she leaned halfway out her door and scanned the hallway.

Strobe lights flashed from red to blue as the alert siren blared.

An armed Purist in a balaclava left one of the rooms lining the hall, having cleared it. When he saw Janice, he raised his handgun.

She slid back into the room just as he shot two rounds at her.

She leaned back out and returned fire. Her bullets zinged past him. He pointed his gun at her to shoot again, but then four bullets ripped open his back.

The Purist went down, revealing Sam behind him—pistol warm, fury burning in his eyes. "Janice, you okay?" he shouted over the wailing siren.

"Yeah!" She hurried to him. "Thanks for the save."

"I didn't think this would ever happen."

"Well, it has."

Gunfire roared inside the building.

Sam said, "Come on, we need to help hold down the fort."

They rushed toward the operations center, where the heart of the battle was raging. Once they entered, they opened fire on the invaders.

Bullets flew back and forth across the operations center.

On one side of the room, RISE members hunkered behind electronic equipment, pinned down. On the opposite side, a phalanx of Brotherhood Purists guarded the breach they'd blasted in the wall. They were going to ensure that no RISE member would escape.

More Purists, all in tactical gear and balaclavas, poured through the opening, joining the firefight against their hated nemesis.

Sam and Janice had taken cover behind a console. They fired, killing three Purists. Bullets zipped back at them, forcing them to duck.

Gunfire pummeled thousands of credits' worth of machinery and equipment. Showers of sparks erupted. Computer screens shattered into fragments. Damaged electronics popped and sizzled, smoke flowing into the air.

Automatic fire from the Purists' weapons mowed down RISE members, leaving the room draped in gore.

Janice rose from her position behind the console and squeezed off two rounds. One bullet put a hole in a Purist's neck; the other penetrated his heart. Before his body crumbled, Janice had already taken out another Purist.

Bullets whisked in her and Sam's direction, destroying more equipment. One slammed into her chest, and she fell backward.

Her gun hit the floor.

"Janice!" Sam unloaded a few shots, then crouched beside his wounded comrade.

Blood pooled beneath Janice. Her breaths came shallow and weak.

In a faint voice, she said, "This . . . is it for me. Goodbye, Sam."

"No! You can make it! Stay with me!" Sam clamped his hands over the bullet hole, desperate to staunch the bleeding. Janice's white shirt turned crimson under his palms.

A RISE member shouted, "Incoming! Move!"

A grenade exploded.

A cacophony of screaming and cursing filled the air.

Hanging on by a thread, Janice said, "The fight . . . is over . . . for me, my friend." Her eyes shut, and she stilled. She was gone, her final resting place RISE HQ—a sanctuary for immigrants.

Sam's eyes misted over as he stared at his bloodied fingers, but there was no time for tears.

Purists hurled Molotov cocktails, glass shattering across the floor. Flames and smoke consumed the room.

Sam coughed. He choked on his words as he shouted, "Everybody, out!"

The two sides charged, merging like colliding tidal waves.

Sam and the remaining RISE members fought their way past the Purists blocking their escape, clearing a path out of the building.

Six of Sam's bullets hit their marks, dropping six Purists. He found satisfaction in every body that fell. *For Janice.* He dashed past the corpses of fallen friends. *We'll get the Brotherhood for this. All of them.* Smoke clogged his nostrils, making him cough.

He and the surviving RISE members barreled through the thick, acrid smoke, finally bursting out into the night air. But they weren't free, far from it. They stared down the barrels of more guns than they could count.

Paul took his place at the head of the assemblage. "End of the line, RISE!"

Sam's bones quaked at the familiar voice. "Shaffer!"

Paul dragged off his mask, unveiling a devilish grin. "Yep, it's me. The one and only!"

"We always suspected you were a Purist," Sam said, his tone as sharp as a knife. "And it was *you* who killed Simone, wasn't it?"

"Yes, sirree!" Paul admitted proudly. "But knowing that doesn't do much for a dead man."

"I'm not dead yet, Shaffer."

"Oh, that's about to change. Now, I already know Jay's one of your little RISE friends. My boys and I paid him and his pretty wife a visit, tortured your location right out of him."

"What? What did you do? If you've harmed them, I'll—"

"You'll what? Kill me?" Paul laughed darkly. "I gave Mark and Dan permission to get rid of Jay and his wife once I confirmed the coordinates were legit. They would've taken care of their little girl too, if she'd been there."

Sam's eyes twitched.

"Don't worry, you'll be joining them soon," Paul said. "Oh, and by the way, Damien Sykes sends his regards. He wanted to make sure you die knowing it was him who finally took you all down. He really wished he could be here to watch you die, considering how much of a pain in the ass you've been."

"Damien? So he *is* the Brotherhood's leader."

"Yep. And let me guess, Akane's part of RISE too. That's why you, Jay, and she are always so chummy, having your little sidebar powwows."

Sam stayed silent.

The Purists' guns clacked as they took aim.

RISE members held their ground, fingers on their guns' triggers.

A standoff.

Sam couldn't stop thinking about the RISE members who'd already been killed. "What is this all about? It makes no sense! We're *all* human beings!"

Paul replied, "If you still don't get it, you're dumber than I thought. Let me spell it out for you. This is about saving the New Humanity. Saving it from colonist domination. Saving it from politicians who are working to ship half of us nonimmigrants out to make room for your kind. Saving it from ruin."

Sam bared his teeth. *Typical Purist nonsense.*

"Alright, finish 'em off, boys," Paul ordered.

Both sides fired their weapons. Though they took some Purists down with them, the outnumbered RISE members were slain.

• • •

Akane landed her flyer beside the burning remains of RISE HQ. Jay's flyer touched down next to hers.

The canopy of Akane's flyer popped open. She jumped out. Bodies were everywhere. *Oh, no. Is everyone . . . gone?* She swallowed the bile rising in her throat.

Sam, lucky to still be alive, sat against a tree. Blood seeped from the stab wound he had received from Paul during the frantic melee. Paul had wanted him to die a slow, painful death. He wanted Sam to be haunted by the sight of his fallen friends as his life ebbed away.

When Akane saw Sam, she gathered her bearings and raced to him.

Jay trailed right behind her, guilt twisting in his gut. *This is my fault.* **I** *gave up RISE HQ.*

Akane knelt next to Sam, the orange glow of the fire washing over her face. "Sam, you're gonna be okay, right?" The sound of flames crackled in her ears.

"I don't think so, Akane," he replied weakly. When he saw Jay come up, he thought, *Well, I'll be damned. He's okay.*

Part of RISE HQ's roof caved in. The loud crash startled Akane and Jay, debris tumbling into the inferno.

Sam forced himself to speak. "The Brotherhood ambushed us. Shaffer was here, leading the charge. We were right. It was him who killed Simone."

Of course it was, Akane thought.

Jay looked visibly ill. "This is my fault. I gave them our location. I—"

"No," Akane cut in, "don't blame yourself for this. Shaffer and his dirtbag crew tortured your wife."

Sam struggled to nod. "She's right, Jay." His skin had gone

pale, and sweat drenched his brow. Had he not been neohuman, he might have been dead by now. "Damien Sykes did this. Paul admitted Damien's the Brotherhood's leader. He sent Paul, Mark, and Dan to torture you and Nicole. He sent the Brotherhood here . . . to wipe out RISE. If you want to blame someone, Jay, blame Damien."

Irrevocable anger scorched Akane's veins. "Sykes is gonna pay!" she vowed. "Shaffer too!"

"Right now, Akane, just . . . let it go," Sam said, strength slowly withering. "RISE's fight . . . is over. Forget about this . . . for a while. You can still make a difference, though, in the CDF."

Akane's eyes were ice-cold. "No. Sykes can't get away with this, and he won't. Maybe Reza was right. Maybe a good old-fashioned public execution is what's needed to make a statement." She ran off, fighting back tears.

"Akane, wait up!" Jay called out.

"Jay—"—Sam coughed—"keep her safe. Go."

"What about you?"

"Go, Jay. That's an order, damn it."

The wail of emergency vehicles grew closer, and CDF flyers were approaching fast. Stacie had finally reached Conlan.

Jay peeled his eyes away from Sam, who might be dead by the end of tonight, and ran after Akane. *Hopefully, those emergency responders will get here in time. Hang in there, Sam.*

Randy and Stacie's flyers landed, along with those of the CDF and emergency responders'.

Fire crews disembarked. They grabbed the hoses attached to their vehicles and blasted suppressant foam over the burning building.

Randy left his flyer. His blood froze as he surveyed the mass of dead bodies. When he spotted a medic about to roll Sam away in a capsule gurney, he broke into a sprint. Stacie followed close behind. It was obvious that she had left home in a hurry—she had tied her hair in a messy ponytail, and she wore a T-shirt and sweatpants.

Randy said to the medic, "I'm Guardian Randal Scott. He's stable, right?"

She replied, "Yes, he is."

"Good, I need a quick word with him."

"Sorry, I have to—"

"It's okay," Sam told her.

The medic turned to Randy. "Ten minutes. That's it." She delivered her words with an indignant bite.

After the medic moved away, Randy started speaking to Sam. "Is everyone—"

"Yeah, everyone's gone, Scott," he responded. The life-saving fluids and healing accelerants being siphoned into his veins had him feeling better. "Except those who live offsite. And guess who was leading the assault on RISE HQ? Our buddy, Paul Shaffer."

"Yeah, I learned he was a member of the Brotherhood earlier," Randy said. "Akane beat me here, right? Where is she?"

"She and Jay took off. And Akane's pissed. She's going to kill Damien. He's responsible for this. He's the leader of—"

"Yeah, he's the leader of the Brotherhood, their Headmaster," Stacie interrupted, coming up beside Randy. "We found that out already. But this Akane can't kill him. The CDF's about to raid all his estates and the Brotherhood's compound tomorrow, and they're going to take Damien into custody. He's involved in intergalactic trafficking of weapons and women. DFI needs him alive to tell them more about his operation, to tell them where more innocent victims are being held."

"Not to mention, Michael Conlan would stop at nothing to

find who assassinated the target of a DFI investigation," Randy interjected. "If Akane kills Damien, she'd eventually get locked up in an orbital prison. I can't let that happen. She's my friend."

"Friend?" Stacie said inquisitively.

"Yeah, she, Jay, and Sam here are members of Vanguard Alpha. They're the three RISE members who've been trying to recruit me. I guess you could say we became close." Randy asked Sam, "Do you know where Akane and Jay are?"

Sam thought about Akane's words: *Maybe Reza was right. Maybe a good old-fashioned public execution is what's needed to make a statement.*

"Nope," Sam said. "But I'm betting they'll crash Damien's rally tomorrow and take him out there."

Stacie scoffed. "The rally's going to be swarming with security. Fat chance anyone gets close enough to Damien to fire even one shot."

"Akane's not going to do this stealthily, sneaking past security and all that bullshit," Sam replied. "She's going to do it publicly and blatantly, with Jay's help. And with a Shell, she can slaughter anyone who gets in her way, which she just might, seeing as how pissed she is right now."

Stacie's eyes went wide. "Where the hell's she getting a Shell from? She can't just check one out of a military installation like a book from an old-school Earth Era library."

"Our bunker," Sam said. "That's where she ran off to. We acquired seven Shells and stored them there. Six are M-X02s— four male type, two female. The other's an M-X01. All security parameters have been deactivated."

"Where's this bunker?" Randy demanded.

"Behind the Sejuela Trees. The access panel's actually built into one of them, the lone one farther off from the rest."

Stacie asked, "How the heck did you guys heist some Shells?"

Right now, that was irrelevant to Randy. "Who cares, Stace?"

The medic returned. "Time's up." She pressed the close-lid command on the gurney's keypad, and the transparent sliding cover hissed shut. Then she took Sam to an ambulance flyer.

Randy said, "Stace, I . . . I need your help to stop Akane. I can't take her and Jay by myself."

"You don't have to take on *anyone*. Let's just inform Conlan. The CDF will put out an APB on both of them, and—"

"No! If Akane's captured, she'll be put away! Right now, no one else knows she's a member of RISE. My dad and Conlan don't even have her name. All they know is that a woman and two men from RISE befriended me. They don't know those three RISE members are Guardians in the ETF. What I want to do is save Akane, save her from herself—from her rage."

"So you're going to deradicalize her? You haven't been able to talk her into leaving RISE so far; what makes you think you can convince her to abort her assassination mission?"

"I have to try."

"This woman means a lot to you, doesn't she?"

"Yeah, she's the first person to treat me like a comrade and a human being since I came back to the CDF from leave. She's my *friend*."

"Did you two Link?"

"Yeah, so?"

"Well, I know you. You're not Linking with someone unless they're pretty special to you. Did you . . . sleep with her?"

A wrinkle appeared between Randy's eyebrows. "Yeah, we had sex, Stace. What's that got to do with anything?"

"I'm saying your judgment might be impaired by your *feelings* for this woman," Stacie said, gesturing emphatically. "If we try to stop her and her friend on our own—with no backup from the CDF or law enforcement—and we screw this the hell up and they kill Damien, it's on *us*, Randy.

"I stomached a lot to help DFI get dirt on Damien. You don't know what it's like forcing yourself to be in the company of someone you despise. I let Damien *touch* me, feel me, kiss me. I did that so he could be brought to justice.

"If the CDF puts out an APB on Akane and her friend, they can scour this *entire* region state to find them. This could end tonight. There's no need to risk fouling DFI's investigation into Damien—fouling all my efforts, everything I tolerated."

Randy was determined to save Akane. There was no talking him out of it. "So let's not screw this up, then."

Stacie shook her head. "Unbelievable."

"Akane has lost everyone she knows and loves. She came to Eden with other immigrants. You know what happened? One of her friends threw herself off a building after prolonged exposure to immigrant discrimination. Another was shot in the head during his and Akane's BCT, just for expressing his *unpopular* opinion on the civil war. Then Paul Shaffer killed her best friend, a Guardian named Simone who took her in. Now her RISE family is dead, and it's all because of *Damien Sykes*.

"Destroying RISE was the last straw for Akane. That's why she's on a rampage. So if we alert DFI and they nab her, convict her, and destroy her career, it'll be because of Damien. Do you really want to let him do that to this young woman, who's already suffered enough? She's just nineteen. You want to let Damien have another win, ruin another life?"

Stacie said nothing, letting Randy's passionate speech marinate in her thoughts.

"Stace, I'm asking you to help me, please. You know I'm right about this. Destroying Akane's career and her life by getting her locked up would be unfair to her and her parents."

Oh, fuck me. Stacie sighed. *I don't know why the hell I'm doing this.* "Okay, Randal, *fine.* I'll help you stop these two. But *if* your friend doesn't listen to reason, she might be a lost cause, and we might have to put her down. Just sayin'."

"We won't have to." Randy knew it might take a fight to get Akane to stand down, but he wouldn't have to take her life.

"So what's our play?"

"Sam said RISE had seven Shells. That means there's five more. We'll need two to stop Akane and Jay."

"So now we're stealing government property?" Stacie didn't want to face theft charges from the government.

"You got a better idea of how to stop two shelled Guardians hellbent on assassinating a Chief Executive candidate? You wanna what, throw sticks and stones at them? Don't worry, we'll ensure the CDF gets its hardware back."

"Alright, we'll do things your way."

"Okay, so we'll come back here in the morning,"—Randy glanced at the Guardians and police combing the area—"when the place isn't swarming with Guardians and law enforcement. I doubt they'll find the bunker. Sounds like it's well hidden. The CDF and the cops aren't searching for access panels built inside trees."

"Okay, so I'll see you back here at . . . noon?"

"The rally starts at fifteen hundred. Are you sure that'll give us enough time to transport the Shells? And where are we going to stage, anyway?"

"I'll take care of transporting the Shells. Noon's plenty of time. Leave the staging ground to me."

"Okay."

Stacie headed to her flyer. "See you tomorrow."

Randy's eyes drifted over the fallen RISE members. Tomorrow, the Brotherhood would be finished. He looked forward to hearing about the raid on their compound, and he hoped every one of those bastards would be killed.

He climbed into his flyer and went home.

• • •

Akane and Jay sat in the attic of a RISE supporter's home, trying to cope. Randy knew where Akane lived, so they couldn't risk going back to her place.

Sullen-faced, they finished their meals. Then they set their ceramic plates on the floor beside them.

Akane drew her knees to her chest. "It's still hard to believe, man. Everyone is gone. Just about." RISE had been her family away from her family, and they were now dead, thanks to the Brotherhood.

Jay placed a hand on her shoulder. "We'll get Sykes tomorrow—for them."

The attic's sliding floor panel creaked open, and an old woman poked her head up. "Are you two okay? Is there anything I can get you?"

"No, we're fine, Ms. Simmons," Akane replied.

"Alright, just let me know if you need anything."

The panel slid shut.

"Come on, let's try to get some sleep," Akane said, curling up under the covers of her makeshift pallet.

Jay lay down in his pallet and shut his eyes, trying to purge the macabre image of slaughtered friends from his mind. He thought about his wife and daughter. To keep them safe, the Brotherhood and every other anti-immigrant extremist group had to be eliminated.

As Jay slept, Akane prepared to go take care of Paul Shaffer. She wore leggings, a shirt, and a hoodie for her mission. *Gotta do this one solo, Jay.*

She remembered the day she discovered Paul might be Simone's killer . . .

Akane stormed up to Sam. "Why didn't you tell me about Shaffer?"

"What are you talking about, Akane?" Sam replied calmly.

"Why didn't you tell me he was the bastard who killed Simone?"

"Who told you that? Was it Jay?"

"Doesn't matter. It's true, though, isn't it?"

"We strongly suspect he's the one who killed Simone."

Akane whirled around. "That's it, I'm gonna—"

Sam snatched her wrist with so much force that she nearly tripped. "You're not doing anything, Akane."

Oh, yes the hell I am. She wiggled her wrist, struggling to escape Sam's grasp—the only thing delaying her from exorcising her bloodlust.

Sam said, "Listen to me. Shaffer might be an immigrant hater and a jerk, but we don't just kill everyone who despises us. I promise you, when we're one hundred percent sure he killed Simone, you'll have your shot. But not before. Understood?"

Akane reluctantly obeyed Sam's orders. He was a leader within RISE, after all. "Yeah, Guthrie, I got you. I won't harm a hair on Shaffer's head until you give me the green light, 'kay?" Her words held the sting of acquiescence. She'd defer vengeance, but patience had an expiration date, and it was approaching fast.

Sam unclasped her wrist. "Good. You have my word, Simone

will not go unavenged." He wanted Simone's killer dead too.

At the destroyed RISE base, just before Akane left, Sam confirmed Paul was Simone's murderer. It was finally time for Akane to unleash hell. Tomorrow, she and Jay would deal with Damien, but tonight would be Paul Shaffer's reckoning. The inferno inside Akane wouldn't die down until she had blood.

• • •

Paul, riding in an air-cab, guzzled the last of the liquor from the bottle in his hand. He'd celebrated tonight's victory with strippers and alcohol. It was a damn good time.

Funny, he couldn't get in touch with Mark or Dan. Maybe they were out partying too. He figured they'd check in by morning.

The cab touched down outside his apartment complex. Paul got out, tossed the empty bottle into a trash receptacle, and headed inside, ready to sleep off the buzz.

He entered an elevator and pressed the button for the sixth floor. Once there, he walked down the hallway to his apartment and pressed his palm to the biometric reader. A chirp confirmed the security scan, and the locks disengaged.

Yawning and stretching, he stepped inside.

The door hissed shut.

Before he could activate the lights, he heard a click from behind him. He spun around. A slender figure holding a plasma knife lunged from the shadows, the red eyes of their mask glowing.

Paul reacted fast. He flung the coffee table at the intruder.

It crashed into her, knocking her off her feet. The knife flew from her grasp, skidding across the wooden floor.

Paul charged. As the intruder scrambled to get up, he seized her throat with one hand, slamming her back against the wall.

"Lights on," Paul commanded.

The room lit up. He saw the intruder was wearing a hockey-style mask that had glowing infrared insets.

He jerked off the mask. "Akane!" He chuckled. "Trying to take me out, huh, pipsqueak? Ballsy, but dumb." His fingers dug into her throat, throttling the life out of her.

The edges of Akane's vision blurred as her lungs begged for oxygen. *Not gonna let this motherfucker do me in.* She drove a knee into Paul's groin.

He howled. "Damn it!" His hand released Akane's throat. "*Fucking* little import!"

Akane sucked in precious air. "That's for all the shitty days of heartache!" She shoved past Paul, diving for her knife.

Doing his best to ignore the throbbing in his groin, Paul tackled Akane from behind, ramming his body into hers.

They both hit the floor hard.

Akane clambered to her feet, body aching. Paul, still on the floor, caught her ankle and yanked, sending her crashing down face-first.

He stood, still holding her ankle.

She kicked free, throwing him off-balance. As he stumbled backward, she sprang upright and scooped up her knife.

She pointed the blade of energy at him, her murderous eyes promising his demise. "This *import's* about to send you to Hell."

Paul rolled his shoulders, joints cricking. Then he cracked his knuckles and assumed a fighting stance. "That so?"

Akane slashed at him, aiming to take off his head. "For Simone!"

He dodged.

With stormy eyes, Akane screamed and raised the knife high. She brought it down fast, as if she intended to cleave Paul in two.

He caught her wrist before the blow could land. "Still crying over that dead bitch," he taunted. "How touching."

They scuffled, fighting for control of the knife. Paul's grip tightened to an unbearable intensity, forcing Akane to drop it. With both arms, he lifted her above his head and tossed her across the room. She slammed into a couch, her flailing foot kicking a vase off the side table.

Paul picked up the knife. "Say hello to Simone for me." He stalked toward Akane to finish her off.

Akane's yearning for revenge wouldn't allow her to be defeated. She rose onto all fours, grabbed the fallen vase, and launched it at Paul. It struck his face, breaking his nose. The excruciating pain fogged his head and wrenched the knife from his fingers.

"You little shit!" he roared. He buried his face in his hands as warm blood flowed from his nostrils.

Moving on pure adrenaline, Akane retrieved the knife. While Paul was still stunned, she blasted herself at him and lodged the energy blade into his chest, making him pay for all the tears she had shed.

Paul wailed in agony.

Yes, suffer, asshole, Akane thought. The heartache from Simone's death flared up, not to ebb until Paul was a corpse.

He crumbled backward, lifeless eyes staring blankly at the ceiling.

Akane leaned over, ripped the blade from his chest, and clicked it off. *I got the son of a bitch, Simone. I finally got him.*

She picked up her mask and drew her hoodie over her messy hair. Body hurting all over, she limped her way out the door.

● ● ●

Jay woke at the creak of the attic's floor panel sliding aside.

Akane hobbled up the stairs with scrapes on her face, a swollen bottom lip, and bruises under her clothes.

Jay propped himself up on an elbow. "Akane, what the—?"

"Yeah, I look like shit, right?" Akane slipped into her pallet.

"What happened?"

Exhausted, Akane curled up and tugged her hoodie low over her head. "I took care of Shaffer."

"Hey, you could've let me come—"

"No, I had to do it alone."

Though Jay would've preferred Akane let him help, he understood. "Well, I'm just glad you're safe." He was also glad Simone's death had been avenged.

"Let's get some sleep. Sykes is next."

Without another word, both closed their eyes.

CHAPTER SEVEN

Satellite One
Colony Four

RISE's council—Tristan Gelano, Franco DeFalco, and Julian Hurst—sat at a table in the room of a run-down building.

Franco stroked his gray beard in consternation. "It's still hard to believe the Brotherhood destroyed everything we built."

Tristan was tough. The enemy's victory wouldn't eclipse her resolve. "It's tragic. But there are countless immigrants on Eden hungry and willing to take up the fight for equality. RISE is an idea, and ideas never die. RISE will be reborn."

A determined expression settled on Julian's weathered face. "Indeed. That's why we're here, to discuss the rebirth of RISE."

Knuckles rapped against the rotting wooden door.

"Our guests have arrived," Tristan said. She stood and opened the door.

Sergei and Arson walked into the dilapidated room.

Tristan hugged Arson. "It's good to see you." She turned and embraced Sergei. "You too."

Sergei felt defeated but refused to let it show. "These are unfortunate times."

"Yes," Franco replied, his hands clasped together on the table. "But when you get knocked down, you get back up. We will rebuild RISE stronger—better."

Julian said, "Arson, Sergei, we appreciate you joining us today."

At the roar of vehicles reverberating outside, Franco jumped to his feet and yanked aside the ragged canvas covering the window. He saw BUSs unloading Guardians. "The Commonwealth Defense Force is here."

Tristan froze in place. "What? How did they find us?"

"No one tailed us; I'm certain," Sergei said.

Julian shot up from his chair. "We need to leave. There's an underground exit—"

Arson whipped his handgun from its holster. "No one's going anywhere."

Sergei pulled his own weapon, aiming it at Arson. "Of all people, I never expected you to betray us."

"RISE is dead, and it's going to stay dead," Arson declared. "There needs to be peace among all the Commonwealth's peoples, but that can't happen while extremist groups are manipulating elections and recruiting the youth into their madness."

Sergei's voice erupted. "I thought you were a changemaker, a revolutionary!"

"I was a revolutionary. The Coalition fought and won the civil war to remove corrupt leaders, free the netscape from censorship, and clean up the central government. It was supposed to be the people who chose their new leaders, through honest, fair elections. But groups like RISE and the Brotherhood are sabotaging that."

Sergei was about to fire.

Arson beat him to the punch, blowing a hole into his arm.

Sergei staggered backward, the pain causing him to relinquish his weapon.

"Nobody else move!" Arson barked. "I don't want to kill anyone, but I will."

Guardians filed into the room, bringing their rifles to bear.

"You're finished," Arson said to Tristan, Julian, and Franco.

The Guardians cuffed the council members and Sergei.

Arson stared at Tristan, his eyes reflecting the anguish of having to apprehend her. "I'm sorry. Know that I support RISE's cause, just not their tactics. If you guys had been open to changing them, maybe this—"

"Save it," Tristan snapped.

A Guardian grabbed her arm and led her away.

The Brotherhood's next, Arson thought. The CDF would raid their compound today, along with Damien's estates. They would also take Damien into custody after his campaign rally.

• • •

Randy and Stacie stood atop a half-finished building overlooking Damien's rally site, a property Stacie now owned. She had secured it as their observation post for today's stakeout. On the rooftop docking platform sat a boxy transport flyer. It contained the Shells they'd gotten from RISE's underground bunker.

Both Randy and Stacie were suited up in the sleeves Randy had obtained for them.

Stacie's team of chasers was stationed at the rally site below, eyes peeled for Akane and Jay, while she and Randy monitored the situation from above.

The area around the stage setup had reached full capacity, packed with clamorous Damien Sykes supporters. The overflow crowd gathered along the barriers lining Damien's limo route, desperate for a glimpse of their champion.

305

Randy lowered his binoculars. He and Stacie had a clear line of sight over the rally. Whether Jay and Akane were among the mass of people remained to be seen. But they'd presumably attempt to take out Damien in their stolen Shells, not civilian attire.

He'd heard a news report about authorities finding Mark MaCallum and Dan Maddox dead in Jay's basement. Akane told him the Brotherhood forced RISE's location out of Jay by roughing up his wife, so it was clearly self-defense. The report also mentioned that Paul Shaffer had been stabbed in his apartment. Randy didn't need to guess who the culprit was. He had to stop Akane from killing Damien too, from ruining DFI's operation, from staining her hands with more blood.

Beside him, Stacie lit up a cigarette to quell her nerves. She regretted not telling Conlan about Akane and Jay's plan to assassinate Damien, but it was too late now. She and Randy had taken matters into their own hands, for better or worse.

The potent scent of nicotine traveled into Randy's nostrils, and he coughed. "I thought you quit."

Stacie plucked the cigarette from her lips, exhaling smoke in a slow stream. "Still working on it," she snapped.

Randy faced the rally site once more and gathered his thoughts. He wanted to make peace with Stacie, even if they couldn't get back together. He figured he might as well try again. *Here goes nothing.*

He turned to Stacie. "Stace, I don't want to be enemies. I know I hurt you, and for the hundredth time, I'm sorry. The truth is that no other woman has been the right fit for me. Not Kesley. Not anyone. Not even . . . Akane, apparently." He edged closer to her. "I'm not asking you to get back with me, but after everything we've been through together, I don't want to lose you as a friend. I don't want to be on bad terms.

"When I was in a dark place, you brought light to my life."

Stacie listened, her cigarette simmering between her fingers.

Randy said, "Hell, maybe I would've gone insane after my mother's death if it weren't for you. I *need* you, Stace. Just . . . do me a favor. Link with me. *Just* for a minute."

His eyes pled with her. "You'll see I'm serious. You'll feel how sorry I am and how lost I've been without you. This isn't some rehearsed kiss-and-makeup bullshit. I mean every word." He paused. "If we can't get back what we had, fine. But I don't want us at each other's throats. So please . . . Link with me."

Linking, the ultimate empathy bridge, had helped mend things between him and his father. He hoped it could do the same for him and Stacie.

"I just want you to know I'm being sincere," he said.

Stacie remembered how Randy stood by her side when she was bedridden during BCT, how he cheered her on when she wanted to quit, how he motivated her and pushed her to finish. She wouldn't have graduated from BCT without him. It was because of him that she had been a Guardian—major brownie points in her book.

Loud, excited voices from below interrupted her reflections as she considered whether to Link.

She tossed the cigarette away. "Hey, sounds like the program is about to start. We need to watch out for Akane and Jay."

Randy sighed. "Right." He returned to the parapet, without an answer from Stacie. Then he lifted the binoculars up to his eyes and tapped the zoom function. *When are you gonna show, Akane?*

Stacie spoke into her wristcom. "Jason, report."

Jason moved amid the flood of bodies. He had on casual

clothes and dark sunglasses.

Rally-goers, packed shoulder to shoulder, chanted for Damien.

"No sign of our targets yet," Jason said to Stacie. "But Eli, DeShaun, and I are staying on our toes."

"Copy," Stacie replied.

Air-lane traffic had been suspended within a twenty-mile radius, and authorities had blocked every entry point except one to control the flow of people.

A paunchy middle-aged man, sporting a "Vote for Damien" pin on his shirt, nudged Jason's shoulder with his elbow. His eyes gleamed with unsettling fanaticism. "Guy's gonna save the republic, man. He'll stop the immigrants from takin' over and make sure all those Coalition traitors get what they deserve."

"Uh, yeah," Jason mumbled awkwardly, eager to distance himself from the man. He slipped away, eyes scanning the restless crowd for any sign of Jay or Akane.

The air pulsed with venomous chants of "Kill the Coalition filth," "Deport the immigrants," "End the lottery," and "Put Amaechi behind bars."

So much rage. So much hate, Jason thought, unnerved by the sight of hundreds of bitter, angry faces.

Eli and DeShaun, dressed in plain clothes, went up to him.

"Insane. All this animosity, I mean," Eli said to Jason, shaking his head. "And there are some real oddballs here."

"Yeah." Jason tamped down the disquieting feeling that was prickling his skin and refocused on the mission. "Stay alert, you two. We can't let our assassins slip by us. Odds are they'll show up in those stolen Shells, but . . . you never know."

"Right," DeShaun said.

The team split off.

One by one, prominent public figures took the stage. Each

delivered speeches filled with hateful rhetoric—overblown, inflammatory, and utterly turgid.

• • •

Oviereya, sitting at her desk in the Executive Office, watched a live stream of the rally on her laptop. She'd known there would be backlash after she exonerated all Coalition fighters. But it was the right thing to do, given that the rebellion had arisen from years of government neglect. Even the Union leaders had stated that the rebellion wasn't treason but rather a justified reaction to systemic oppression.

After Damien was arrested and exposed as a criminal today, his enraged supporters wouldn't simply disappear. They would still demand that Coalition fighters face trial, and they would fight, protest, and riot to preserve the status quo. And when another anti-reform politician inevitably emerged to take Damien's place, they would flock to him, their next self-proclaimed savior.

The election for the Chief Executiveship remained an uphill battle. Yet, Oviereya held onto a fragile hope. After learning about the government's mistreatment of the colonies and hearing reports about violence against immigrants, some citizens began to reevaluate their perspectives. But the divisions ran deep. The Commonwealth would remain a fractured society for some time, unless some catastrophic event suddenly brought everyone together. Oviereya prayed such a thing would never happen.

• • •

At the rally, the moment everyone had been waiting for arrived.

Flanked on both sides by boisterous supporters pressed against the crowd-control barriers, Damien's limo slowly made its way to the stage.

Fists pumped the air. Hurrahs thundered. Hands clapped.

Damien sipped a martini in the back of his limo and peered out the one-way glass windows. His adoring fans' effusive praise energized him.

His father had taught him to be the best at anything and everything he pursued. Weakness and defeat were unacceptable.

Damien had respected his father, a man of strength, power, and fortitude. Now, he was gone, stolen from him by Arman Reza's death squads—by the Coalition. And Chief Amaechi had just let those insurrectionists walk free.

Damien swore he'd set things right. He'd overturn Amaechi's exoneration of the Coalition fighters and hold them accountable. He would also make proud the second most influential figure in his life, Atticus Hancroft.

Everything was coming together. He was certain he'd win the Chief Executiveship, and it seemed Stacie was back in his life. But was she really? What was this game of cat and mouse she was playing?

He didn't fully trust her yet, and with good reason. That was why he'd kept her blindfolded while they traveled to and from the Brotherhood's compound. That was why he had someone watching her. So far, his operative had reported nothing concerning. That was a good sign, because he'd hate to eliminate her. But he would if necessary.

I wonder how Ms. Evasive is doing. Damien sent Stacie a message on his wristcom.

She accessed the message, frowning. Did she really have to keep playing along? If Damien somehow evaded indictment, she might have to continue helping Defense Force Intelligence. So yes, for now, it was best to play along.

Damien: How are you, my dear?

Stacie: Stellar. I'm at home watching the rally. Quite the fan base you've got.

Damien: Indeed.

Stacie: Rooting for ya! Go get 'em!

Damien: See you tonight afterward?

Stacie: Most definitely.

Stacie rolled her eyes. *I can't wait for this creep to get busted today. I just have to keep those two RISE lackeys from killing him.*

Damien's limo pulled up next to the stage.

The announcer bellowed over the sound system, "Now here he is, the next Chief Executive of the Commonwealth, Mr. Damien Sykes!"

The crowd roared.

Damien got out of the limo in a posh burgundy suit. He ascended the stairs, stepped onto the stage, and strode confidently to the lectern.

Paul Shaffer was supposed to be onstage with the other two bodyguards. Damien had heard about his death on the news, which he assumed was the work of RISE remnants. He hated losing a good soldier, but the show had to go on.

He spoke into the mic. "First, I want to thank every one of you for your support." The crowd burst into cheers and whistles. "Why does a man who has everything—everything he could ever want—run for Chief Executive? The reason is simple: I refuse to sit by and watch our republic sink into the abyss. I refuse to watch men and women who committed the greatest atrocity in Commonwealth history walk free. And yes, I said greatest. I refuse to let our republic be destroyed."

Stacie scowled. *You're running because you're a narcissistic egomaniac.*

Randy noticed the telling look on her face. "What's the deal between you and Sykes? You said you two had a 'thing' going?"

"Yeah. We were involved. My parents found out and put an

end to it. Eight children don't intermingle romantically. But Damien and I kept secretly hooking up. In hindsight, it was a shitty relationship."

Randy sensed there was more to Stacie's ire than just a past relationship she regretted. Her expression right now practically radiated repugnance. "I get the feeling he's wronged you pretty badly in some way."

A muscle in Stacie's cheek twitched. "I introduced Damien to a close friend of mine, Cassie." The memory of Cassie sobbing after the jury's verdict flashed through her mind. "Damien played her, manipulated her into thinking he actually loved her. She was just another trophy to him. Another conquest. A fucking pet. A plaything. Like the rest of his bedfellows." Her voice darkened as she said, "And he slapped her around more than once." The desire to rip Damien's heart out boiled in her veins. "She and I took him to trial. But he got away scot-free."

"What happened to Cassie?"

"She took a job with Galactic Excavation Incorporated, one of the big players in its industry. They've got her traveling to different worlds, studying minerals to gauge their value to the Commonwealth. She just got back to Eden recently."

"Have you talked to her?"

A deep longing for her friend shone in Stacie's eyes. "I haven't spoken to her since the trial. It's obvious she blames me for introducing her to Damien, for everything that happened, for that circus of a trial." She wrapped her arms around herself as a wave of self-reproach crashed down on her.

Stacie's emotions were like a palpable weight descending upon Randy. "Sounds like you're just guessing," he said encouragingly. "You don't know that for sure."

"Oh, I know." Shame flooded Stacie's soul. "The way she

looked at me outside the courthouse, before she got in that air-cab . . . It was silent and as cold as ice. That said everything.

"She ghosted me after the trial, never answered my calls or messages. She didn't even tell me about the new job that would send her into the depths of the galaxy. I heard about that from a mutual acquaintance. So yeah, I'd say she's pissed at me, in my humble opinion."

"Still, you don't know how she feels for sure. And you shouldn't blame yourself for what happened. It was Damien who hurt Cassie, not you."

Stacie, burdened by guilt, felt a heavy feeling in her chest. "I'm the one who introduced them. I ignored the warning signs . . . things about Damien I should never have brushed off."

"Like I said, *he's* the one who hurt your friend, Stace. Not you," Randy said in that hero voice that came naturally to him.

He's always trying to make people feel better or give them hope, Stacie thought. One of Randy's many irritatingly good qualities. "Yeah, well, anyway, he's finally gonna pay." She oriented herself toward the rally. "Normally, I wouldn't care if your friend killed him. But DFI needs him alive to gather information about his trafficking operation and save women who are probably being used as playthings right now. That's why I put myself in risky situations to get close to him."

She thought about the kiss she gave Damien at the Brotherhood's compound to allay his suspicion. "I despised every second of being around him. I didn't suffer through all that bullshit just to let this fall apart. DFI's investigation is more important than your friend's vengeance."

"That much, we agree on," Randy replied.

Switching gears, Stacie asked curiously, "So, how's Jarius?"

Randy smiled a little. "He took my advice, decided to

commission into the Ambassador Corps. He's at Officer Candidate School."

"Good for him."

Randy returned his attention to the rally.

The crowd clung to Damien's every word.

"The pundits call me 'extreme,' a 'loose cannon,' a 'wildcard,'" Damien said. "Well, I'm all that and more!" An applause boomed. "We don't need some coward in office, or a spineless centrist that tries to walk the middle line. We need someone who'll preserve AEGIS's framework for humanity. Someone who won't let Amaechi tear down our military's proud culture. Someone who'll hold Coalition fighters accountable for their untenable actions. I will be that person."

Damien's political bombast made Stacie's head throb. She wished he would just shut the hell up.

Randy lowered his binoculars. "Stace, Akane and Jay will probably make their move soon. We need to get shelled and head down there. We can't stop them from up here."

"Let's suit up, then."

Stacie pulled up her wristcom's holographic interface and pressed an icon on a drop-down menu. The transport's sealed doors swung outward, and a platform extended from the cargo hold, delivering the two standing M-X02 Shells to her and Randy.

She tapped another icon. The platform clicked free from the track it was connected to and hovered into the air. Using the interface's directional controls, she guided the platform down in front of her and Randy.

The rear paneling of her Shell opened, and she entered the rubberized interior. Then she grabbed the helmet from the magnetic catch on her hip and slid it over her head. The faceplate zinged shut. Brackets locked, and the CPU's wetware uplinks synced to her implant. Icons, readings, and diagnostics scrolled across her HUD.

Smart fibers contracted to fit her frame. Telescoping tiles of Kryoplaste shifted, rearranging themselves. The Shell morphed into an extension of her body, every joint optimized for mobility.

After the CPU completed its diagnostic check, Stacie flexed her wrists and arms. Mind/machine integration complete, the CPU's unmatched computational power flooded her implant with information. Her mind instantly registered the approximate headcount of rally attendees, possible enemy approach vectors, and even small details such as the building's exact height. Yet the constant data stream never felt like a neural overload.

With enhanced strength and speed, an arsenal capable of leveling a building, and cerebral access to the entire netscape, Stacie felt like a combat goddess. The Shell's power vibrated her bones. It thrilled her every time she suited up. The mechanized battle suit was a formidable weapon, and now the unthinkable had happened: Two extremists had control of two Shells and were about to use them to carry out a public execution.

Randy's Shell completed its user configuration, tailoring itself to his proportions. He rolled his shoulders and tested the fit, punching the air with a one-two combo. *Fits good.* He flicked his wrist. *Click.* He'd worried the hacked suits wouldn't be fully operational, but they were, aside from comms. They also lacked the latest Nerve Center software updates, but that wasn't a showstopper.

"Stace," Randy said.

"Yeah?"

"We've got no C-comms or audio comms. We should Link."

Stacie's brows soared. "What? No way. I'm—"

"I get it. I know we're not . . . together anymore, and yeah, you're not crazy about the idea. But we need to maintain communication. It's not going to kill you. Come on, just for the mission."

Stacie hesitated, deliberating. Randy was right. "Okay, Randal. Fine."

Silently, Randy concentrated and sent the Link request.

Stacie's implant pinged. The reestablished Link allowed her to feel Randy's love for her, his self-disappointment, and his longing to be with her again.

Randy wasted no time, proceeding with the mission. "Stace, let's get into position."

Staying on task, Stacie brought herself out of Randy's mind, but his feelings continued whispering to her amygdala. "Okay."

They transitioned into stealth mode. The Shells' holographic cloaking skins shimmered, reflecting their surroundings like liquid glass.

Randy hopped down to platform one of the construction scaffolding. Stacie thunked down beside him. Together, they leapt from platform to platform until they reached the ground.

Damien said, "The Coalition dropped onto our soil—*Eden* soil —and launched an invasion that killed service members simply defending their land! Why is it that the Coalition fighters lose nothing for taking those lives? They just get to continue living with no punishment, no repercussions!"

The crowd booed.

A man in the sea of attendees shouted, "That ain't right! That's a buncha bull!"

Damien heard him and seized the moment. "Exactly, my friend. It's time to make them pay! It's time to—"

CRASH!

Something plummeted onto the stage, spiderwebbing cracks

into its wooden surface.

The crowd gasped.

Two camouflaged figures stood in front of Damien. They were Akane and Jay in their Shells.

The two bodyguards behind Damien grabbed pistols from inside their jackets and opened fire.

Bullets hit the Shells, rippling their holographic skins. Of course, no damage was done to the armor.

The crowd screamed and scattered in every direction.

The Shells' cloaks disengaged.

A wrist gun unfolded from the housing on Akane's forearm. She fired tranquilizer darts into the guards' chests, and both collapsed onto the stage instantly.

Akane leveled her arm at Damien. A simple thought switched her wrist gun to plasma-burst mode.

Damien raised his hands in surrender. "Easy there."

"Your fate won't be as merciful as theirs, you murdering bastard," Akane said.

She activated her external sound port, which amplified her voice like a bullhorn. "PEOPLE, I AM FROM COLONY THREE. I'VE BEEN MARGINALIZED BY AN OPPRESSIVE GOVERNMENT SYSTEM, BY A SYSTEM DESIGNED TO KEEP PEOPLE LIKE ME DOWN. BUT I DECIDED TO FIGHT BACK. YOU MAY NOT APPROVE OF MY METHODS, BUT I REALLY DON'T GIVE A DAMN.

"AND I HAVE NO SYMPATHY FOR THIS MAN, DAMIEN SYKES. HE'S A PIECE OF TRASH. HE ORDERED THE MURDER OF MY FRIENDS, GOOD PEOPLE WHO WERE TRYING TO MAKE A DIFFERENCE. FOR THAT, I SENTENCE HIM TO

DEATH."

Rally police shouted to the fleeing masses, "Move! Move! Move!"

Jason, Eli, and DeShaun pushed against the flood of bodies, converging on the stage.

"Hey!" Jason yelled at Akane and Jay, drawing their attention.

The chasers fired their pistols. Bullets ricocheted off the Shells' armor.

Jay aimed his wrist gun at them. "Knock it off!"

Akane pivoted back to Damien. His arms were still up, but he'd taken several steps backward, ready to make a break for it.

From within the stampede of fleeing bodies, Randy and Stacie, Shells cloaked, power-leapt into the air. They landed in front of Damien, blocking Akane and Jay from their target.

The cloaks deactivated on command.

"Enough, Akane," Randy said. "You two don't have to do this."

"Like hell we don't," Jay retorted.

Stacie motioned for her team to fall back. Jason nodded, and they set off at a run.

The crowd was gone, leaving the plaza to be an arena for the inevitable fight.

Police officers still on the scene kept their distance, speaking into radios and monitoring the standoff.

Stacie stepped closer to Akane and Jay. "DFI has evidence linking Damien to the same criminal operations as his parents. He's going to be taken into custody. There's no need for you to kill him."

"What evidence?" Damien asked demandingly.

Randy looked back at him. "You shut up."

Akane shook her head. "There's no jail in the universe that can keep him locked away. He'll just buy his freedom with all the money he's made off his criminal empire. Shit, he's probably got a château in Hell waiting for him—after I send him *there* to make sure he never hurts anyone else."

"We can't let you do this," Stacie said. "DFI needs him alive to interrogate him."

Damien's brows arched as he processed the familiar voice. "Wait a minute. Stacie, is that you?"

Stacie's faceplate slid up, and she spun on her heel. "Yeah, it's me. Surprise."

Damien's face flushed. Stacie had played him. Paul Shaffer had been right. "You *bitch*. I should—"

Stacie blasted a tranquilizer into his shoulder. His body tensed as the drug took hold, and he fell back-first onto the stage. "I've heard enough of you for today." She lowered her faceplate, ready to engage Akane and Jay if she needed to.

The police continued holding their position, watching warily.

Stacie, huh. So Randy's teaming up with his ex-girlfriend, Akane thought. "Move!" she ordered. "I don't wanna hurt you guys, but I will!"

< *Stace, get Damien as far away from here as you can,* > Randy said.

< *That'll leave you here alone with both of them.* >

< *Yeah, I know. No choice.* >

< *Okay, just . . . be careful.* >

Stacie leaned down, preparing to hoist Damien over her shoulder.

"No you don't!" Akane lifted her arm as her wrist gun powered up, glowing hot. It was seconds from firing.

Stacie paused and contemplated her next move, leaving Damien on the stage's floor.

Randy intercepted Akane before Stacie could. A compartment on his chest clicked open, and a disruptor mine shot out. It clamped onto Akane's Shell and discharged a crippling field of plasma energy that destabilized her implant-to-CPU connection. The feedback slung her backward off the stage, leaving her incapacitated.

That shock should keep her down for a few minutes, Randy thought.

"Akane!" Jay roared. An energy blast from his wrist gun zapped Randy's shoulder. Another blast grazed Randy's side, shaving away bits of Kryoplaste. The damaged areas crackled.

Jay's weapon flared again, but Randy activated his barrier shield just in time. The glowing dome enveloped him, deflecting the next volley of blasts and protecting Stacie and Damien, who were behind him.

Stacie hefted Damien into her arms. *<Randy, you good?>*

Energy blasts splashed against Randy's shield. *<I'm good. Move!>*

<Be careful.>

Stacie slung Damien over her shoulder and power-leapt, clearing twenty feet and landing atop a car. She jumped again and leapfrogged across vehicles.

"You're not getting away!" Jay vaulted into the air to go after Stacie.

Randy dissolved his shield and leapt. Midair, he tackled Jay with a bear hug, and they spiraled downward together, barrel-rolling until they crashed into the ground. Shattered phyocrete exploded upward like a geyser and then rained down, pelting their Shells.

Randy exhaled and rolled onto his back, away from Jay. Staring up at the sky, he saw Akane soaring over him to pursue Stacie. She had already recovered from the disruptor mine's shock. *I have to stop her.* He got his feet beneath him, his Shell sparking from the damage done by the fall.

Jay grunted as he stood, his armor dented and scarred. "You're on the wrong side today, Scott!"

"No, you're the one on the wrong side, Jay!"

Randy fired a succession of shots from his wrist gun. One blast slammed into Jay's torso, but the rest veered off target, striking empty vehicles and blowing chunks out of nearby buildings.

Randy's Shell's public-protection protocol pushed an advisory across his HUD:

Local environment: Urban / Dense civilian population
Property-damage probability: High
Enemy assessment: One hostile / Equivalent offense and defense capabilities
Resolution recommendation: Convert to gladiator mode / Close-quarters engagement only

Randy's Oracle said, "It is strongly recommended the user accept the proposed resolution to minimize public-property damage and reduce civilian risk."

Randy understood that engaging in mechsuit combat within a civilian area was dangerous. "Proceed," he ordered.

"Converting to gladiator mode," the Oracle responded. "Reallocating power to enhance close-quarters abilities. Disabling all long-range offense to prevent unintended discharge."

A diagram of Randy's Shell appeared on his HUD. The fists, knees, and mechboots glowed red, showing that energy had been rerouted from long-range weapons to boost striking power. Mobility indicators flashed, signaling a thirty percent speed increase.

"Gladiator mode activated," the Oracle confirmed.

Jay's Oracle issued the same protocol. His Shell transitioned into gladiator mode as well.

At blurring speed, Randy and Jay exchanged strikes and counter-blows, pushing their Shells to the limit.

The CPU, the AI Combat Assistant called Oracle, and the user all operated as a seamless unit. The CPU analyzed the enemy's movements, predicting their next actions. Those predictions were then transmitted directly to the user, while the Oracle provided real-time offensive and defensive recommendations based on them. The Oracle also served as a safeguard, overriding user control when necessary to execute blocking maneuvers.

Both Jay and Randy thrust plasma-charged fists at one another. They were basically concentrating plasma energy into a single component of their Shells and propelling it outward as a condensed micro-field.

Randy's glowing, powered fist collided with Jay's chest plate dead center, delivering a loud, percussive dong. At the exact same instant, Jay's fist whammed Randy's chest in the same spot. Sparks of energy scattered as both bodies twisted backward from the sheer force of the impact. Knocked off-balance, the two men floundered for stability, their mechboots clacking.

A dark scorch mark and scuffs marred Randy's armor where Jay's strike had landed. He reset his combat stance, exhaling three breaths. "Stop it, Jay."

Jay mirrored the stance. "So you can gang up on Akane with your friend? I don't think so, brother."

They circled each other, fists poised.

Both searched for an opening and watched for the next attack.

Jay said, "No offense, but I knew you weren't cut out for RISE, Scott."

"No offense taken."

"Just to let you know, I don't hate you or anything. I still respect you for what you've done for the colonies. Right now, we're just on opposite sides."

"I appreciate that. And hey, I get it. Your friends are gone, and you want Damien to pay. He will, but not your way."

"Gonna have to disagree there."

Sorry it had to be like this, buddy. Randy made his move. His jumper struts propelled him into a leaping glide, fast enough to look like he was skimming the air, about five inches off the ground. Guardians had coined the trick "air sliding." He rammed his shoulder into Jay, hurling him ten yards away.

Jay's Shell clanked to the ground and skidded to a stop. He sat up. "Deploy short-range defense agents," he ordered his CPU.

Three golf-ball-sized drones ejected from his Shell and levitated above Randy. They zapped him with laser beams, chiseling away at his armor.

Enough. Randy summoned his plasma saber, a flicker of energy extending into a full-length blade. Flustered, he swung at the drones, but they zigzagged and darted here and there while shooting at him from all angles.

Randy's Oracle activated his barrier shield as a countermeasure. The ballooning dome of energy expanded outward, swatting the drones from the air. They tumbled across the ground, sparking and steaming.

"Thanks, Oracle," Randy said.

"User is welcome."

The barrier shield dematerialized.

Jay bolted toward Randy, plasma saber flaring, ready to strike him down if necessary.

A flash-bang shot out from under Randy's wrist. It exploded in a burst of blinding light, stopping Jay mid-charge and stinging his eyes.

"Damn it!" Jay used a forearm to cover his visor.

As the light faded, he lowered his arm, eyes still burning. Randy hadn't moved. He appeared to be standing there, waiting.

Jay said to his Oracle, "Abort civilian-protection protocol for ten seconds and re-enable wrist guns." Override completed, Jay fired. The blast went straight through Randy. It was a decoy, a diversionary holo. "Where—?"

A blast struck Jay from behind. Randy had temporarily deactivated his civilian-protection protocol too.

Jay fell face-first. Randy jumped, and as he came down, he drove a plasma-charged knee into Jay's back plate.

He screamed from the bone-crushing impact.

Randy, with one knee on Jay's back, reached down and ripped the helmet off his head. After tossing the helmet aside, he said, "Lights out, Jay." He dispersed a mist of knockout gas from the micro-sprayers embedded in his fingertips.

"You can't—" Dizziness and nausea overwhelmed Jay as he blacked out. He'd be unconscious for at least three hours.

Randy palmed the Shell's manual release and stood. Then the armor expanded and retracted from Jay's body.

He turned to the policemen keeping their distance and hollered, "My name's Randal Scott. I'm a Guardian. He's down. You can arrest him now."

Radios crackled, and five officers advanced to take Jay into custody.

Now it was time for Randy to find Stacie.

Stacie huffed, catching her breath. She was on the rooftop of a tall building. Damien lay nearby, still unconscious from the tranquilizer. *I hope Randy's okay. Now to—*

Akane leapt onto the rooftop. She landed in a crouch just feet from Stacie. "Gotcha!"

Damn, she tracked me. Stacie was impressed. "I know Damien's the leader of the Brotherhood. I know he sent his goons to kill your friends. I hate him too, maybe more than anyone. He abused a friend of mine, treated her like trash. But I can't let you kill him. I went to great lengths to help DFI gather enough evidence to take him down properly."

"Tough." Akane's plasma saber ignited, casting a purple glow on her armor.

She swung in a wide arc, the energy blade cleaving away a piece of Stacie's shoulder plating.

Stacie jumped back, staying outside the saber's reach.

Her Oracle then said, "Public-protection protocol recommended."

"Negative. I'm on a fucking roof. There aren't any civilians up here."

"It is suggested the user reconsider," the Oracle urged.

"No!"

Akane lunged, swinging wide three times.

Stacie dodged two of Akane's attacks, but the third carved a deep gash down the center of her Shell.

She's not kidding around, Stacie thought.

With lightning-fast reflexes, she ducked under Akane's side-sweeping strike. Then she sprang up and locked her arms around Akane's waist. With a powerful heave, she suplexed Akane onto her back, falling with her.

Akane's teeth chattered from the impact.

Stacie kipped up and drove her mechboot down at Akane's helmeted head. Before Akane could throw up an arm to block,

Stacie's stomp connected, cracking her visor and rattling her brain. Zigzags of static and red error messages flickered on Akane's HUD.

Stacie raised her mechboot for another stomp, this one infused with plasma energy.

Akane rolled, and Stacie's foot smashed into the rooftop, creating a web of cracks.

Lying on her side, Akane aimed her wrist gun at Stacie and fired. As the blast hit Stacie's chest plate, her torso arched backward, but she kept her mechboots grounded.

Akane got up, knee actuators groaning.

Stacie recovered fast. She engaged her jumper struts, catapulting herself into a somersault. The moment she landed behind Akane, she wound her arms around Akane's helmet, trapping her in a headlock.

Akane struggled to break free, growling.

Stacie yanked back on her grappling hold.

In a firm, no-nonsense tone, Stacie said, "Stop it. I'm trying not to hurt you, for Randy."

"That so?"

"Yes. I could snap your neck right now, and I should. You're a criminal. Your whole organization is criminal."

"Criminal? Wasn't it not too long ago that you and your team of chasers were breaking the law by being in X-Quadrant, to go after traffickers not assigned a bounty? My, my, aren't you morally flexible? You're just a damn hypocrite."

"That's right, you're a member of Randy's task force. So you were there, huh?"

"Yep."

"Well, I didn't shoot up a fundraiser like your friends did. They put *noncriminals* in danger. Maybe some were discriminators or dirtbags, but they weren't criminals." Akane clawed at Stacie's arms, but Stacie only tightened her hold. "Damien was the target, and honestly, I probably would've been happy if he had caught a bullet to the skull. But RISE's assault team sure wasn't worried about everyone else in the line of fire, me included. I was there undercover for DFI."

"I was there too, bitch. Guns had a safety mechanism. Stunner rounds only for undesignated targets."

"Do you know what happens when a stunner round hits someone in the eye? Not pretty, kid."

"Just let me go!"

"Request denied," Stacie said. Akane snarled. "Randy shared your tragedies with me. I understand you've been damaged by—"

"Damaged? You're talking like I'm a wrecked car or someone fried my brain. Try marginalized. Oppressed. Bullied. Disadvantaged. Stigmatized. Disempowered. Or simply treated like shit." Akane's mechboots thumped against the roof as she fought to free herself from Stacie's ironclad headlock.

"Okay, terrible choice of words. I'm just trying to say I under-"

"No, you *don't* understand." Akane made every effort to crack Stacie's grip. No success. "What would a richling like you know about what immigrants like me deal with? People like you love to patronize us with your snooty commiseration."

That got Stacie pissed. She wrenched harder on Akane's neck. "What would I know? Oviereya Amaechi, the Commonwealth's Chief, was my mother's midwife, and she's like a mother to me."

Akane blurted, "What?"

"You heard me."

"So let me guess, your parents took pity on her, the poor immigrant, and gave her a job."

"Yeah, something like that. But they never treated her cruelly.

I'm not saying they didn't believe they were her societal superior. We were a family of the Eight, the so-called 'alpha' of all Edenites. To my parents, no one was on our level. But my point is that I grew up with an immigrant as my caretaker, a woman who'll be immortalized as one of the most important figures in Commonwealth history. I don't *patronize* anyone. I don't think I'm superior to any human being. So don't paint me with the same brush that you paint the people who marginalize you."

"Enough! You're in the way of me killing Sykes, the enemy of my people! That's all I know!"

Akane drew on her Shell's augmented strength, bending forward to hurl Stacie over her back.

Stacie crashed onto the rooftop, a metallic clang ringing loudly.

Damien was still lying unconscious. It was an easy kill for Akane. She leveled her wrist gun at him. *Sayonara.* The gun's accumulator hummed to life, collecting plasma energy.

Randy descended behind Akane. Launching himself into an air slide, he rammed his elbow into her back at full speed, throwing off her aim. The blast discharged from her wrist gun zoomed through the air and evaporated before it could hit anything.

Akane rose. "Just because I like you—and the sex was bomb—doesn't mean I'm not gonna hurt you, Randy."

Touché, he thought. "Please, Akane, stop."

"You know, I don't get it. You fought with the Coalition. Why wouldn't you fight with RISE?"

"The Coalition had an ethos. They had honor. They didn't plot assassinations or rig elections. They disrupted supply chains, blew up weapons depots, used digital activism to promote change."

"They had their tactics; we had ours. Move, Randy."

"I can't let you kill Damien. But this isn't about protecting him. I don't give a shit about that asshole. I'm doing this to protect *you.*"

"How touching," Akane said, sarcasm in her voice. "What about protecting RISE, my family? You gave them to DFI."

"I was hoping you could warn everyone before the CDF's raid. Then . . . maybe they could go on living normal lives. And with the council gone, maybe the organization wouldn't start up again." A clash of emotions and principles roiled within Randy. "Despite RISE providing shelter for immigrants, legal aid, and other services, it had to end. But anyway, it was the Brotherhood who got to RISE first. They're responsible for your friends' deaths—not me, not the CDF."

"Which is why I'm killing Damien. Outta the fucking way!" Akane fired both her wrist guns at Randy. The weapons' recoil sent vibrations up her arms.

Randy brought up his barrier shield, blocking the blasts. He had to stop Akane from getting herself imprisoned. There was no way he could let that happen, not after all the kindness she'd shown him.

Suddenly, Akane's HUD displayed a danger advisory: HOSTILE APPROACHING FROM BEHIND.

She stopped firing at Randy and whirled around.

Before Akane could discharge a single blast, Stacie sprinted and slid across the rooftop on her armored knees, sparks trailing behind her. Executing a sweeping kick, she knocked Akane off her feet.

Randy powered down his shield and followed Stacie's attack, a barrage of blasts from his wrist guns hammering Akane's Shell. Her battered armor sparked, crackled, and popped under the assault.

Akane's HUD flashed a warning: MOBILITY REDUCTION 75%. Refusing to give up, she forced herself back to her feet. Limbs sluggish from the damage, she found it hard to move.

Randy watched her sway. *It's over, Akane.*

329

Akane's Shell was in critical condition, and her body was exhausted, but grit kept her standing.

She was a fighter, a goddamn survivor. And survivors like her didn't go down easy, even as fatigue screamed at her to quit.

Though her jerky, pixelated HUD impaired her sight and she could barely defend herself, she staggered toward Randy, one stiff step at a time—to keep fighting, to get to Damien.

Stacie finished the fight, driving a plasma-charged high kick into Akane's helmet.

Akane felt like her brain was banging against her skull.

As the world around her spun, she thumped to the rooftop, unconscious.

Randy took off his helmet and caught his breath. He glanced down at Akane, then turned to Stacie. "Thanks for your help, Stace. Thanks for not going to Conlan, for not having an APB put out on her. Saving her means a lot to me. I owe you."

Stacie removed her helmet. "You don't owe me anything. My pleasure. What now?"

"Contact Conlan so the CDF can take care of Damien." Randy's eyes shifted back to Akane. "I'll take care of her."

CHAPTER EIGHT

kane groaned awake. She was in a bed, but where? She squinted, her vision blurry, her mind struggling to think.

"Akane," Randy said. He approached the bedside, hands tucked in his pants' pockets.

"Randy, you—" Akane tried to move. Chains clinked and rattled. Randy had cuffed her wrists and ankles to the rails of the headboard and footboard of the bed. It wasn't his bed, though. "So, what? Are you turning me in to the CDF?"

Randy sat in a chair beside her. "Akane, RISE is gone, and Damien's behind bars, awaiting trial. It's over." His face and voice were stern. "No one knows you killed Paul Shaffer. No one knows it was you in that Shell trying to assassinate Damien, because I covered for you.

"Technically, I'm aiding and abetting a felon." He sighed. "And why am I doing it? Because I care about you. Move on, Akane. Focus on your CDF career. Just . . . go live your life."

"Someone's gotta fight for equality. My ikigai is to—"

"I get it, Akane," Randy cut in. "Colony and immigrant equality can and *will* happen. The Coalition made that possible with Operation Hammer Fall. The net is finally what it was meant to be: a free information system. No filters. The government no longer controls the flow of information. People can speak freely—to the entire Commonwealth—about their welfare, about their grievances.

"Change won't happen overnight. It may take years. But it will happen, piecemeal."

"I'm not gonna lie down like a dead dog and let my friends die for nothing! Someone has to continue RISE's fight! Someone has to stop Purists!" Akane yanked on the restraints. "Now lemme go!" That stubborn fire of hers wasn't going out anytime soon.

"*No*," Randy replied assertively. "And the Purist movement is about to be in shambles. The Brotherhood, the largest Purist group in the Commonwealth, is about to fall. The CDF's hitting their compound soon. The other Purist groups will be walking on eggshells, knowing they could be next."

Akane's brow furrowed. "You can't fucking keep me here, Randy."

"I don't intend to, but here's what you're going to do." Randy's tone implied that he wasn't open to compromise. "You're going to contact Breckenridge and tell him you're taking a leave of absence, effective immediately. Go home to your parents. You told me the last time you saw them in person was before you left for Eden. Pay them a visit."

Akane's eyes watered as she thought about her mother and father.

Randy said, "What would they think if they knew you were running around committing illegal acts, jeopardizing your career as a Guardian? You want to honor them, right? Go home for a while, Akane."

Akane stammered, "Wha-what about Sam and Jay?"

"Emergency responders took Sam away. He's alive. He was probably questioned about what he was doing in the area. Whatever lie he told must've worked. And since the Brotherhood wiped out RISE's base, there's no evidence linking him to the organization anyway. So yeah, he's lucky.

"As for Mark MaCallum and Dan Maddox's bodies in Jay's basement, it was self-defense against intruders. But after our fight, the authorities took Jay into custody. He's in jail now. I don't know how bad his sentence will be. It could be light, since Damien wasn't killed.

"And it's not like I'm happy about Jay getting locked up. I'd rather he got no jail time. I know how hurt he was, seeing all his friends dead. I tried to get both of you to stand down, but it didn't happen, and actions have consequences. Who knows, since we have an immigrant Chief in office, maybe he'll be pardoned.

"You'd be locked up too if I'd turned you in. I'm giving you a second chance. Make your parents proud, by fighting for equality the right way. If you come back to Eden and I find out you've joined another extremist group, or you're still messing with elections or pulling stunts like this, I will drag you straight into Defense Force custody. Don't test me. Understand?" He'd be torn if Akane risked getting arrested again.

Yeah, Akane wanted to honor her parents and make them proud, but she also wanted to honor her friends' sacrifice. "No promises, man."

"Then for now, just go home. Go heal."

Akane closed her eyes as she thought about NeoJapan, her home. "Yeah, I think home is what I need right now."

Her RISE family had been destroyed, but her biological family was still alive, and they were yearning to see her in person—to hug her, to comfort her, to love her.

Randy unfastened the restraints on her wrists and ankles.

Akane sat up and swung her legs over the side of the bed. "Is this your place?"

"No."

"So whose place is it?"

"I brought you to someone who could watch over you while I explained what happened to Conlan and returned the stolen Shells. He's a friend of yours. You told me about him. With CDF resources, it wasn't hard to track him down."

There was a knock at the door.

"You can come in," Randy said.

The door whistled open, sliding aside.

"Hey, Akane," said Jacobi. His friendly smile sent a jolt of warmth to her chest. He wore a white dress shirt and dark slacks.

Akane stood and hugged him, crying. "Jacobi, it's been a while, man."

"Yeah, I know. It's good to see you. Randy told me everything. You gonna be okay?"

Akane sniffled. "Yeah, I'll be fine."

"Good." Jacobi held her closer, leaving no space between them. "You've come a long way. I'm sure your parents are proud of you, and . . . I'm sure Skylar is proud of you too. She's looking down on you from above. I know it."

"Thank you."

"And . . . I know this activist organization you joined is gone, but you can still find other ways to fight for equality, ways that won't get you in trouble." Jacobi kissed Akane's forehead. "I don't wanna lose you, Akane."

"I appreciate you, J. I really do."

Randy exited the room to go take care of some business.

• • •

Brotherhood Compound

The doors to the Brotherhood's headquarters blew open. Guardians in BDUs and body armor stormed into the building's vestibule.

"Hands up!" a sergeant barked.

Lying in wait, the Brotherhood Purists opened fire.

A bloody firefight erupted throughout the building. After the dust settled, the Guardians stood victorious, having suffered not a single casualty. The Brotherhood was finished.

• • •

THE NEXT DAY

Chief Executive's Manor

Oviereya was streaming a state-of-the-republic livecast to the citizens of Eden and Satellite One.

She stood on the stage of the Manor's lawn, speaking into the lectern microphone as reporters snapped photos and recorded the address. "People of the Commonwealth, extremist groups have been operating within our republic, attempting to advance destructive agendas. One such group was the Brotherhood for Humanity's Salvation. Its members were Purists, bigots dedicated to oppressing immigrants and colonists. Unfortunately, the Brotherhood is not the only Purist group in existence. There are others. Similarly, there are extremist groups advocating for equality.

"Last night, the CDF conducted a raid on the Brotherhood's compound. They discovered that Damien Sykes, now in custody, was leading the organization under the guidance of the Purist founder, who called himself Quinn. Based on a comprehensive analysis of communications data and the raids on Damien's estates, investigators confirmed that Quinn is actually Atticus Hancroft, the last living creator of AEGIS. He has yet to be apprehended, and intelligence suggests he may have already left the planet.

"Additionally, two suspected members of an immigrant extremist group called RISE are believed to be the assassins who attacked Damien's rally. However, investigators are still working to confirm those details.

"RISE was the largest immigrant extremist group known to us. I say 'was' because it has been dismantled. Sadly, it was the Brotherhood that dismantled it. The CDF intended to offer RISE a peaceful opportunity to surrender, but regardless, they are gone.

"As I mentioned, the Brotherhood is no more, but Purism—the ideology that birthed the Brotherhood, Quinn's ideology—remains. RISE is gone, but the extremist mindset it embodied has not disappeared.

"To all citizens of the Commonwealth living on Eden and Satellite One, do not allow these extremist groups to lure you into their dangerous crusades. I realize that our society is deeply divided. Some of you demand Coalition fighters face trial. Others desire political reform and long to see reformist leaders win elections to drive change. But none of those causes justify supporting or joining extremist movements.

"The Brotherhood and RISE both interfered in our electoral process. In response to their interference, no election results will be certified until investigators determine the full extent of the damage. Once the facts are clear, I will work with the Parliament to decide next steps and implement reforms to fix the vulnerabilities within our election infrastructure.

"Beware: Purists and radical activists have entrenched themselves in our institutions, which include the government, the

CDF, and the police. We will root this cancer out of our society. There must be peace between immigrants, colonists, and native Edenites. Extremist groups, regardless of how righteous they believe themselves to be, are obstacles to peace and equality.

"Our fractured republic faces great unrest, and I understand that healing will take time. Opinions, hearts, and minds cannot change overnight. But together, all of humanity must make steps toward reconciliation.

"We cannot allow extremist groups to continue spreading their toxic ideologies. And you, the people, can help. If anyone tries to recruit you for an extremist group, or if you know of anyone involved in such groups, report them immediately to Defense Force Intelligence or the police.

"Wherever you are, may blessings fill your life."

The livecast ended.

• • •

TWO DAYS LATER

On a balmy day, Stacie sat under the awning of the outdoor seating area of the last restaurant she and Cassie had dined at. She'd reached out to Cassie via text message, inviting her to reconnect over lunch. To Stacie's surprise, Cassie had said yes.

Nervous, Stacie fiddled with a strand of her hair. She then stared down at the table, once again mentally rehearsing what to say. It had been such a long time.

The clicking of heels neared. "Stacie." It was the unmistakable, lovely voice of Cassie McCanns.

Stacie lifted her chin. Cassie wore a vibrant yellow sundress, and her hair was twisted into a long braid. "Oh, wow, you look wonderful, Cassie. Come sit," Stacie said softly.

Cassie sank into the second chair at the table. "Stacie, it's so

337

good to see you." Her warmhearted greeting completely undercut Stacie's assumption that she was furious.

Stacie stilled, searching for the right words. Cassie didn't seem defensive, upset, or angry. Not at all. "Cassie—" She paused. The right words still eluded her.

Cassie's brows quirked in confusion. "Stacie, why are you acting weird? What's going on?"

Stacie bit her lower lip. "Cassie, I want you to know I'm so incredibly sorry for what happened to you. But I got him, Damien Sykes. I helped the CDF put him behind bars. I wanted to make up for putting you in harm's way."

Cassie lowered her eyelids briefly. "Oh, Stacie, I never blamed you for what happened."

"But you left without a word. You never told me about your new job. I figured you were mad. Mad about the way the trial ended. Mad at me for Damien's abuse and the tabloids that called you a liar. It was all my fault, after all." The salty taste of tears reached Stacie's tongue as her cobalt eyes flooded. "I'm really, really sorry, Cassie. Please believe me."

"No, you're not responsible for what that monster did. You don't control him." Cassie's voice quavered. "After the trial, I just needed to heal. Damien smacked me around, but I kept going back to him. Then came that awful trial, which he walked away from unscathed. I felt humiliated, but not because of you.

"I had to get away, to forget the scars, the bruises—all of it. So when Galactic Excavation offered me a spot on their expedition team, I took it. And you weren't the only one I ghosted. I ghosted a lot of friends and family. I retreated into isolation.

"I'm sorry I didn't talk to you after the trial. I just needed to be alone . . . until it was time for me to leave off-planet. But I was never angry at you."

Cassie recalled storming out of the courthouse toward her air-cab after the verdict. Stacie had run after her, and just before getting into the cab, she'd given Stacie a tearful look of disappointment, the one etched in Stacie's memory. "That look on my face wasn't about you," Cassie continued. "I was disappointed in myself for not having the dignity to walk away from Damien. I was young and naive."

Stacie rubbed her teary eyes. "No, you were strong. You were strong enough to walk away in the end."

"With your help, sister. And for that, I'll always be grateful. I'm sorry you've carried that guilt all this time. I owe you an apology."

Stacie muffled a cry. "Thank you, Cassie."

Cassie smiled. "But . . . I *am* glad you helped take down that son of a bitch."

Stacie laughed. "Me too."

Watching a newscast on his wristcom while waiting for his meal, a man at a neighboring table exclaimed, "No way, Sykes is dead?"

Cassie and Stacie shared confused looks.

Stacie brought up a news site on her wristcom. "Let's see what's going on."

The holowords of the article hovered in front of her:

Yesterday, Defense Force Intelligence, aided by a covert inside informant, took Damien Sykes into custody for his involvement in the domestic extremist group known as the Brotherhood, and to question him about his ties to trafficking. Guards found Sykes dead in his cell an hour ago. There is no known cause of death, no camera footage, and no evidence. The investigation is ongoing.

"Do you think one of the Purist groups did it?" Cassie asked. "Maybe they were afraid he'd squeal to DFI."

Stacie's features pinched. She knew Purists wouldn't take out their *champion*. They'd sit back and hope that he'd win his trial. "No, it wasn't any Purist group that got to him."

"How do you know?"

Stacie's brows drew together. "Because I know the Seven Elite. It's forbidden for any of us . . . *them* to run for Chief Executive. I'm guessing they voted to get rid of Damien, after giving him time to withdraw his candidacy. The right opportunity must've finally presented itself."

"Well, either way, he's gone."

"And *that*, my friend, is something I'll toast to."

They picked up their cocktail glasses from the table and clinked them together.

As Stacie sipped her drink, her mind wandered to the information Damien's confession could've exposed, such as the players involved in his trafficking operation. But her efforts to bring him down hadn't been entirely in vain; the CDF had likely retrieved valuable intel during the raid on his estates.

CHAPTER NINE

Satellite One
Colony Three
(Sector 07)

NeoJapan, cultural pluralism at work. Everywhere, signs of the citizens' Japanese heritage were visible: street art, clothing, jewelry, and more.

Akane walked along an unpaved road, a duffle bag slung over her shoulder. The aroma of skewered meats roasting on food vendors' grills teased her senses.

Merchants flagged down pedestrians. Bicycles zipped through narrow alleyways. Buskers performed for small crowds. Children cavorted in the road. Akane was home, and it felt good to be home.

She reached her parents' housing unit and paused. It'd been so long. *Here goes,* she thought. Haltingly, she went up to the door and knocked.

She almost cried when she heard her mother say, "[It's open.]"

Akane stepped inside.

Voices shouted, "[Surprise!]"

Tears ran down Akane's face as she saw her closest friends gathered for her homecoming, a lovely meal and cake waiting on the table.

"[Akane, oh my gosh!]" her friend Kimiko exclaimed. "[How is Eden? Is it as awesome as they say?]"

Akane sobbed. "[Kimiko!]" she shouted, squeezing her friend in a hug. *Thank you, Randy, for giving me a second chance.*

• • •

Randy lay awake in bed, watching the blue sky outside his window fade into dusk. *Akane, how are you doing out there, my friend?* She'd definitely left her signature on this chapter of his life, and he missed her.

His wristcom chirped, drawing his attention. It was a message from Akane.

Akane: Randy, I'm doing well. Thank you for not turning me in. Thank you for this second chance.

Randy smiled and messaged back.

Randy: No problem. Stay out of trouble.

Akane replied with a two-finger peace emoji.

Randy was right about Akane needing to go home—to heal, to start over. And he was right about something else: Stacie was really the woman for him. He treasured the heartfelt, unforgettable moments he and Akane had shared; however, it seemed they weren't meant to be an item forever. He hoped she would avoid getting involved in any further extremist activities once she returned to Vanguard Alpha.

Thinking about Stacie, he wondered how she was doing, so he sent her a message.

Randy: Hey, Stace, we made a good team out there. How are you doing?

Two minutes passed, and then a response popped up.

Stacie: Yeah, we kicked ass. I'm doing okay. I reconnected with Cassie. It turns out you were right. She didn't blame me for what happened. After the trial, she just needed space. How are you?

Randy: It's been a rough few days. Honestly, I'm feeling kind of lonely right now.

Stacie: Yeah, I feel you. I've been through a lot lately too, from going undercover to trying to run my parents' organization the right way. Can you imagine me running an intergalactic megabusiness like my parents'? Tremendous responsibility! Yikes! I'm only twenty-two and barely know the first thing about their operations. I've got a lot to learn.

Randy: Hey, wanna meet up and continue this chat over dinner?

There was a thirty-second pause, which felt longer to Randy.

Stacie: *Smiley Emoji* Yeah! Sounds good, babe!

Randy: Let bygones be bygones?

Stacie: I think I can do that. Where are we meeting?

Randy: How about your favorite go-to spot, Ultimate-Taste Cuisines?

Stacie: You remembered. I'm down. What time?

Randy: In an hour?

Stacie: I'll see you there.

Randy headed to the door, grateful for second chances.

Acknowledgments

Every author needs a good editor. I would like to thank the editing duo of Xyana and Leilani Dewindt. I didn't realize it at first, but there were moments when my characters' actions or words didn't quite align with who they are. Thankfully, Leilani's sharp eye for developmental editing caught these inconsistencies, leading to rewrites that helped keep my characters true to themselves. She also encouraged me to "show, not just tell."

One example is Skylar's suicide. In the original draft, the scene began with the aftermath of it, Simone entering the apartment to find Akane sitting against the wall, knees drawn to her chest, devastated. Leilani suggested placing the reader directly in the moment, allowing them to experience Skylar's suicide as it unfolded and truly feel Akane's emotional response.

Leilani also pointed out that Akane should show more resistance when Randy asked her to go home. I had originally written her as more compliant, but Leilani reminded me that Akane, being the stubborn woman she is, wouldn't go along so easily. I rewrote the scene to give her the attitude she's known for.

Thank you, Leilani, for helping me stay true to Akane's character. And thank you to both you and Xyana for your thoughtful edits and recommendations. I can't list them all here, but they absolutely helped refine *Republic Under Siege: Threat from Within* and make it a stronger novel.

I would also like to thank Ann for her illustrations of Akane. You captured exactly how I envisioned her. And my cover designer, Ida Jansson, did a phenomenal job as always.

Lastly, I would like to thank every single reader. Your time and support mean everything to me.

Credits

Author

Michael J. Brooks holds a BA in Art and an MFA. He is a member of the Independent Book Publishing Professionals Group (IBPPG), and his debut novel, *Exodus Conflict*, was a finalist of the 2013 Next Generation Indie Book Awards, in the sci-fi/fantasy category; earned honorable mention from the 2013 London Book Festival, in the science fiction category; and received five stars from *Readers' Favorite*. He has been featured on The Authors Show and in the Spring 2022 edition of Review Tales Magazine.

Editors

Xyana and Leilani Dewindt are two creative sisters who graduated from the University of California, San Diego. Xyana has a BS in Cognitive Science with ample experience in academic research and editing journal articles. Additionally, Xyana is specialized in unique product, studio, and lifestyle photography. Leilani has a BA in Literature/Writing and is specialized in editing fiction and non-fiction novels, journal articles, and admission essays. She has been editing such works for the past four years and was an editor for UCSD's literature magazine.

Illustrator

Ann is a Russian freelance artist who provided the illustrations of Akane. She loves to draw and paint. You can find her artwork on Instagram at anygoart.

Cover Designer

Ida Jansson has been working with authors and publishing houses since 2010, designing covers, book interiors, websites, and all sorts of promotional materials. Ida works under the company name Amygdala Design. She also has a background in Biomedical Science and Psychology with special interest in the brain.